PENGUIN F
THE TUTOR O

Manjushree Thapa's published wor
a political history of Nepal; a travelogue, *Mustang* ...
Fragments; and translations of Nepali literature. *The Tutor of History*, her debut novel, was published by Penguin India in 2001. Her essays and short stories have appeared in several anthologies, journals and magazines in Nepal, India and USA.

Manjushree Thapa lives in Kathmandu, where she helps to manage Martin Chautari, a centre for public interest and advocacy.

Praise for *The Tutor of History*

'The schism between Nepal traditional and Nepal emergent and its anguished resolution is the essence of [Manjushree Thapa's] novel...Her main characters are typical yet very convincingly individualized. There is a kernel of indestructible humanity in them, which relentlessly urges them to reach for fulfilment...Manjushree Thapa's accomplished first novel will not be a one-time hit. She will be a recurrent success story.' —Indra Bahadur Rai

'Against the brooding degeneration of a once mythical landscape, Manjushree Thapa poignantly evokes the simplicity and strength of small lives: where love peaks in the midst of frustration, rice fields ripen despite urban dereliction, private dignities persist in the face of collapsing public ideals...An evocative glimpse into the truth and turbulence of today's Nepal.' —Anees Jung

'Remarkably for a first attempt, Manjushree Thapa details her characters with a thoroughness and finesse that leaves the reader gasping...The novel's description of electoral dynamics can give the best study course on the subject more than a run for its money. Nepal emerges under its own sun...as a proud nation, stubbornly awaiting its heroes and narratives. The whiff of difference is delectable.' —*Deccan Chronicle*

'Thapa's book reminds one of *The God of Small Things* in the way it effectively captures the local idiom, but it is free of the sadness and suppressed fear that lie subsurface in Arundhati Roy's book. Thapa is more full of fun and sarcasm. Tongue in cheek, Thapa...weaves a tale of political stratagems and blends it cleverly with everyday life and sub-plots of an evolving love affair and adolescent infatuation, idealism and rivalries...[*The Tutor of History*] gives the reader a taste of rural Nepal with the beginnings of modern awakening. It makes for engaging reading.' —*Business India*

'Thapa is firmly grounded in the social reality that she depicts in her novel. This sensitive story looks far beyond the clichéd image of smiling people living in the shadows of the mighty Himalaya…Thapa fails neither the English language nor the Nepali circumstances…For a reader familiar with Nepal, there is nothing dreary or repetitive in the tale, its cast, or its context. For those for whom Nepal is merely an exotic country, the book is a wonderful, non-wearisome introduction to its society…whatever the perspective that is brought to the reading of this novel, it is clear that it is a well-crafted and commendable work that points to a future of promise for Nepali literature.' —The *Kathmandu Post*

'Manjushree Thapa's debut novel about the politics and identity of a small town in Nepal has a compelling range and sweep of vision…Thapa writes about her complex and marginalized society with sincerity and authenticity.' —*Outlook*

'An artful and riveting story in which contemporary Nepal and the relations of its members are described in a fascinating way…Even though written in English, the novel clearly reflects the author's skill and creativity in writing unhindered, as though having earned the voices of the characters…and in depicting local and national politics in ways that are, in some senses, more poignant than anything found in Nepali-language literature.' —*Kantipur*

'Manjushree Thapa…reveals to the world more about Nepal—the land and its people—than anyone has ever done…with the country's first major English novel, she's gone beyond the exotic and looked at the places behind the touristy names.' —*Sunday Review*

'*The Tutor of History* abandons the importance of being neurotic to tell a story about a place, a time and its people—in this case, Khaireni Tar, an impending election and the lives of those impacted by it…A worker of broad brush, [Thapa] attempts an accurate translation of cultural sensibilities. The protagonists of *The Tutor*…don't speak English. Happily for Thapa, they speak in their own voices.' —*India Today*

'A valiant and expansive effort to depict the interconnectedness of several lives in a complex society and polity…The writing is evocative and intelligent.' —The *Telegraph*

'[*The Tutor of History*] is an ambitious social saga, a portrait of contemporary Nepal caught between tradition and modernity, that is ultimately a story of idealism, alienation and love.' —The *Daily Star*

'To depict Nepal in all its messy politicization is also to tell an important truth…above all, [*The Tutor of History*] is a moving story of ordinary people in a changing society, living one day at a time and trying to figure out what to do about their craving for intimacy and meaning…a perceptive and memorable portrayal of a more-or-less contemporary Nepal, coloured by "the permanent unrest of those who move unseen through the land."' —Sawnet Reviews

the tutor of history

manjushree thapa

PENGUIN BOOKS

PENGUIN BOOKS
Published by the Penguin Group
Penguin Books India Pvt. Ltd, 11 Community Centre, Panchsheel Park, New
Delhi 110 017, India
Penguin Group (USA) Inc., 375 Hudson Street, New York, New York 10014,
USA
Penguin Group (Canada), 90 Eglinton Avenue East, Suite 700, Toronto,
Ontario, M4P 2Y3, Canada (a division of Pearson Penguin Canada Inc.)
Penguin Books Ltd, 80 Strand, London WC2R 0RL, England
Penguin Ireland, 25 St Stephen's Green, Dublin 2, Ireland (a division of Penguin
Books Ltd)
Penguin Group (Australia), 250 Camberwell Road, Camberwell, Victoria
3124, Australia (a division of Pearson Australia Group Pty Ltd)
Penguin Group (NZ), 67 Apollo Drive, Rosedale, North Shore 0632, New
Zealand (a division of Pearson New Zealand Ltd)
Penguin Group (South Africa) (Pty) Ltd, 24 Sturdee Avenue, Rosebank,
Johannesburg 2196, South Africa

Penguin Books Ltd, Registered Offices: 80 Strand, London WC2R 0RL,
England

First published by Penguin Books India 2001

Copyright © Manjushree Thapa 2001

Grateful acknowledgement is made to Sajha Prakashan for permission to
quote from Gopal Prasad Rimal's poem 'Aamako Sapana'.

All rights reserved
10 9 8 7

Typeset in Sabon by Mantra Virtual Services, New Delhi
Printed at Chaman Offset Printers, New Delhi

For Aama, Ba, Dai and Birdie

To those who stay, the soil.
To those who leave, the pathway.

acknowledgements

A great number of people helped me write this novel, and I am indebted to each one. Maya Sonenberg and Shawn Wong read the first preposterous drafts of the manuscript and did not balk; their early advice proved invaluable till the end. Later drafts benefited greatly from Tej Thapa's dauntless critique: 'Cut all this. What's wrong with you? Tch. Let your characters fall in love, yaar.'

At Penguin, Ravi Singh has been an insightful editor, always tactful about devastating criticism. I am thankful to David Davidar for his support for work from far-flung outposts, and to Thomas Abraham for not writing off Nepalis after witnessing, first hand, the baffling Hrithik riots. H.K. Dua and Vinod Mehta graciously mapped out literary Delhi for my disoriented self. Khushwant Singh did the great good turn of shooing me, with briskness, wit and affection, into the publishing world.

Before I got to Delhi, though, I gained much in Kathmandu from Wayne Amtzis, Kesang Tseten, Joel Isaacson and other English writers. Discussions with Nepali writers and poets Khagendra Sangraula, Narayan Dhakal, Govinda Bartaman, Shyamal, Rajav and Bimal Nibha have helped hone my aesthetics, while Banira Giri, Manjul and Susmita Nepal have offered encouragement. Outside the literary circles, Pratyoush Onta and the fiercely intelligent folks at Martin Chautari sustained me intellectually as I wrote this novel: my faith in Nepal's democratic civil society is affirmed by this and other gatherings of engaged intellectuals. Dr Chandra P. Gurung's visionary work in the Annapurna region has informed my description of mothers' groups; it has been my immense good fortune to work with him. Kanak Mani Dixit eventually stopped hectoring me for my antisocial streak, and readily extended help when called upon.

The Fulbright Commission of Nepal and the creative writing programme at the University of Washington helped turn me from a well-paid NGO worker to a paisa-less writer: Penny Walker was particularly helpful in this process. Malcolm Griffith, Charles Johnson, Ranji Khanna and David Shields offered valuable literary guidance along the way. My teachers Tsoknyi Rinpoche and Chyoki Nima Rinpoche have conferred light and grace to my writing efforts, and indeed to my life. In addition, many close friends in Kathmandu, Seattle and other corners of the world have kept me going through years of aimless scribbling (typing). I am deeply thankful for their camaraderie. To Aavaas the added dream that we may all someday live, love and create free of societal tumult.

Most of all, I could not have written this novel without the help of my family. From early on, my parents Bhekh Bahadur and Rita Thapa offered me the greatest privilege possible, that of liberal love. They also tossed their common sense to the winds to abet my bohemian proclivities. My brother Bhaskar and sister Tej, and their families, Sumira and Barune, Ciaran and Maya (cooing in earnest), offered solidarity from afar. My uncle Deepak and aunt Jyoti Thapa made it possible for me to keep writing as the house fell apart around me. I came to rely on them—too much—and am greatly obliged to them and other relatives who have helped me negotiate Kathmandu.

Finally, there is in Nepal an actual Tanahun District, and in it an actual Khaireni Tar. I beg indulgence from the people of these areas, for, as they can judge for themselves, the communities in this novel are entirely fictional. Neither should the depictions of political parties be read as definitive: Nepal's parties created the democratic space in which a novel such as this finds public expression, and their members are surely committed to more than power endgames.

rain through the nation today

1

Originally from the town of Khaireni Tar in Tanahun district, west Nepal, Rishi Parajuli had lived for twelve years in Kathmandu, taking several lodgings, each less cheap, less mean than the previous. He gave private tutorials in history. In the throng of the city, he was easily lost: a small man in his mid thirties with dark parchment-like skin, curly hair and fine bones; a single man who could live through an entire day without meeting a familiar.

He started each morning by reading vernacular weeklies and daily newspapers in the blue light of dawn. Today again his light eyes skimmed the papers, seeking facts. The caretaker government had just appointed a new chief for the Election Commission. Rishi recognized the man's name, and thought back to himself, years ago, spending foggy winter mornings in a room full of thieves, murderers, rapists and activists, all huddled back-to-back on the cold dust floor. The new chief of the Election Commission had been in the Panchayat government when Rishi was jailed during a students' demonstration for democracy. Now, a decade later, the man was back in power, administering elections.

Such ironies were rife in today's Nepal, this rocky scrap of land that brothers squabbled over without end. No one bothered to disguise their interests here. Scanning the papers, Rishi saw that the communist parties had become aggressive in their bid to oust the Congress party from Parliament. One communist weekly had printed a story about the 'pharmacy scandal', accusing the Health Minister of taking bribes from foreign pharmaceuticals that sold expired drugs. Another had printed a story about the 'spinach scandal', claiming that the Minister of Agriculture helped vegetable cartels to hike the price of spinach. In a vernacular paper affiliated to the left there was a story of the 'border scandal', an incident six months before in which the Home Minister had sold land along the Nepal-India border to an Indian businessman.

In the Congress-backed weeklies the accused ministers decried communist misinformation tactics and hurled accusations of their own. Rishi read these stories too, with disinterest. Wasn't it true, one Congress columnist wrote, that the splintered communist parties had lost support in their own ranks? The columnist was popular enough to have a picture of his square face printed at the top of the page. Rishi had seen him on the city's streets. The columnist wrote: And wasn't communist ideology outdated? 'Not even China,' he concluded, 'believes any more in communism.'

Rishi pulled up from the papers. He got a kind of clarity from these back-and-forth debates which, with crude efficiency, created the broad setting within which lives like his floundered. He set aside the papers and got ready for the day, collecting papers into a book bag. The room he lived in was spare: a bed, a bookshelf, a desk and two chairs. His presence in the city was slim. In his birth village he had a fuller identity—he was so-and-so's grandson, so-and-so's son, a member of a select caste and class—but in Kathmandu he was anonymous, a slip of a man like all the others, a shadow moving against a wall and disappearing when the sky clouded over. He could assume any bearing he liked here. Today he was dressed too well for his means in thick corduroys and a plaid shirt. To look at him, he might have been born to a middle-class Kathmandu family.

Leaving his boarding house, he entered an alley off bustling New Road, then entered a narrower one filled with the cloying scent of temple incense. He passed dogs curled up in doorways, worn out from a night of barking. A woman sweeping the sidewalk was raising up a small dust storm. On a wall there was a poster of a Hindi movie, torn, another identical one next to it, also torn. Scraps of paper shifted as he walked. He squeezed against a wall to allow a farmer to pass with a load of fresh bananas. The wall smelled warm, like a body. Passing by groups of people he heard tongues: Nepal-bhasa, Tamang, Magar, the mixed languages of the city. Rishi walked till he came out of the narrow alleys onto the vegetable bazaar in Asan, some stalls set up with fresh watermelons and tomatoes, others still bare. A young girl was putting up a canvas canopy to shield her sweet peas from weather.

He stopped awhile at the centre of Asan, in front of the temple of Annapurna, the goddess of grains and of fulfilment. One of his students lived not far from here. But exams were a long way off, and the boy had been slack. Rishi got no satisfaction tutoring him. Like his other students, this boy couldn't remember which king succeeded which, let alone appreciate the intricacies of Nepal's history. Once this would have upset Rishi. He used to live with large ideas about the nation. Once he had seen a role for himself in creating fresh new democratic histories. But over the years he had grown into a less ambitious person, earning what he could in a city that begrudged opportunities to migrants like him.

He stood, now, feeling reluctant to start the day. Above him, the low, dark clouds rumbled, and a few slanting drops of rain swept against his bare forearms. He moved beneath the temple's gold-plated eaves. People around him began to scuttle for shelter. Men crowded into him beneath the eaves. Rishi looked at them: men who had long faces, protruding cheekbones, furrowed brows; men with moustaches, the cartilage of the nose soft and padded in some and sharp in others. Some men held his gaze, others glanced away and turned back when they thought he'd looked away. Some men had skin as dark as molasses, others were fair like wheat. Some had curly hair tucked into colourful caps and others had beards—thick beards, thin ones, or stubble from a few days of neglect, like his own.

All the men waiting for their day's fortunes to begin. The rain began to patter hard. It occurred to Rishi that he might stay all morning beneath the eaves of the Annapurna temple. Or he might leave the city . . . And go where? If not forward, then back: if only to awaken from inertia, to will a move, right or wrong. He might catch a bus and go back home to Khaireni Tar.

So much water beating down. If all this rain were rum—no, vodka—then all one needed to do was stand beneath the crying sky with face turned up and mouth open. Giridhar smirked at the thought. If all this rain were vodka there'd be no need to rove Khaireni Tar's brew shops, no need to sneak drinks when no one was looking, no need to conceal plastic bags in the folds of his crumpled shirt or stash telltale bottles at home. There'd be no blame or censure hurled his way. Ho. Giridhar gave in to this vision. All nature would writhe, twitch and twirl inebriated. Clean astringent waters would seep into the land and permeate everything, so that when eating the rice that grew in the fields one would get drunk. When taking a sip of water one would feel intoxicated. Even a baby could suckle alcohol from its mother's breast!

He was sitting on his front porch. It was only the middle of the day, and vaguely it occurred to him that perhaps he was being silly: silly, useless thoughts came to him sometimes these days. But—eh, why not let them? Why not enjoy life, motherfuckers? He wasn't a drunkard, he wasn't a good-for-nothing *raksyaaha*. Wasn't he entitled to small diversions?

He took out a quarter bottle of Khukuri Rum from his shirt pocket, took a long swig from it, and tucked it away. Then he turned back to the rain. So much rain. If all the rain shimmering down beyond his front porch—if all this rain were vodka! The whole world would be afloat—

Having served everyone tea, Binita kept her back turned to the men who had come in on the latest bus. This was her way with customers. In all the years since she'd opened her teashop in Khaireni Tar, she had maintained reserve with strangers and townspeople alike. A lone woman, still young, draped in a gray widows' fariya, a woman unloosened from the custody of men: she tried to ward off critical voices by subduing herself. And she'd found some good uses for tradition: it was with cool deliberation that she had decorated her teashop with posters of Shiva and Parvati in the high himals, the goddess Saraswati riding a swan, Radha and Krishna embracing in the woods, a dancing Ganesha, and Laksmi bejewelled and bright. Men didn't misbehave in these sanctified surroundings. Men didn't think to move in on her.

She reached for a textbook belonging to her young cousin sister who was learning letters in an adult literacy class. She traced the outlines of the alphabets with her fingers. क ख ग घ... Letters, like the ones she had used to reach out from school to college, from college to the world.

'One more cup here,' a customer called out from across the teashop.

Binita drew to attention.

The customer was an out-of-town traveller who had arrived on the Kathmandu bus, just another nameless man passing time in the teashop. He was listening to a handheld radio. As she served him tea, Binita caught the weather forecast: 'There will be rain through the nation today.'

Monsoon: there would be rain for another few months. Outside the teashop, Khaireni Tar was deceptively lush, a misty land of slanting rain, damp earth and rich foliage. The town

appeared so temperate in this season. Binita would not be placated
by it today. She wouldn't be lulled by this season's charity. Most
of the year, Khaireni Tar was a parched, desiccated land.

   She turned away from the window and returned to her cousin's
literacy textbook. Today she wanted to remember all she'd lost
by leaving her studies on a whim, all she'd risked for the love of
one man. All her failed gambles. She was trapped in a stunted
life. She wanted to feel out her confinement today. She wanted a
hard honesty.

The rain had let up by evening time. Darkness was closing in on
Khaireni Tar, amplifying the sounds of crickets chirping, people
calling out to each other, dogs barking and radios broadcasting
news. Om stood by the front door of his house and looked out at
the town, thinking, as he often did on such easy evenings, of his
life, the life of this town.

   Fourteen, fifteen years it had been. Fourteen, fifteen years
since he'd left Hong Kong and—after wandering through
Kathmandu taking on business ventures which brought him money
but no inner satisfaction—he'd finally settled back in his own
birthplace. We must pour our energies into bettering our town,
his own dear wife Asha had counselled him. So one fine day, Om
had decided to spend all his savings on an English-medium
boarding school with standards as high as any Kathmandu school:
the Pure Hearts Boarding School. Five years into operation Pure
Hearts made barely enough money to support itself, let alone
pay back his investment, but still Om believed deeply in the
enterprise. He felt rewarded by his work and knew he was
contributing, in some humble way, to his society as it sped towards
modernity, searching for wealth. Not that modernity was bad,
not that wealth was unimportant. It was for a taste of the modern
world, and for economic security that he himself had served in

the British Gurkhas. But he had disliked something about Hong Kong, its aspirations to slickness and sterility, the way people trained their hearts to fit into strict grids. In order to develop, he felt, one needn't forsake one's humanity, needn't fray the fine links of emotion that connected one heart to another. This was what he hoped the students would learn at Pure Hearts.

For there was a rich humanity in Khaireni Tar. In fact there was so much humanity here it was a challenge at times to attend to each individual life. Society was dense, obligations were aplenty, and oftentimes people couldn't be as considerate to others as they should be. Too often children grew up pell-mell, the elderly were shown brusque behaviour, husbands and wives shared more grief and anger than affection. Bereft of good counsel, people wandered astray, knocked against hardship, found companionship among others, and there if they were lucky to find a kind of selfless, brotherly love, they returned to the straight path. Most people returned to the path, thankfully. This was what made Khaireni Tar worth living in, and worth working in.

People were big-hearted here. In times of need, they always helped each other. Inevitably, there were always a few souls willing to guide those who had lost their way. It made Om feel good to think about this. He felt a certain aching love for this place, a kind of yearning or wistful affection. This was the soil on which he was born, the place where he would pour all his efforts, right or wrong. His town. He looked out at the darkening landscape, suffused with a sense of all the town's people huddled together in their houses, eating, talking, laughing, and spinning gossamer threads of communication linking everyone in a web of fellowship.

rumours of government
collapse confirmed

2

'In headline news, rumours of government collapse were confirmed today as parliament dissolved amidst infighting in the House regarding multifarious corruption charges against Minister for Housing and Physical Planning. The collapse happened when independent and small party MPs switched without warning to support the vote of no-confidence tabled today against ruling Congress party by opposition UML party. Such a break has been speculated for previous four months. In a tense atmosphere, talking to the press after the collapse, Minister for Housing and Physical Planning denied he did engage in any corrupt activities such as taking bribes, cuts and commissions and giving his nephew two multinational contracts as accused. According to democratic Kingdom of Nepal Constitution (1990), if there is a failure of other parties to make a majority coalition, His Majesty the King shall declare snap elections, the Minister said. He further opined that upcoming elections must be conducted in free and fair manner in keeping with ideal of glorious democratic principle. The Nepali Congress Party and Nepal Communist Party (UML) and all small parties and independents are anticipating for elections this upcoming winter, it is surmised.'

3

Khaireni Tar was a roadside town along the snaking Kathmandu-Pokhara highway, set apart from the others by its tropical vegetation, uncommon in the hill regions. Ringed by rich green rice fields and spotted with jacaranda, gulmohar and bougainvillea plants, its bazaar was slightly less drab than most highway bazaars. Its narrow alleys were littered with dirt, bits of torn schoolbooks and plastic wrappers, shards of light bulbs, snarls of chicken wire, fallen leaves and stubbed-out cigarettes. Most of the buildings were huddled together in an unattractive clump and there was no view of the himals from here. Still, it was a good place to live in. It wasn't remote like the villages off the highway. It wasn't a sleepy hick settlement. The bazaar had a police post, a high school, an agriculture office and an intermediate-level college campus; it even boasted a private English-medium boarding school for those who earned handfuls of cash. A few of the shops sold posh city items like handbags, sunglasses, nail polish, and leather belts. Khaireni Tar was a middling kind of town where it was common, while walking through alleys, to enter a twilight of cultures: to hear the screech of Nirvana on a transistor radio while passing a group of women carrying loads of freshly scooped dung. Young men from the town's finest families no longer just joined the British, Indian or Nepali armed forces but went to work as migrant labourers in Seoul, Osaka, Australia and Dubai. From abroad they sent their families a hundred, two hundred, three hundred green dollars a month. Young girls no longer consented to illiteracy but clamoured to go to school. Occupational caste tailors, cobblers, metal smiths and singers rehearsed liberation slogans under their breath. In the bazaar people could be heard speaking Nepali, Gurung, Magar, Hindi, Kumhale—and bursts of English: 'Ta-ta, bye-bye, hello Sir.'

The town's physical structure mirrored its changeling ethos. A new church stood at the edge of the bazaar, near the caves where a Hindu ascetic lived off alms. The newer buildings of the bazaar had firm stone walls, and tin roofs were in demand among the well-to-do. But most of the older houses were made of clay and thatch, and their uneven walls and mismatched windows bore prints of the hands that had built them. Some of the town's houses were covered in red clay, others in house paint, while others weren't decorated at all. Some had metal rods on the windows, others didn't even have glass. Some had electric wires, others were bleached at night by the bright white light of kerosene lamps. Each house contained, in this way, an archaeology of its own, its artifacts bearing testament to Khaireni Tar's growth and development.

At the centre of town was a sacred twined-together bar-peepal tree which concealed, with its dense banyan and bodhi foliage, the fumes of the trucks and buses that rolled into the bus stop at all hours of the day. Every morning vendors gathered on the stepped platform beneath the bar-peepal tree to sell seasonal fruits and vegetables, ready-made snacks, candies and biscuits, hair oil and hair threads, and aluminum and plastic trinkets. On days when it wasn't raining the Musalmaan bangle seller set up a display of glass bangles of the latest designs. When people got off the buses, all the vendors vied for attention: 'Bananas so cheap they're almost free!' 'Cheeseballs-chips-a-locket-for-your-daughter!' 'Peanuts? Peanuts? Peanuts?' The bangle seller alone waited in peace for her customers, bargaining with no one— 'Fixed price, baba'—even as people around her haggled, made counteroffers, cried foul and defended their honour.

After the announcement of elections, a few changes took place around the twined-together bar-peepal tree. A few more passengers than usual disembarked from the Kathmandu buses. After looking around uncertainly, the newcomers asked for directions to their party offices. The bazaar thickened each day with unknown faces.

One morning the communist UML party office, which stood next to the bar-peepal tree, hoisted a tattered red hammer-and-sickle flag above its door. The next day the party assigned its workers to repaint its sign board so that it could be read from afar: NEPAL COMMUNIST PARTY (UNITED MARXIST LENINIST). From then on, a number of UML workers began assembling in front of the office each morning, some sporting Lenin goatees, Marxist beards, Castro fatigues and Che Guevara t-shirts, and others more ordinary in village homespuns or in ragtag student uniforms. As more and more workers arrived at the UML office, they spilled into the adjoining crockery store, talking politics in hushed tones among the store's displays of aluminum plates, iron pots, stainless steel utensils and plastic buckets.

Next door to the crockery store was a cloth shop which carried fine Indian cottons and Chinese rayons. The Nepali Congress Party office was beyond this shop, and the current Member of Parliament was often seen in front of this office—till the day the party abruptly announced that it was fielding another candidate. The new Congress party candidate, a tubby Bahun man whom no one had ever heard of—but who was said to be a member of the dynasty that ruled the Congress party—then showed up at the office, constantly surrounded by hordes of young followers he'd imported from Kathmandu.

The small conservative Rastriya Prajatantra Party had no following in this electorate, but it had decided this year to field a woman from here—because the five per cent quota for women candidates had to be filled somehow. The RPP office was located a few houses from the Congress party office, between some fruit stalls and the Himal Lodge Restaurant Bar. But the RPP's lady candidate was too shy to come to the party office, and the lone office guard, nodding off at the door, gave the building an abandoned, dispirited look.

The blind shopkeeper Shankar's grain store was next to the RPP office, its spacious airy interior displaying stacks of rice, daals, grain, spices and oils, as well as odds and ends like cigarettes, chocolates, biscuits, cheap dolls, plastic earrings and Chinese umbrellas. Next to Shankar's grain store was the radio and watch repair shop, a canvas stall dwarfed by a two-storey yellow house decorated with stucco pineapples. (The ostentation

of the yellow house always prompted newcomers to guess: 'A
former British Gurkha's house?') For its first two meetings the
People's Party had gathered here, relying on the hospitality of
homeowner Om Gurung. No such meeting had been held in the
past few years, and the People's Party didn't even have an office
in town.

Beyond Om Gurung's yellow house was a wood mill, and
past that, the arid uncultivable plains which dried like dung as
soon as the monsoon rains ended, giving Khaireni Tar its name:
ashen flatlands.

Inconveniently for all the political parties, Khaireni Tar's
Telecommunications Office was located on the north side of the
highway, away from the bazaar. All day, political workers were
seen scurrying across the highway to this one-room office to place
STD trunk calls and telexes. Everyone knew that the operator
was efficient at her task; they also knew that her supervisor listened
in on conversations from his rented room above the office, where
he spent half the day lolling in his bed with stained yellow sheets.
People talked cautiously over the phone:

'I'm calling about *that* matter.'

'*That* one or the one before that?'

'*That* one, that's the one I mean.'

'Not the *other* one?'

'No.'

A little distance away from the Telecommunications Office
was Binita's teashop. Binita was a retiring woman who—everyone
knew—had never recovered from the shock of her husband's death
in a bus accident. When his mangled corpse had been brought
home, the whole town had watched her change, almost before
their eyes, from a brash youth to a recluse. The more conservative
Chettri-Bahun families of the town shunned her for her unseemly
decision to continue living alone, with only her little daughter
for company till the arrival of her young cousin about six months

back. But the more liberally inclined townspeople, and those who appreciated Binita's fragrant milk tea, tended to frequent her shop.

Binita's teashop served no alcohol, and it didn't attract men in search of raucous exchanges to pass the evenings with. Such men went to other places at the southern end of town, shabby bamboo-and-thatch stalls erected overnight by landless settlers from other districts. These settlers' backgrounds were sometimes hard to determine—some had dark southern faces but ethnic Gurung-Magar surnames, while others had rounded features but Chettri-Bahun caste names. They seemed to bring with them no past, and sometimes no qualms or strictures. Their radios were always on, their food was cheap and their alcohol strong. Their clients included government employees addicted to card games, bus and truck drivers staying the night, unemployed men, local hooligans, youths who hadn't made it into the army, and boys just out of school. In these dens talk now veered to the elections:

'Let's see who wins this time.'

'It's UML's turn.'

'Congress won't give up.'

'Doesn't have a choice.'

'Did you hear about the People's Party? That party— remember?—of intellectuals.'

'Eh them. Are they fielding a candidate?'

'Giridhar Adhikari—the son of Baburam Adhikari.'

'Hah, he'll never win.'

In his house in the hills north of town, the chairman of the People's Party district committee, Giridhar Adhikari, knew that the bazaar was whispering about him, laughing, saying, have you heard, did you know—insinuating, spreading rumours, implying that he'd been fired from the bank due to incompetence, and he deserved it, he wasn't capable . . . There was no place for him in the world. Giridhar's Khaireni Tar was an intimate one where everyone knew him and talked about him in demeaning ways, declaring him to be a hollow man. The town crowded him out of its space.

Years ago Giridhar had been dismissed from his position as bank manager. It wasn't his fault: there had been civil service reforms, and everyone who'd worked for more than twenty years had lost their jobs regardless of capability, regardless of qualification. It was a matter of regulation. It didn't reflect on his ability. For he'd been an excellent bank manager, hadn't he?

These past few years, Giridhar had begun to spend long days lost in the unsteady grounds of his mind, in cracks and crevices that led back past a day's memory, past a week's, a month's, a year's, to areas sown thick with catastrophe. Today he sat despondently on his front porch, looking out at the terraced rice fields below his house. The silver rains of the monsoon had drenched the town these last few months. The fields had turned a succulent green. Giridhar owned a plot of land at the bottom of the hill: its harvest was his only income now. Beyond that plot was the path into Khaireni Tar. He could make out the bazaar from here, a scraggly row of houses along the highway. His friend Om had invited him for dinner tonight. But he didn't feel like waiting till dusk. He wanted to be in the bazaar now, amid its stone and cement and cracked plaster, its spat-on walls and dark rooms, its shifting people, the new faces arriving on buses, telephone messages, the push of bodies, talk of the latest, men whispering—have you heard . . .

But they never made room for him there.

Once, Giridhar used to oversee hundreds of thousands of rupees' worth of transactions. He used to know what happened in the power centres of the district: who was spending money for what, and how. He used to know. But now here he was. His days embarrassed him with their idleness. He spent all afternoon straying into the past and scrambling back to the present. He did not feel he had the courage to venture onto future grounds— ambitions, achievements—all too precarious to support him.

Sheltered by his wife's floral umbrella, former Rifleman of the British Gurkha's Second Regiment, Om Gurung, stepped out of his yellow house into the bazaar. A heavy rain shower beat down as he made his way slowly from step stone to step stone. Puddles everywhere; his new safari suit was sure to get stains. He anchored each step for balance.

Om was a man of abundant flesh and unhurried movements, at forty-six, no longer young but by no means old. His face was wide and radiant, always poised for laughter. He greeted a few shopkeepers sitting in the dry interiors of their shops. At the centre of the bazaar, the usual vendors were huddled on the stepped platform beneath the bar-peepal tree, sheltering their soggy biscuits, peanuts and potato chips with makeshift plastic canopies. Om stopped at the grain store to exchange pleasantries with the blind shopkeeper Shankar: 'The monsoon's been long this year.' The blind man could tell the value of bills just by feeling them, and he intrigued Om, who found his eyes uncannily watchful. But he didn't tarry with Shankar today. Om had arrangements to make. His dear friend Giridhar was coming for dinner. No doubt Giridhar would talk about the elections. No doubt he'd say something about the People's Party's plans to field a candidate from this electorate.

At the Himal Lodge Restaurant Bar, the proprietor Thakalni-aama's youngest daughter was minding the front dining room. The daughter was slight and chaste, and Om felt coarse buying alcohol from her, so he enquired after her health, then asked,

'And that wonderful mother of yours, where would she be?'

The daughter glanced at the kitchen door.

Ho yes. Om went into the kitchen with a cheerful cry, 'Oho, what I'd do for a cup of tea from Thakalni-aama's hands.'

The old grandmother was sitting at the stove. She turned and smiled, her aged face creasing. She cooed, 'In this cold rain you came just for tea?'

Om was always mindful of the need for courtesy in conversation. To him, talking to people was like weaving a web of gossamer threads which snapped at indelicacy, rudeness. He took a seat beside Thakalni-aama. 'Could a little shower keep me from that special tea of yours?'

Thakalni-aama laughed, and set about preparing him tea with imported full-cream New Zealand powdered milk, which she made only for family and friends. The smell of wood smoke stirred in Om deep feelings of well-being. He settled into a chair. As the tea boiled, Om asked after Thakalni-aama's populous family, and she asked after his wife and children. Both his daughter and son were enrolled in his own boarding school. 'The students in your English-medium school, they're studying well?' she asked. 'They'll become big-big people, eh?'

It was only after the old grandmother had poured him a cup that Om explained, 'So I was hoping, Thakalni-aama, to find a bottle here. Something good, see?'

To Om's recollection, Thakalni-aama was now as she had always been, as far back as he could remember: astute and wily, but ultimately of good heart. 'I have new quarter-bottles of Everest whisky,' she said, testing to see whether he really meant *good*. 'And there's always Khukuri Rum.'

'Oho-ho!' Om feigned horror. 'Local booze I can find anywhere.' He flashed his most charming rake's smile. 'Maybe you have something special hidden away, a bottle of Red Label?'

'So you've become too good for your wife's home brew?'

'Me myself, imported whisky: no. But there'll be guests, see?'
Thakalni-aama smiled. 'I'll check the storeroom, then.'

When the old grandmother left the room, Om began to mull
over what he wanted to say to Giridhar tonight. The situation,
he thought, was delicate. On one side was his dear friend, who
badly needed to head up in life. Since his forced retirement,
Giridhar had lost the sort of direction he'd find again running for
Member of Parliament. And he was, strictly speaking, qualified—
a former bank manager, he was now the district chairman of the
People's Party, which was a not-inconsequential post to hold. He
was a well-educated, worldly man; and furthermore he was a
local man. He knew each corner of the electorate.

But on the other side was the former cinema hero Nayan Raj
Dahal, who lived in Kathmandu, but was originally from Khaireni
Tar. Nayan Raj had dominated Kathmandu's silver screen
throughout the seventies, starring in all the leading roles of that
time. He later portrayed a revolutionary in a movie about the
democracy movement, *Ma Maanchhe Hun*. The movie had been
a big hit ten years ago. A few years back Nayan Raj had been
appointed the national spokesman of the People's Party. Ever
since, he'd been in the papers and on the radio, making pithy
and hard-hitting statements about democratic reform. He enjoyed
more stature than Giridhar, and the fact was, the party's leaders
in Kathmandu would probably give the ticket to him.

Thakalni-aama returned with a bottle of White Horse which
was open but, she swore, unadulterated. 'My son and a friend
had one peg each,' she said, setting it by Om's side. He tactfully
placed beside it a sum of money which covered its cost. Thakalni-
aama ignored the money as she sat down once again at the stove.

They chatted a while yet. The old grandmother offered Om
more tea and he declined and she persisted and he acquiesced,
'Only because it's so special.' A half-hour passed before he put
on his gumboots, picked up his wife's floral umbrella and made

his way back through the rain with the White Horse tucked in his pocket.

There must be some place, some place he could go, Giridhar thought as he dashed, hunched and cold and shivering, into town. He was being smacked by raindrops as hard as hail. Rum tingled in his blood and he felt off-balance. There must be some place in this closed-off town. He stopped beneath the eaves of a house but rain bounced off its edge and onto him, so he ran back into the downpour, heading for the first open door.

He reached a small shop—the town's only cobbler's shop, a shack nailed together with tin sheets. Inside it was dark, and the drumming of rain on the roof was deafening. But it was dry.

The cobbler was sitting in a corner, surrounded by a display of rubber slippers. Giridhar crouched on a bench near the door. A cobbler's shop on this grey day: was this any place for him to be? He felt the cobbler's gaze bear down on him, and the weight of his judgment. Anyone could see he was drunk. Guiltily, he made a show of examining his slippers, and was lucky to find a hole in the right one.

Without a word he handed his slipper to the cobbler, who began to examine it. A transistor radio was propped up on a window ledge, and Giridhar turned it on. A woman was moaning about her lover's tragic death. Giridhar needed a drink.

'These Indian slippers are no good,' the cobbler shouted above the din of the music and the rain. 'They look nice but don't last a month. Look at this.' He fingered the rent in the heel. 'Our own Elephant Brand is better. Cheaper too.'

Giridhar tried to look interested.

'Nepali rubber is better than you'd think,' the cobbler went on. 'We think, don't we, that Indian, Chinese goods are better. But no. And someone like you shouldn't walk about in this state.

Look.' He pointed at a row of gleaming new Elephant Brand slippers. 'Only thirty-five rupees.'

Giridhar shook his head.

'Thirty-five rupees only.'

Giridhar mumbled no.

'Thirty-five rupees, hajoor.'

Giridhar spat out, 'But who has thirty-five rupees?' He didn't like the cobbler's tone, its inferences and implications. Did the man think he still managed the bank? He said, 'Everyone knows I'm not in government service anymore.'

The cobbler made a face like an iron pan: all rusty surface, no expression.

'I'm an ordinary man,' Giridhar cried. 'And so I dress like one.' He jutted forward a leg. 'Look at this rip in my pant. Look, this stain on my shirt. Why shouldn't I wear torn slippers, Bhai? What difference between you and me?'

And the cobbler turned his rusty face away, and the rain drummed hard against the tin roof, and a cool wind swept in from the door and Giridhar's anger slowly dissipated.

Still, this wasn't the right place for him.

The woman on the radio wailed in anguish. Giridhar stood up, suddenly desperate to leave. He shouted, 'Isn't it fixed?'

The cobbler mumbled something—impossible to hear above the radio's clang of cymbals.

'Give me that.' Giridhar yanked his half-mended slipper from the man's hands, and tossed him a few rupees—for what? Had he even patched the hole? Money just went like that.

'Give me a bit more,' the cobbler protested. 'What's a few rupees for a big, rich man like you?'

No, a cobbler's shop was no place to be. Giridhar thought of the Sub-Inspector of Police: his good friend. The Sub-Inspector would give him a drink. And his quarters weren't far from here.

He stepped out and submitted to the frigid slide of rain on his skin.

'I won't have it,' Asha said, wiping the sitting room sofa with a wash cloth. 'To love him as a friend is one thing, but to drown yourself in drink because he does: I won't tolerate it.'

'Eh, love,' Om clucked, setting the bottle of White Horse on the coffee table. 'He's my old, old friend. A little drink. And things are happening in politics—you don't know.'

'Your politics!' Asha was a big-boned woman as tall as Om, and striking in her red batik lungi and gold fineries. They had married long-distance while Om served in Hong Kong; his bride was a colour photograph for the first six years of his married life. In flesh she had proved to be engagingly complex, and after decades of living side by side Om still marvelled at her.

'Your politics,' she said, 'are just an excuse to gossip all night.'

Om agreed. 'It's a useless thing, politics.'

'Because who's going to vote for a drunk, you tell me. Who's going to vote for a drunk?' With great vigour, Asha wiped the mirror's gilt frames, the cotton-covered sofa, the coffee table and its cut-glass ashtray, the television set covered with a needlepoint scarf, and the embroidery on the wall that read, in English, WELL-COME HOME SWEET HOME.

Om could only hope she'd expend her anger by the time Giridhar arrived. There were relatives in the kitchen. Perhaps they would distract her. He went to the porch to wait for his friend.

Giridhar arrived late with a trampled air about him. He was usually a bit sloppy, but tonight his trousers were soiled and his shirt was discoloured. Ashen rings circled his eyes.

Om was perturbed by the sight of him. 'Eh friend,' he said,

taking Giridhar's hands. 'It's been too, too long.'

Giridhar responded with a faraway smile.

Om led him into the house, observing the slackness of his shoulders and the lurching rhythm of his steps. Had he been drinking already?

In the sitting room Giridhar seemed to startle at the sight of Asha. 'Namaste, Asha-bhauju,' he mumbled, hastily joining his palms.

Asha returned his greeting watchfully. 'Namaste, Giridhar-dai.'

Om sat his friend down on the sofa. 'Look what I found,' he said with a grin, picking up the bottle of White Horse. 'Old Thakalni-aama was hiding it, but I managed to wheedle it from her.' His wife was watching on from the WELL-COME HOME SWEET HOME sign. He flashed her a conciliatory smile. 'That Thakalni-aama,' he said, fixing two drinks. 'She's got everything in her lodge. You just have to ask and she'll provide.' He handed Giridhar a glass. 'To King and country.'

'To King and country.'

This was their usual ironic toast. Giridhar clinked his glass against Om's and then gulped his drink. Om noted this, and thought it was true that the Chettri-Bahun castes drank too much, as though making up for their ancestors' abstinence. Om also saw that Asha had moved forward, studying his friend.

He attempted lighthearted chitchat: 'That blind shopkeeper Shankar. Sometimes I swear he's pretending. The way his eyes follow you.'

To this neither Giridhar nor his wife responded. Nevertheless it was important to place everyone at ease, so Om continued with emollient intent, 'Meaning, there he is running a grain store. But how does he tell mung from rahar daal? Simply by touching? By smell? What fragrance does daal have, I wonder?'

The ceiling light cast harsh shadows on Giridhar, giving his face a sunken, cratered look. Om said, 'What if Shankar-dai's been seeing everything all these years? What if— '

'So,' Giridhar broke in.

Om sat up. Talk of elections. 'So.'

'I found a hole in my slippers today.'

'A hole,' Om said, surprised.

'A hole.'

'Eh.'

'Elephant Brand slippers are the best,' Giridhar added. 'Without Indian, Chinese rubber. Only thirty-five rupees.'

'Only thirty-five?'

Asha chose this moment to speak. 'I think Giridhar-dai should get the ticket,' she remarked with her usual directness. 'I know the cinema hero's more famous, but Giridhar-dai's a local man and also our favourite.'

Giridhar turned to her. He opened his mouth to say something, then closed it without a word.

To relieve the awkwardness of the moment, Om reached for his friend's glass, which was already empty. He made as if chiding his wife, 'Won't you offer your Giridhar-dai something to munch on?' Then he made an event of pouring two more drinks, drawing out the scrapes and clinks of their glasses against the growing silence.

Asha was being wilful, though. 'It's true,' she said, holding a bowl of spiced peanuts in front of Giridhar. 'Take a handful, Dai. I spiced them fresh for you.' Then with a daring that even through his dismay Om admired, she said, 'We want you to run for elections because you're the best, Dai. But you've got to start acting like the best. Because everybody's heard about your drinking. Nothing stays secret in this town. A man wasting his life in drink—who's going to vote for him?' She turned to her husband and offered him peanuts. 'That's the kind of counsel a friend needs to give,' she said. 'A friend needs to tell a friend difficult truths.'

Then she placed the peanuts on the coffee table, mumbled something about food, and left for the kitchen.

Om turned to Giridhar with a grin. 'She talks too much, my woman. Like a child—hardly knows what she's saying. I tell her: some things you don't know, you must accept this fact.'

Giridhar asked, 'Ticket?'

'The elections,' Om said, and realized at once that Giridhar hadn't heard the news. How could he not have? 'It seems there's going to be elections,' he said delicately. He added, 'Or that's what I thought the radio said yesterday.' He was uncertain about how to go on. 'And I was thinking,' he ventured, 'from this electorate, who deserves the ticket more than you?'

Giridhar's face took on a flat abstracted look, as though the life had drained out of it. Om had said the wrong thing. 'What I mean to say,' he corrected himself, 'is . . . contest, don't contest these elections, it makes no difference to me. It's just that a friend like you, a local man—managing whole banks by himself . . . And Nayan Raj, who is he? Not that he's not famous—but a cinema hero? Versus a man who knows the district inside out? I mean, where does Nayan Raj live? But you, in Khaireni Tar. Tch.' Om tried to smile. 'The fact is, there are going to be elections.'

A depressed air descended upon the room. Giridhar's bewildered look pulled down Om's mood. He could hear Asha in the kitchen, laughing with their relatives.

'Give me another drink,' Giridhar finally spoke, coming to life.

Om grimaced.

'It's too light.' Giridhar narrowed his eyes into dark black slits as Om poured him a peg. 'Eh friend, don't be so stingy with the juice.'

'Moola,' Om said, for he was himself getting tipsy. 'When have I ever been stingy with you, you turnip—you're a brother to me.' He added a dash of whisky to Giridhar's glass. 'There. Drink all you want.'

Giridhar lifted his glass. 'To the People's Party,' he spat out. 'To our cinema hero Nayan Raj.'

'No, to you, to you,' Om said, lifting his glass. 'You're the best, my friend.'

Giridhar gulped down the whole glass and collapsed back into his seat.

Om sat back limply, feeling dismayed.

Stumbling in the middle of the night through rice fields, Giridhar swerved off the narrow path, slipped on moss, felt the sharp edges of rocks on his feet, trampled tender shoots of rice, and swerved back onto the path, his body meeting each sensation with a shuddering of veins and quaking of flesh. Spots of blue and black danced in his eyes. The Shiva-moon was a crisp swaying crescent of white. After dinner at Om's house he'd gone back to his good friend the Sub-Inspector of Police to prove that he'd known earlier about the elections, to say, 'What—you think you're better than me, you ullu ko pattha son of an imbecile you!' He had stayed on for two, four shots of XXX Khukuri Rum and bragged: 'I'm getting the party's ticket. A future Member of Parliament! An MP of our nation!' He'd live in Kathmandu, in brick-and-cement quarters paid for by His Majesty's Government. He would ride a car to Parliament House. He would attend every meeting and serve the nation and his countrymen.

Eh, dreams.

4

Having survived the usual dangers of mumps, measles, rubella,

diphtheria, meningitis, whooping cough, polio, tetanus, typhoid
and hepatitis A, and the aftereffects of malnutrition and neglect
(for she was orphaned young), Sani, the comely cousin sister of
the widow Binita, had grown into a teenager whose prospects of
marriage were excellent. For wasn't there a mole on her chin,
and didn't her face radiate like the moon on a summer's night?
And she worked all day without tire, without a word of complaint.
'That orphan is a shiny jewel,' even the most envious neighbours
had to concede. 'An ideal daughter-in-law she'd make.' Sani had
done well to make people forget her own misfortune and her
widowed cousin's reputation when judging her. There was indeed
little doubt—even in Sani's own mind—that she would soon catch
the eye of the family of a young man who was, if not in the
Indian Gurkhas, at least in the Nepal army.

Ultimately what made Sani so attractive was that she seemed
oblivious to her own perfection. Unconcerned by the mud that
sullied her well-proportioned feet, she stepped now into her
cousin's fields to check for mealy bugs; yesterday a neighbour
had seen maggots in his fields. Sani didn't care much for Binita-
didi; she would never have come to live in this ghastly town had
her uncle and aunt not forced her out of their village. Still, she
had to fulfil her duty to her cousin sister. Binita-didi's fields lay
on a steep hillside of terraced fields just outside the town. Sani
reached into the growth, collected brown and brittle shoots and
scrutinized the base of their leaves. There were no mealy bugs
here. Then she broke into a duet, first deepening her voice like a
boy's:

Me, I'm a boy from the flatlands,
A boy from the flatlands.
Eh young girl, won't you run away with me?
Let's ride off in a taxi-car.

She hopped down to another terrace, soiling by mistake her hitched-up kurtha-sural. But what did it matter, a mud stain? Pitching her voice high, she refused her own marriage proposal:

You, you're a boy from the flatlands,
A boy from the flatlands.
You can't earn enough for yourself, let alone for me.
I won't ride off with you in a taxi-car.

The surer Sani became that the fields were free of bugs, the more melodiously she sang:

Me, I'm from the bazaar,
But you're from the hills.
Eh young girl, how pretty you are!
Let's ride off in a taxi-car.

Reaching the bottommost terrace she replied:

You, you're a boy from a bazaar,
A boy from a bazaar.
How can a hill girl trust a boy like you?
I won't ride off with you in a taxi-car.

Then, still humming, she stepped out of the fields and took the footpath back to town. Scrabbling past a slick, washed-away portion, she happened by chance to turn back and catch sight of a figure in the distance. The tune stopped abruptly on her lips. It was the Khadka boy.

He was standing at the edge of his landlord's fields, silhouetted by the sky, and Sani couldn't see his face but she was quite sure he had that look of distressed rapture he wore whenever he saw her. She turned back to the footpath, a sheen of heat rising on her face. Why was the stupid boy gawking at her? Did he take her for the kind of girl who'd talk to boys alone in the fields? A skinny corpse like that!—the Gurkha recruiters would die laughing at him. Eh, not even the Nepal army—not even the Nepal *police* would enlist a corpse like that.

Glancing back she saw that the Khadka boy was behind her on the footpath. He was following her! Her heart raced. She quickened her pace. Binita-didi's house wasn't far from here: Sani rushed past the abandoned cowshed and clambered over a fence to take a shortcut home. She must dodge this boy.

For she was a proper girl. To meet a boy in the fields, to look into his eyes and to talk to him—it would court gossip. Because no one in all of Khaireni Tar—except for the Khadka boy himself—would deem it fit for Sani to waste her youth on him.

She reached her cousin's backyard and stumbled through the vegetable patch, heading straight for the teashop. Thankfully Binita-didi wasn't there. 'Skinny corpse,' Sani cursed beneath her breath. 'Skinny, skinny corpse!'

But she had no time to sit at leisure cursing the Khadka boy. The afternoon buses would arrive anytime, and the teashop would fill with customers. Sani despised having to serve tea to common strangers. Instead she set a pot of lentils to boil. Binita-didi's daughter Tripti would return from school, hungry for snacks. And there was the evening meal to prepare. She curried fresh pumpkins. She washed the rice for the evening meal. Soon she regained her composure. In time she even broke into a gentle smile that understood the folly of others. She was not wholly insensible as to why lovelorn boys might chase after her. But she was a good girl. And she sat at the hearth now, endowed with all thirty-two qualities of unblemished womanhood.

5

Within days of the announcement of elections, Khaireni Tar's bazaar was being altered by the hubbub surrounding the UML, Congress and RPP party offices. Men, boys and a few girls and women began gathering around the twined-together bar-peepal tree, talking, asking questions, wondering who would win: would their party come into a majority this time? Some of the newly arrived party workers were young and urbane, wearing dandyish slacks, shirts, windbreakers and skirts. Older workers wore traditional bhotos, homespun fariyas or pajamas tailored in their villages. The UML workers had by now colonized the crockery store next to their office. Much to old Thakalni-aama's profit, Congress workers had begun to patronize the Himal Lodge Restaurant Bar. The RPP party office remained quiet, for their lady candidate was still refusing, out of shyness, to visit it. There was talk among those gathered beneath the bar-peepal tree that the ethnic rights Janamukti party might also field a candidate: a Gurung-Magar man would voice the resentment of the minorities towards Chettri-Bahun caste domination. People also whispered about the Maoists, who had taken control of several far-western districts by waging a guerrilla war against democracy. The possibility of violence worried many. 'Pipe bombs . . . petrol bombs, pressure cooker bombs,' people said vaguely. 'The Maoists are better stocked than the police. They carry rifles, pistols and khukuri knives.'

Every now and then someone mentioned the People's Party, but this small party was quickly dismissed. 'That gathering of disgruntled intellectuals, what chance do they have of winning here?'

'No chance.'

'Not unless the cinema hero Nayan Raj runs.'

Binita, who was Nayan Raj Dahal's sister-in-law, had heard in passing about the elections, but she didn't know that there was talk of her brother-in-law running for office. Her teashop was located in the cinema actor's ancestral home, a modest stone structure with cement additions to the front. In the parched surroundings the house was considered well placed. A public tap near by provided enough runoff to support the year-round cultivation of vegetables in the backyard. There was a shed for water buffaloes in the back, and a modern-style outhouse. A stone wall around the property allowed a measure of privacy.

Even before her husband's death, Binita had had little contact with her actor brother-in-law in Kathmandu. She had no communication with members of the People's Party. But she was acutely attuned to the signals that buzzed around her, and she noticed, now, that people were suddenly paying her great attention. In the bazaar the vendors beneath the bar-peepal tree took more note of her than usual. 'From my own yard,' one of them said once, placing two bananas in her hand. 'Give them to your daughter.' Another day another vendor stopped his shrill cry of 'Cheeseballs-chips-trinket-for-your-wife' to ask her how she was. Binita knew that such gestures were fraught with meaning. Even the blind shopkeeper Shankar, hearing her voice in his shop, stopped his transactions to ask after her health. Passers-by pressed in to hear her reply.

Her brother-in-law must be in the news again.

He must have done something remarkable, because there was also a surge in the number of customers in her teashop, unusual in such rain. Most of the customers were boys—high school age, maybe in their college intermediates. They were bold. They looked straight at her, trying to get her to talk to them. They wanted something from her. Binita turned her back to them as she prepared tea: black, milk, special or readymade, with or without sugar. A woman's back gave off few messages. Face to face she acted so stony that she intimidated these boys into silence. Still they kept staring at her, trying to decipher her.

What was it they wanted?

She found out on a day that began inauspiciously with a recurring blood-red nightmare. The morning was marred by small tensions. Binita's daughter threw a rare tantrum at having to wear torn socks. The line at the tap was long, and her cousin Sani grumbled about having to share water with those of unknown castes. The kerosene was diluted, and it smoked up the teashop. Then two out-of-town customers left without paying. The day turned hot and sultry, and by midday Binita felt worn.

Outside, the monsoon clouds had parted, giving way to sunshine. During the afternoon lull Binita left Sani in charge of the shop and set down two buckets of water by the banana plants in the backyard. She placed a towel within easy reach, took off her plain brown fariya and blouse, and pulled her petticoat over her chest. Then she squatted on the ground and drew a mug of water.

Her neighbour Phool Devi stopped by as she washed.

Binita didn't like Phool Devi and was wary of her few visits, which always left her feeling intruded upon.

'Having a bath?' Phool Devi sat on a rock beside the outhouse. She was dressed in a fine nylon fariya, her hands resting in a way that showed off her gold ring and spangled red bangles. Her hair glistened with oil, and in the parting she wore a splotch of bright vermilion, marking her marriage, Binita thought, with boastful relish.

Phool Devi launched at once into a story about a cloth vendor she had bargained down: 'Fifty-five rupees per metre, he says. For cotton spun in Nepal! I tell him, what kind of useless price is this? With my own eyes I've seen this cloth sold for thirty-five rupees...'

The number of words people used in order to say nothing—.

Binita, crouched awkwardly, allowed small gestures to be taken as indications of attention: a slight nod, the raising of a chin. Phool Devi chattered on: 'Transport costs, the vendor says. I say, did you carry it all the way? Are you charging us for the meals you ate along the road?'

Surely her neighbour hadn't come to chat about a cloth vendor. Phool Devi always wanted something.

'Things will probably change for you, then,' the woman finally said as Binita poured the last of the water onto her covered legs. 'With your brother-in-law returning.'

Binita hesitated for a beat, revealing her surprise.

'Surely you've heard.' Phool Devi's eyes widened. 'The cinema hero's running for elections! I heard it from my husband who talked to the watchmaker, who was in Kathmandu—he actually visited your brother-in-law. Did you know that Nayan Raj lives in a newfangled house made of Chinese bricks? That's what the watchmaker said.'

'Chinese bricks are cheap in the city,' Binita said, to hide her surprise. She covered herself with a towel and gathered her clothes.

'So things will change for you, no?' Phool Devi continued, following Binita to the house. Her bangles chimed as she gestured. 'Maybe his children will move here too. His wife! His workers! The house will be full of people! Aren't you lucky. You won't have to mope the way you do now—all alone, you poor widow.'

There were two doors at the back of the house, one leading to the teashop, the other to the alcove and upstairs rooms. Binita stopped at the door. Phool Devi waited awhile, and then, as it became obvious that she wouldn't be invited in, she declared, 'Well, I'm off. We women never get a moment's rest.'

Upstairs in her room, Binita put on her fariya again, pleating and tucking it slowly. Her brother-in-law, running for elections. Nayan Raj-bhai was many years younger than Binita's husband had been. He was already a famous actor in Kathmandu when

Binita had eloped with his brother, and too far removed from Khaireni Tar to be affected by the small-town scandal they caused. Her husband and Nayan Raj-bhai hadn't been close. Binita had met her brother-in-law, but she hardly knew him.

Now he was coming back. Or maybe Phool Devi had picked up false rumours. Binita went to a window and scanned the hills north of town, searching out a small white house above the terraced fields. There. Giridhar Adhikari would know. If she asked him, though, she would expose her ostracism from her husband's family. Binita's husband's relatives must also know whether or not Nayan Raj-bhai was returning. The family patriarch Kainlo-kaka surely knew. He hadn't bothered to tell her. He wouldn't.

Buses rumbling in the distance, a radio song wafting, a crying child. Binita listened to the separate, distinct sounds of the town beyond her window. Apart from these sounds she felt out her own silence. This silence was what she had. Elsewhere there was a hum of conversation. Elsewhere her husband's family was talking about things that pertained to her. Here there was only silence.

Downstairs there was still a lull in the number of customers at the teashop, with only two young men at a corner table. Binita sent Sani to bathe, and soon fell into everyday routines, washing glasses, stacking plates, tending to the fire and checking to see how much milk was left. A half-jug: enough for the day. The afternoon's dust had settled, and she began to wipe the tables and straighten the benches.

Then one of the customers asked from across the room, 'Is Nayan Raj really running for elections?'

Binita pretended not to have heard him, and ducked out the back door.

A week or ten days after his friend came to dinner, Om made the steep climb up the northern hills. He hadn't heard from Giridhar, and this worried him. True, the two of them weren't inseparable as they had once been. There was a time when Giridhar would drop by every day, and spend hours talking about anything that came to mind. That was back when Om was freshly Hong Kong-returned. The two of them had found in each other a similar worldliness, exposure, and social concern. They spoke of their experiences, they spoke of the world, they spoke of their aspirations. In those days Giridhar practically lived at Om's house. Gradually, over the years, his visits had begun to grow less frequent. Nowadays he rarely came without an invitation. And Om, busy managing his school, hadn't been able to visit Giridhar as much as he would have liked.

Blessed as he was with the heft of those who have enough to eat, Om had considerable difficulty climbing the uphill trail. In his years since Hong Kong, he hadn't done a single push-up, running drill, curl, stretch or arm lift. In fact he had been lucky to avoid all physical stress and any emotional or spiritual distress. Such were the comforts of being unshackled from military regimentation. By the time he reached his friend's house at the top of the terraced fields, a sheen of sweat covered his face, and he was wheezing hard.

He found Giridhar's wife sitting on the porch. Laksmi-bhauju stood when she saw him and covered her hair with the end of her fariya. Om found such Chettri-Bahun modesty quite unnecessary. He raised one hand in a half-namaste. 'Oho, Bhauju. I couldn't resist the thought of fresh tea from your hands.'

These words were meant to produce a smile on Laksmi-bhauju's lips, but she just slipped into the house like a servant following orders.

Om sat alone on a pallet laid out on the front porch, till Laksmi-bhauju brought him a glass of tea. 'Such green fields,' he said of the rice terraces below the house. 'The harvest will be excellent this year.'

Laksmi-bhauju retreated into the house without a word. Om sighed. In all these years he'd never known how to draw Laksmi-bhauju into conversation. She was one of those women, he knew, who only talked to other women. Asha and she, they sometimes spoke.

After a while Giridhar's aged father shuffled out the front door. Om stood up. 'Ba, namaste. I was beginning to think maybe no one was home.'

Giridhar's father was in his late seventies, a landlord with considerable holdings. He leaned on Om as he settled on the pallet, then turned towards him. 'My son,' he said, his eyes blinking behind thick glasses. 'He's in his room.'

'I thought I'd visit him.'

The old man frowned. He had Giridhar's fierce eyebrows and chiselled lips, and the same grimace of resolve. When he spoke his words were cautious: 'He doesn't answer when we call. He only comes out to eat. He doesn't talk—not even to his sons. He's been doing this every day. Locking himself in.' After a pause he added, 'He's drinking.'

Om thought at once that Asha was right: he shouldn't have let Giridhar drink at their house that night. Or perhaps something had happened—something calamitous. He asked, 'Did he get any word about the ticket? Anything from the party leaders in Kathmandu?'

Giridhar's father sank into the pallet like a deflated sack. 'Yesterday the peon from the telephone office came all the way to say there was an STD trunk call from Kathmandu. But my son didn't go.'

Om saw that Laksmi-bhauju had come to stand at the doorway. It seemed, from her servile stoop, that she was asking for help.

'I'll talk to him,' Om said, getting to his feet.

Giridhar's father said, 'Maybe he'll listen to you.'

The inside corridor was dark and cave-like. Om pushed Giridhar's bedroom door, but it stuck. The latch was fastened from within. 'Eh friend,' he said, leaning against the plywood. 'I've dropped by to chat.'

He got no response.

'It's me,' Om said. 'It's been days. My old woman is saying, "Why hasn't our Giridhar-dai come back, is he angry with me?" I wanted to see how you are.'

Om waited awhile. A year-old calendar hung next to Giridhar's door. The corridor walls were stained with fingerprints. Om knocked on the door. 'Are you asleep, friend?' Then he used a cajoling tone: 'I have an important matter to discuss. A party matter.' Then, in a matter-of-fact clip, he said, 'Are you sick? Should I fetch the doctor?' He finally begged, 'Just open the door, once.'

But he heard not a creak nor a shift.

It disturbed him. 'Eh friend,' he cried, beating at the door with the broad of his palm. 'It's me. Let me in. It's me!'

Locked securely away from the jeering hordes Giridhar slept, his heavy-lidded eyes obeying the command of his cravings. When he awoke, he sat up, stumbled to the window. There was an election. The yellow-brown stains at the back of his eyes gave way to the sight of rice fields. The bones of his legs throbbed. He turned back in. He must get the ticket. There was disaster in his room—the bed askew, clothes crumpled on the floor, the smell of sickness and sweat. He was overcome with exhaustion just thinking. Everyone knew. He was a drunk. There'd be no ticket for him.

Voices called outside the door sometimes. Knock and knock. Giridhar wished he never had to see anyone. Any face. Unbearable, the eyes that watched him. His wife. Her eyes cast down, and the straight, oiled part in her hair. If he could slip in between the broken tones of her voice as she called out to him... Between her syllables, in the silence there, he'd be safe. His father had an insistence to his words. 'Your friend has come to visit.' A long pause. 'He's waiting to meet you.' Hours later, or so it seemed, his father spoke again. 'Your friend is gone now.'

Giridhar's face sagged. The weight of his body brought him down like a corpse. He must pull himself up, stand, walk. He must go to Kathmandu and demand the ticket. But as the days progressed, he felt weighted down by his lurid materiality, the crusty dried saliva of his self. Days passed or not, he wasn't sure any more. He drank from one bottle, and then another. Sometimes he could hear Om pleading, oppressing him with his expectation. Giridhar wanted to grind himself into the flatness of his bed till he became immaterial. His head ached and his eyes smarted. His limbs felt bloated and insensate, and a sour taste coated his tongue. Sometimes he stumbled outside in the night and made his way to the outhouse. He came back and checked on his bottles and drank unmindfully from them. At other times he felt inebriated without even drinking. A whole afternoon he sat on the floor with a cheek pressed against the wall, seeing the surface of the wall ripple. Once, he lost feeling in his right arm. Bile rose to his throat—and he knew he must suffer through the solidity of this town, his body heavy in it till he evaporated. His eyes closed. He curled into bed. There was no election.

6

So eclectic was the character of Khaireni Tar, not all the townspeople were affected by public events; and in fact, many people still remained oblivious to the elections. Sani, for example, remained fully occupied merely adjusting to this uncouth town.

It was becoming clear to her that Binita-didi's ill repute could all too easily jeopardize her own good name. Why else would boys dare hound her?

A girl couldn't be too guarded: Sani knew this. That was why she covered her arms with full-length sleeves and made sure her kurtha's neckline maintained propriety. Binita-didi should consider herself lucky that Sani didn't waste her earnings on gaudy bangles, earrings, nose-rings and trinkets the way her friends did—touched as they were by youth. Sani never so much as checked a mirror to see which side-part suited her best. Nevertheless, walking with the town's girls, she was always deemed the prettiest. 'She's the prettiest,' said all the other girls.

She was in a group of girls now, heading to the grasslands far south of town to collect fodder for their cows and buffaloes. The younger girls were gossiping:

'No! Really?'

'If not, I'd eat a cow.'

Apparently someone had said something to someone, who'd said something back a few days ago. Sani never paid any mind to such chatter. Her attention wandered instead to a trail that dipped down the side of the flatlands to the Akala-mai shrine. There was no place as sacred as this tucked-away shrine, she had heard, where the blessed could hear the tinkling of divine bells. Only true devotees could hear these bells, and only if the mother was pleased with them.

She nudged her friend Gaumati, walking next to her. 'Let's listen for Akala-mai's bells.'

Gaumati wasn't the pious type. 'Nobody actually hears them,' she said. 'There aren't even any bells at the shrine. It's just a story old people tell.'

'I have a feeling we'll hear something today.'

Gaumati balked. But Sani had already hopped across a fence to a plot of fallow land, so she reluctantly followed her.

The shrine lay beyond an expanse of brushes and brambles. When they reached the middle of the expanse, Gaumati stopped. 'Doesn't this land belong to the witch?'

Sani also stopped. True: this land belonged to the witch who wandered through the town babbling madly.

The girls exchanged looks.

'She'll eat us raw!' Gaumati shrieked. She broke into a sprint, running past scrubs and brushes. Sani ran behind in panic. The ground was slippery, and she lost a slipper, but managed to keep running somehow. The two of them finally reached the dilapidated shrine and collapsed, flushed and out of breath, on a patch of damp grass.

When their fright wore off, they turned back to the witch's land. There was no one there. Eh Akala-mai! The witch hadn't seen them! Gaumati began to giggle. 'We almost died,' she gasped. 'We almost died! The witch almost caught us today!'

'She wouldn't kill us.' Sani glanced back at the land. 'And she's a madwoman, not a witch.' Sani tucked down her kurtha. 'Quiet now. Let's listen for the bells.'

'She almost ate us raw!'

'Tch!'

Gaumati finally stopped giggling, and the two of them pricked their ears.

But the only sound they heard was a squelch: the sound of someone stealing through damp undergrowth.

Gaumati shrieked, 'The witch!' and was up and running in a flash.

Sani bolted after her, and in confusion the two girls crossed back through the witch's land. They flew over the fence, landing hard on the main trail—and only then did they realize that they hadn't been chased.

Gaumati started giggling again. 'I thought we'd died again! I tell you, I thought we'd died once more!'

Sani giggled too, out of sheer relief. She saw that she had cut her foot. Then she caught a movement across the flatlands. A slip of a shadowy figure, all bones: a man. It was the Khadka boy. 'Let's go,' she snapped, and rushed off without waiting for Gaumati.

7

Seeing the UML, Congress, and RPP parties set up for elections it occurred to Khaireni Tar's revenue collector of yore, Lord Krishna devotee, husband of two, father of seven sons, grandfather of twenty-two grandsons and founding member of the People's Party, Jimmawal Sharma, that he must find out whether his party was entering the moral battlefield of politics. Because he had a modern house completing construction...and who better to rent it out to than his own party? Till now it had been a mistake, associating with this party of losers. He had joined only after receiving Giridhar's word that the party would reward its members. But all they had to give was useless ideas and big-big words. Now there was this new house of his—the party could rent it for three, four, maybe five thousand rupees a month. He would finally reap benefits. 'Niskama kama,' Jimmawal-baaje murmured to himself, quoting the core teachings of the Bhagavad Gita: Act without attachment to the results.

When the monsoon rains began to abate, he left his home and nine-stalled cow shed, and headed to the bazaar, polluted though it was with defiling non-Hindu influences. He himself was a religious-minded man who dressed in simple cottons to express his liberation from the material world. Muttering mantras under his breath he buzzed and manoeuvred through the alleys, taking quick, sprightly steps and keeping his eyes and ears wide open.

Stopping beneath the bar-peepal tree, he studied the push and pull of men in front of the party offices. So many new faces. It surprised him.

'There goes the Congress candidate,' he heard the cheeseballs-and-chips vendor say to the Musalmaan bangle seller. 'They say he's a nephew of the Congress Prime Minister.'

Jimmawal-baaje followed the bangle seller's gaze and saw a tubby Bahun man at the door of the Congress party office.

The bangle seller said, 'All thieves, baba. These politicians are all thieves.'

The banana vendor said, 'The UML candidate is a Magar boy, something Ale. A boy of thirty, thirty-five.'

'Baaje,' the cheeseball and chips vendor turned to Jimmawal-baaje. 'Is it true that Giridhar Adhikari is running from your party?'

'Yes no,' Jimmawal-baaje replied, quickly turning away. He waved his hands in an indeterminate gesture. 'The party hasn't decided.'

Then, as he passed Shankar's grain store, the blind man asked, 'Is it true that cinema hero Nayan Raj is running from your party?'

'Discussions are ongoing within the party,' Jimmawal-baaje replied curtly, walking on. The situation was critical, he saw. He must rent his new house to the party—immediately! It had no glass on its windows yet, but it could be ready within a week or ten days. Where would the party find a more suitable office? A solid house, made of cement, with four large rooms, even an indoor toilet—with tile-chips on the floor! And it was located close to Nayan Raj's ancestral house, where that widow ran a teashop. Lord Krishna, he prayed—three, four, maybe five thousand a month!

Without a moment's thought, he bounded off in the direction of the northern hills, to meet the chairman of his party. It took

him no time to reach Giridhar's house. But he was disappointed
to find no men at home. 'My husband's away,' Giridhar's wife
said in a guilty, lying voice. 'He's out meeting friends.'

'Meeting which friends?' Jimmawal-baaje asked sharply.

She looked away.

Drinking at a den, more likely. Being himself reluctant to
hunt through the dark, shabby quarters that fallen men like
Giridhar frequented, Jimmawal-baaje decided to wait for the man's
return. Giridhar's wife seemed unhappy about this decision, but
she was resigned: 'I'll bring tea.'

'No!' He shuddered at the thought of accepting food from
the hands of women other than his own two wives. This woman
might well be menstruating. Not all women observed strict
separation these days. 'I never eat food prepared outside my own
kitchen. There'll be no tea for me.'

Giridhar's wife retreated into the house.

Jimmawal-baaje went to a row of lima bean stalks, picked
one pod, and chewed on it. He was startled, then, by a screech.
Giridhar's two sons had run out of the house and were hitting
each other with schoolbooks. 'Tch, tch, tch,' Jimmawal-baaje
clucked. 'You act as wild as bears!' The boys ignored him and
lunged for each other's hair. Jimmawal-baaje turned away in
distaste, grateful for his own sons and grandsons: each one of
them could recite lengthy passages from the Puranas from
memory.

But where was that drunkard Giridhar? Jimmawal-baaje
waited, he sighed; he sighed, he waited. When the sun reached
the centre of the sky, he decided to leave. But as he made his way
down the hill, cursing Giridhar, he caught sight of two figures
behind the house. The British Gurkha Om Gurung, talking to
Giridhar's aged father.

Jimmawal-baaje headed towards them, hollering. 'If I'd
known!' he cried. 'Hours I spent waiting on the side of the house!

If only I'd known you were here.'

Giridhar's father smiled uneasily. Om Gurung shuffled a few steps away. The man was wearing one of those slick nylon rain coats that cost a thousand minimum. Jimmawal-baaje wasn't fooled by Om Gurung's nearly-bankrupt school: with his generous foreign pension the man was rolling in money, and getting as fat as a breast-fed five-year-old.

'I had an urgent matter to discuss with Giridhar-bhai,' Jimmawal-baaje said. 'An important party matter.'

'Eh.' The loquacious Gurung man seemed short of words today. 'You've received word from Kathmandu?'

'No, no.' Jimmawal-baaje gestured towards the east. 'Who knows what our leaders are up to in the capital...but meanwhile I've had an idea. And the idea is this.' He lowered his voice. 'We must open a party office.' Then, without allowing Om to object, he explained that everyone was wondering about the People's Party: was it fielding a candidate, and if so, who? 'Such matters only our leaders in Kathmandu can decide,' he said. 'But in the meantime we must look like we've entered the battlefield. We must create a commotion. We have to open an office.' He flashed a smile. 'And my new house has large south-facing windows, so new, so smart, with white coats of paint, and best of all, an indoor toilet with tile-chips on the floor. And since I'm a party member, the rent will be reasonable.'

Giridhar's father wandered off. Om cast his gaze skyward.

'We need a party office.' Jimmawal-baaje poked Om in the chest. 'If I talked to our Giridhar-bhai he'd tell me to go ahead.'

Om sighed.

There was something abnormal going on. Both man were acting as though Jimmawal-baaje shouldn't be here. 'The truth is I'm concerned,' Jimmawal-baaje said, sidling up to Om. 'Our Giridhar-bhai is a busy, busy man, I know...and I'm not criticizing him. But where is he? At this time of national instability we party members should be united under his leadership...but instead we're scattered like leaves in a storm.'

Om shuffled from one foot to the other. 'He's sick,' he finally said. 'Giridhar-dai's got a cold.'

Jimmawal-baaje perked up. 'He's home? But his wife said he was out.'

'It's a bad cold.'

'I know just the remedy!' Jimmawal-baaje made for the house. 'A pinch of turmeric and salt in hot water—clears the system like that.'

But Om blocked his path.

'Inactivity induces phlegm,' Jimmawal-baaje insisted. 'A man like our Giridhar-bhai who tends, like yourself, towards fleshiness...he should stroll about in the fresh air to dispel the accumulation of phlegm.'

But the Gurung man seemed intent on keeping him from the house. Placing himself squarely before Jimmawal-baaje, he said, 'All you want is to open a party office, right? Go ahead. I'll pass it with Giridhar-dai.'

Jimmawal-baaje stepped back. Ho yes. 'I'll hang a sign on the door at once,' he agreed. 'The People's Party of Nepal, it will say. In large-large letters that everyone can see from the bar-peepal tree.' Then he hesitated. 'But the rent...So many sons and grandsons to feed. A poor Bahun like me. My cows, with distended bellies...and the Agriculture Office rates for the medicine for colic! I wonder if the rent will be fair...'

'I'm sure the rent will be fair.'

Jimmawal-baaje was thrilled. Gurung-Magars were, he knew, true to their word. Such loyal soldiers they made. He cast a last glance towards Giridhar's house. 'La ta, all right then,' he said, then he skipped down the rice fields.

At the edge of town, he slipped into a side alley to avoid a large puddle near the Telecommunications Office. Across from

the alley he caught sight of Nayan Raj's widowed sister-in-law
in her backyard. She would be an important woman if her cinema
hero brother-in-law came back! He should greet her. The widow
was standing underneath the thatched eaves of her porch, and
looking straight at him. He shuddered. There was something
unnatural in her gaze. He raised a hand to wave, but slipped,
and had to balance himself again. The alley smelled powerfully
of dung. When he looked back at Binita, she was still looking at
him. A witch who sucked her husband's blood till he died!

Whores and drunkards everywhere in these dark kaliyuga
times. Jimmawal-baaje gave up on greeting Binita and hurried
home. 'Mothers of my sons!' he shouted, rushing past his cow
stalls. 'The party will rent our new house!'

The house was particularly quiet that evening when Giridhar
woke up, alert after weeks of haze and fog. He must steady himself,
he thought. He must place his body in the world and find reasons
for it to move. He must stop poisoning himself with drink. That
was what he must do.

He picked up a pencil. A long time passed before he knew
what he wanted to do with it. Delving deep into his knowledge of
his home district he sketched, on a scrap of paper, a map from
memory, reciting to himself the names of each village—at once
familiar and entirely unknown. Majhkot, Arunodaya, Gajarkot,
Sundhara. Black lines leading from village to village. He must
move into the world using this map, people must make way for
him. Then he felt his energy draining away, and he succumbed
to sleep. He dreamed of the retired army men who used to come
to cash cheques at the bank, of parents who came to deposit the
money that their sons had sent them from abroad. He awoke in
the middle of the night, saw faces in his mind and remembered
favours he'd extended to people. The next day he made notes

about these people. They were from Kihun, Chhang, Bhanumati, Bhimad. He dotted each Village Development Committee on his map, and wrote its name in capital English letters. TANAHUN DISTRICT, he wrote, at the centre of Nepal. His hand trembled with the weight of the pencil.

Again he slept, depleted. A few hours later he awoke. He turned over in bed and found the map at his cheek. He sat up, studied it. TANAHUN DISTRICT. Its third electorate had fifteen Village Development Committees with a total of sixty-five thousand voters. A sixty per cent turnout made it thirty-eight thousand voters. In a close three-way race, any party that won fifteen thousand was sure to win the elections. Giridhar marked Khaireni Tar on the map. Dimly he thought that Kathmandu was an eight-hour bus ride away.

He emerged from his room after two weeks of isolation looking wrecked, with his clothes rumpled and twisted. He couldn't feel his feet, but knew they were moving by the way the walls swung past him. He reached for the corridor wall. He tried to call for his wife, but his voice dried in his throat. He could hear glasses chink in the kitchen. He reached the door and caught sight of her. 'A bath,' he said hoarsely.

Laksmi blinked, and blinked again. Without a word she reached for a bucket. She was about to pass him when he reached out to place a hand on her neck. She cringed in anticipation. Giridhar knew he'd hurt her again; he always hurt her. He was her wretched fortune. He moved closer, seeking support. She eased, and timidly placed her shoulder beneath his arms. Her steps guided his as they walked through the hall to the tap at the back of their house.

Outside, the light of day blinded him. He submitted to his wife as she sat him down, took off his shirt, then his trousers and his brown, stained underwear. She gathered water in the bucket and collected soap. Her touch on his back was light and child-like as she lathered him. Her fingers reached into the warmth of his armpits, the broad curves of his hips. 'Close your eyes.' She poured water on his face. 'Lift your arm.' She nudged him into obedience. She had done this before—led him out of his room and prepared him for the world. Her hands were neither forgiving nor unforgiving. She didn't say anything. She just felt him, bathed him, knew him.

That morning Giridhar let Laksmi tidy the room, and then he locked himself in and remained in bed for the rest of the day. He pretended to be asleep when he heard voices outside his door. Om. Om oppressed him with his expectations. As the afternoon wore on, Giridhar pored over the map he'd drawn of his district. His body the map, his flesh the paper. His wrinkles the lines. A man deserved a chance. Majhkot, Arunodaya, Gajarkot, Sundhara. Kihun, Chhang, Bhanumati, Bhimad...He would go to Kathmandu and ask the party for the ticket.

At night he packed a change of shirts into a plastic bag, then slunk out of the house. His father and wife didn't say anything as he left. His sons, bickering on the porch, stopped and looked up at him. They wanted to see a man they could admire. Giridhar was glad to be dressed in his best clothes: black trousers, a shirt, an office jacket. On his feet were his good pair of leather shoes. He strained to smile. 'I'll bring you biscuits from the city,' he said. His voice sounded false. Then he flashed a torchlight ahead of him and stole into the night, like a thief.

The rice fields were greyish-blue in the moonlight. The beam of his torchlight swayed on the track. Khaireni Tar was lit up below him, warm yellow windows in the dark. A flare of light glided along the highway. The night bus was coming in. It would park for half an hour beneath the bar-peepal tree before heading east to Kathmandu.

He kept his torch trained on the ground, illuminating mud, torn plastic wrappers, twigs and fallen leaves, a broken GI pipe, stubbed-out cigarettes. At the bottom of the hill he stopped, feeling tired. His torch lit up a pool ahead of him, a puddle so large it blocked the path. There was a narrow alley to the side of the Telecommunications Office. Giridhar knew each alley of this town by heart. He knew he wouldn't encounter anybody in this alley. He didn't want to talk to anyone, to justify his ambition. Far off, he could hear radios playing in the night dens of Khaireni Tar. The sound of people getting on with their lives harrowed him.

When he scrambled into the bus he felt free at last.

gaps—.

8

Kathmandu. One day after another in a lifetime of rambling. One day after another, as though they had some order. Rishi followed a set routine, but it was a routine that lacked purpose. Every day he walked the city's tortuous alleys to the house of a student. There he reviewed the student's homework, made corrections and assigned the boy textbook pages to study more carefully. The student's mother brought him tea. Sometimes she also brought two slices of bread. Most days she didn't. Biding his hunger, Rishi watched the boy struggle to understand simple facts. In the background he could hear family members in the inner rooms, which he had never been let into. A scrape. Creaks. Footsteps sliding on the linoleum floor. The easy rhythmic sounds of bodies at home.

From there Rishi headed to the house of another student, who was richer, and to another. At both houses he was fed snacks. He stopped at evening time to read papers at a pavement stall, and then at the end of the day he made his way through the halogen-lit city to Hotel Tanahun. That was his day. That was his drift.

Hotel Tanahun was a street-side diner owned by a couple who had migrated from Rishi's home district. Many of their clients were also from the district, but Rishi didn't know them. He sat apart in a corner, watching everyone through the steam that rose from his tea: men holding out plates for second helpings of sour rice and vegetables oversalted to hide their staleness. He eavesdropped on the exchanges that took place around him. 'I work as a peon at a factory.' 'I'm a driver at a hotel.' Entire lives compressed into short sentences. 'I arrange visas for boys to go to Korea.' 'I have a farm in the district.' Some sentences were longer: 'I didn't weigh enough to qualify for the army, but I'll try again next year.' All these people who thought they knew who they were.

He was, himself, unwilling to respond to queries about what he was doing in the city. He no longer felt he needed to know. When anyone asked he said he was a tutor of history. 'A teacher?' No, a private tutor. 'Eh.' People assumed he was in between jobs on the way to a more stable position. The truth made them uneasy: he was cut off from his family and he had no friends in the city. He had no connections and couldn't find a job. Since he left the UML party's student wing, he had no political patrons to look out for him. He'd been working five years as a tutor, and this life wasn't leading him anywhere.

Sometimes Rishi would lie. 'I teach at a local school,' he would say. When people asked why he was still unmarried, he would say, 'I'm already engaged.' And he had been, once. But now he couldn't imagine starting a family with the pittance he earned. When he was pushed for more detail, he extended the lie. 'My family adopted a Bahun name, but we're actually from the lower castes,' he would say, deriving a sharp pleasure when people shrank from him. Casually, he steered himself into the bare jutting walls and cold corners of his pariah's place. 'Actually, my father died in a landslide,' he would say. 'My mother took up with another man whose name is Parajuli.' Why not? In the city he could shrug off identities or wear them like a shawl to cloak himself. This was the mobility he'd sought when he had decided, years ago, to leave home.

Heading back at night to his boarding house on New Road, Rishi was all eyes. A man with ropes strapped to his back: a porter waiting for work. A child washing dishes in a restaurant. Three men talking in Gurung tongue. He stopped and watched an auto-rickshaw driver arguing with a customer. He watched a man come out of a house reading an air-mail letter. He mimicked the hand gestures of a teenage girl and adopted the rolling gait of a foreigner. This was what it meant to live unnoticed in the gaps of Nepal's history: to grow unrecognizable, unknowable to others and to himself.

Yet every now and then Rishi felt overwhelmed by the hardness of his life, its abjection and lack of charity. On such days he felt tugged by untenable desires. Unlike his college friends he didn't want to go to Osaka to wash dishes, or to Kuwait to tend gardens. He didn't want to earn vast sums of money. What he wanted was a modest life which would let him live with his mind in flight. At times he thought he might return to Khaireni Tar and work as a teacher there. But for what? Home. The accusation of his father and reproach of his mother. The tenacious orthodoxy of village society—. He couldn't return. He could neither move backward nor could he spring forward. All he could do was lose himself.

To commit himself to his straying, Rishi had hewn a map onto the city of Kathmandu, with one constant path leading from his boarding house to Hotel Tanahun. The shifting community of the diner's customers—villagers coming to Kathmandu on errands—was his only link to home. Sometimes he even recognized people there—family acquaintances, friends from childhood, shopkeepers he had bought grains from, long ago, in Khaireni Tar bazaar. He kept his distance from them. One evening he spied his old schoolmaster from Khaireni Tar, and he turned away to avoid him. The next night the schoolmaster was in the diner again, surrounded by other men. The following evening, Rishi stayed away from the diner. When he came back the day after, he found the schoolmaster there, sitting with someone. It was as though the man had never left.

Rishi took his place in the corner of the diner, facing his old high school teacher. The schoolmaster was probably in his sixties

now, and he looked hard, whittled with age. His silver hair was
unkempt and his eyes were narrowed onto the man he was talking
to. He exuded the same aura of heedlessness that had impressed
Rishi as a boy, with his steeled look of someone who'd survived
disaster intact. It was he who had recruited Rishi into the UML
party. The schoolmaster glanced up, scanned the room, seemed
not to recognize Rishi, and looked back at the man he was with.

Rishi lowered his head and listened to the clatter of steel
plates and spoons, and the distant moaning of radio songs. A
mosquito whined near a light bulb. The man with the schoolmaster
was talking about the elections. The UML must win a majority
this time. The woman who ran the diner put a plate of rice and
daal in front of Rishi. Some men sitting by the door guffawed.
The schoolmaster mentioned Tanahun district's third electorate.
Rishi leaned in to hear what he was saying. 'The People's Party
will make it a three-way race.'

'They'll cut votes from the Congress.'

'We need sixteen thousand.'

'If they were to cut three, four thousand...'

The schoolmaster's words rustled beneath the din of the city,
and Rishi remembered late meetings in a dark room in Khaireni
Tar, lectures on Bolshevism in this voice at once forceful and
hushed. He remembered a distant blue moon, crickets rapping at
night and the schoolmaster's steps pattering behind him.

The schoolmaster looked up several times during that evening,
but his eyes always swept past Rishi, who puzzled at his own
taut spine, at his disappointment in not being recognized. When
he finished eating, he left feeling empty. It was raining outside.
The city flickered behind a sheen of reflected halogen. It didn't
look real. Rishi submitted to the nostalgia welling up inside him.
He was a boy caressed by the warm rains of the hills. He was
running barefoot with pebbles grinding into his toes. Swallows
flitted above. Marigolds grew thick along the path. He came to

a hillside. He was stumbling on rock steps, his pants were torn. Steep slopes. He was sliding home.

The next evening, Rishi walked up to the schoolmaster and introduced himself. Almost as soon as the schoolmaster's eyes steadied in recognition, another man joined them. Before turning away, the schoolmaster said to Rishi, 'I thought it was you.' He slid aside to make place for him on the bench, then turned to the other man. They seemed to be resuming a conversation they were holding earlier, about the Minister of Agriculture.

Rishi settled into his seat. The bench was warm with the schoolmaster's heat. Even though the conversation had nothing to do with him, he felt included in it by the way the schoolmaster sat, their shoulders touching. There was allowance in that contact. The older man's voice vibrated against Rishi's arm. The Minister of Agriculture was to be watched, the schoolmaster was saying. Who came from and went to his house: it could be useful to know.

The other man glanced uncomfortably at Rishi.

'We can talk freely,' the schoolmaster assured him. 'This comrade is my former student. He was with us during the protests. He was—weren't you?—one of those jailed during the democracy movement.'

'I was.'

Rishi settled in and listened to the two of them plotting for scandal. The woman who ran the diner brought three plates of food and they ate in silence. Afterwards, when the other man left, the schoolmaster turned to Rishi, casually. He didn't inquire about Rishi's present life but asked instead after his parents, as though he didn't know that Rishi hadn't been back to his village or even to Khaireni Tar in all these years. Rishi responded to his queries as best he could: 'They're probably in good health.'

'Old people in the village, they get sick,' the schoolmaster murmured vaguely. He didn't dwell on this topic. 'The students of Khaireni Tar are still renowned for their political will,' he said, and his words took on the rustling tone familiar to Rishi. 'The rally they organized last May Day was the biggest in all of Tanahun district.'

Listening to such talk, Rishi felt contained by the past—memories of himself running away from home to spend fervid nights with the schoolmaster, listening to his lectures on Marx, Engels, Lenin, Mao and proletarian and peasant revolutions. The split between the Soviet Union and China, its repercussions on a country like Nepal. The schoolmaster now began to talk about district-level politics, and how people had suffered these last few years under a Congress MP. Rishi remembered falling asleep on a mat in the man's room. 'And now these elections,' the schoolmaster said. 'This time we're sure to win a majority. The first majority communist government to be elected democratically. We're sure to win.'

Rishi didn't tell the schoolmaster that he had long stopped paying party dues. 'That's what I hear,' he agreed. 'The UML may form a majority government this time.'

When he arrived at Hotel Tanahun over the next few evenings, Rishi now scanned the dining room, seeking out the schoolmaster's silver hair as it caught the light of a naked bulb. There was usually a group of men gathered around him. The schoolmaster nevertheless nodded at Rishi, and invited him to sit with him as he directed his conversations at the other men. They talked about the elections in Tanahun. In the last elections the UML had lost by only two thousand. 'What we need to do,' the schoolmaster said, 'is to get the cinema hero Nayan Raj Dahal to run from the People's Party. That party can cut maybe three-four thousand votes from Congress. That'll help us win.'

The other men, who were also from the district, argued the merits of this strategy: 'Every seat is critical'; 'A three-way race will make it difficult for Congress'; 'All we have to do is to keep the People's Party from penetrating our strong areas.'

Rishi felt privileged to be included in such conversations, to witness the first flawed drafts of history being written. Like anyone who kept abreast of current affairs, he knew about Nayan Raj, who had joined the People's Party after his career on the silver screen had stalled. He had played a revolutionary in his last movie, and when he joined politics people had laughed that he now wanted to be a revolutionary in real life too. But he and his party had gained credibility of late. In the last elections the People's Party had surprised sceptics by winning two seats in parliament.

The UML activists at the diner slowly formulated a plan. Each day one of them would send a few people from Tanahun to visit Nayan Raj, to voice their support and urge him to run. They would create an illusion of popular grassroots support. Being a democrat, Nayan Raj would bow to the wishes of the people. He would run, he would cut Congress votes—and help bring the UML to victory.

When the men disbanded, the schoolmaster stayed awhile with Rishi in an easy silence. He patted his former student on the shoulders before leaving. Rishi noticed that he never asked him to help execute their plan, and he felt pangs of regret at having left the party. He walked home alone in the cold, damp night, and returned to Hotel Tanahun earlier and earlier each evening, listening to the buzz of conversation around him till he saw the schoolmaster arrive.

9

At the bus park on the northern end of Kathmandu, Giridhar

stood beneath an awning, shying away from a downpour that looked like hard silver coins dropping onto cement. The air was cool. In his hands was a plastic bag with a change of shirts. Ahead of him was a row of local buses that went into the city. He wasn't sure which to catch, and so for a while he pressed into the building behind him, just watching the mêlée. Men disembarking from buses scuttled out of the rain, and women smiled, embarrassed to be running in the fineries they'd worn for their city trip. An old man, frail and sick, was being carried on the back of a young man. Giridhar watched a young taxi driver adjust the black goggles on his face, and another one argue with a customer. A taxi nearby suddenly started up and sputtered away.

It was dawn: Giridhar's watch said quarter past six. He had a few hours to while away before the party office opened. He felt muddled from the night spent on the lurching, rattling bus. Throughout the ride he had reviewed the course ahead. He would meet the party's national chairman and spokesman, and give them justifications for why he should get the party's ticket in Tanahun. The reasons were many. One: he was the chairman of the party's district committee, a man who had lived his whole life in Khaireni Tar, a man who knew the electorate by heart. Two: he was qualified, an educated man with more than twenty years in government service. Three: he had created a network of supporters during his years at the bank; men he'd loaned money to would remember how fair he'd been, how he had approved their loans, how he had pardoned payments which they couldn't— in some cases—make. Four: his family was respected in the district. And five: he had a good name. He must get the ticket, therefore.

These arguments must be made with conviction, or else they would sound feeble.

A mist was spraying up from the pavement, dampening his shoes. Giridhar covered his head with his plastic bag and dashed to a row of buses. At the first one, he asked the conductor how to get to Sinamangal.

The conductor pointed at a green minibus.

Giridhar ran to the minibus. Inside, he huddled into himself for warmth. He studied the others in the bus, observing the neatness of their clothes, the way their backs were straight, the animation with which they talked with one another.

As the bus left the bus park, Giridhar looked out and saw that the city looked as beaten down as he felt, with its ragged concrete structures and exposed bricks, its walls of peeling paint, its thick electrical wires. The telephone lines in the city always impressed him. All these crowded houses connected to each other. The streets were sometimes lined with sidewalks. Where were all these people going? To work? He saw umbrellas, black, striated, patterned. Smart young women dressed in suits. Men on motorbikes, blanketed by raingear. He started when the conductor nudged him. 'Sinamangal.'

He stepped onto a brick sidewalk. It was still too early to go to the party office, so he ducked into a teashop, asked for a glass of tea, and sat looking across the street at the two-storied building that was the People's Party's central office. It was a lurid pink house which belonged to the national chairman, who lived upstairs with his family. The office was downstairs, but senior party members were always holding meetings upstairs. Giridhar had been here once before, for a party convention years ago. Streaked by rain, the building now looked run down, as though to match the paltriness of Giridhar's own ambitions: to be a candidate of one of the multitudes of small, inconsequential parties that had flooded the country after democracy. The United People's Front, the Nepal National Party, the Nepal National Unity Party, the United Democracy Party, the Make the Nation Abhiyan, the National People's Rule Party, the Peace Party Nepal, the Nepali Citizen's Party. There were six Congress parties alone: the main

Nepali Congress Party, and then the Nepali Congress (Socialist), Nepali Congress (Democratic Socialist), the Nepali Congress headed by Subarna, the Radical Nepali Congress, and the Real Nepali Congress. No one could keep count of the socialist and communist parties in the country. There was even another People's Party—the Nepali People's Party—different from this, the People's Party of Nepal. But who would give *him* a ticket to run? And why? As he sat in the teashop across the party office, his ambitions, which had seemed so paltry, now felt ridiculously presumptuous.

The traffic on the road thickened as the morning wore on. So many cars coming and going, so many three-wheeled tempos, minibuses, jeeps. People walked with purpose here. Giridhar straightened his back and imagined himself walking in this same determined way. The party must give him a chance. He lost confidence and slouched again. His shirt was still damp from the rain. He was a wreck. Who would vote for him? The sweet smell of milk in his tea comforted him. He must speak with conviction. But he didn't deserve the ticket, he knew.

No, he didn't have the will. He'd go to the party tomorrow.

The next morning Giridhar apprehensively approached the gate of the party office. Holding onto his plastic bag, he stood for a while in the front yard, taking shelter beneath a flowering jasmine vine. Its yellow buds dropped onto him like the blessings of a mocking god. He'd had a bit of homebrew at a cheap lodge last night, and he felt separated from himself, his thoughts lagging behind his movements. It was important to stay alert. The splotchy pink building was depressing. He didn't actually know any of the party members of the central office. Two men stood at the door, talking. They looked, like him, to be from rural districts— they were villagers with stains about them, with clothes inappropriately small or big or warm or summery. He patted down his hair. His pants were soaked through at the ankles. He fought off his dread and moved from the jasmine vine towards the door.

'I'm here to meet the spokesman.'

The men at the door shrugged. One of them said, 'I don't know if he's come to the office today.' But he stepped aside to let Giridhar through.

The hallway inside was full of moving shadows. Giridhar waited till he could make out the figures swarming in the dark. Conversations swirled around him. 'Do this first.' 'And he said no?' He sought out faces, a man with a profile that looked familiar, but people were hard to recognize in the dark. Someone said, 'Came all the way from where?'

'Giridharji.' A body pressed up near him and he turned to see a man addressing him. His face was familiar. They'd met before, eh, ho at the party's convention.

Giridhar was able to reply, 'It's been years.'

The man beckoned for him to follow. 'Make way, make way.' The others parted to let them through. The man—what was his name? Which district was he from?—led him into a dark back room. He showed Giridhar an empty bench. 'How long have you been in Kathmandu?'

Giridhar tried to mirror the ease of the man's gestures, but he only managed to perch oddly at the edge of the bench. 'I'm just coming in.'

The man had a kindly face, and Giridhar remembered that they had become good friends at the convention in the easy way strangers sometimes do. The man—what was his name?—said, 'You've already talked to Nayan Rajji?'

Giridhar shook his head.

'He's upstairs. He's been anxious to talk to you. I'll send him a message.'

The man beckoned a young boy and sent him off with a slip

of paper bearing Giridhar's name. Then he eased into the bench, and Giridhar tried to do the same.

'We want to win six seats this time,' the man said, becoming serious. 'We're trying to field forty candidates. Any electorate we've got a chance in, we're considering. Like your electorate. Even more unlikely places—the far west, the east. We must increase our seats by a hundred per cent.'

Giridhar tried to follow him, thinking he should remember all this. The man then talked about other parties and about national and international scenarios. Now he was onto the problems of democracy in the Third World. 'In the name of democracy an unbridled open market...Democracy and social justice are not, as we know, incompatible. So liberty and equality both—without social and economic equality what good is liberty?' Then he started to explain what kind of coalition the People's Party was willing to form with future governments. To Giridhar all this sounded familiar and exotic at the same time, like things once known but long forgotten. This was how people talked in the central office. He felt he should say something. Hearing the other man talk of European socialism, he said, 'Economic democracy matters,' but the man was already onto another topic. He was now talking, if Giridhar wasn't wrong, about the influence of India on Nepal's politics. 'Not a decision gets made without the Indian embassy's approval.'

The messenger boy returned with a note to bring Giridhar up. Taking leave, Giridhar remembered the other man's name. But it was too late to make anything of this. He slapped together a hasty namaste and followed the messenger boy.

Walking up the stairs, it seemed to Giridhar that people were looking at him, and they could look through him and see that there was nothing inside. The hallway echoed with whispers. He

saw lips pursed. Men were crowding the upstairs landing. The
messenger wound his way through a hall and Giridhar followed,
arriving suddenly at a room filled with dazzling light. He stopped
at the threshold, blinded. When he regained his vision he saw
men sitting on a row of sofas along a glass wall. Someone looked
up. 'Here he is.' And everyone turned to look at what a hollow
man he was.

They'd been talking about him, he could tell from their sudden
hush. He joined his hands in namaste, looked from one man to
another. They looked familiar, but their black hair, brown eyes,
their pale city complexions confused him. He couldn't tell them
apart.

A tall man among them spoke. 'We're glad you came.' His
tone was gracious and his features pale. With his jet black hair
combed neatly and his freshly ironed clothes, he looked store-
bought and unreal. A film star—Nayan Raj Dahal. He showed
Giridhar a sofa. 'This is your home too.'

Giridhar stooped awkwardly to take off his shoes. When he
took a seat, though, he noticed that none of the others had taken
off their shoes. He knew he should say something to Nayan Raj
but couldn't find words. He gripped his plastic bag close to him.

Another man said, 'We've been phoning to get news of the
district.' He was older, and dressed in a cotton tunic with a gold
ring prominent on his fingers. The national chairman.

'The district,' Giridhar said. He wasn't sure what to say, so
he said, 'I took the night bus, arrived yesterday.' This statement
belonged, he realized, to the conversation he had been having
downstairs. He mumbled, 'The ride was long.'

The chairman said, 'We've been discussing your electorate
for the past few weeks. We've called every day. Just yesterday
we were told you'd left town.'

'Yes I came here.'

Nayan Raj leaned forward. 'Everybody says Tanahun three

is a strong electorate for us.' He stopped and looked down at the ground, as though reflecting on something. He was a man, Giridhar saw, made attractive by the clean contours of his features. His scrubbed and polished look gave a spark to his every gesture. And though he was no longer young, he could easily star in a cinema even today. Nayan Raj continued, 'As you know, our party decided at last year's convention—you couldn't attend, am I right?—to field a candidate from there. A lot of people from the electorate have visited me, and have assured me of their support. Our party leaders are also urging me to run. But I wanted to hear from you, our chairman for the district. Tell me.' He seemed to look through Giridhar. 'What are our chances of victory?'

'Victory.' Giridhar tightened his grip on the plastic bag and rummaged about his mind, trying to find the right response. He needed to sound worthy of the ticket. He said, 'We have party members. We've got members in Khaireni Tar.'

Another man with a slack-jowled face broke in, 'Everyone says we can win. The man on the phone—what was his name?—said that the new party office has made a large impact already.'

Giridhar didn't understand.

Someone said, 'Jimmawal Sharma.'

The slack-jowled man said, 'He said people are eager that our spokesmanji run.'

'Jimmawal-baaje,' Giridhar said. What party office? And why were they talking about that old man? 'The old revenue collector from Khaireni Tar?'

Nayan Raj looked at him squarely. 'We're glad you opened an office,' he said. 'We're on the verge of deciding, but I've been hesitating. Without talking to you I couldn't say. The truth is I haven't ever…Grassroots politics—I'm not *local*, like you. I was born in Khaireni Tar, of course. And I feel very close to the people. But I won't run if you don't give your support.'

His words pattered like a distant rain shower around Giridhar, who found himself enveloped by a kind of shield which kept his mind out of the place he was physically in. He needed to ask for the ticket himself. But everyone was acting like the ticket had already been given to Nayan Raj. The whole room was watching Giridhar. He had to say something. From far away, he heard himself saying: 'Could I not support you?' There was nothing else he could say. His throat had gone dry and there was a bitter taste on his tongue. 'Could I not support you one hundred per cent?'

Nayan Raj looked hard at him, as though deliberating over this statement. 'I'm honoured,' he finally said.

Giridhar felt far removed from the room. Coolly he said, 'It's decided so fast?'

Nayan Raj said, 'We were waiting for you to decide.'

The other men in the room started chatting among themselves. 'We need four-five seats this time. Tanahun three is a strong place for us, we have to win there.' The light from the window hurt Giridhar's eyes. He tried to keep focused. He became aware that Nayan Raj had turned to him. The man was saying something: how long did he plan to stay in Kathmandu, would he come to his house later on in the day, did he need a place to stay?

'Eh I can't stay,' Giridhar said, feeling confused. 'I have to head home at once.'

'You've only just arrived. There are many things to plan.'

'No.' Giridhar felt angry now, and disgusted. He was just as capable as this cinema hero—more capable, even. From his pocket, he fetched the map that he'd drawn of the electorate. 'See for yourself.' He laid it out on the plastic bag on his lap. 'Here is the district.' With a finger he traced the black lines that looked like the wrinkles of his own hands. 'I know people here, here. Here. I know the village leader here. I met him years ago at the bank. I can still see his face.' He couldn't help sounding quarrelsome. 'All the ward members of this VDC are relatives of mine. Now this whole flank is a UML stronghold. Our chances are better in this half, where Congress is popular. Like Dhor.' With his forefinger, he circled half the electorate. 'We should penetrate Dhor. If we can penetrate Dhor we'll break Congress.'

He realized, then, that Nayan Raj wasn't looking at the map. Big men like him wanted to talk about the national agenda, not about local strategies. Giridhar's concerns were laughable. Desperately, he thrust the map into Nayan Raj's hand, giving away the chart to his own future. 'Keep it,' he said. 'Everything's written down.'

Nayan Raj put aside the scrap of paper without even looking at it. 'I can't come to the district for another month,' he said. 'There's too much to do at the centre. Fundraising, organizing. And our platform needs revision.' He frowned. 'We're focusing more strongly, this election, on what we mean by democratic reform. It must be clear to everyone that we hold high values, Giridharji. We must wrest our democracy away from those who just want to focus on power politics. We must focus on people at last.'

An actor performing his lines. Nayan Raj kept speaking of such fine-fine ideas, but Giridhar was no longer listening. The man already looked, he thought, like a victor, with his combed-back hair that presented his attractive features to the world. He talked with such exaggerated humility. How could he not become the candidate? The actor concluded, 'I hope you'll come back soon so that we can discuss how best to sound our call for true democracy.'

'No, no.' Mustering all his strength, Giridhar got up from the sofa. 'Planning, plotting, organizing cannot be done in Kathmandu city.' He joined his palms in namaste. 'These things I will be doing at home. You—.' He tried to control the hoarseness of his voice. 'If you send me a note with instructions, I will follow all of them. All you have to do is send me your orders. I will follow one hundred per cent.'

Without waiting to be dismissed, he fled.

Later, he thought the problem was the bigness of this city, its indifference, its people pushing against each other not knowing the backgrounds of those they talked to, its assumptions, its way of controlling the talk, its colours, its crowds, its lives swarming forward at a clip, its disguises, its secret wires of communication, its whispers and its hidden power. Pacified with sweet rum in his veins, Giridhar wandered through New Road, lost. He couldn't even guess where he was. In a village a man was confined. Here, spaces unfolded, promising to hide him from others, from himself. But open spaces were dangerous. A body in vast spaces got lost. He belonged in small spaces, he belonged in spaces which trapped him. He needed to feel the sharp edges of life and know what the limits were. In Kathmandu it was possible to disappear into gaps and silences. Gaps—. He felt himself a wisp in this mire. In the din of the city, who would hear what he said?

10

'In press release statement today, People's Party of Nepal Spokesman Nayan Raj Dahal confirmed that he was "running for the sake of democracy" from Tanahun District electorate number three. Similarly, seven other People's Party members confirmed their candidacy. "The People's Party is an illustrious and honest party of the people and we will serve the people as deserved," party members opined at press conference. Speaking afterwards to this scribe, former cinestar said that he was proud to actualize his main philosophy of democracy reform by running

for elections. This makes overall forty candidates from the People's
Party in a bid to become major political contending party other
than Congress, UML and various others. Overall, 41 of 93
registered parties have announced candidates so far, although
rumours are going round saying some of smaller parties are
established only for sake of receiving free telephone line from
government, as regulation quota permits allow.'

11

Tutoring his student, Rishi watched the boy, trying to fathom his
incomprehension. One king followed another—all he had to do
was remember their names, one king after another inheriting this
country and its subjects. What was confusing about this? When
Rishi was a boy, history had been for him the explanation behind
palpable everyday events. His own family's backwardness had
been caused by the tyranny of the kings who wouldn't let their
child-like subjects grow into enfranchised citizens. Linking his
life to national events had given him a reason to memorize these
quaint names: Pratap Singh Shah, Ranabahadur Shah,
Girwanyuddha Shah. Black Devanagari script printed with
smudged ink. His student's dull eyes roved listlessly over the
surface of his textbook. It was not Rishi's job to motivate the
boy. He was paid to make boys like this—born into the comfort
of middle-class Kathmandu homes—receive passing marks in
year-end exams. That was all he could do.

    Today the boy's mother brought him a cold piece of toast
with jam smeared on top, which Rishi accepted with relief. He
spent the rest of his day distracted. He had read in the vernacular
papers about Nayan Raj's candidacy, and had made up his mind
to talk to the schoolmaster. He wanted to say, Why don't you
ask me? Why didn't the schoolmaster ask Rishi for help with the

elections? If he asked, Rishi would give himself up to the party again. He had decided to.

After the last tutorial of the day he stood by the pavement news stall looking at the evening papers, but not reading anything. He was lost in thought.

The mistakes of youth multiply. At first Rishi had made a mistake, then to spite himself he had purposefully ruined things, and then that spite had become habit. Years ago he had quit a teaching job after an altercation with the headmaster about unfairly high tuition fees. That hadn't been a mistake, but it had bred mistakes. At that time he had Radhika—they were waiting for him to find a job to support them both after marriage. They waited too long, far past the limits of their yearning, far past their ability to contain desire. And then they took the only option they could afford: they overpaid a disdainful obstetrician to have the foetus aborted illegally. Rishi remembered standing to one side of a plywood partition, alert to every word, cough and movement on the other side. When it was over, neither he nor Radhika ever mentioned it. The decision had been made together, but its sorrow had changed Radhika, and its remorse had changed Rishi too. He had disappeared from Radhika's life without ever telling her why.

The mistakes of youth. His passions had been uncertain, too paltry to confront life with. He had always lacked conviction; always waited too long.

That night Rishi arrived at Hotel Tanahun ragged and depleted. His curls were in disarray and his eyes gleamed unnaturally. His clothes, usually tasteful, were mismatched and crumpled from neglect. His dishevelment wasn't like the schoolmaster's, though; it didn't give him the same look of someone who'd been burnished by hardship. He just looked debased.

The schoolmaster hadn't yet arrived. Rishi sat at a table

next to the radio and turned it on. The news was over, and a current events show announcer was stumbling over his words to discuss the atmosphere of doom among the country's intelligentsia. 'Ranked as the second poorest country by the UNDP, Nepal has one of the lowest GDP rates...'

The show ended, and was followed by love duets. Rishi ate his dinner listening to songs praising love's virtues and the beauty of the himals. At nine, the schoolmaster entered the diner, and sat at another table with two other men. Rishi waited. When, after an hour, the schoolmaster stood to leave, Rishi followed him.

Outside, the older man sensed Rishi's presence and slowed to let him catch up. Rishi caught a sparkle of amusement in the schoolmaster's eyes. But he didn't ask Rishi to explain anything. He just started speaking, filling the darkness of the city with his easy, rustling voice. He spoke, for some reason, about his underground years, the decades after he stopped teaching in Khaireni Tar. Wanted by the government, he had gone to live in east Nepal with his brother, selling wholesale onions. 'I took up alien identities at will,' the schoolmaster said, his voiced tinged with wonder. 'But I found myself that way.' He walked step to step, shoulder to shoulder with Rishi. 'Sometimes you find yourself in false identities.'

He spoke in his familiar drone. He didn't seem to want Rishi to respond, but did seem to appreciate his audience. His tone was confiding. He steered Rishi at intersections, placing a hand on his arm. The two of them walked for a long time along the broken grids of Rishi's Kathmandu, into dark alleys lit by the sudden yellow of motorcycle beams, past groups of young men gathering at paan shops, past fluorescent-lit restaurants with love songs blaring, past idling taxis and packs of stray dogs. They went wherever the city streets led them. Rishi leaned in towards the schoolmaster, his eyes, with lashes as thick as a girl's, focused

on the older man's angled face. Sometimes the schoolmaster
stopped to look: a woman offering flowers at a way-side shrine,
her face lit by oil lamps; a window lit up by the flickering blue
light of a television set inside. Sometimes Rishi stopped to look
at similar things: a man walking down the street wearing bright
new Adidas.

All the while, the schoolmaster talked about the disguises
he'd taken up while he was underground. Rishi knew he was
being inculcated into the schoolmaster's ethics, into his vision.
His old teacher was teaching him the vocabulary of his politics,
its grammar and expression. He was showing Rishi that he too
could find himself in the UML. The two men stopped and looked
at three prostitutes walking into a cheap lodge.

The schoolmaster said, 'The things people do in life.'

The next day, Rishi drew another line on his map of Kathmandu
city: one leading from his boarding house on New Road to the
UML office on the edge of town. He followed this line and found
the schoolmaster at the end of it. 'I want to join the party again,'
he said, cringing at the way his own voice sounded in plea. 'I
want to help the party win in Tanahun three.'

'I knew you'd come back to us, Comrade.'

Afterwards, Rishi sat in his bare room pressing his
membership slip into his hand, throbbing with nostalgia for home.

love that was gone

12

In the fields the girls of Khaireni Tar were taking a break from uprooting rogue weeds and grasses. They were talking about the upcoming harvest: groups of boys and groups of girls would work together, as they always did. There would be bantering and teasing and flirting, there would be singing, and there might be love...Every few years a girl eloped at harvest time.

'Remember the girl who was captured last year?' one girl said. 'In the end she didn't agree to marry the boy, so he had to give her back to her parents.'

'Then she ran away with another boy,' said another girl. 'They're living in Kathmandu now.'

Someone quipped, 'Why don't you run away too, so you can live in Kathmandu?'

The girl protested as the others snickered.

Sani disapproved of girls who only talked about boys, boys, boys—such behaviour smacked of commonness. It surprised her that her friend Gaumati was chuckling along with the other girls. Gaumati said, 'I know a good boy, if anyone wants to run away with him.'

The first girl laughed, 'Be quiet, whore!'

'You're the whore,' Gaumati shot back with an obscene gesture.

Sani was appalled.

Gaumati turned to Sani. 'There's a Rawal boy coming from India,' she said, poking her with a hoe. 'They say his arms are made of steel.'

'Is the rest of him also made of steel?' another girl squealed, and the whole group erupted in scandalized cries.

Sani grimaced. 'Let's not waste time,' she said sternly. 'Quick, let's weed the fields.'

Gaumati poked her again. 'I bet the Rawal boy'll take a liking to you, and grab you with his steely arms.'

Everyone started to laugh.

Sani blushed fiercely. A girl like her becoming the target of such base talk! She shook her hoe at them. 'The weeds! What, you want to spend all next year eating weeds?'

The girls stared at her blankly.

Was she the only girl of proper breeding here? Sani suddenly lost all sense of decorum. 'Did you come to the fields to work, or to talk about boys, boys, boys?'

Then, having said something so righteous, there was nothing to do but march off in a huff. This was exactly what she did, standing up with a stamp of her foot which expressed her indignation.

The girls tittered as she stomped off.

'Come back,' Gaumati called out. 'We'll be very, very good, like you.'

Was Gaumati mocking her? Sani marched on. She headed towards town, then suddenly stopped: there he was ahead of her, the Khadka boy, standing with his head bent and his toes pointed in.

The skinny corpse!

Much to the surprise of the girls, Sani rushed back to the fields and sat down among them. Then she began fumbling with her hoe, uprooting weeds.

The water tap next to Binita's house consisted of a trickling PVC pipe affixed with a leaky nut and washer, which stood near a row of bottlebrush trees. Sani came here each morning to collect water; but no matter how early she arrived, women were already in line, waiting their turn. One couldn't tell, by looking at the faces of town people, which caste or ethnic group they belonged to. It made Sani feel impure to drink water from a tap so commonly used. But such was her broken fate. Today there were six women in line. Sani stood behind them with her brass jug hitched to her hips. Visible on the other side of the bottlebrush trees was the bar-peepal tree. Vendors were already setting up on the stepped platform beneath. Beyond the bar-peepal was the bazaar: a dark huddle of buildings. Sani had been to the bazaar only twice—once when she arrived in this ugly, crowded town six months ago, and then the time Binita-didi had taken her there to buy her new clothes. She hated the bazaar, people took too many liberties there. Shiftless, mannerless people pushed and nudged as if they owned the world. And common shopkeepers acted familiar. She was not Binita-didi, she wanted to tell them; had she a choice, she wouldn't be living with a woman like her.

Something appeared amid the bottlebrush trees to block her view of the bazaar. Sani shifted, but the obstruction shifted with her. She peered and saw, in the dim light—she wasn't sure—ssss: there was a figure standing there, a boy, an ugly boy, the Khadka boy. He was ogling her from behind a tree!

Then the boy actually stepped out of the trees, and Sani almost screamed. The whole skinny length of him was less than ten paces away! Her heart pounded. Her shock increased when she saw the boy's face. Ssss, he was so ugly! Small-boned and unmanly, he shifted from foot to foot, carrying a cheap tin pail in his hands. A boy collecting water: she sucked in her breath.

The other women at the tap were also looking at the Khadka boy in astonishment.

'I—' his voice was high. 'I just came to collect water.'

'Hare Shiva, Shiva,' an elderly woman cried. 'A boy doing women's work! What a sight to see!'

The boy fluttered an uncertain gaze over everyone. He said, 'I usually come earlier, before dawn—so that no one will see me.

People laugh...it's humiliating.' His eyes settled on Sani. 'My mother died giving birth to me, so I've grown up this way, doing women's work.'

Sani's shock turned into disgust. Cornering her in public like this, evoking the name of his dead mother, begging for love: the boy was pathetic.

The other women were moved by his plight, though. 'Poor thing's been deprived of a mother's love,' said one of them. 'Boys like that always have a sickliness about them. They need a woman's care.'

The woman at the head of the line made room for him. 'Here, boy, fill your pail, you don't want the rest of the women to see you. They'll die laughing at you.'

The Khadka boy stepped forward, and Sani stepped back in horror. Tch, he was so distressingly close. Luckily for her the other women quickly surrounded the boy, plying him with questions. 'So who cooks at home? Every day you cook every meal?'

'Your father—he doesn't treat you like a son? He—he doesn't love you, what?'

'No wonder the poor thing's just skin and bones.'

Sani waited till the boy was encircled. Then she sneaked away.

The next morning, Sani asked Gaumati to fetch her water. 'I cut my foot in the madwoman's land that day—remember?—and it's hurting,' she said, showing off the gash in the arch of her right foot. Gaumati willingly complied. Sani then turned to chores in the teashop. The best way to prevent meeting the Khadka boy was to stay at home. Let him search the rice fields for her, let him roam every last alley, let him even fall off a cliff and die!

Binita-didi was resting today, on the first day of her monthly

cycle. Reluctantly, Sani served steaming hot tea to all the
customers who came in on the morning buses. Most of the men
complimented her by asking for second and third cups. Some
tried to talk to her, but Sani refused to be lured into conversation.
At mid-morning, the crowd had thinned, and she sat down at one
of the tables, leafing through her literacy textbook. It was at
Binita-didi's insistence that she'd enrolled in the evening class.
There were fifteen other women enrolled. Sani was the youngest
one. She didn't particularly enjoy studying. For a whole month
she hadn't understood a thing the Sir taught. Nowadays, though,
she was beginning to recognize letters. Like this letter: she placed
a finger on a swooping black sign. She knew it. She knew it.
What was it? She opened her mouth to read it out loud.

'Sani,' said a voice that wasn't her own.

Her spirit leaped clear out of her body.

She turned to see the Khadka boy standing right there, in the
teashop, just an arm's reach away. Sani was stunned. She
considered running to the back porch—but if she moved he might
try to stop her, which meant he would touch her. Eh gods!

The Khadka boy's narrow shoulders were drooped and his
face was contorted in anxiety. His hair stood straight up on his
head. He was, Sani realized, not even taller than she. 'Sani,' he
repeated in his feminine voice. 'How...' His gaze flickered away
from her as he hesitated. 'How luminous you are.'

A flash of contempt brought Sani to her feet. She waved
about like a madwoman, and finally spluttered, 'Go!'

The boy's shoulders crumpled and his eyes drowned in a
pool of tears.

Ssss, she was being cruel. 'Go!' Sani warbled, choked with
confusion. 'Go!'

And, like a beaten dog, the boy turned and slunk out the
door.

Sani remained standing, quaking, and poised for aggression

should the boy return. When he disappeared down the front steps, she collapsed on a bench and started to sob in dismay.

What a stupid boy! How ugly he was! Why did he force her to see his pitiable self?

What if anyone had seen him talking to her? They'd think she was a hussy, like her cousin sister. So rattled was Sani by this incident that she spent the whole day flitting in and out of the teashop, wringing her hands. Only when Tripti returned from school did she realize that she hadn't prepared any snacks.

For days afterwards, Sani was anxious and tense. How was she to get rid of the Khadka boy? She feared his lunacy. And she was convinced that someone would hear that she had actually spoken to him. She couldn't leave the house without feeling afraid. She was vigilant when she went to the water tap. She was vigilant when she went to the fields. She wished she didn't have to collect grass for the buffaloes, or fetch firewood. Walking in a group of girls didn't assure her any more. She didn't even feel safe in Binita-didi's teashop.

She finally decided to ask Gaumati for help. She chose a time when the two of them were perched side by side on a chestnut tree, chopping branches for firewood. Other girls were perched on nearby trees, just out of earshot. They were in the patchy forests on the hills north of town.

How to begin? Sani's full-moon face clouded. Her lips pursed. The mole on her chin twitched. 'Gaumati,' she finally said, 'I don't know what to do. And your grandfather's second wife's son is the stupid boy's grandfather, so I thought …'

Gaumati turned towards her.

Sani flushed. 'Nothing's actually happened,' she said. 'But he follows me, everywhere, in the fields, at the tap—he even came into the house!' She dared not look up to face Gaumati's judgement. 'A girl, all alone...What if anyone had seen? Don't tell anyone. Swear, swear, swear you won't tell anyone!'

Gaumati tucked her sickle into her waistcloth and clambered over to Sani, perching next to her on a sturdy branch. 'Tell me what happened,' she said avidly. 'I won't tell anyone.'

'I'll die if you do,' Sani whimpered. 'Ssss! What will people think?'

'I won't tell,' Gaumati promised. 'But who's the boy? Which one of my grandfather's second wife's son's grandsons are you talking about?'

Sani shrugged unhappily. 'I don't know his name, but he's a Khadka boy and he's thin and he speaks like a girl and he doesn't have a mother and he collects water by himself every morning.'

'You've talked to him about all of this?'

'I'd never!'

Gaumati's face lit up. 'It must be Harsha Bahadur! Does he have hair that stands up? And the face of a goat?'

Sani nodded.

Gaumati grinned. 'That imbecile!' After glancing about to make sure that no one could hear, she whispered eagerly, 'Some say he's not even his father's legitimate son! He's sickly, you know, and pale. With a father who's dark—his mother was dark too, she died giving birth to him. People wondered, when Harsha Bahadur was born, if his father hadn't killed his mother out of rage. But anyway—. His father's so poor. He's so, so poor. A boy like that targeting you—it's ridiculous!'

Sani felt comforted. She moved closer to Gaumati and said, 'So I thought, since you're his distant relative, maybe you could tell him...I don't know. No, don't talk to him, don't tell him I said anything. Swear, swear, swear you won't...But maybe you could tell him to just go. Just go and—join the army or something.' Then she remembered what a skinny corpse he was and she lost her composure. 'He wouldn't get in, though,' she scoffed. 'Who'd want him, he's so skinny, and he's ugly too. Even the Nepal police would die laughing at him. Tell him to go jump off a cliff and die!'

Gaumati gasped. Sani was shocked by her own cruelty. Tears welled up in her eyes. She hid her face in shame.

Hearing her cry, the girls on the nearby trees turned. It wouldn't be long, Sani realized, before they came to find out what was wrong. She thrust out her right foot. The gash on it could serve as a good excuse. And she pleaded with Gaumati, 'Just tell him I'm a good girl, I want to be left alone. Tell him I won't marry him. But don't tell him I said it. Just make him go away!'

The trees began to rustle as the other girls made their way over.

13

Rejection was the swift dive you took when slipping on bamboo leaves: no time to reach out for balance. Rejection was the stench of rotten feed that cows had urinated on. Rejection sounded like an old witch laughing at a naked boy. How swiftly it moved, rejection, a sudden hailstorm pelting down from calm blue skies. Rejection soured the guts and blackened the blood. It throbbed, and it tasted like iron in the mouth: it was the tang of your own mortality.

Harsha Bahadur Khadka had heard this on the radio once: a poet had recited it. It was strange how each word came back to him now, as he tried hard to keep calm with Gaumati standing before him, bearing witness to the miscarriage of his love. His distant cousin from the wealthy lineage of his grandfather's family, Gaumati was born to look down on him. 'She's too good for you,' she said vindictively. 'Sani—and you! It's beyond ridiculous!'

Harsha Bahadur wanted to protest that his love was a pure, ungrasping thing. After what Sani had said to him in her cousin's teashop, it was clear that his fate was to admire, from afar, the radiant glow of her starlight. She had made her wish known and he would obey. He wanted to tell Gaumati all this, but his cousin wouldn't let him speak.

'So there's a Rawal boy coming to work on the fields next month.' Gaumati was clearly relishing hurting him. 'He works in a hotel in India! All the girls are saying he's certain to fall for Sani. They say she's the prettiest and he'll fall for her.'

Ssss, no. Harsha wanted not to hear this. The thought of someone else marrying Sani made him quiver in dismay. Not that he stood a chance...and yet it was true that even now he allowed himself to see deep dreams of themselves. Flesh skin tendons bones blood bile and excreta: he prayed that his sickliness would be healed by Sani's healthfulness. He imagined that one day, in their union, he would give her his air, and she him hers, and they would breathe together.

'The Rawal boy's stronger than you, and richer and more handsome,' Gaumati went on. 'And he's high-school passed. Furthermore he's got steely arms.'

Gradually Gaumati's voice drifted like a fading memory— and so was it an illusion? Because when Harsha Bahadur blinked, and the tears began to flow, Gaumati was gone.

But then he saw, no: she was still here, his cousin, standing before him with a look of scorn on her face. It was the dream of Sani which was winking and fading. It was love that was gone.

In utter grief, Harsha Bahadur decided to spend his life crying, eating nothing so that he would vanish, and drinking no water so that he'd run out of tears to cry. And endless tears he cried. He spent whole mornings, whole afternoons and whole evenings beneath a dried-up lemon tree behind his father's shack, curled into a ball and sobbing, sobbing without end. He managed none of the household chores, and he left the tree only at night, to curl up exhausted on the wood planks of his pallet. Day after day, he cried so much that his body got parched. His face wrinkled, his bones ached and his insides contracted as he tried to weep away his soul.

The neighbourhood boys began to gather around. They'd heard of Harsha Bahadur's questionable parentage, and they knew his father treated him with contempt, making him work like a daughter instead of pampering him like a son. What if they asked him why he was crying—and he spoke unspeakable family scandals? No one really wanted to hear of his misery. The boys pitied Harsha Bahadur, but they also disliked him for being so pitiable. A deep melancholy pervaded his spirits. He was sensitive. He was annoyingly frail. Some of them wanted to be nice to him, but didn't know how.

'So, what, unh, did something, ke, happen?' a boy ventured one day. 'What, you—unh, you seem unhappy.'

'Ho yes,' another boy said. 'Did, ke, something happen?'

'You can tell us,' said another boy. 'We're your friends. We—won't we?—yes, we'll help you.'

Harsha Bahadur held in his misery and held in his misery—till he could contain it no longer. 'She hates me,' he finally sobbed out loud. 'All I wanted was to breathe the air…but she hates my air.'

Eh, it was love gone awry. The boys sighed in relief. Now they knew what to do. They started at once to coax the girl's name out of Harsha Bahadur, who in a moment of anguish, wailed: 'Sani!'

The nickname Sani was a common one, though, and it took a while for the boys to guess which Sani Harsha Bahadur was wailing over.

'Sani? That cousin of the widow Binita?'

Harsha Bahadur nodded miserably.

A few of the boys laughed. 'Check the size of your gullet before swallowing a bone,' someone said. 'You can't expect to get a girl like her.'

A few boys tried to be kind to the suffering fool. 'You've got to forget her. Who is she, after all? To think you're not good enough.'

'A boy doesn't cry over a girl,' another boy explained. 'He makes her cry over him.'

'Ho. The girl has to cry over the boy.'

Harsha Bahadur looked up from his tears and saw a world, wobbling and wet, filled with people who didn't understand what it meant to love. 'She must never cry,' he hissed.

Another boy suggested cavalierly, 'Find another girl, friend—there are so many. Find another girl and ask your father to fix your marriage with her.'

'You should just forget her.'

'Or go to the city, take a job—but you'd need connections for that.'

'You should do karate, kung-fu and boxing and build up your body.'

'A boy needs money to impress girls. Go to Kuwait and work as an Arab sheik's servant.'

'But you'd need money to pay your way abroad.'

Harsha Bahadur groaned.

'What you want,' someone advised, 'is for her to realize she's wrong. You have to keep trying to meet her, keep trying to talk to her. A girl wants a boy to be persistent in proving his love.'

'I still think,' the first boy said, 'that he should try to forget her. Who does she think she is? An orphan. Doesn't she realize how—sincere—this poor boy is? Doesn't she realize what a frail, sickly person he is? A shock like this can destroy a poor boy's life. Especially a boy as weak as him.'

'Ho, he's quite weak.'

'He's puny.'

'From this angle he looks like a skeleton, in fact.'

Ssss! Harsha Bahadur started to cry even harder. True, he wasn't the handsomest richest smartest most dashing boy in the world, but he had a loving heart. Was the world blind to this?

Then opinion turned against him. Someone in the group said, 'I mean, she's a most comely girl.'

Another boy said, 'With a face as radiant as the moon.'

Everyone sighed. A girl with such a well-placed mole on her chin: it was natural for her to reject Harsha Bahadur.

Intuiting this silent verdict, Harsha Bahadur curled into a tight ball, and wept.

'Now I see you've been soiling my good name by sitting beneath the lemon tree out back, weeping over some girl. It doesn't suit a boy to cry over love tragedies. You never were a hearty fellow, though—you've always taken after your mother, so weak of spirit she died birthing you. She had your same look of a dehydrated chicken. Now listen, I won't have any son of mine being the talk of the neighbourhood. I don't know what's gotten into you, maybe the witch took your spirit away. But toughen up boy, you need to spend more time in the fields. Such feebleness: I should have never sent you to school. What do they teach you in those books? To sit beneath trees and weep? Now I know you're tenth-grade fail, and I haven't studied at all, but this much I know: a boy needs rigour, a boy needs discipline, a boy needs a taste of the cane. Next year I'm enrolling you in the army whether you like it or not. After you've been beaten by your captain major general for being such a ninny you'll finally learn what it means to be a man.'

Harsha Bahadur was confirmed in his suspicion that his father wasn't really his father.

The spectacle of Harsha Bahadur sitting beneath the dried-up lemon tree finally caught the attention of his Maoist second cousin from his own poor lineage, who was an intermediate-level student at the Khaireni Tar campus and a most brilliant boy. 'Bourgeois girls want to marry bourgeois boys,' this cousin explained gruffly, sitting down next to Harsha Bahadur. He had the jagged profile of a revolutionary, but straight-on his face was as soft as a teenage boy's. His wispy beard didn't suit him at all. Silhouetted dramatically against the sky, he declared, 'That's the way of reformists in this multinational imperialist broker capitalist age of exploitation. The bourgeoisie never redistributes its wealth— or their women. The Rawal boy is the son of a rich landlord and it's no surprise that he should deprive you of your girl.'

'But it's Sani who rejected me,' Harsha Bahadur groaned. 'The Ra...The Rawal boy didn't steal her from me, she made her own choice.'

'Choice!' His cousin hissed. 'Her class character won't let her love you.'

'Ssss. Her character—so flawless—.'

'Her character is governed by her class!' His cousin was almost shouting now. He held up an instructive forefinger and wagged it angrily. 'The bourgeoisie won't let its daughters love poor landless men. That's how they train their girls to think, that's how they'll think—till the workers' and peasants' revolution liberates them and makes them realize that we're brothers, all!'

This thought gave Harsha Bahadur pause. 'So it's not her fault,' he said, searching his cousin's face for hope. 'Society makes her not love me because I'm poor.'

His cousin smirked. 'That's why we're fighting, my brother,

for a Maoist republic. We live in the turbulent transition time
from a feudal to a capitalist system. But capitalism creates a
bourgeois society that won't give us what we deserve.
Parliamentary democracy is just a pawn of the rich, that's why
we workers and peasants must reject reform efforts and fight for
true revolution—we must claim what is rightfully ours: Education!
Jobs! Electricity! Roads! A wholesale landslide gale-storm kind
of cultural revolution!' He tugged at his beard in excitement,
'Look, brother, the Maoist people's war is the best option for the
heartbroken. You think you're the only sad Nepali? Aren't
millions of others suffering? Is any of us free from the
multinational imperialist broker capitalist exploitation of our
parliamentary democracy? You must awaken, brother, and fight!'

Harsha Bahadur wasn't sure he agreed with all that his cousin
was saying, but he felt comforted by his confident tone. 'There
are so many other people in the world,' he agreed, 'who live in
unhappiness. The poor, the sick, those whose homes get washed
away by landslides and floods.'

His cousin almost pounced on him. 'That's why you must
join me in sabotaging these upcoming elections! If people won't
help us boycott these elections, we'll make them, with the use of
petrol bombs, automatic rifles, pistols and khukuri knives!'

What? Harsha Bahadur looked up, startled. What happened
to talk of love?

One look at his cousin and it was confirmed: Maoists were
scrappy and rough, forever rabble-rousing. They spoke too fast,
and they stayed up late and looked at each other with piercing,
blood-shot eyes. Harsha Bahadur himself was a peaceable soul
who just wanted to be happy in love.

He sank deep into despair, not knowing what to do.

cinema hero this-that this-that

14

Giridhar had returned from Kathmandu in a muddle, spent four rowdy days drinking in the dens in the southern end, then collapsed into the isolation of his home. His inchoate utterances provided just enough drywood to kindle fast-spreading rumours on the topic of Nayan Raj:

'He's running, I heard it from his own chairman. That one-time number one cinema hero, he's running from here.'

'Ho yes, I heard the same thing...'

Soon shopkeepers were gathering in the eaves of the bazaar houses and gossiping away their afternoons, speculating on only one prospect: 'Will the cinema hero win, will he lose...what will happen?'

'Well, he *is* the most well-known candidate. His famous movie—*Ma Manchhe Hun*—they say it brings tears to the eyes.'

'Ho, I saw it, it was excellent. I've seen all of his movies, every last one. Personally, me myself, in my own view I believe that he'll win.'

'The only problem is his party's unknown.'

'And it's got a drunk for a chairman.'

The vendors on the stepped platform beneath the bar-peepal tree kept coming back to the topic of Nayan Raj in their talk. 'Today or tomorrow, he's going to arrive,' the peanut vendor said. 'The radio interviewed him the other day, and he said he wanted to devote his whole life to grassroots politics from now on...Peanuts, anyone?'

'I heard that interview,' said the cheeseballs-and-chips vendor. 'He talks seriously, that man.'

The town's watchmaker, sitting at his canvas stall near by, had suddenly become an authority on all matters pertaining to

Nayan Raj, since he, in a trip to Kathmandu, had actually visited
the actor at his home at the urging of the old schoolmaster of
Khaireni Tar. 'I myself wouldn't vote for him,' the watchmaker
said prudently to the UML and Congress workers who flocked to
his stall to gather information. 'A cinema hero. What does he
know about the district?' When non-partisan townspeople asked,
though, the watchmaker was more candid. 'The hero, he has a
certain grave look. Even when he smiles, it looks like he's thinking
about serious things. I thought he'd be arrogant—such a famous
man—but he's not. He remembered my name till the end.'

Thainlo Nepali, from a nearby settlement of Gaine-caste
singers, listened attentively to the watchmaker's account. 'Is it
true,' he finally asked, 'that the parties will give us money if we
sing for them?'

The people at the stall dismissed him with a laugh.

Thainlo Nepali was in earnest, though: he needed to put at
least one son through school. Political parties had money to throw,
that's what everyone said. He drew a bow against his fiddle to
sound a frolicsome riff. 'This new party—this cinema hero
master—won't he need a singer to wander the villages singing
about how illustrious he is?'

The watchmaker pointed at the People's Party office across
the highway. There wasn't a hint of movement in the building.
'Go there, old man, and ask how much they'll pay to listen to
your bleating.'

The others at his stall guffawed, but Thainlo Nepali remained
unfazed. During the last wedding season he had gone from village
to village carrying news of the latest couplings: so-and-so's virgin
daughter was being given to so-and-so's virgin son of such-and-
such village. 'How touching your melodies,' people told him,
their stony hearts softened by his soulful tunes. 'I could sit and
listen all day.' Thainlo Nepali knew he could enthrall even an
audience of deaf mutes. There was no reason why political parties

shouldn't pay him to sing their praises.

He turned to study the shiny new party office across the highway.

Not everyone was interested in news of Nayan Raj's candidacy, though. Sitting peaceably at her stall the Musalmaan bangle seller remained thoroughly unimpressed. A cinema hero turned politician—who needed it? The RPP lady candidate actually bought a dozen bangles from her the other day—now *she* was the kind of politician the bangle seller liked. The lady had size four-two hands, and she'd chosen the multicoloured bracelets that the high-fashion ladies of Delhi-Calcutta-Bombay were wearing this year. This Nayan Raj Sayan Raj fellow—he was just a good-for-nothing creator of small-town hubbubs. Above all the bangle seller didn't want hubbub—especially not near her stall, where she had to attract lady customers.

The rest of the town's women also had no time for politics. A month ago the first-ever adult literacy class had started in Khaireni Tar at the insistence of Hom Kumari, the elder wife of the Sub-Inspector of Police. Like the other women enrolled in the class, Hom Kumari was too busy learning letters to bother about the elections. Yes, she was learning letters at the age of forty-five. Naturally, people laughed. Even she hadn't stopped giggling the first day of class. A mother of four going to school! 'Our women are getting bold,' the town's men had joked the first time she walked to the evening class. 'I wonder what their Sir looks like, to attract flocks of women like this!' Some were more uncharitable, and sniped that the women just wanted to walk freely at night, like whores. But there were other men who believed in literacy for women, and the women students got more determined as the class went on—except for Hom Kumari's neighbour, whose husband beat her so badly she couldn't see for two days.

By now the pencil no longer felt foreign between Hom Kumari's fingers, and she knew all thirty-six letters of the alphabet.

Every night the Sir lectured the women about women's development. 'You should form a mother's group,' he urged them constantly. 'Then you can do things for the development of women. Don't forget, women occupy half the earth and hold up half the sky.'

Such notions! Hom Kumari could hardly be bothered about this Nayan Raj hero.

But generally, whether or not they cared for the actor, the people of Khaireni Tar spread word of his candidacy. Even the ascetic who lived in a cave near the Seti river far south of town heard of Nayan Raj from a passing alms-giver. The ascetic was himself once high in the Congress party's ranks, but now he shrugged to hear news of politics. To him politics was a field of base temptations. Offered so many chances for graft, bribes, kickbacks and payoffs, even the best men succumbed. He himself had. Thankfully, the gayatri mantra gave a man a chance to purify himself. Om bhoor bhuba subaha, the ascetic chanted all day, willing his atma towards all-pervasive Brahma. Om tat sabitur barenyam. Only the gayatri mantra could cleanse a man of base hungers. For wrongdoing began in the stomach; the stomach was the cause of all evil. Bhargo debasya dhimahi, the ascetic chanted. Dhiyo yo na prachodayat. He lifted his shirt to watch his stomach move, like ocean waves undulating. Only when every politician mastered his stomach would the country be liberated from corruption. Om.

Though Nayan Raj's name was on many lips, and though a few townspeople began to think of voting for him—'What's my one vote, after all'—nobody actually went up to the People's Party's office to enquire if they could join. The party office was just too stark to be welcoming. Sometimes the old revenue collector Jimmawal Sharma could be seen scuttling towards it, and at

other times Om Gurung was seen heading there on his way back
home from his boarding school. Giridhar Adhikari was the man
to talk to—but he never came to the office at all. With a chairman
like him, what kind of campaign would the party run?

Besides, wasn't it foolish to help a tiny party at a time of two
big parties—the Congress and the UML? True, the big parties
kept letting the voters down with their corruption and infighting.
With their ineptitude they'd even brought democracy under threat:
the monarchists on the far right had begun rallying to restore the
king to absolute power, and the Maoists on the far left were
waging an armed 'people's war'. The People's Party was formed
by men of vision, it was said. Its leaders enjoyed clean reputations,
so rare in today's politics. Their call for democratic reform had
gained much credibility among Kathmandu's intelligentsia. They
sounded dignified on the radio. And yet—how remote it sounded,
their talk. For no matter how irresponsibly the big parties acted,
they appeared—well, fated to power. In a daily that had reached
Khaireni Tar two weeks late, a columnist had written about these
parties: 'They suffered for many years underground, and now
they are like the disloyal sons of Nepali governance—allowed to
seize their father's properties solely by birthright, not by merit.
Such is Nepali custom, such are the ways of the land.' These
small new parties—they seemed good, but who *were* they,
actually? Would they prove any better once elected? Wouldn't
they too show their greed the first day they came into power?

The fact was that in Khaireni Tar the People's Party was
little more than a list of names inked into a moth-eaten ledger
that had come, by everyone else's neglect, to fall into Om Gurung's
custody. It was only at the national level that the party
commanded attention. Locally, the party had languished under
Giridhar's considerable lack of direction. Most of the party's
original members had drifted into inactivity, or switched parties,
or migrated from the district. Some had even died. Few of the

remaining party members knew that their party was fielding a candidate this time, and fewer yet cared.

So scattered a force was the People's Party, that no one even knew that Khaireni Tar's wealthiest man, the construction contractor Chiranjibi Joshi, was an officially registered party member. This was because Chiranjibi had never told anyone. With a rare impulsiveness he had signed up at the party office in Kathmandu, talked into it by Nayan Raj after they met by chance at a government office some four years ago. The actor's words had for some reason impressed the contractor. 'People used to say we'd never have democracy,' Nayan Raj had said. 'And now they say, yes we have democracy, but what of it? Has it brought faster development? Is it suited to a poor country? Is it better than the king's rule? Can we really manage freedom, do we need it?

'But we mustn't forget, Chiranjibiji, that the 1990 constitution only laid the grounds for democracy. We have yet to spread social values, build institutions and systems which actualize democratic ideals. First we have to rescue party politics from those who use it to fulfil their greed. Liberty and equality, equality and liberty: these are our twin ideals.'

How well he spoke, and with such easy conviction. His words, so fine and precise, seemed to echo with uncommon integrity. Chiranjibi had visited the actor at the party's central office in Kathmandu later that week, and to his own surprise he'd taken membership.

But Chiranjibi was a pragmatic man, and upon returning home he had kept his membership secret. This was easy given the party's low profile in Khaireni Tar. Now that Nayan Raj's candidacy had been announced, the contractor worried that his membership would be exposed. This would not do. Early this monsoon, the district government had announced a tender for a new school building, and Chiranjibi had placed a bid. The bids were due to be opened soon. It would jeopardize his profits to be affiliated with any party, least of all a party as far from power as the People's Party.

Chiranjibi lived a short distance away from the People's Party's new office, in a sprawling construction complex behind the wood mill that he and his brother owned. He was a plain-faced man of moderate manners who could slip in and out of rooms, groups and landscapes without drawing attention to himself. He dressed more simply than he needed to in simple ready-mades, and the steel frames of his glasses were held together with Sellotape. Despite his wealth, others rarely envied him because of the sad effect created by his looks. Seeing him people said: A man so rich, but with six daughters, no heirs. They felt sorry for him.

This morning, Chiranjibi went early to the wood mill. His younger brother was already busy with workers, measuring fresh-cut logs. In their partnership it was his brother who managed construction work. Wood beams, cement, iron rods, mortar and tin sheets didn't concern Chiranjibi: his work was to make deals and to keep the books. The partnership between the brothers was so efficient that they rarely had to exchange more than a few words to understand each other.

'New stocks,' his brother said as Chiranjibi entered the mill.

Chiranjibi replied, 'The school tender's as sure as won.'

For a while the two of them watched the wood being measured. Then Chiranjibi nodded, bringing an end to their communication.

He went to his desk surrounded by planks and perfumed by a crisp bouquet of pine, saal and redwood. The desk was made of teak, with a sleek surface that gleamed like a vision in this setting of sawdust and wood shavings. Chiranjibi sat down and produced from his pocket the bid for the school tender. Fourteen lakhs, a fourteen and five zeros, to build seven classrooms: cement, plaster, steel girders, cheap Indian glass, wood beams and a tin roof. For a long time he studied the bid, its numbers adding up to fourteen lakhs at the bottom of the page, beneath the words SUM TOTAL. One, four, zero zero zero zero zero. He wasn't focusing on the figures, though. It was the invisible equations that took place outside these figures that he was thinking of, slippery human equations beyond the empty precision of simple math. To secure the bid he'd have to cover the hospital bills for the District Education Officer's mother, who was dying of bone cancer. He'd have to offer a job here, a round of beer there and cash in brown envelopes all around. Such were the calculations he had to do for human greed to add up.

Chiranjibi put down the bid and sighed. The truth was, it had begun to lose charm, this life. He slid a hand on his desk. Choice teak as lustrous as a pool at night with no winds to disturb its stillness. It had been irresistible when he'd seen it in a Kathmandu furniture showroom: that limpid surface, those paisley carvings on its legs. He had trucked it all the way.

It was during that same Kathmandu trip that he'd met Nayan Raj. He thought back now to something the actor had said: 'Any pure ideal is impossible, Chiranjibiji, perhaps it can never be realized. But to seek it—to strive for democracy—that is our dharma.'

Was Nayan Raj just acting when he spoke with such conviction? Chiranjibi was mystified. But how could a rational, intelligent man hold up an ideal that couldn't be realized? How could he expect a contractor to do the same—commit himself to something so blatantly uprofitable? It had been foolish for Nayan Raj to ask him to join the People's Party. It had been foolish of him to agree. To join politics was to forfeit the cycles of bidding, bribing, winning and constructing, and all this to pursue a goal so lofty that not even its basic equations were defined.

From his pocket Chiranjibi took out a box of Yak cigarettes and lit a stick. What for did people do something as absurd as politics?

15

Weeks after Nayan Raj's extended family had heard of his candidacy—and had plotted their futures over it—Binita was still wondering whether he would run, and if he did, what this would mean for her. He would come back—if not for ever, at least for the campaign. He would want to live in his ancestral home. He had a right to. By law the property belonged half to him, half to her.

But it would be strange to have him here. She could hardly imagine her carefully groomed, stylish brother-in-law living in these semi-rural conditions. Binita had met Nayan Raj-bhai twice, once when he stopped by to meet her husband, and the next time after the bus that careened off course, killing her husband, brought the entire Dahal clan to Khaireni Tar for the cremation. Her husband used to laugh at his younger brother's film roles, at his poor lip-syncing and gyrating dances, and at his fame—'Our Nayan,' he would laugh, shaking his head, 'a star!' The two brothers were chance survivors after many miscarriages and stillbirths: the only sons of aged parents. But they had parted soon after their parents' deaths, and they rarely met. Binita's husband used to teach at Khaireni Tar's college campus when Nayan Raj-bhai rose to fame. Nayan Raj-bhai was married to a woman from Kathmandu. They had two children, but Binita had never met them.

Would the whole family move to Khaireni Tar for the duration of the elections? A complete family; people of means—.

Binita felt diminished just thinking about it.

To prepare for the eventuality of her brother-in-law's return, Binita began to stack her possessions into small piles which were ready to move. She didn't have much in the room. The browns and beiges of her fariyas fit neatly into one aluminum trunk, along with her shawls and sweaters. Her blouses and petticoats fit into a few plastic bags, and her nightdresses and underclothes formed a small bundle. Her towels and sheets, comb, hair oil, threads and face mirror she placed on the windowsill.

Phool Devi walked in while Binita was tucking and folding her clothes, rearranging the sparse furniture and clearing dust from hard-to-reach corners. 'Preparing to leave,' she said knowingly. Then, in a bid to become a close and confiding friend—for Binita was now—so suddenly—well-linked—she launched on lengthy tales of errant servants, prodigal relatives, querulous acquaintances and ungrateful friends. Binita was tempted to ask her neighbour what she'd heard about Nayan Raj-bhai, but she was ashamed to reveal to her—and through her to the town—her isolation from her husband's family. It reflected badly on her that Nayan Raj-bhai hadn't sent her word of his plans. She wasn't respectable enough to merit such courtesies. And so Binita brooked Phool Devi's chatter without revealing her own doubts. When her neighbour left, she returned to stacking, piling, organizing; preparing for changes that might or might not come.

Then one morning Binita's husband's uncle Kainlo-kaka paid her a visit. Kainlo-kaka was the patriarch of the Dahal clan, and he lived an hour's walk south, across the Seti river. It was raining when he arrived. A few customers at Binita's teashop were speculating on whether there was a fear of root rot setting into the rice crops. Binita was sitting at the counter watching Sani puzzle over a word she had learned in last night's literacy class. 'This loop goes before the letter ka,' Binita explained, trying to clear the girl's confusion. 'That turns the letter ka into ki. And the na makes it kina. Kina: why.'

There was a shuffling at the back gate, and when Binita went to the window, she saw two figures, their faces hidden beneath black umbrellas. She immediately recognized Kainlo-kaka's loose-jointed knees and knobby hands. The other man was his son. Binita left the teashop, responding more to alarm than to the demands of protocol. She patted her fariya to make sure it was in place.

In her first year of widowhood, Binita had been urged—hounded—by Kainlo-kaka's tradition-bound wife to come and live in their family house: 'You can't defile the kitchen, of course, but you can build a clay stove outside for yourself and your daughter.' Binita, who'd broken with her own orthodox family when marrying a wrong-caste man twice her age, saw no reason to obey the old crone, and decided to live alone. The extended Dahal clan had immediately launched a faultfinding campaign. 'No daughter-in-law of the Dahal clan has ever done what you're doing,' Kainlo-kaka's wife had said. 'You married a Dahal, we have a name to keep. You live by the rules of our family.' When Binita started her teashop their criticism became vitriolic. 'A young widow selling tea to unknown men,' Kainlo-kaka's wife warned her. 'People will think she sells much more than tea.'

Binita and Kainlo-kaka hadn't talked for years now. The distance between their houses had provided them a convenient excuse to avoid each other. The old man had aged, Binita saw. There was a slight stoop in his posture, and he climbed gingerly over the bamboo poles of the gate.

In the teashop, Sani began to prepare tea. Binita checked again that her fariya was in place. Kainlo-kaka walked through the backyard with the affected nonchalance of one acutely aware of being watched. His son followed behind, bumping into him like a herded goat when he stopped at the tomato vines. Kainlo-kaka poked at the vines with his foot, frowning at the growth. Then with a proprietary nod he made his way to the back porch.

'Binita-buhari.' He shook out his umbrella, avoiding her eyes. Binita felt her movements become automatic as she bowed. There he was: a crooked man raising his crooked hands in blessing. His son then bowed to Binita. Formality. Binita raised her hand and made the required gestures. Her movements were controlled, her mood wary.

Kainlo-kaka said, 'I came to check the arrangements.' He wasn't looking at her, nor she at him. He turned towards the backyard, frowning in disapproval at the buffalo shed. 'My nephew called last week. I said, stay with your uncles, all your relatives are eager to help in your election campaign. But,' he waved vaguely towards the house, 'he says you should prepare his rooms, make arrangements for his stay.'

Binita tried not to bristle at the commanding tone. She couldn't of course say no—but she didn't want to say yes. There was nothing to say, then. An obstinate silence emanated from her.

Kainlo-kaka turned to look at the house. With the same disapproving look, he took a reading of the door to the teashop, then went to stand by the other door, which led to the rooms. He said, 'He'll need to meet a lot of people. I told him, how can you meet people in a public shop? There's no room, you should stay with us. Workers, party members and we, your own people— where will you meet everyone? Where will you talk to your voters? How will this house meet the needs of a man of your stature?'

Again Binita found nothing to say. She looked at Kainlo-kaka, and saw that his face had become skeletal. The skin on his cheeks had dried, his moustache had greyed and his eyes had sunk. He seemed drained of some of his old force.

Avoiding her gaze, Kainlo-kaka turned again to the backyard. His son shifted from foot to foot, looking at the rain clouds overhead. Kainlo-kaka also turned his attention skyward.

When Binita finally spoke, her tone was cool. 'Will he come with his family?'

'Wife and children, no.' Kainlo-kaka smirked, though Binita couldn't understand why. He said, 'His wife, you know, works at an office. If she stops earning, how will my nephew afford politics?'

Binita decided to put an end to his visit. 'So I'll ready the upstairs room,' she said.

Kainlo-kaka shot back a withering look. 'That's what my nephew wants.' Then he opened his umbrella, and his son did the same. 'I just came to check,' the old man declared, as though his intentions had been questioned. 'We being relatives. I wanted to see that the right arrangements are being made for my nephew.'

Binita heard herself say that all the right arrangements were being made for his nephew.

'Good.'

Then Binita watched herself bow to receive his blessing, she watched herself blessing his son, she watched herself standing at duty as they made their way through the vegetable patch. At the edge of the patch, Kainlo-kaka stooped to pluck tomatoes from the vines. A flash of animosity flared up in Binita.

Sani arrived with a tray of tea. 'But I made tea.'

'They wouldn't touch our tea.' Binita watched Kainlo-kaka and his son walk off without bothering to shut the bamboo gate behind them. And she stood helpless to the rages that gathered inside, preparing to storm through her.

When Binita had opened her teashop, years ago, she had quickly learned the value of family. Within months of her husband's death, her first customers—friends and colleagues of her husband, some government employees—had begun to treat her with an unpleasant presumptuousness. At first Binita tried not to interpret too much in their manners. But soon overtures came, veiled as sympathy. 'A young widow like you,' her husband's closest friend had asked one day, 'how do you satisfy your...nature has sent down every person with—desires, it's natural.' There were two other men with him, watching her, waiting for her response.

By the time a year had passed, Binita found that more and more of her customers leered at her, their eyes roving over her as though she, and not her tea and snacks, were on offer at her shop. If anyone were to wish them harm, she and her daughter Tripti would have no protection. Everyone knew that her own family, from the neighbouring district, had responded caustically to her overtures to return to them. Her neighbours like Phool Devi found her too deviant to socialize with. She was vulnerable to mistreatment. She had decided to repair her frazzled ties with Kainlo-kaka's wife and family.

The loneliness of her widowed life had also become unbearable by then. The hours she spent ruminating on her husband—his roguish laugh; the way he stood millimeters away, leaning into her; the sinews of his shoulder blades; his ardour as he moved to her—these hours alone relieved her desolation, which returned with spiteful intensity as soon as she remembered that he was gone now: he was a trick of her mind. Her past pleasures wrought despair in their wake, and the present afforded her no comfort. She was desperate for a salve.

Kainlo-kaka's wife had fairly crowed to see Binita return, defeated, to her house. 'Now we know you threw away your caste when you married our nephew,' she cried. 'But you're a Dahal now and you can't throw away our name too. Stop your life of buying-selling and come to live with us like a woman of good birth.'

The younger female aunts had echoed her orthodox tones. Kainlo-kaka, though, had acted more forgiving. Without actually apologizing for his wife's harsh words, he let Binita know that he was more moderate. 'A girl at an age to wear nice things and eat well,' he lamented when no one else was present. 'A bus turns, a man dies, a woman's life darkens. A mere girl is forced into widowhood.' So relieved was Binita to receive his sympathy that she tolerated his wife's criticism each time she visited them. She liked escaping the constrictions of her home and teashop to take the hour-long walk along the Seti river. She enjoyed the busy, peopled feel of Kainlo-kaka's house. With each visit she became less unwelcome. A kind of compromise was reached between herself and Kainlo-kaka's wife: neither of them changed their ways, but they got used to each other.

Then one day Kainlo-kaka followed Binita to a shed at the back of the house, and suddenly pressed in behind her, clamping down her neck. 'Fidgety girl, fidgety girl,' he whispered, knocking her against a pile of loose bricks, his lean body suddenly animated with surprising strength. She realized with shock that he was tugging aside her fariya. 'This will calm a fidgety girl like you.' Numbed by confusion, Binita hadn't known what to do but stay still as he heaved himself onto her. 'This will pacify a fidgety girl like you.'

Afterwards he had laughed strangely and pushed her away.

For weeks afterwards, Binita had been terrorized by the prospect of pregnancy. When she bled at last, she was still menaced by the thought that she might have had an illegitimate child: it was this, rather than the actual rape, that set off her deepest dread. She never went back to Kainlo-kaka's house. Neither did she receive any word from his family.

It was then that Binita had withdrawn from society. The years she'd spent with her husband seemed meagre recompense now for the life she was left with. All the choices she'd made in

youth seemed regrettable. She should have been more cautious.
Everyone had warned her. Her professor—how easily she had
been entranced by his seduction, his reckless play. And she had
deferred to his worldliness. All for his lips on her breasts, his
breath on her skin, the surprise of being brought to abandon.
She'd thought their delight more important than her security.
One incautious move: a life of being preyed upon. The threat of
catastrophe shimmered around her after he left. She could think
of no way to protect herself from possible harm than to retreat
into herself.

After Kainlo-kaka's visit, Binita felt shaken by the same fears
that had haunted her after the rape. Her brother-in-law was
coming: there would be unknown men coming to the house. She
must protect herself, Sani and Tripti. But which decisions would
be right to make, which would be mistakes? Which decisions
would lead to danger, which would keep them safe? How could
she tell what was correct to do?

At sixteen, Sani was still more of a girl than a woman, and
understood little of what went on around her, accepting blindly
the old rules of the village. And Tripti was shy and reserved.
Binita didn't like this, but she wasn't sure whether or not to steer
her cousin and daughter towards rebellion, towards risk. In the
days after Kainlo-kaka's visit Sani hummed around the teashop,
setting to chores with a superior air. In the evenings she went to
her literacy class, and she sometimes came back excited. 'Today
our Sir taught us how to hold a pen so that its nib presses exactly
on the lines on the notebook sheet,' she said. 'Ka, he taught us.
Ka. It's funny how the sounds we make look when they're written.
Ka kha ga gha nga.'

Binita listened to her voice. The voice of early youth, with
its rising tones, its dips, its brief hesitations. She tried to gain

some strength from the fortune of this girl—she had years, a
lifetime, to shape her life. Time to test life, live it, and, if she
chose, to dare it.

In Tripti's low voice Binita heard more of her own wavering.
'When is Nayan Raj-kaka coming, Aama? Aama, when will we
have to move?'

It had always been her way, poor guileless girl, to expose
her rawest fears and doubts. Tripti had her father's lips—thin on
top and full at the bottom, with a plaintive curl. Her long lashes
were Binita's, though, as was the sharpness of her nose and the
bones that protruded already from her cheeks and chin. Each
night she asked, 'When will he come, Aama?'

For her Binita steeled her will. For her she kept her mood
light. 'He'll come soon, my baby. We'll move down then. We'll
sleep with your Sani-didi, all together downstairs.'

A few days later, Binita went to the Himal Lodge Restaurant
Bar. She needed Thakalni-aama's help, and she knew she would
get it. Acting on some inscrutable private ethic, Thakalni-aama
had always helped Binita through difficult times. She had been
the first to befriend her after Binita had eloped with her professor.
She had helped Binita through her pregnancy, and later, when
she was widowed, had scolded her out of her grief and helped her
start the teashop. Binita wasn't the only one Thakalni-aama
helped, and for long periods the grandmother would forget about
Binita. At difficult times, though, she was the one person Binita
trusted to approach for help or advice.

The sprawling structure of the Himal Lodge Restaurant Bar
looked beaten down by rain, with green lichen spotting the facade.
It had been years since Binita had come here. The front courtyard
looked more shabby than she remembered. The dining room was
overrun with men—Congress workers with party flags pinned to

their shirts. Some of them turned to look at her. She shrank from them and made for the kitchen door.

Thakalni-aama was sitting cross-legged at a wood-fire stove, presiding over a score of helpers—daughters-in-law and unmarried daughters, nieces and cousins, a swarm of female shapes in the dimly lit room. There were two kerosene stoves on full blast, and their hiss filled the air. The room smelled of mustard oil, cumin and coriander, and of sweet onions fried till brown.

'Binita,' Thakalni-aama cooed, seeing her. 'I've been meaning to visit you, but look.' She pointed to the dining room. 'The Congress party captured my booth.'

With a nudge, Binita took over the work of Thakalni-aama's youngest daughter, stooped over a mortar on the floor. For a while Thakalni-aama examined Binita, as though judging her ability to pulp garlic. Then she sat back and assumed an advising role: 'I was thinking, you, all alone in that house, and your hero brother-in-law returning—you do know the date of his arrival, don't you? Last night the Congress boys were saying two weeks from now. Now you, all alone, how will you manage?'

'Of course there's your cousin sister now,' she continued. 'That orphan has grown up strong; those who suffer in youth are blessed in their later years. But you, you won't be left in peace any more, you'll have to accept that. Look.' She pointed again to the Congress workers in the dining room. 'That's what your house will be like.' Then Thakalni-aama turned to a daughter-in-law frying potatoes. 'Fry them till they're crisp, those boys will enjoy that.' When she turned back to Binita, her tone was low. 'Use the hero's return to your advantage. Family—some give, some take. Favours and obligations. Don't give up the chance.'

The old woman's scheming tone jarred on Binita. What give, what take? What favours and obligations? She nodded as though she'd understood, but her only goal was to seek protection. She said, 'It'll be awkward, Thakalni-aama. A house full of females alone with my brother-in-law.'

Thakalni-aama seemed to have anticipated this. With a swift nod she turned to a woman at a nearby kerosene stove. 'Eh Pramila!' she called out, then turned back to Binita. 'I don't need Pramila to work for me. She'll work for you when your brother-in-law comes.'

The woman came over, wiping her hands on her cotton fariya.

'You say there's never enough work for you here,' Thakalni-aama laughed. 'Well here's your chance. Binita's brother-in-law is the cinema hero everyone's talking about. You work for him. You'll become famous just serving him food and washing his dishes.'

A pink scarf tied around Pramila's hair gave her a prankish look. She grinned. 'I can also sing, and I can dance!'

'Maybe he'll give you a heroine role.'

It was arranged that the woman would move into Binita's house when her brother-in-law came.

Binita finished pulping the garlic, then stayed a while longer, enjoying the flurry of activity in the kitchen. She left the Himal Lodge Restaurant Bar feeling clear. On the way home, she stopped in the bazaar and bought a framed picture of the goddess Parvati to hang next to a picture of her husband, one from long before she'd known him, before they had met, when her life could still have taken a different course. She thought about what Thakalni-aama had said. Give and take. Opportunities. She would move all her belongings downstairs today, she decided. She must make the most of Nayan Raj-bhai's return. For the duration of the elections she would take care of her brother-in-law. She would feed him, wash his clothes, clean up after him, cook for him, make his stay comfortable. This was what she would do. After the elections, her brother-in-law would want to repay his debt. He might ask if there was anything he could do for her. She might ask him for some recompense. This was family: impositions, opportunities.

But Binita wasn't given to calculating, and her thoughts easily wandered. A week after Kainlo-kaka's visit, she was sitting at the teashop window staring at the trickle of rainwater down the trunk of the bougainvillea plant in front of her teashop, feeling in her body the runnels and causeways and stray drippings of the desires which bloomed, thrived and wilted within her in perfect privacy. How acute longing became when held in secrecy: how distilled, how combustible. Binita had been distracted all day by the subtlest of sights and sounds, by the stippled surface of the buffaloes' udders, by the squish of rain-soaked hay underfoot, by the crinkle of plastic wrappers, by the ridged tin sheet covering the porch, by fine films of dust on her husband's picture. The feel of every surface she touched lingered in her skin: loose skeins of wool, brittle barks, slippery windows and ciliated stems, the tack of resin, ripples, scales, flakes, burrs, grain. She could feel her husband's hands slide over her belly. He used to watch her intently as he stroked her, as he sank into her, as he roused her to pleasure. He would watch keenly for her shuddering—. Outside the teashop, a late monsoon storm stuttered and coughed. The rainwater on the bougainvillea tree quivered, slipped, slipped.

17

With a mere week left till Nayan Raj's arrival, the revenue collector of yore Jimmawal Sharma couldn't believe he was the only one who'd armed the party for the moral battlefield that was politics. For the only thing the party had done was to open its office. 'And *that*—' Jimmawal-baaje was quick to point out to Om Gurung, 'was because Lord Krishna gave me the foresight: what is a party without an office?'

Jimmawal-baaje and Om met frequently at the new party office—not so much out of design but because both, for different reasons, were anxious that the building, so visible from the bazaar, look as though it were being put to use. Each time they met, Jimmawal-baaje exhorted Om to remember the sacrifices he had made for the party. 'With our Giridhar-bhai...indisposed.' He chose his words carefully, for he knew that Om was loyal to that drunkard. 'With Giridhar-bhai indisposed, it's a fortunate thing that the gods helped me rent my house to the party...at such a reasonable rate!'

Om murmured vaguely. These days he never said anything that extended beyond formality. And he never revealed anything about Giridhar. This heightened Jimmawal-baaje's curiosity. Why wasn't Giridhar coming to the party office? Was he really drinking himself to oblivion, as everyone said?

Hoping to joggle a few words from Om, Jimmawal-baaje poked at the man. 'Don't you agree, Om-bhai, it was a lucky thing I had this house to rent, and—oho what a fine shirt you're wearing!' He reached over to rub the cloth. 'Imported, it looks: ssss. Tremendously lustrous.' A feeling of envy prickled through him. How plush was the former British Gurkha man's life, how rich with satiny affluence. He pulled back and tried to remember what he'd been saying. Eh ho. 'Don't you agree? It's been up to me...to me and you...to sacrifice for our party?'

'Hmm,' Om said.

Hmm hah! In fact it was only *he* who was doing all the sacrificing. With his vast foreign-earned riches, the Gurung man couldn't be said to be sacrificing anything. Whereas Jimmawal-baaje himself, who had no more than his wits as wealth...now *his* efforts entailed true charity.

With an acrimony he couldn't help, he asked, 'And when shall we start receiving regular visits by Giridhar-bhai?'

Om gave no response, and Jimmawal-baaje turned away

disgusted. Such party members he had.

He left Om downstairs, and went through the narrow hallway, up the stairs. The two capacious rooms upstairs still thrilled him with their newness—the sleek white walls, crisp windowpanes, modern light sockets and oiled hinges. In the sunnier room, he stopped by the window and looked across the highway, past the bazaar's bar-peepal tree, to the nine-stalled cow shed in front of his house. Hail mother cow. Hail, he thought. And he suddenly received, like a boon from mother cow, this thought: the party needed a peon boy. Ho. The party needed a peon boy to sit in the office all day, a boy who was lettered, a boy who could make intelligent responses to public queries about the candidate, a boy undefiled by non-Hindu modernity...His seventh son.

Jimmawal-baaje was pleased with this thought. He flew back downstairs to Om. 'Can it be that the first month's rent is almost due?' Jimmawal-baaje started off with a question that came to him from nowhere...a distraction, but an important one. 'Hard to believe it's been a whole month since we opened the office.'

'We'll pay rent when the candidate comes,' Om said.

How casually the rich spoke of money. 'Yes,' Jimmawal-baaje said. 'What's money, after all? It comes, it goes, at the whims of the gods. Money means nothing in this fleeting two days' long world.'

Then he proceeded to the more pressing matter of his seventh son. How to broach the topic? He circled Om once, he circled Om twice, then said, 'I've been thinking, Om-bhai. My seventh son can man the office for us. He can come here every morning, open the doors and windows, make sure only party members come to the building, that kind of thing. A brilliant boy...he can work as the party's peon boy, I thought.'

For a while Om stared at him in incomprehension. Then there was a stirring on his forehead. Jimmawal-baaje could almost see him thinking no. Finally, Om said, 'Hiring-firing is up to Giridhar-dai.'

Jimmawal-baaje wouldn't give up so easily. 'But with him so...indisposed.' He smiled. 'Really, Bhai, I know he's your friend and I know he's our chairman for the district, but if we wait for Giridhar-bhai to do everything...Well, what can I say.'

Om sighed.

Such placidity! 'Bhai,' Jimmawal-baaje squawked. 'We cannot enter the moral battlefield of politics without our men in place. King, commander, troops and orderlies... How can we demolish the enemy without a king, commander and so forth?' Om wasn't listening, and this enraged Jimmawal-baaje. 'It's not enough to have a king,' he cried. 'It's not enough to have a commander.' He waved his hands to stress his point. 'How can there be an office without a peon boy? Who's ever heard of such a thing!'

'Hiring-firing is up to Giridhar-dai.' Om repeated.

But there was a hassled look in Om's eyes. Ho yes. Jimmawal-baaje saw at once that he could wear down the man's resistance. With a little more perseverance, with a few days of nagging he would achieve results.

18

A boy skipped school to steal oranges from his neighbour's backyard: and he grew up to suffer cataclysm, Om thought. The boy used to scour the edge of the forest with slingshot in hand, killing pheasants with his keen aim. He spent hours picking gooseberries from mountainside thickets, he waded through deep streams to fish. In school he scratched alphabets on his own slateboard and others'. A rambunctious boy, a boy full of pluck. He grew into a dazzling teenager who quizzed his peers over minute details of history, oddities of grammar, complex chemical compounds and lengthy algebraic formulae. He matured into adulthood raring to meet his vocation as a civil servant. Work, family and society all came under his command as though ceding to his ascendancy. And then he entered middle age and lost his job, and suffered, somehow, a cataclysm of the mind.

How could one accept this?

Om spent much time musing over Giridhar, and over the riddle of human frailty. He had felt hurt when his friend slipped off to Kathmandu without telling him. But when Giridhar returned bearing news of his thwarted ambitions—'Motherfucking corpse kept the ticket for himself'—he had put aside his misgivings and set about helping Giridhar adjust.

This help was difficult to provide. After days of defiant, swaggering drinking, Giridhar had finally collapsed in his bed reeking of rum, his features bloated beneath a greyish, translucent complexion. 'We must speak to him kindly,' Om advised his father and wife, 'but urge him to think of all the bright suns yet to dawn in his future. We must show him that he is surrounded by many, many people who look to him with affection and esteem.' He suggested confining Giridhar to the house, and weaning him, firmly, from alcohol.

This Giridhar's father and wife did. But as though in retaliation, Giridhar wouldn't meet Om any more. Like a hurt child he locked himself in his room every time Om visited. Om tried not to mind. And though there were quite a few matters to attend to at his school, he began to spend only morning-time at work, heading immediately after lunch hour along the path to the northern hills. Most days he spent a few hours with Giridhar's father, trying to dispel his pessimism. 'When the habit of alcohol leaves his body, he'll return to his old self at once,' Om assured him. 'There's nothing we can do but wait, Ba.' To Giridhar's wife he said, 'Laksmi-bhauju, I give you my word he'll get well soon.'

A few days before Nayan Raj was due to arrive, this prediction finally came true. Giridhar was sitting on the wooden pallet in his front porch when Om arrived, and he didn't leave when he saw Om. And he actually looked presentable, dressed in ironed trousers and a dark jacket that was only slightly short at the arms. His hair was oiled and combed back, giving his features a harsh, handsome prominence. There was even a ruddiness in his cheeks which caught the generous light of the porch.

'Finally the monsoon is looking to end,' Om said brightly, gesturing at the rice fields below the house. 'A few more weeks of rain, and all the roots would have rotted.'

Giridhar didn't seem to be listening.

Om sat beside him on the pallet. 'At the school,' he ventured, figuring that his friend might benefit from everyday chitchat, 'we're thinking, maybe, if they're not too expensive—we've already almost decided, but we don't know yet—we're thinking of buying computers.' He pointed at the school building, visible far below. 'Just think. Computers in our town!'

Giridhar kept staring at the rice fields.

It didn't matter. 'The problem is,' Om continued, 'the school keeps losing money no matter how hard I try keeping our costs in check. It's no use.'

There was no reply from his friend. For a while, the two of them sat in silence. Om reached over and turned on a transistor radio lying on the pallet. There was a woman crying at her abandonment on some drama show. He turned it off. And he tried to radiate a comforting serenity, but in truth it disturbed him to see Giridhar staring so hard at the rice fields, as though some mystery were revealing itself there. What dense, dark world was his friend lost in? He thought: the human heart sprawls with unexpected outcroppings and makeshift alleyways. The heart grows messy shanties like an unplanned town. Tch. In trying to accommodate growth, the self expands without design, grows irregular, and mars its own symmetry. It bickers with itself, tangles itself in misunderstanding and strife. It becomes a slum, the soul.

But to his delight, Om found Giridhar in the front porch the following day too. It almost seemed like—yes it could be—his friend had been waiting for him. Om tried to expand the scope of their talk today to include party matters. 'That Jimmawal-baaje,' he said with a laugh. 'It's always money, money, money with him. He wants to get his son hired. The party must hire his seventh son, he says.'

Giridhar turned to him, exposing his scarred face to the light. 'Hired by our party?'

'As a peon boy that we don't need,' Om laughed.

Giridhar actually smiled. 'Money, money, money,' he said a little flatly.

'The man's only passion is for money,' Om said. 'Every day I meet him at the party office, he says we must hire his son.'

And then, the next day, Giridhar actually initiated conversation: 'The party office. It's—where?'

'It's in that new building right by the telephone office.' Om pointed at the town. He smiled broadly, in relief—he couldn't help it. 'You come down the hill, take the alley behind the telephone office. It's right there.'

'Unh eh.'

And Om thought: one must take heart at such signs of recovery.

But when he arrived the next day, sweaty and out of breath, his friend was shuffling about the front yard, whispering about annihilation. There was nothing Om could do to make Giridhar sit down, or to make him stop raving like a madman. He shouldn't have mentioned party matters yesterday, Om thought. He had reminded his friend of painful things, and now—with only a few days till Nayan Raj's arrival—Giridhar had succumbed to despondency.

Or insanity. The day after that Om found Giridhar kneeling in the backyard, muttering about too much rain, uprooting squash plants from their beds, scrutinizing the roots for signs of rot and killing them in the process. Laksmi-bhauju was struggling to drag away her sons, who were wriggling away from her grasp to see what was wrong with their father.

Om firmly guided his friend back into the house and onto his stale-smelling bed. He couldn't imagine how to help him. Perhaps he should follow Asha's advice, perhaps he should tell him difficult truths.

'One must think about the long term,' he exhorted Giridhar. Then he faltered. But Asha was rarely wrong, so he went on: 'I was thinking, and it's true, you'll agree with me, friend—Nayan Raj's candidacy is the best thing that could have happened for you.'

Om waited a moment, then said, 'Look: our party won't win this time no matter who runs. No one will vote for an unknown party like us, not even if they admire Nayan Raj. We don't have a base in the district. We have no workers, no supporters. No one recognizes our ballot symbol. But by the next elections,' he said, and he really meant this, 'we'll have a party structure in place; we'll have workers and supporters all over the electorate. We'll be in a position to win then.' He took his friend's hand. 'And who'll get the ticket then? You! You prove yourself a good chairman now, you'll get the ticket, no doubt. You are the People's Party's future MP, my friend. You'll win the elections next time.'

Giridhar looked at him vacantly.

Impossible to tell if Om's words had helped or hurt. 'Rest,' Om said, leaving his friend to the solitude he preferred.

In the cave-like corridor outside, he assured Giridhar's father. 'What harm will come if he rests a few weeks? Even after Nayan

Raj comes, he'll be busy meeting his own family and friends. He won't notice if we're not all there.'

'At least he's stopped drinking,' said Giridhar's father, blinking hard behind his thick glasses that magnified his eyes. 'The more he mixes in company, the better he'll get. Visit him whenever you can, Son. You're busy running your school, but visit him when you can.'

'Yes, Ba,' Om agreed. He saw that Giridhar's wife had come to listen. She stood morosely, covering her hair with the end of her fariya, her face looking pinched by grief. 'Really, Laksmi-bhauju, he'll be well soon, wait and see.'

She grimaced in an attempt to nod yes.

And then—demoralized by the unhappiness of the house—Om left.

His own cheery yellow home offered him great comfort when he got back. Relatives were flitting through the front hall, prattling with Asha: 'How are the children faring in their father's school, has the school turned a profit? Tell your old man not to pamper his students so. An English-medium school running at a loss—who's ever heard of such a thing!' A neighbour had dropped by, and two former army men had come to chat. Asha was serving them snacks in the sitting room. 'Eh, my old man,' she was happily complaining, 'he sees a child in need, he can't stop himself. Seventy-five, eighty per cent of his students are on scholarship. He won't feed us on his earnings from the school.'

Om settled into the sitting room sofa, his mood immediately restored. 'Enough, enough.' He turned to the army men for witness. 'Look at this house, look at my girth, look at the gold on my old woman—does it look like I haven't provided?'

Asha laughed a full-throated laugh.

The television was on, showing a Bollywood movie. 'That, in the background—that's Switzerland,' the neighbour said. 'That himal looks like our own Machhapuchhre himal, but it's actually a peak in Switzerland.'

'Is that right? It looks like our own Nepal.'

The evening meal passed amid merry exchanges.

Later, though, when they were in bed, Asha asked, 'You visited Giridhar-dai?'

Om sighed. 'It's like he's been trampled.' Against him, his wife was all smooth skin and firm, springy flesh. He nestled against her, fitting curve to curve. He said, 'A man like him who helped so many—alone now...bulldozed by unfortunate events.' He sighed. He was exhausted by the day's efforts. He said, 'We, his friends, must bring him out of the night...Otherwise the heart grows into a slum, in sad times. I worry for him.'

Asha reached for his hand and placed it in the space between her breasts where he kept it while sleeping. 'All the time you're spending with Giridhar-dai,' she said, 'will it yield any good?'

Om snuggled closer against her. 'But he needs to be loved, love.'

19

On the morning of Nayan Raj's arrival, Giridhar forced himself to walk into town early. He was ready to fill the space of the district's party chairman. His mind had cleared and his body had been restored in this brutal month of abstinence. At times he felt a limberness in his joints, and in his arms sudden surges of vigour. If he kept his attention narrowly focused on what was before him, he didn't slip into doubt. He was ready for the elections.

The monsoon clouds had finally tapered off in the past few weeks. The sky was deep blue, but the air was still humid. There were a few yellow sheaves of rice in the terraced fields. The crop could be cut in a month.

Even before Giridhar reached town, he saw the party office: impossible not to see it. So new. So white. The building presented him challenges that he didn't feel like meeting yet. He crossed the highway, drawn by the familiar squalor of the bazaar's shops and houses, their facades stained by rain marks at the end of the monsoon. The shops were still closed, but the peanut vendor had already set up his stall beneath the bar-peepal tree. He called out, 'Peanuts, Chairmanji?'

Chairmanji. Giridhar joined his palms. 'Namaste.' He thought: there are dimensions a chairman occupies. 'No peanuts,' he said. Then he walked past rapidly, hoping to exude confidence.

He passed the UML office with its hammer-and-sickle flag, and then the crockery store. The fruit stall near the Congress office smelled of persimmons. The RPP office next door had a deserted air, but the Himal Lodge Restaurant Bar was packed with Congress workers. So Congress was patronizing Thakalni-aama, Giridhar thought, stopping to consider this. He must talk to the old crone, and remind her of their long ties. He must tell her: take Congress's money, but vote for us.

Beyond, the blind shopkeeper Shankar was opening the wooden slats of his grain store. Giridhar headed there, formulating full sentences in his mind before speaking: 'Shankar-dai, you know my party's joined the elections.' He wondered if the man could hear, from his voice, that he'd spent months stumbling about drunk. 'We'll be needing your support.'

Shankar rewarded him with a gracious response, 'You can rely on me.' The blind man's smile was kind. 'Of course I'll support you, Chairman-bhai.'

Chairman-bhai. Giridhar was genuinely touched. 'I'll count on your help,' he said.

Ho. From there Giridhar doubled back to the party office, taking the alley of the cobbler's shack. He stopped there. He should make up for his last misadventure there. The cobbler was sitting in a corner of his shack, stooped over a rain-sodden shoe. 'Bhai,' Giridhar said. 'I've come to buy slippers from you.'

The cobbler glanced at Giridhar's leather shoes. 'You'll be wanting Indian, Chinese slippers?'

Giridhar pulled out thirty-five rupees. 'I'll take our own Elephant Brand.'

The cobbler sniffed as though placated. He reached for a white pair of slippers and packed them in the pages of an old notebook. Then he turned to Giridhar. 'Forty rupees.'

'Thirty-five. You told me just a month ago that it was thirty-five rupees.'

The man shook his head. 'Inflation. The prices just keep going up.'

Five rupees in one month? Giridhar immediately thought to quarrel, but he restrained himself. He handed the man five more rupees, feeling cheated. But he kept his voice genial: 'You know my party's contesting elections. We can't win without your priceless vote, Bhai. I'll count on your vote.'

'I'm not registered to vote.'

'We'll get you registered.' Giridhar liked the way that sounded. 'There's still a month left to write your name in the voters' list. Come to our party office, we'll get you registered.'

'And I'll have to give you my priceless vote in return?'

Why the snide tone? Giridhar said, 'It doesn't matter who you vote for, Bhai. But it's your duty as a citizen to vote.'

The man shot back, 'The kingdom of god is where I've taken my citizenship, hajoor. In Jesus's eyes we're all equal. I've already voted for him.'

What kind of impudence was this? 'Don't vote for me then,' Giridhar snapped. 'You think I'll grovel for your two-paisa vote? Don't vote—what do I care?'

'You'll care on your judgement day.'

'Eh moola!'

But the man didn't back off. 'We'll all have to face judgement day, hajoor.'

Giridhar turned away, rattled.

He approached the party office feeling unnerved. The front door was open. There was a large room downstairs, and a toilet with tile chip floors. Upstairs were two sunny rooms. Giridhar was startled to find a skinny boy in one of them.

The boy had Jimmawal-baaje's sallow face. 'Namaste, Sir.' He sprang to attention. 'An honour for us to meet you on this auspicious day of our candidateji's arrival. We are very proud to be receiving the opportunity to serve the party to the best of our abilities. As you know we've been manning the office building at our respected father's suggestion, even though we're not being paid a paisa...yet. But with your kind mercy and the generous blessings of the gods, Sir, we hope to keep serving the party.'

'I can't hire you,' Giridhar snapped. 'There's nothing for you here.'

The boy smiled slyly, as though he knew better. 'But Sir, today is the day of the inaugural ceremony for which we have made all due preparations.'

Giridhar left the boy and went to the other room. It was the bigger of the two, and completely bare. He needed to be by himself. He had to feel like he was in command of this office. He tossed aside his new slippers, and had only just settled on the floor when he heard Om's voice in the hallway, accompanied by scrapes and bangs. 'Careful, ho yes.'

The door opened and in stepped two porters with chairs a d benches tied on their backs.

'Oho friend!' Om's bright red parka dazzled Giridhar. Om said, 'You here: I knew you'd come. It's gratifying to see.' He gestured at the furniture that the porters were unloading. 'For the office. I thought I'd bring some furniture from the school. Just old pieces lying around.'

The room was soon crowded with two scratched benches, two creaky chairs, a few cane stools and a cane bed, several straw mats and a table riddled with cup marks. It looked, Giridhar thought, like a furniture storeroom. He felt Om tugging at him, so he got up from the floor.

Om led him to the bed. 'Come, now, sit properly.'

Sit properly. Was Om judging him for having failed to buy furniture?

'I bought a new membership log,' Om said, spreading a notebook on Giridhar's lap. 'Most of the people in the old log aren't in the district anymore. Some—that old landlord from Tharpu—even died. So I thought let's start a new one, let's fill it with new members and people willing to work hard to bring our party to victory.'

'Yes,' Giridhar said. 'Let's start anew.'

'That's an excellent way to put it, friend.'

There was something distinctly fawning about the way Om spoke to him these days.

Just then, the door to the room once again banged open. 'May Lord Krishna bless us!' Jimmawal-baaje swept in, dressed as usual in spotless white daura-suruwal. 'With Saturn eclipsed and the moon entering a new phase, this is a most auspicious day.' He turned and revealed his seventh son, standing behind him. The boy was carrying a spool of red ribbon and a pair of scissors. Jimmawal-baaje said, 'For the inaugural ceremony. My own son suggested it. A clever boy he is, so eager to serve...we'll discuss his wages when our candidateji comes. In the meanwhile, Son, let's you and I tie the ribbon on the front door.'

'Make sure the door still opens,' Om joked. 'Otherwise our candidate will inaugurate the building with us inside.'

'Oho Om-bhai, you are so very witty,' Jimmawal-baaje shot

back insincerely. 'But my son is multi-talented, Om-bhai. He'll
tie the ribbon so cleverly, even a fat man like you will fit through
the door.'

With this he and his son took off.

Om laughed and turned to Giridhar. 'That greedy old man.'

Giridhar felt unduly pressured to smile. There were too many
people around. The window was pouring in too much light. It
was hard to think here.

Om seemed oblivious to his flustered state. 'A revenue
collector in youth,' he said gaily, 'a money collector till he dies.
Forever invoking the name of the gods—to what end, I wonder.
Has he found liberation from his worldly concerns? Has his
devoutness helped society? I feel—don't you feel, Giridhar-dai?—
what's the good of blind devotion? Meaning, I believe in the
gods; who doesn't? But people matter, too. People have gods in
them. These gods—the deities in us—they deserve more attention
than stone idols, don't you feel?'

Quiet, Giridhar thought.

Then suddenly there was a distant slam of car doors, followed by
a shrill yelp from Jimmawal-baaje—'He's here!'—and Giridhar's
balance slipped. Om rushed to the window. 'The candidate's
arrived,' he said breathlessly. 'Come, friend. Let's welcome him.'
There was a tug at Giridhar's sleeve, and he followed Om as
they headed—must they hurry so?—to the stairs, colliding against
each other. He felt severed from his surroundings. Outdoors, in
the blinding midday sun, were people, people, people, and there
was Nayan Raj, tall, pale, smiling, returning the namaste that
Giridhar's hands had somehow formed. The blue van he had
come in was parked near by. A small crowd stood gaping—'The
cinema hero.' Giridhar tried to speak, but his tongue wouldn't
move.

Jimmawal-baaje pushed through the crowd. 'Namaste, Candidateji!' The old man bowed. 'To see you here is to see the face of God in our humble town. Heartiest welcome home...to your loyal constituency. I myself, friend of your late father, founding member and proud landlord too, on behalf of my family and my seventh son'—he yanked his son forward—'are eager to serve you.'

Nayan Raj's jet black hair caught the sunlight and glittered. Was it dyed? Giridhar squinted. The man's clothes were simple— a homespun Indian cotton shirt and black trousers—but they were unnaturally clean. He was looking directly at Giridhar now.

The sun was hot, and blinded Giridhar. He should say something, but his body wouldn't move. Om, ever-prepared to meet the demands of the social world, stepped forward and launched into speech:

'So many things to talk about, so much to do. Perhaps, Candidateji, we should hold a committee meeting today? If you see fit. But first, come, your relatives are waiting at home. Let's get you comfortably settled.'

'I'm so glad to be here at last,' Nayan Raj said.

Giridhar sneered at the man's genteel tone.

Then he felt a crush of bodies directing him as Om led the cinema hero towards his ancestral home. Giridhar tried to keep Om's red parka in view as he followed behind. Pushed up against Nayan Raj as he walked, he felt driven to smear the whiteness of the hero's clean shirt, but when he lifted his hands the whiteness eluded him. The landscape juddered as they crossed the Telecommunications Office. There was a bougainvillea plant in front of the widow Binita's teashop. Giridhar was thrown off by the colour of its fuchsia buds. Steps. A door. There was a crowd of faces in the teashop—Nayan Raj's relatives? They pushed and pulled and crowded out Giridhar, and it wasn't till he was sitting on a bench that he found some steadiness again.

It was cool here. The orderly rows of tables and the posters of the gods soothed Giridhar. Nayan Raj stood at the centre of a crowd which bore great resemblance to him. Relatives. Om had come next to Giridhar, and was looking at him anxiously. This needled Giridhar. It made him feel like he had to perform. He stood, patted down his hair and straightened his shirt, then approached the cinema hero. 'We were planning,' he said, but Nayan Raj was busy talking to someone else. Giridhar poked the man's white shirt till he turned. 'We were planning to inaugurate the building today.' He was speaking very slowly; he had decided this was what he should do to sound normal, to sound like he was in charge. But already he wasn't sure this was the right approach. 'Candidateji will eat,' he continued, frowning. 'Then we will fetch you. Then you will inaugurate the office. Then we will hold a meeting.'

Nayan Raj smiled heartily, like a hero spying his heroine in a secluded garden. 'Why don't we eat together, Giridharji? I'm sure our Binita-bhauju will oblige us with a meal.'

At the stove his widowed sister-in-law shot everyone a stiff look.

A relative laughed. 'Ho, this is a teashop, after all—it's open to the whole public and their sons.'

At this Jimmawal-baaje protested, 'Me, I never eat anything prepared outside my home. My seventh son too. Never.'

Giridhar too shook his head, though he had no idea why he was refusing. 'I will come here after you eat,' he said. After a pause, he added, 'And on behalf of all our party members, welcome.'

Then, avoiding Om, he rushed out.

He went home and ate in silence, thinking nothing—and by some grace, by the time he finished eating, he discovered how to occupy the spaces that made him act normal. It took moving his body quicker than usual, making gestures that exuded self-mastery, and adopting an even, steady tone when speaking. He had spoken slowly at the end, he thought. He must speak slowly again—while moving as though he were speaking fast. He felt he could do this now.

He went back to the cinema hero's home. Om and Jimmawal-baaje were already there, chatting with the hero's relatives. Everyone headed together to the party office. At the office door Nayan Raj cut the red ribbon that Jimmawal-baaje's son had tacked up. Curious onlookers joined in the applause of party members and relatives. Then, with a confidence that surprised even himself, Giridhar led everyone to the large upstairs room. The first thing he saw were the slippers he'd bought this morning. He kicked them aside and straightened the furniture. The cinema hero sat on one of the good chairs, and Jimmawal-baaje and Om sat on the bed. Seeing that a meeting was about to take place, the hero's relatives remained in the hallway. Jimmawal-baaje's seventh son lingered by expectantly till Giridhar shut the door on him.

'It's a nice building,' Nayan Raj said. He looked a little shorter here than in Kathmandu, and slightly less polished. He looked less unreal. 'This room is sunny,' he said. 'Let's make it our regular meeting room.'

'It's an honour to rent the house,' Jimmawal-baaje said.

There were important matters of strategy to discuss, and Giridhar didn't want to get distracted by niceties. He said, 'I've been thinking about the best strategy for our party.' He stopped as everyone turned to him. Beside him, Om smiled. Why? Was Giridhar telling a joke? Giridhar turned away and tried to remember what he was saying. Eh ho. His plans, dammed all month in his mind, suddenly rushed out: 'I see three stages to the election—the first—we have to recruit workers, this isn't easy.

Because other parties have taken all the boys. The first stage—so first we take anyone we can find. Boys, old men, anyone in Khaireni Tar. We need party workers to volunteer time. The second stage—.'

The cinema hero raised a hand. Giridhar braced for judgement. But the man only said, 'How many workers are we aiming for, and what kind of people do we want?' He spoke in the tone of a philosopher. 'I'd like to recruit only the best workers and educate them about our party's principles.'

Sharp quarrels formed in Giridhar's mind. Who could afford to pick and choose workers at this late hour? Who had time to train them? Trying to hide his irritation, he said, 'We'll need twenty, twenty-five workers within two weeks. Then we'll have mass rallies which will attract more workers, later we'll have to recruit workers in each village, but.' He was speeding too far ahead. 'That's the second stage.'

Om said, 'So far it's an impeccable plan.'

Giridhar winced.

Nayan Raj said, 'I'd like to talk to each worker myself, share our vision with everyone. They should all represent the party in the same way. They're our ambassadors to the people.'

It took a very silly man, Giridhar thought, to describe the motley bunch of boys they'd end up using as 'party ambassadors'. He felt bolstered: only a local man knew what had to be done. He said, 'We'll have several publicity groups. They'll travel the electorate, putting up posters, painting slogans in every village, publicizing our ballot symbol. Our party's teacup symbol must be known to everyone when they go to the voting booth. Teacup, teacup. Everyone must recognize us as the teacup party.'

He stopped. No one said anything. He continued, 'We ourselves will form two groups, travelling from village to village campaigning, recruiting men. Our most important task is to form booth committees.' Then he caught a lost look on Nayan Raj's face, and thought—what, didn't the hero know anything? Giridhar explained, 'There are thirty-three booths throughout the electorate. Each booth needs a committee from our party manning it on voting day. We need to establish these booth committees in phase two.'

The cinema hero said, 'So, at the end, we'll have thirty-three booth committees?'

Giridhar produced from his pocket a scrap of yellow paper. The night before, he had reproduced the map he'd given Nayan Raj in Kathmandu, and he had plotted an alternate future over it. He trailed a finger along each dotted village and spotted trail. 'Here,' he said, pointing to the southern village of Kihun. 'They block-vote for communists here.' He pointed at another dot. 'But I have a friend near by who's an old village leader, he'll help us break this block.' His finger slid to the top of the map. 'Most of our votes will come from Congress areas. This whole area.' He palmed half the electorate.

'Such knowledge you have of the villages,' Om said appreciatively.

His doting tone annoyed Giridhar. 'Anyway that's phase two.' He put away the map. 'Phase three starts two weeks before election day. We finalize our strategies in each booth, decide which booths to focus on, where to give up. That's phase three.'

The cinema hero said, 'That sounds like an excellent plan.'

'It's impeccable,' Om added.

Giridhar snapped, 'That's how campaigns are conducted.'

Jimmawal-baaje broke in. 'In my opinion what we need, foremost, is a peon boy. What kind of party office lacks a peon boy? Congress, UML, everyone has a peon boy. People will laugh if we don't hire one—'

Giridhar lost patience. 'I was hoping maybe one of us could see to office management.' He turned to Om.

'Tell me what to do,' Om said readily. 'In the mornings I

must manage the school. But I'll dedicate my afternoons to the party.'

Jimmawal-baaje shot up. 'We're not going to hire my son?'

Giridhar said, 'Om-bhai can take care of the paperwork.'

'But, but.'

'Let's wait,' Giridhar snapped.

Jimmawal-baaje sat down sulking.

Both the details and the larger designs were fixed, then. Having proved his competence, Giridhar sat easier in his chair. Nayan Raj started to speak about his deep commitment to democratic ideals, but Giridhar stopped listening. Instead, he began to evaluate his own performance. He had spoken well. He had laid out a plan and it was good. Good enough? He could have written down his points beforehand. He could have presented them more slowly, more convincingly. He had spoken–too rapidly. He hadn't sounded entirely dignified.

The cinema hero, though, looked won over. 'So I'll count on you all,' he was saying when Giridhar came to attention. 'I left the district as a boy, I don't know the villages. You must teach me. If I'm going to represent the people here, I must become one of them. All of you must guide me.'

Om said something most charming, and Jimmawal-baaje added something ingratiating, but Giridhar felt too spent to reply. He was shaky; he needed some strength.

A few days ago, the Sub-Inspector had visited and said, 'Now that you're running a party you don't stop by for a drink—what, you think you've become too good for us, you motherfucking corpse you?'

Nayan Raj then started to talk about democratic reform. He spoke about the ideal of free and fair elections, and said that the party's ideals were more important than winning. He spoke about the poor, the downtrodden, women. Such grandiloquence. He said, 'We must give people an understanding of real democracy.

We must conduct a fair campaign.'

It was very pretty, the way the hero moulded his words. Giridhar sat up in his seat, thinking that he must stop behaving so fitfully. He must learn to speak with eloquence. He must claim without apology the space his body was allowed to occupy in the world. The chairman's space. True, he wasn't as sharp as he should be, but he was being the sharpest it was possible to be, given—. Given his drinking. But that was over. He was trying, now, and he must continue to try; he must try and try, and he mustn't—tch—squander his life on efforts that always—no, not always failed.

20

All morning she had bent in front of those who begrudged their blessings. Relatives, some women, many of whom Binita had stopped recognizing. 'How are you, poor thing? How is your poor daughter?' Barbed and insincere words had ricocheted through the teashop: 'And why don't you ever visit us, your own husband's cousin sisters?' Relatives had pried into every space of the house. 'This is the shop? And where are the rooms? Where will our nephew sleep? And you?'

Binita had maintained form, not responding to attempts at fellowship, acting on none of her anger, or her urge to defy. Quietly she had deferred to Kainlo-kaka and his battalion of kin. When Nayan Raj arrived, there had been nothing for her to do but to serve everyone as the family's daughter-in-law.

Then, as soon as Nayan Raj-bhai left for his party office, she was shown her worth: all the relatives followed him out of the teashop. Her house was rapidly emptied after being occupied, all morning, against her will. The teashop was left in a shambles. The tables and benches were askew, scraps of food were scattered

about. A teacup had broken, and its shards littered the floor.
Everything felt defiled. Binita felt debased. She paced near the
stove feeling made use of, choked by frustration at being made to
go along with her own submission. She hadn't uttered a single
hard word all morning. Very obediently, she had betrayed herself.

A stack of dirty dishes was piled up at the sink, polluted with
the spit and saliva of those who would deny her meagre freedoms.
After pacing a long time, Binita finally closed the teashop,
brusquely turning back a few local men who came in with
questions on their faces. She ordered Sani to clean the room,
sending her scuttling with her sharp tone. Then she sat at the
sink. Leftover rice grains on dirty dishes. Yellowish mung daal,
the green juices of watercress and stains of spice-coloured oils.
She stayed with the sullied feel of half-eaten food, apprenticing
herself to her servitude. Kainlo-kaka's spit and saliva. She must
inure herself to him.

She was still sliding her hands through the dishes when Pramila
arrived from Thakalni-aama's house, carrying a rolled-up
mattress and a bag full of clothes. 'I'm ready to begin my service
at the Binita Teashop,' she said with a grin. Binita could barely
muster a smile in return. Pramila seemed not to notice. She said,
'Thakalni-aama found out that the cinema hero had arrived and
she sent me at once.'

Binita put aside the dishes, then led Pramila to the alcove.
She knew she should say something to make the woman feel
welcome—but she couldn't. Not that Pramila seemed to mind.
She had a talkative disposition, and her voice rang through the
whole house. 'All the women sleeping in a row,' she remarked,
laying out her mattress beside Binita's and Sani's beds. 'Four
women to guard one man.' From her bag she pulled out a pink
scarf and tied it over her hair. 'Now tell me what to do.'

In an effort to shrug off her melancholy, Binita forced a smile.
Pramila set to work at once. After helping Sani sweep up,

she began to take stock of her surroundings. 'Forty glasses and not a single one chipped,' she exclaimed, studying the shelves. 'Sixteen—no, seventeen cups; but only twelve saucers. Plates, saucers, forks and spoons. Look at this saucer—it's got two cracks.' She felt the shelves for dust. 'Come, Sani. Let's clean the racks till they shine.'

Binita returned to the sink. Grains, granules, juices and oil, filmy suds glistening with grease. Her purpose in this house was to cook and clean. Slowly she began to lather each aluminum plate, each steel glass and serving spoon. Her motions untangled some of her feelings. She no longer controlled the house: it was best to acknowledge this. Nayan Raj was master from now on. His relatives were loyal minions. She thought of Kainlo-kaka's furtive glances at her this morning. He would come here every day, flanked by family, and he would summon her to serve him. She would move as he bid her to, never rebelling, only protecting herself.

A shame to have to live in such fear.

Pramila meanwhile had finished cleaning the shelves and was squatting on the floor now, chopping onions, garlic and ginger for the evening meal. She seemed to be in the habit of commenting on everything. 'This Radha-Krishna picture, how bright it makes the room,' she said to no one in particular, looking up at the wall. As Binita cleaned a thermos, Pramila remarked, 'Chinese thermoses aren't like they used to be. You knock them once and they break.' Seeing the leftover food from the morning meal, she said, 'A woman's feelings get hurt if you don't finish her food.'

Binita found her a bit loud. But Sani, finding a willing audience in the new woman, launched into stories about what her Sir had said in the literacy class. Binita didn't like Sani's smug tone. 'Sir says, women cover half the earth and hold up half the sky,' Sani said, making a face.

Pramila laughed. She had hitched her fariya above her knees

so it wouldn't encumber her. 'What else does your Sir say?'

'He says the silliest things. Like women can be just as strong as men, but first we have to form groups to fight the men...the patty-arcky.'

'See what happens when you educate girls!' Pramila cried in mock horror.

'I wish he would stop lecturing us and just teach us letters, like he's supposed to. Yesterday he taught me how to write my name—sa-aakar, na-eekar. Then I gave him my real name so I could learn to spell that too. Ma-aakar, dha-ukar. Madhu.'

'Madhu—a nice name.'

'Sir was asking about Nayan Raj-kaka. Tonight I'll tell him he's here.' Then, turning to Binita, she added, 'He'll live here, sleep here. Won't he, Binita-didi?'

Sometimes the girl tested Binita's patience. Binita ignored the remark. She finished washing her dishes, then piled them up in the cleaned-out shelves, preparing to serve everyone again at night.

Her brother-in-law returned in the evening, accompanied by party people: Giridhar Adhikari, Om Gurung and Jimmawal-baaje. Kainlo-kaka, his son and some distant nephews also returned, crowding around their famous relative. Binita bowed to Kainlo-kaka for the second time today. The old man proffered indifferent blessings.

Nayan Raj-bhai was busy talking to his party members, but he stepped aside to ask Binita—with a consideration he hadn't shown this morning—if it was possible for them all to eat at the teashop tonight. He might have just ordered her: could she say no? She figured he needed to feel like he wasn't imposing on her. 'I should have asked you a few hours ago,' he said. 'With these last-minute invitations, I'm burdening you.'

'I've already prepared enough food.'

The men settled in the front portion of the teashop. Binita sent Sani off to her literacy class, and took refuge behind Pramila at the stove. Tripti was in the alcove doing her homework. In the teashop the sharp light of the naked bulb cast a cheerful light upon everyone, but Binita remained watchful. She felt vaguely ashamed that the teashop was open at night—it looked like a drinking den. The sound of men's voices made her feel guarded. She caught Kainlo-kaka glancing at her once, and was glad to have Pramila near her. The woman's loud, banging movements lessened her anxiety.

'I can feed ten, twenty people at a time, no problem,' Pramila bragged, pulling out a stack of aluminum plates. 'I've fed fifty, hundred men at Thakalni-aama's hotel. Up to twenty, I can feed with my eyes closed.'

Binita tried to respond normally. 'Thakalni-aama manages so much.'

Pramila said, 'That old grandmother rules her empire like a queen.' Across the room, the men laughed at something that Kainlo-kaka had said. 'Eh she's sharp,' Pramila continued. 'She fools you with her soft looks, but she's always been as tough as a man.'

As the rice was cooking, another group of relatives arrived at the teashop. Nayan Raj started greeting them and asking for their blessings. Binita silently placed more rice on to boil. Then, because protocol demanded it, she went to bow to the new guests. One old uncle said, tactlessly, 'The teashop—I didn't realize it was so decent.' Another distant uncle agreed, 'It isn't like I thought it would be.'

From a nearby table, Om Gurung said, 'It's every bit as homey as one's own kitchen. I don't feel like leaving at all.'

Returning to the stove, Binita thought, yes, this was it, her life in the next few months: being judged by strangers who stood as her proprietors.

Thankfully, no need arose for her to address Kainlo-kaka: he didn't leave his table the whole evening. Having finished her homework, Tripti came to sit on a chair at the counter, quietly studying the unfamiliar commotion in her house. Sani, returning from her literacy class, was startled at the number of people in the teashop. She stared unhappily at the crowd, and flashed Binita a disdainful look. Pramila alone seemed unperturbed. She banged about the stoves throwing more and more vegetables into the simmering pot. 'What a blessing to be able to feed so many people! It must be my fate to feed hungry mouths all my life.'

When time came to serve the meal, Pramila did so with clatter and dash. 'It's terrible food but eat it as though it were good,' she cried, placing plates of steaming rice, daal and vegetables in front of everyone. 'It's not good, but eat it as though it were.'

Then she began, almost at once, to offer seconds. 'You'll go home hungry if you don't take more.'

With Sani helping Pramila, Binita was free to feed Tripti. Her daughter tended to pick at her food, especially when she was nervous. 'Eat,' Binita coaxed her. 'You'll never grow taller than me if you don't eat.'

'I'm not hungry.' Tripti's gaze kept going back to her uncle.

'Eat this much and then you can go.'

Later, there was another round of bowing and scraping as everybody left. Binita, washing Tripti at the sink, pretended not to notice so that she wouldn't have to bow to Kainlo-kaka again.

Then it was just the four females and Nayan Raj-bhai. Binita felt unsure about how to approach her brother-in-law, and waited for him to turn to the stove. But he just stood near the door, looking at the poster of Saraswati on a swan.

He stayed like that while the women cleared up. Tripti was

looking from her mother to her uncle. Nayan Raj-bhai's posture was relaxed. Surely he wasn't contemplating the gods, Binita thought; he didn't look given to religion. His hair was as black as Binita's husband's had been, and from this angle he looked very much like pictures of her husband as a young man. His bearing was more austere, though. Even now, standing at rest, he looked controlled. He had none of the sleepy charm of her husband, none of his tousled appeal.

After a long time Nayan Raj-bhai sighed. When he turned, he looked tired.

'There's a bucket of water outside to wash up,' Binita offered.

'You've seen to everything, Binita-bhauju.'

Binita led him to the back porch, where Sani had placed a filled bucket. 'There's a towel in your room,' she said. 'I'll fetch it.'

She left him there, and went to the upstairs room she had cleared for him. Her brother-in-law's surprisingly small bag stood to one side of the room, still unopened. A city man: he would find the room too spare. When she reached for his towel, she heard him coming upstairs.

'My old woman sent some mementos,' he said, entering the room. 'They're just small things. She selected them herself.'

Binita waited as he emptied what seemed like half of his bag's contents. 'She would have come,' Nayan Raj-bhai said, turning to her. 'Her office, though. She can't take leave.'

Binita took the gifts and handed him his towel.

'My old woman kept wishing you'd visit us, Binita-bhauju. She's always wanted to make you feel like our Kathmandu home is your home too. She sends her fond remembrance.'

Binita couldn't think of a proper reply. Then, because it seemed best, she turned to leave.

'Binita-bhauju.' Nayan Raj-bhai stepped up, leaning into her at the same angle her husband used to when talking to people. 'I wanted to say—my presence here will disrupt your life. Relatives will visit, party members will drop by. There'll be endless rounds of tea, snacks, meals.' There was a hint of exasperation in his voice, as though he hadn't enjoyed meeting so many people earlier. He said, 'It'll be months of having people walking through the house.'

This was his way of apologizing in advance, Binita thought. He was clearing his mind of blame. She didn't have the guile to contradict him, to say that his presence was welcome and his guests a pleasure to serve. She waited for him to continue, and when he didn't, she made to leave.

But he wanted to keep talking. 'It would be wrong for me to impose on you,' he said, staying her at the door with his voice. 'I wanted to ask—my party's going to need a canteen, a mess where workers can eat.'

He needed to hear her say that she was willing to serve them.

He said, 'One option is for me to contract the work to someone who'll run a canteen at the party office. That would make things easy for you. The other option is you, here, like today...' He paused. When he spoke again he was apologetic. 'The teashop is your source of livelihood, it's what's sustained you. If you close it to the public, you might lose customers. And so I wanted to give you the choice, Binita-bhauju, whether you'd like me to contract out the work or whether you'll accept the contract yourself.'

He looked up at Binita, who turned her face away in surprise. He was being considerate, she realized: but rancour flashed through her. How could she turn him away? Her own brother-in-law refused to eat food cooked by her hands, people would say. She could almost hear her neighbour Phool Devi sniping.

'The choice is yours,' Nayan Raj-bhai said.

Binita tried to feel the choice: but there was none. 'I can cook for your party,' she said.

'I'm grateful.' Nayan Raj-bhai strode over and placed an envelope in her hand. Money. Binita withdrew in surprise, but he placed the envelope more securely in her grasp. 'For the first month. You must keep tally of how many people you feed, and the next month's expenses will cover those costs.'

The exchange of money confused her. 'I'll go now,' she said.

Nayan Raj-bhai took leave from her with a formal bow, oblivious, it seemed, to Binita's discomfort at having taken money from him.

A woman who sold to men.

In the alcove, Binita tucked the envelope into her blouse. She couldn't, of course, have afforded to feed party workers by herself. Neither could she have charged relatives for their meals. Her brother-in-law was being pragmatic—and even considerate. But something about the give and take made her feel ashamed. She had to remind herself that Nayan Raj-bhai wasn't Kainlo-kaka; he didn't bear the same judgements of her. But how could she be sure?

In the teashop, Pramila whooped when she saw the gifts. She immediately unbundled the package and pulled out whatever caught her eye. 'A red sweater! It's just Sani's size. Is it for her?'

'It's for her.'

Sani reluctantly accepted the gift.

Tripti said, 'A picture book. And colouring pens!'

Pramila nudged Binita. 'There's a fariya for you. A nice colour, it'll suit you.'

Binita saw that the fariya was green, a shade that she was unlikely to wear. 'You take it,' she said to Pramila.

Pramila bit her tongue. 'How can I make off with your brother-in-law's gift? He'll think I'm a chicken thief. No, no—I can't.'

Binita smiled. The fariya was pretty, she saw. It was made of a fine silky material, and was a colour between gray and green but more green than gray, the velvety shade of eucalyptus leaves. After seven years, only the most orthodox widows shunned colours the way Binita did. Her reasons were purely pragmatic: a widow's indulgence in colours revealed her pleasure, and invited criticism—or harm. She wore drab clothes to guard herself. Now she reached over and fingered the green. Once she would have thought nothing of placing this hue next to her skin. She lingered a while, observing how unusual the colour looked against her hand. What a pity to grow from an intrepid girl into a wrecked woman. She fingered the green.

'Aama, my friend said he saw a ghost walking by the river, it had no head.' Tripti lay with Binita in the bed she had laid, in the alcove. Next to them Sani was asleep already, her back forming an untroubled curl. Pramila too was snoring. The lights had been switched off long ago, but Tripti was cavilling about going to sleep. She said, 'The ghost was trying to cross the river but couldn't find the bridge. It was going to kill people on the other side, Aama.'

'That's the cowherd who was killed in his stall.' Binita pulled her daughter closer into her. 'His killers crossed the river and were never found. So he wanders up and down the shore looking for a way to cross to the other side.'

'And if he finds the bridge, Aama?'

'He's looking for the old bridge. It's not there any more, it was swept away. That's the only bridge he can cross.'

'So he won't be able to come this side and kill anyone?'

'He'll never be able to cross the river.'

Tripti took in this information. 'Aama,' she then said, reaching for the edges of her mother's nightdress. She was trying to prolong her time awake, and Binita yielded to her child's desire. Tripti said, 'Aama, a girl in my class can eat ten bananas at the same time. She showed me yesterday. Aama, will papaya seeds grow in your tummy if you swallow them?'

Binita could feel her daughter's voice vibrate through her skin as Tripti prattled on about her friends and their world of small feats and marvels. She responded to her daughter when she had to, but mostly she just listened. Tripti was unsettled by her uncle's arrival, she could tell. Binita could almost anticipate her daughter's principal question, which came, eventually: 'Aama, is Nayan Raj-kaka Baba's own brother?'

The girl's need for assurance was so palpable that Binita embraced her, warm and bony, into the heat of her stomach. 'He's your Baba's own brother.'

'Is he a good man?'

With all the conviction she could muster, Binita said, 'Yes he's good.'

'Will he stay here from now on, Aama?'

'He'll stay for three or four months, little one. Beyond that I don't know. If he wins the elections, maybe he'll always stay here.'

Tripti stayed quiet, thinking this over.

Binita began to stroke her fine, straight hair, and soon her daughter's breathing deepened. Binita lay her head next to hers; and they fell asleep in a tight embrace.

21

In the days following the number one hit cinema hero's arrival in Khaireni Tar, townspeople began to loiter in public spaces—at shops, in the pathways, at the bus stop, at the platform beneath the bar-peepal tree—allowing their gaze to wander, as if by chance, to that part of town which housed the Telecommunications Office, to that part of town which housed not only Nayan Raj's ancestral home but also the People's Party office. Not that anyone

would admit they were waiting to spot the cinema hero: no. An
indifferent veneer was maintained by all. But if one should catch
a glimpse of Nayan Raj as he came out of his party office, say—
then one could see with one's own eyes whether he still looked
like he did in his cinemas, couldn't one? Just a look.

The peanut vendor folded a scrap of newspaper into a crisp
cone, filled it with peanuts, and handed it to a customer who was
eyeing the People's Party office, across the highway. 'They say
he's not haughty,' the vendor commented.

His customer started at his remark, as though he'd been caught
theiving. 'Yes,' he said, paying for the peanuts with a tatty rupee
note. Then he slunk away.

To no one in particular, the peanut vendor repeated, 'They
say he's not haughty at all.'

The banana vendor agreed. 'They say he's a simple man,
the hero of *Ma Maanchhe Hun* right here in our midst.'

The Musalmaan bangle seller remained unmoved by this
cinema hero hubbub. An actor turned politician—all nonsense,
baba. Much to her chagrin, the bazaar was now filled with the
faces of politicking men, men, men. To one side of her sat two
Congress workers, talking about America. To her other side stood
communists, glaring about with mistrust in their eyes. She wished
these men would go away, and clear room near her stall for lady
customers.

The watchmaker, though, was eager to meet Nayan Raj. He
wanted to see if the cinema hero would remember him from
Kathmandu; but he felt too shy to approach him. One day, as he
rested beneath the bar-peepal tree, he was rewarded with a sighting
of the actor. 'Look, look,' he pointed to the People's Party office.
'I'd recognize him anywhere. So tall, such black, black hair.'

The vendors followed his gaze.

Across the highway, Nayan Raj could be seen coming out of
the party office, a slim, angular man. He was dressed, for all his

fame, in humble cottons. Giridhar Adhikari was with him, as was Om Gurung. The rest of the people following him had the clannish look of relatives. Nayan Raj was walking at the centre of the crowd.

For several days, townspeople watched the goings-on across the highway. They looked, they lingered—but they hesitated to go and meet the cinema hero. Then one morning, in plain view of all the bazaar, the Gaine singer Thainlo Nepali stepped up to the People's Party office. It was that time of day when the sun had already yellowed, but the air hadn't lost the crispness of dawn. Thainlo Nepali's son was with him, a tiny duplicate of his father with his skinny build and solemn face, and his tunic patched in ten places. Both father and son waited in front of the office building, waiting for Nayan Raj to emerge.

Their presence there gave other men an excuse to gather around. 'Play us a tune, why don't you?' a passerby called out, stopping in front of the party office. 'Play us a sweet, sad tune.'

Thainlo Nepali plucked at the strings of his sarangi fiddle. 'The song doesn't come like that, hajoor,' he said with a wistful smile. 'The song doesn't come just like that.'

'Here.' The man tossed the son a five-rupee note. 'Sing us a sweet song now.'

Thainlo Nepali waited till his son had pocketed the bill, then began to slide his bow on the taut strings of the instrument.

They say democracy's come to the land
To free all of us wretches who live by our hands...

He was hired later that day by Nayan Raj.

After that, one by one, other townspeople stepped across the highway to meet Nayan Raj and to volunteer to help him.

The first such volunteer was the failed army recruit Juddha Ale, a man frankly frustrated with life. Skinny boys on the verge of tuberculosis got recruited to the army because of connections, while he, fit and trim, had been rejected on a technicality: he hadn't met the height requirement by mere millimeters. One needed the patronage of the powerful, Juddha had realized. The King and his courtiers were weak now; the parties ruled supreme. If he helped the People's Party in these elections, Nayan Raj might help him in the next round of army recruitment.

A few of Juddha's friends also joined him.

The gatherings in front of the People's Party office gradually swelled. One day some female students from the college campus stopped before the office building. 'What are *you* here for?' A man called out. 'The hero's autograph?'

One of the students was a distant relative of one of Nayan Raj's aunts. 'His wife works at an office,' she said. 'She's a modern woman. We're here only to ask the candidate what's his commitment to women. The parties never do anything for women. Does he also see us as mere chattel of our fathers-brothers-husbands, or does he believe in women's equality?'

Some of the men around cackled.

Standing not far off from the girls, turned contemptuously away from everyone, was the hooligan BB—'BB-Gun'—Thapa, who knew that his presence here was being noted by the Congress boys at the bar-peepal tree—boys belonging to his rival gang. Striking a pose that showed off his build, BB-Gun looked more like a cinema hero than Nayan Raj did—like the Hindi cinema hero Salman Khan, BB-Gun was all tight muscles and merciless good looks. He ruled supreme in the alleys of Khaireni Tar. No one dared challenge him. And this—well, was beginning to bore him. Last week he'd bloodied a low-caste Kumal boy but hadn't even enjoyed it. It had become too easy, his life. He fought and he fought and he fought, he wielded nun-chucks, chains, bats, secondhand guns; he did weightlifting, judo, karate, kung-fu. His gang members were loyal to him. Rival gangs shook and shivered at his sight. Now what? He would show up the Congress boys by joining the People's Party. BB-Gun's fellow gang members, decked in bandanas, earrings, ripped T-shirts and Chinese Reeboks, stood by him, mirroring his breezy look.

Nayan Raj met each volunteer separately, and impressed everyone equally. With Juddha Ale and other aspiring army recruits, he spoke of reforming the system: 'The army belongs to everyone, not just to the well-connected.' He argued for women's rights more passionately than the female students: 'Our women haven't been granted full citizenship yet.' With boys like BB-Gun he even bantered: 'Handsome young boys like you should be starring in our cinemas.' His versatility impressed people. As the days progressed, more and more townspeople began to go and meet him, and the People's Party office acquired an open, accessible look.

There were of course those who remained indifferent to Nayan Raj's arrival, or were even put off by it. When the town's cobbler saw the growing swarm at the party office, he descended into a foul mood. 'Politicians,' he said to the Sub-Inspector, who was getting his boots resoled. 'Every election they come to our settlements and say they want to help—but will they touch our children, will they share their water taps with those they deem untouchable?' He shook his head. 'No, Sub-Inspector Sah'b, no. But Jesus will reach out and pat my children's heads. The kingdom of god is the only place for those suffering in the kingdom of Nepal!'

The Sub-Inspector frowned to hear such cow-eating Christian talk, but instead of shutting up the cobbler, he opened his mouth and yawned. He was tired, he'd been up all night. Some months ago the Sub-Inspector had brought home a second wife, and there was no woman as beautiful as she, a Magar girl from the neighbouring district, as plump as an apple, as pleasing as the velveteen blouse she wore on their wedding night. Eh gods her supple, supple skin. How sorely the Sub-Inspector longed to slip to his private quarters to partake of his duties as a husband. For his new wife he spent all his mornings loafing around Chiranjibi Joshi's mill, mumbling vaguely about regulations that needed following. For her he spent his afternoons harassing truck and bus drivers. He jeopardized his standing in the community for his younger wife—while his older wife waged war on him, carping about him with all the women in her literacy class.

There was no winning with women. The Sub-Inspector yawned. He badly needed a rest.

Equally unimpressed by Nayan Raj's arrival was the town's Doctor Sah'b, a retired health post peon who ran the only medical shop of Khaireni Tar. The Doctor Sah'b grew sullen at the very thought of politics. For in this world with so many people, and so many problems, and so many needs that couldn't be met, politicians were utterly useless, like rocks in the middle of fields, taking up precious space. Or like planks that were too small to bridge turbulent rivers—what was the use? Voters were like aged bulls given away to lesser castes so that they could kill them discreetly and eat them. Helpless to catastrophe: that was how voters were.

Yesterday a woman had come to the medical shop, bleeding from the place that women bleed. 'My husband's away in the army,' she said. A woman who'd gotten pregnant while her husband was away...she had walked two days after an abortion failed, and was now having a less-than-spontaneous miscarriage.

Bleeding, anaemia, infection, septicemia, cervical scarring, hysterectomies. How wretched it felt to charge such patients large sums of money. The emotional cost the Doctor Sah'b paid! But look at the way his daughter wilted waiting for a boy who'd marry her, look at the way his son coveted brand-name shirts. Look at the desires naked on their faces and tell him he was wrong to overcharge his patients. Was any politician in a position to help? Voting: what was the use?

Near the medical shop roamed the madwoman who had strolled Khaireni Tar's alleys for years now, babbling insistently about things no one understood: 'Eat that goes raise run at health,' she said to passers-by. 'Splayed on very so the retreat does rail—heat regrettable love of upon fly shout reward for hand.'

She too wasn't concerned about Nayan Raj.

At his desk in his fragrant wood mill, the contractor Chiranjibi Joshi tried hard to ignore the whisperings of the nearby workers. 'Cinema hero this-this-this,' he heard them say as they looped measuring tapes around logs. 'Cinema hero that-that-that.' What were they saying about Nayan Raj? Chiranjibi tried not to eavesdrop, but his ears pricked up at the mention of the actor's name. Chiranjibi needed to focus on an important matter—he'd just received a letter from the District Education Officer informing him that he'd won the bid for the school building. He had to respond at once. But Chiranjibi found himself dilly-dallying, trying not to listen to what the workers were saying. 'Cinema hero this-that, this-that.'

It was natural that people were interested in Nayan Raj. It wasn't just that the man was a famous actor, Chiranjibi knew. No, he had a magnetism to him, a human spark. The way his eyes settled on those he spoke to, his respectful tone, the way he leaned in to listen to others: he believed in other peoples' worth, in their humanity. It was this conviction that Chiranjibi had responded to when he'd let Nayan Raj talk him into joining his party. Of course the man might have changed in the intervening years...Chiranjibi had dealt with scores of politicians in his contracting work, and knew that they were shifty creatures. A principled politician? Even the most upright leaned at the sight of zero zero zero sums placed in envelopes. In his view, they weren't really people, politicians: they were more like price-tags that moved, walked and talked, price-tags that had to be met in order to get work done.

'Cinema hero this-this-this.'

'Cinema hero that-that-that.'

Impossible to focus on the task at hand. Chiranjibi rose from his desk. On the other side of the mill, his brother was counting stacks of freshly sawed saal trees. How rapt his brother was in his work: how absorbed he was in his world of wood beams, bricks, iron rods, mortar and cement.

Outside the mill, a young woodworker was hunched over Chiranjibi's Honda motorbike, inspecting its mileage metre. The boy couldn't be older than sixteen. He moved his hands tenderly over the curves of the bike, its leather seats and gas tank. He inspected himself in the mirrors, then placed a hand on the gears and made believe he was driving.

People and their desires. The contractor stepped aside quietly, not wanting to interrupt the boy's fantasies. Across the highway was the People's Party office, gleaming in the sun. A small crowd was gathered there. Chiranjibi studied it and recognized, with shock, the pale figure at the centre, talking to a group of girls. There he was. Chiranjibi fumbled at his shirt pocket for a pack of Yaks. He lit a cigarette and filled his mouth with its acrid taste. One mustn't be foolish, he told himself, battling a sudden urge to cross the highway. On this side of the highway was his work, he thought. On that side of the highway was his life.

Was it ludicrous? Without allowing himself to halt the astonishing movement of his desire, he tossed the half-smoked cigarette and set off to the People's Party office. Nayan Raj was leading the crowd into the office building, and Chiranjibi felt there was nowhere to go but after him. By the time he slipped in through the front door, he'd lost his breath. His face was flushed and he hardly noticed it when the Sellotape holding together his glasses unravelled. With his unassuming looks, he did not stand out among the other workers. His clothes were as plain as the next man's, and looking at him no one could guess that he was risking millions of rupees worth of contracts, sub-contracts and business deals by following Nayan Raj with such imprudence.

Chiranjibi hesitated briefly, then edged behind a group of hooligans to get a look at Nayan Raj, the neat jet black of hair, the precise features. He was talking to someone about the way social movements deepened the base of democracy. 'The occupational caste movement, the women's movement, the strides our minority ethnic groups are making—all these will set the roots of democracy in Nepal,' he said.

'Our constitution,' Chiranjibi muttered to himself, quoting his first conversation with Nayan Raj from memory. 'Our constitution is just a starting point. We have yet to realize the democratic revolution.'

Was he being fatuous? Chiranjibi stood behind the hooligans, feeling out of place but also bizarrely emancipated, waiting for Nayan Raj to recognize him.

the current sister doesn't save again
electric prod

22

'Respected Congress Party Chairman and Vice-Chairman, fellow party members, distinguished guests, older and younger brothers, older and younger sisters, and well-wishing Nepalis who are gathered:

'Jaya Nepal!

'We have converged, for this rally, today, at this place, all together, to uphold democratic norms, and to honour the fearless martyrs who spilled their blood! A decade ago, fearlessly! Vanquishing the legacy of autocracy, and bringing back to our land the tree of democracy, for which our Congress party has fought and ceaselessly continues to fight. We must not forget the blood—spilled by our martyrs! Or the tears!—that poured forth from the eyes of their mothers-wives-sisters. No! Because if we forget, we dishonour our martyrs! Whose sacrifice is now bearing fruit, by spreading—freedom! We are a backward country. But it is my ardent belief, that our party—which sadly, due to infighting and strife, and destructive power-hoarding tendencies among top leaders, and bitter words uttered nakedly against my uncle the Prime Minister, has not always lived up to expectations—the party must make place for the younger generations like me, who wait, wait patiently, so patiently, to lead our nation of himals and rivers, forests and plains, to the fruits of democracy.

'Democracy will let the free market turn us into Hong Kong-Singapore-Bangkok. Of course not every problem, especially in rural areas, has been solved so far. These problems are very, very complicated. But respected party leaders, fellow party members, distinguished guests, older and younger brothers, older and younger sisters, and all Nepalis who are gathered, I pledge!—with my palms joined in namaste!—if you vote for me, I will let you eat the fruits of democracy, which we all—we *all* deserve to eat!

'Jaya Nepal!'

'Revolutionary UML comrades and guests and older and younger brothers and older and younger sisters and all progressive left forces who are gathered:

'Lal salaam!

'A decade after the dawn of democracy too many among us remain hungry homeless naked! There's fire on the himal's snow peaks! A spectre is haunting the third world—the spectre of capitalism! The free market is thriving on our tears sweat and toil and threatening the sovereignty of our himals rivers jungles plains! Congress leaders squabble while the World Bank IMF and WTO set our policies! We're becoming the pawn of foreign powers! The rich are getting richer and the poor poorer! Our village brothers and sisters are dying every day! Sick babies infirm adults and the elderly are crying out! But who hears the wails of the poor!

'It's true that power play mismanagement money grubbing and a proclivity to bicker and splinter has marked our party too! Some say you Marxist-Leninists are too communist! Some say you're not communist enough! People ask are you socialists or communists? We bear the name of Lenin with pride! But we're not old-fashioned Soviet/China-style communists: that much we assure you! We've embraced the worldwide tide of democracy, we're committed to parliamentary norms, we support globalization and don't oppose capitalism, really. The market: how convenient it is! I myself buy goods in it. The World Bank and IMF are our friends! Let's join the WTO at once! It's class coordination and not class warfare that we seek! Such is our present-day communism.

'This doesn't mean we're mere socialists! Eh we're authentic United Marxist-Leninist communists with red blood pumping in our hearts! We love the poor! We hear their cries! We cry with them! I say, where has the revolution gone? Vote for me! Vote for the UML! Let the red sun rise in Nepal!

'Lal salaam!'

23

In the aftermath of his devastating love tragedy, Harsha Bahadur began to develop a theory about love and his own misfortune. In the body there were places to receive love as a liquid emission, and love became the fine, cool water pervading cells, marrow, tears, the binding matter between ligaments, mother's milk and blood. It was this liquid—this juice—that he lacked, Harsha Bahadur had come to feel. And also air. For humming in each hollow space in the healthy body was breath, like a redolent wind or sunlit breeze. The breath humoured love, let it tumble and run, let it play without limits or rules. No ventilation took place in himself. And this was why his life-flame flickered at the point of extinguishing. There was no regulation of heat in his body. In him there was no steadiness of warmth. Instead, his passions set ablaze in unruly crackles, like wildfires on arid hillsides; his love turned to patches of charred earth. To add to all this, his flesh and bones were as infertile as sand, containing no nutrients. No, his was not the kind of earth in which love could come, linger, reside.

Meanwhile, in the neighbourhood, scandal burgeoned. The boys said, 'Harsha Bahadur had a love tragedy with Sani who acts like an innocent girl!'

'Sani, that comely sister of the widow Binita?'

'She soiled her good name. And she still shows her face without shame.'

Such damaging words. Harsha Bahadur of course had licensed them. In the throes of his misery, he had revealed Sani's name, and had forever stained her reputation. She would never forgive him for this. He would never forgive himself either. Throughout the alleys of Khaireni Tar, Sani was being talked about as a common girl, and for this he was entirely to blame.

Still grieving, he eventually left the dried-up lemon tree behind his father's house and returned to his daily chores. He was in agony, though. He was constantly reminded that he couldn't have Sani: like happiness, she had become unattainable. But her essence throbbed everywhere in his world. Harsha Bahadur could feel her at times when he filled his water jug at the tap, when he cooked and cleaned for his father, when he made his way through the rice fields, inspecting the landlord's crops. The further he strayed from his father's mean house the more overpoweringly he felt Sani in the atmosphere. A vision of deep blue sky. A breeze against his face. The chirp of a flock of bulbuls. She became the smell of earth, the flavour of a fat, ripe guava.

Recently Harsha Bahadur's Maoist second cousin had disappeared from home to go below the ground. He had urged Harsha Bahadur to go below the ground with him, but Harsha Bahadur had dithered too long. One night, his cousin had just vanished. He lived in a tunnel now, Harsha Bahadur figured. He could never came out of it. All that remained was his memory. Harsha Bahadur, too, imagined becoming a memory—just vanishing one day.

'Why are you sitting idly like a goat tied to a stake when there's so much to be done in the house! Go do your chores and stop embarrassing me with your ugly sickly girlish look! Just wait till I get you enrolled in the army—then you'll get beaten to rags by all your major captain generals and know what it means to be a man!'

If he vanished, what would happen? Harsha Bahadur wondered. If there was no father, no family, no tragic past—what place would remain for him on this earth?

If he disappeared, would the part of him that had hurt Sani disappear? Would she be happy again?

And the part of him that loved her: where would that go?

24

A few weeks after Nayan Raj arrived in Khaireni Tar, Rishi took a bus from Kathmandu. It was surprisingly easy for him to give up his room, stow away his few belongings and put Kathmandu behind him. Each jolt of the bus released some of the closefisted feel of that city. The ride was six hours long. They stopped for the morning meal at a roadside lodge run by an old man whose plump daughters the driver eyed lustily. When the bus started up again, Rishi fell asleep, and awoke when his dreams began to smell of schist, brooks, wild grass and sap. Outside the window, the rocky ridges of the central districts had given way to gentle rolling hills. The terraced fields were thick with rice crops. Bougainvillea bloomed beside roadside huts, and whiffs of lemon scented the air.

You're not going home, the schoolmaster had said to him at Hotel Tanahun. You're going underground.

Yet everything felt like a homecoming. A group of schoolchildren waved at bus passengers from the side of the highway, and on a whim Rishi waved back. The tropical air loaned moistness to his skin. He felt limber and light. The bus must be nearing the shortcut to the northern hills—yes, there was the narrow path from where his walk home could begin. Rishi sat up as the bus hurtled towards it. Past a wayside shrine, his

birth village rolled into view, a thicket of trees and some glinting
tin roofs. Automatically he raised his hand to signal for the driver
to stop; but he checked himself in time. The shortcut to the northern
hills shuddered past, a blur of terraced rice fields.

He thumped the side of the bus.

There was a screech of wheels and a forward lurch of seats
as the driver braked. But when the conductor looked at him,
Rishi shook his head. 'It was a mistake,' he said. 'I thought we
were somewhere else.'

'This is the shortcut to hills north of Khaireni Tar.'

'I thought it was somewhere else.'

Not much later the bus rolled to a stop beneath Khaireni Tar's
twined-together bar-peepal tree. It was four by then.

'Cheeseballs-chips-a-locket-for-your-wife!'

'Bananas so sweet they've been bitten by bees!'

'Peanuts? Peanuts? Peanuts?'

Rishi pushed through a throng of vendors and took in the
sight of the town. He'd spent all his school years here, but the
crowded shop fronts and cement houses were new to him, as was
the swarm of men in the bazaar. Political workers, obviously.
He remembered the bar-peepal tree—but the town of his memory,
the place in which he'd been a boy: it was gone. No one looked
familiar. He had hoped as much. Twelve years had passed since
he'd left.

He saw the UML office and avoided it. This was what the
schoolmaster had instructed him to do. Go to the southern end,
the schoolmaster had said. Find witnesses to your new identity.

Rishi walked past an unfamiliar row of houses, and turned
into a lane with a medical shop. Soon he reached the ashen
flatland. He knew this plane well. Memories were strewn across
the barren ground, memories of desiccation. But the flatlands too

had changed. A small cement church stood to one side, and further south was a whole settlement that hadn't existed before.

Rishi headed to the new settlement. There were less permanent structures in this part of town—bamboo shacks, huts constructed out of piled-up concrete blocks, hovels fashioned out of tin—the tentative claims of landless settlers. He went into a house with a painted 'Restaurant' sign tacked above its door. Inside, a group of men were playing cards. Rishi sat at one end of their table. The man who ran the restaurant was squatting at a stove, a skimpy cotton dhoti bunched between his thighs.

'Are there snacks?' Rishi asked.

The man got up and prepared a saucer of tepid potatoes and chickpeas. 'Tea?' he asked, and Rishi nodded. After serving, the man squatted by the stove again, and studied Rishi in the open way of restaurant owners. 'Where are you coming from, Bhai? Where are you going?'

'I'm from Jamune,' Rishi said, choosing the name of a village just outside the electorate. Speak close to the truth, the schoolmaster had said. 'I'm coming to see if I can help one of the parties.'

The restaurant owner nodded, not surprised, it seemed, by this information. Then, testing Rishi, he said, 'The UML says it'll give land deeds to all us settlers.'

Rishi hmm'ed neutrally. The card players were glancing up at him. Rishi said, 'I used to vote UML, but they've proved no less corrupt than Congress. No, I was thinking—Nayan Raj. He has connections, he'll find me a job afterwards.'

The restaurant owner took a judiciously neutral tone: 'He's more famous than the others.'

A card player said wryly, 'Everyone flocks to the famous.'

'We all need patrons to support us,' Rishi shot back.

The man assessed him with a glance. 'Ho, we all need to survive.'

The restaurant owner put an end to the topic. 'Landless settlers, what do we know about politics. You'll have more tea, Bhai?'

After that Rishi walked slowly through town. It felt curious to be so close to home and yet remain severed from the past. The spaces of the alleys were crowded, the measurements of the houses body-sized and cramped. But the rural feel to the town was spliced with urban dereliction. He passed his hand over a cement wall covered with clay, over raw plywood doors and glass windows covered with dust, on electric poles with no wires, along barbed metal signs marking private property, and along a dripping tap. Plastic PVC pipes jutted out of the ground marking abandoned irrigation schemes. Reggae beats drowned out Radio Nepal's agriculture programme. The city had come here to meet the villages, he thought. Nepal's wandering populations had gathered by the highway to make neighbours of farmers and businessmen, of squatters and landlords, of Hindus, Buddhists, Christians, Musalmaans and the godless like him, and of Gurungs, Magars, Chettris, Bahuns, Kumals and indiscernible half-breeds. Everyone, Rishi saw, wore maps on their expressions. The faces that passed by were hewn with ambitions no longer met by local means. In them Rishi recognized his own life of roaming and seeking, seeking jobs, accepting payment for services rendered, paying for food cooked by strangers, and sleeping on hard beds, without dreams.

He circled the bazaar, the landscape of his underground. He stopped by a few small teashops, spreading word to those who asked that he wanted to support the People's Party. All according to the schoolmaster's instruction. All for the masses. 'Nayan Raj is honest,' he said in one teashop, and at another, 'What have the big parties done in all these years?' He spoke loudly, so that everyone near by could hear him.

As evening fell, he asked around for Shankar's grain store. It was closed by the time he got there. Committing to memory its shuttered doors and windows, he headed for the People's Party office. He stopped awhile before the Telecommunications Office. This office hadn't been here when he was a boy. He looked north, towards home. His village was a short walk away. But he was Rishi Lamsal of Jamune. The northern hills felt generations away.

Meet Giridhar Adhikari first, the schoolmaster had said. He was a drunkard, and would be easy to approach.

There was a surprising number of people in front of the People's Party office, even at this late hour. Outside, a Gaine singer was playing his sarangi fiddle, and the bright window lights gave the building a festive air. Rishi asked around, and found out that Giridhar was upstairs in the meeting room. He waited in the narrow hallway, turned away from workers to evade questions. Most of the party's workers were young: boys in their intermediates or still in high school. He could hear a few female voices. A gang of hooligans muscled their way past him. Everybody seemed to fall in, already, with their common identities as party workers. Rishi went out to wait for Giridhar there.

By then the Gaine singer had abandoned the night to the trill of crickets. The sky was darkening, and the northern hills were an inky black stain on the horizon: no electric lines had been pulled there yet. Blue shadows concealed Rishi. Across the highway, dimly lit, was the UML office, rectangles of window light illuminating a few figures in the gloom. The schoolmaster had said he'd come to the district next week. It would be risky to meet him, though. The blind shopkeeper Shankar was to serve as their intermediary from now on.

After a while people emerged from the office, teeming around a figure Rishi immediately recognized as Nayan Raj. He looked for Giridhar Adhikari—'Pocked face, stocky build.' Some older men were walking behind the actor, talking among themselves.

Giridhar must be the middle one.

Rishi went up to him. 'I want to join the party.'

They were near the Telecommunications Office, amid obscuring shadows. The man turned, and his gaze steadied on Rishi. He was heavy-set without being fat, with dark rings beneath his eyes. There was fatigue in his gaze.

Rishi said, 'I came from Kathmandu. I was hoping to work for the party in exchange for food and a place to stay.'

'You want to help the party?'

'In return for food and a place to stay.'

The man made an awkward spasm of his body, indicating that he should follow him. The whole group was headed towards Nayan Raj's ancestral home. Giridhar—if this was him—turned back to the other men and said with sudden vehemence: 'My sources in the hills say everyone's talking about the cinema hero. By the time we hold the rallies, we'll be attracting crowds.'

'At par with the other parties?'

'I guarantee it.'

At Nayan Raj's home they entered a dining room full of religious posters enforcing an aggressive piety. Nayan Raj settled at one table with a group of workers, talking, Rishi heard, about an upcoming mass rally. The man Rishi had spoken to—he heard someone call him Giridharji—sat with another group of workers. Most of the other tables were occupied, and Rishi found himself facing the prospect of sitting with people who'd ask, in the stark light of a hundred-watt bulb, who he was.

He took an unoccupied table, flouting his loneliness in this site of belonging. At the next table, boys were talking about the party's next rally. It felt strange to be let into the party so easily. Rishi was used to the strict discipline, the cross-checks and counter cross-checks and the us-and-them divides of communist party culture. A teenage girl served him his meal. He ate in silence, taken aback by the succulence of the rice grains and the creaminess of the daal. The food tasted of his childhood. There was a loud woman at the kitchen counter, and every now and then her laughter rang over the voices of party workers. A more reserved woman dressed in widows' clothes sat at the counter with a child. The teenage girl offered Rishi second helpings: 'Have more, Dai.'

After the meal, Giridhar came to him and stood looming over his table. 'You can stay at the party office,' he said. 'The driver sleeps there, a few village boys join him when they're in town. I'll show you.'

Outside, Giridhar led Rishi through the town, walking with uneven, lurching steps. He seemed to have no interest in talking, or in conducting the kind of interview that Rishi had expected. Was this all it took to get in? Were there no questions about his family, his political commitments, his plans, his qualifications, his past?

'I'm MA-passed,' Rishi offered. 'It's been years I've worked giving tuitions in history. I was hoping Nayan Raj could help me get a teaching job afterwards. If I helped him he'd help me, I thought.'

Giridhar stopped in front of the party office. They'd been followed by a few stray dogs, who also stopped with them. 'MA-passed,' Giridhar said. He seemed uncertain about what to do with this information. The light from the building lit his face, its pocks and blemishes. 'You said you're from?'

'Jamune.'

'Name, caste?'

'Rishi Lamsal.'

'Related to Dhana Raj Lamsal of Jamune?'

'He's a distant uncle.'

'You offer tuition?'

'In Kathmandu.'

Abruptly Giridhar turned away, and led Rishi to the party office. A row of foam mattresses had been laid out in a downstairs room. Three men were sitting together on one mattress. Giridhar made perfunctory introductions—the party's driver, party workers. 'Make room for the new worker,' he said to them. Before leaving he said to Rishi, 'Tomorrow we'll assign you work.' Then he stumbled away.

So effortless it had been to change his identity. Rishi took a corner mattress. He placed his bag at the foot of the bedding and straightened the flower-patterned sheets. Then he took off his shoes, rolled off his socks and began to unbutton his shirt.

'You want to join us?' The driver took out a bottle that he must have hidden at the sight of Giridhar. The two others— teenage boys—were edging up to him to resume their interrupted drinking session. The driver held up a bottle of Everest whisky. 'Join us, Sir.'

He looked like a pleasant man, but Rishi didn't intend to befriend anyone here. He shook his head.

'Don't be shy.' The driver smiled indulgently. 'We working men need our fun. Just a small peg, Sir.'

'No.' There was too much surliness in Rishi's voice, but instead of softening it he turned his back on the others and began to unpack his clothes. Two shirts, an extra pair of pants, underclothes, three pairs of socks, a cardigan for the winter months. He also took out the hand held transistor radio he'd bought before leaving Kathmandu.

It was past the time for the news. As the others poured drinks, Rishi allowed the voice of the radio to blast him with stories of worldwide barbarism—so many kidnapped, so many slaughtered, so many displaced and raped and tortured. In front of him was a powdery white wall. The ceiling above him was clean. Behind him the others were exchanging the fey, feckless quips of men at drink. When the BBC World Service began, Rishi put the radio to his ear. Flowing capital, tightened borders, labour disputes and demonstrations, failed negotiations and a recession: stories

of the vanquished in a time of victors. He belonged with the
invisible of the world.

25

After Nayan Raj's first public rally there was untrammelled chaos
in the People's Party office. Boys and men kept pouring in with
advice about how the party should proceed, and boasts about
their own hold on important local leaders. They spun long tales
of their past, offering intricate personal histories and in-depth
explanations of why they wanted to support the People's Party.
They gave subtle or not so subtle hints about what they expected
in return. It was joblessness, invariably, which brought them here.
'I'm hoping the party will find me work afterwards.' Most of the
new recruits were in their twenties or thirties. Many came from
other towns along the highway, though some from villages further
off: 'I'm from Puttar'; 'I'm from Bhimad.' Even city boys who'd
migrated from the district had returned in search of jobs: 'I'm
from Kathmandu.'

Tch, the state of the nation, Om thought as he signed up
Rishi Lamsal. An MA-passed boy seeking the patronage of a
political party—sad to see. Very good for the party, ironically—
how would any of the parties conduct campaigns if boys—men—
like Rishi didn't abound? How would the political machinery
run? Om wasn't one to savour such irony, though. He felt upset
signing up Rishi.

Om had arranged things at the school so that he could devote
his afternoons to party work. Of course, there was much going
on at school, too. But Giridhar needed him now. Om spent each
afternoon rubber stamping new membership cards with the party's
teacup symbol. He welcomed new recruits and did his best to
make them feel valued. 'Congratulations, you've joined the teacup

party.' Wanting to forge links with everyone, he delved into their
life stories. 'And then you went to India, and found work as a
doorman?' Life led each person along such winding paths; Om
found people so interesting. 'Didn't you feel insulted being called
Bahadur? For fifteen years you answered to that name? It feels
good, doesn't it, being back home?' To each worker he said,
'We're truly blessed to have you helping us'—and indeed, given
its late and unpromising start, the party was blessed to attract so
many volunteers.

Meanwhile Giridhar paced through the office without rest,
without refreshment—and, in Om's view, a bit distracted by
whatever appeared in front of him. New recruits whose names
Giridhar hadn't even learned kept asking what to do, where to
go, whom to talk to, what was the campaign strategy. And without
taking a moment to think Giridhar assigned them tasks—'Here's
a bucketful of paint, a group of you go and paint teacup symbols
in the town.' Or, 'Here's a microphone, take the Gaine singer to
the bazaar and make him sing about Nayan Raj.' Or, 'Form a
group and go from house to house asking people to vote for the
teacup party.' And off the workers would go to spread word of
the People's Party in a haphazard way.

It worried Om. True, the nature of electioneering work was
like this: constant, strenuous and completely disorganized. People
came over to meet the candidate, the candidate went to meet
people, things happened, crises teemed and one met them, and
somehow a campaign got conducted. And a month ago, Giridhar
couldn't have responded to all the demands made of him now.
On days when he paid attention to his appearance Giridhar almost
looked like he used to as a bank manager. The greyish pallor of
his face was gone. He spoke with force and projected the kind of
adamant, commanding masculinity that made even the rowdiest
workers—like that boy BB-Gun Thapa—obey him. But Giridhar
was being pushed too hard, Om could see. He looked tired much

of the time. Though he had clearly conquered his problem with drink.

But still—where was the organization, where was the plan? Om didn't say anything, but he worried. No one in the party was really planning the roadside rallies that had to be held in Kotre, in Dulegauda, in Mouriya, in Tharpu and—the last and biggest— in Khaireni Tar. While Giridhar ran about—well, in disorder, Om thought—Nayan Raj spent all his time instructing new recruits about the party's principles. Each time Om passed the meeting room, he could hear the candidate speaking to groups of workers. 'People say democracy has failed them, they say why not give power back to the palace, or join the Maoists. They forget that the 1990 movement only planted the seeds of the democratic revolution. We have yet to make democracy spread roots in our land.'

During these talks, Jimmawal-baaje always sat near Nayan Raj, nodding obsequiously at everything he said. His seventh son stood by, still waiting to be hired. The contractor Chiranjibi Joshi listened to Nayan Raj as he pulled on one stick after another of cheap Yak cigarettes. The contractor had recently surprised the town by revealing that he had been a party member for years already. He had started to trail Nayan Raj with a devotion that was a little strange, but, in Om's view, quite touching. Like everyone else, the contractor always seemed won by the candidate's words. And indeed Nayan Raj spoke splendidly. The things he said—political democracy; economic democracy—they roused the intellect. Nayan Raj was a dashing cinema hero, a personable man, and also a scholar of some erudition, it seemed. The party was lucky to have such a candidate.

But the fact remained that they were operating without the least coordination—the party's candidate and the party's chairman. This lack of coordination would reflect badly on Giridhar, should the party lose on voting day. Giridhar lacked proper skills, people would say. He was disorganized; he was a drunk.

'You can't keep a buffalo from hurtling off a cliff by taking it onto your shoulders.' This, Om's loved ones said to him again and again when he failed to help poor relatives out of their difficulties, when quarrelling neighbours persisted, despite his intervention, in sowing strife, or when wayward students proved beyond remedying. 'All you can do is to pray Ram, Ram. Sometimes that's all a person can do.' Even Asha nodded in agreement. Usually, Asha reinforced Om's most generous impulses. But now, when Om got home each evening, she asked with sharp tones about his party work.

'Things are going splendidly,' Om lied. 'I have no doubt that our Giridhar-dai will achieve brilliant results.'

To himself he thought: the trick is to make Giridhar slow down.

'Eh friend,' he said one day as he passed Giridhar in the hallway. 'It's been too long since we've talked.' With his ample build, Om tended to block passage in the narrow hallway. He squeezed against the wall to let a few workers pass. He said, 'My old woman keeps saying: What, doesn't he like the taste of our food? Why doesn't he come by any more?'

Giridhar made a swatting gesture, as though flicking a fly from his face.

'You've been busy,' Om conceded. 'And you're doing such a fine job. But you must take time to think, reflect, relax. Decisions are best made with adequate forethought, I find. This is what I tell my students. Come, let's go and sit upstairs.'

'There's work,' Giridhar said. With a nod he indicated the workers.

'Yes, of course.' Some boys were indeed waiting to talk to Giridhar. Om said, 'Then why not come to our house tonight? My old woman will serve us a special meal.'

Giridhar nodded and walked away, and Om left him to attend to his duties.

But his friend never showed up that night.

'Don't you think,' Asha asked, 'that it's like pouring water onto sand? What you're doing for him—do you think it will help?'

Om sighed. 'He doesn't have the same confidence he used to. He isn't fully healed from drinking, love. But he needs us. At this time, he needs our love.'

Asha nodded, but ambivalently.

The next day Giridhar's explanation for missing dinner was: 'There was work.'

'Of course.' Om took his friend's hand to show him that he hadn't minded one bit. But he noticed that Giridhar was taking a tense, bristling stance as though trying to ward off the repeat invitation that he had, naturally, planned to extend. 'Right now you have so many workers to direct, so many decisions to make,' Om said, giving his friend the freedom he seemed to want. 'I chose a bad time. When your work eases you come to us, but. My old woman will be thrilled.'

Giridhar looked away as though embarrassed.

Om knew he must accept his friend's needs right now. But he did wish Giridhar would reciprocate some of his affection. Frankly, there were matters at the school that he would have liked help with. After many months of indecision, Om had decided to purchase computers. Cheap Korean models. Six of them. He would have liked to consult Giridhar about the wisdom of this decision, about the financial sense of it. But he would wait. A friend mustn't make selfish demands at difficult times. A friend must give all he could.

The office emptied on the day of the rally in nearby Kotre town. Almost all the workers piled into a rented bus to lend numbers to the local crowd. When Om arrived at the office, he found Jimmawal-baaje's seventh son guarding the locked front door.

'Namaste, Sir, how nice to be able to let you into our office,' the boy cried, jumping to unlock the door. 'With no senior party members in the building, our father thought it best that we stay and safeguard the premises. The office needs a paid caretaker like us, as you are witnessing for yourself.'

Om pitied the boy's sly manners: a most unbecoming Chettri-Bahunish trait in a wee lad. Not that Om had anything against the Chettri-Bahun castes. Wasn't Giridhar Chettri-Bahun? Wasn't Nayan Raj Chettri-Bahun? Weren't half the students in his school Chettri-Bahun? No, not all Chettri-Bahuns were cunning at heart. But still.

Jimmawal-baaje's seventh son almost bowed after opening the front door.

The narrow hallway looked stained already. The paint on the walls was flaking. Upstairs, Om was surprised to see a boy asleep in the hallway, crumpled against the cement floor. He must have been locked in by mistake. A ragged pair of trousers and an old shirt dangled loosely over the boy's frame. His hair stuck to his head, slick in sweat. He didn't look like anyone Om had registered—though by now it was hard to keep account of all the party's workers. Was the boy sick? Had he fainted? Om crouched beside him. 'Eh boy.'

The boy shot up, terror in his eyes. He stepped back in fear of reprimand, and stood, shivering. For a while he eyed Om uncertainly, then his pinched face contorted as he spoke: 'I was looking for my mita-Ba, Retired Rifleman Om Gurung, Sir, formerly in the Second Regiment of the foggy white British Gurkhas.'

Om laughed. 'The one you've named is me.'

The boy hung his head.

It took Om some effort to guess at who he might be. When

Om was a child, his parents had linked him ritually with several mita-friends. And though by custom mita-friends were to be cherished as dearly as one's blood relations, the vagaries of life had made Om lose touch with them all. He finally ventured, 'You're my mita-friend Hom Bahadur Khadka's son?'

The boy nodded but did not look up.

Amazed by how big the boy had grown—was it so long ago that his father and he had last met?—Om embraced Harsha Bahadur. How fast the years flew by. The skinny boy shivered in his arms. 'Come, Son.' He led him to the meeting room and sat him on a bench. Beneath his shirt, the boy was all bones. The veins on his forehead protruded like snaking blue rivers. Om asked, 'How is my mita-friend? What is he doing? Is he in good health?'

The boy seemed unable to respond.

'Are you all right, Son? Is everything all right at home? How is your father, how is his health?'

The boy said, 'I want to join the British Gurkhas. I want to leave this place. I want to die.' Then, to Om's amazement, he began to weep.

The situation qualified, in Om's view, as an emergency. 'Stay here.' He rushed to the other room looking for someone to mind the office. Nobody. He didn't want to leave the building in charge of Jimmawal-baaje's son: the boy's father would never stop pestering him to hire him. Thankfully, Rishi Lamsal was in the dormitory room downstairs. Om said, 'Bhai, Rishi-bhai, could you stay in the office while I'm gone?'

Rishi agreed. A most dependable man he seemed. Then Om led his mita-son downstairs and took him home. The boy walked with dainty half-steps. How frail, how battered he looked. Om faintly recalled some third-hand or fourth-hand rumours that his mita-friend's wife had died in suspicious circumstances. That was when Om had stopped associating with him. The man obviously didn't treat his son well either. 'So you want to find employment?' Om said. 'You thought you'd ask your mita-father for help? Why not? Your mita-mother will be thrilled to see you. Son, mita-son: they're exactly the same to us.'

The boy responded with a dispirited smile. By the time they reached home, his lips were blue.

Once Om explained who the boy was, Asha took charge of him. She displaced visiting relatives and seated Harsha Bahadur at the kitchen table. Then she turned to Om. 'Love, send someone to your mita-friend's house to find out what's happened.'

By the time Om dispatched a nephew to go to his mita-friend, Asha had served rice and daal onto a stainless steel plate. Adding vegetables and goat stew from the morning's meal, she set the plate before the boy.

He stared blankly at the food.

'Eat,' Asha said.

The boy meekly obeyed.

After the meal Asha assigned Om the task of taking the boy to the doctor. Om led the boy out of the house, talking to him gently. 'Do you want to see a doctor? Have you ever seen a doctor?' With his arm around the boy's shoulders, he guided him through the bazaar to the medical shop.

The Doctor Sah'b was sitting around with the look of someone who'd just sucked vinegar. He was, of course, a retired health post peon, not a doctor, but he served as the town's physician, surgeon, endocrinologist, dentist, eye-nose-throat specialist, midwife and medicine seller. Om put his mita-son before him.

With a wave of the hand the Doctor Sah'b indicated that Harsha Bahadur should sit. The shop was dank and sunless, and it smelled of iodine. Om guided the boy to a bench beside a shelf of dust-laden medicine bottles.

The Doctor Sah'b gave a resigned sigh as he shone a torchlight into Harsha Bahadur's eyes. 'Typical vitamin A deficiency leads to dull eyes weak vision,' he intoned almost before looking. Then he forced open Harsha Bahadur's mouth and directed the torchlight inside. 'Streptococcus type one white spots on the tonsils red ulcerated skin and mucus on the tongue.' With the butt-end of the flashlight he jabbed the boy in the chest. 'Undernourishment caused by who knows what parasite tapeworm ringworm stomach irregularities or simply too little food. An emaciated boy like him could be suffering tuberculosis. He's not coughing blood?'

Alarmed, Om looked to the boy, who shook his head.

The Doctor Sah'b droned on, 'A hundred opportunistic diseases thrive on the malnourished. The boy's deprived of essential nutrients vitamins minerals supplements he'll need tablets to boost immunity and antibiotics for his throat. What good will it do though. What good will it do to adopt curative rather than preventive interventions.' He knocked the flashlight hard against Harsha Bahadur's knees. Then he stepped back. The examination had ended. 'He must take glucose to give him energy and no doubt he's got worms. Who knows what other diseases are harbouring inside him that for lack of laboratory stool sputum blood tests I can't diagnose.'

So chronically grim was the Doctor Sah'b that he didn't even smile when Om paid four hundred rupees. Instead the old man chanted, 'Two yellow tablets twice a day after food one white tablet at night with milk. Never take the pink syrup before food or the blue capsules after food. What good are curative treatments if digestion doesn't improve. Feed another blue capsule per day. Bring him back if he doesn't improve.'

Leaving the medical shop, Om saw, past the bar-peepal tree, that the People's Party workers had returned from the rally in Kotre town. The blue minivan that had taken the candidate, Giridhar, Chiranjibi Joshi and Jimmawal-baaje had returned.

How had the rally been? Had there been a large crowd? Had Nayan Raj's words met with applause? He felt a little left out.

But his attention had to stay with his mita-son, who was hardly able to walk by now. 'This way.' Om led the boy back home. There, Asha handed the boy to an uncle, who led him to the backyard to bathe.

Then she pulled Om into their sitting room, by the WELL-COME HOME SWEET HOME embroidery. 'His father doesn't want him back,' she whispered. 'He says Harsha Bahadur isn't his son.'

'Who is he, then?'

'No, no.' Asha kept her voice low to avoid being overheard by relatives in the hallway. 'Our nephew went and met your mita-friend—who said Harsha Bahadur wasn't, well, wasn't born of him.' Normally Asha wouldn't mind such talk, but she flushed now, perhaps more in indignation than modesty. 'He spoke roughly. He smeared the memory of his late wife, and he said the boy wasn't his.'

'The rogue!'

'So here he is now, without a home to go back to, or a destination to reach.'

Om immediately followed his impulse: 'Then we'll keep him. We'll keep him ourselves and treat him well, as our own son.'

For a while Asha hung her head.

Om frowned. 'Love?'

'Why does it always fall on us,' She finally said, 'to help everyone, to help anyone who shows up in need? All right, someone's got to help. But why us? Why always us?' She shot a glance towards the backyard, where the naked boy was being bathed, his ribcage and hipbones more prominent than his flesh. She sighed. 'I know, what's one more person to feed. This boy, all right, let's keep him. The children's room is free. We can give him your clothes from when you were a lad. We're lucky, we can afford to help him. But that's not the issue. That's not what I mean.' She turned back to her husband, her eyes flashing. 'Sometimes you think you're a buddha, old man.'

'Eh love.' Om took her hand.

'You do. You think you're a reincarnate buddha.'

'But look at all we've got.' Om pointed at the sofa, the television, the shelf full of trinkets. 'Will we ever go hungry? And look around us—a society full of suffering. This boy's come to us. Why not make him feel that our home is his home.'

'You don't have to teach me that,' Asha snapped. 'I said we could keep him, didn't I? But if it were up to me I'd tweak his father's ears and force him to take the boy back. The boy's lucky to have a mita-father who thinks he's a buddha.'

Om teased her, 'It's his mita-mother the boy must thank the gods for. You speak hard, love, but your heart is far softer than mine.'

Asha smiled through her annoyance. 'The two of us,' she said shaking her head, 'we share the same flaws—it's not good in these times to be soft at heart.'

26

Now that he was well, it was impermissible to dwell upon past illnesses, to think back to failings, to remember wasted hours, days, weeks, to wonder what might have been, to imagine, to regret. Nowadays Giridhar moved fast to forestall doubt. The world around him had assumed stability, and his body moved through it roughly in the way it should. In the morning he awoke and his place was clear. With Laksmi he acted as a husband: he took morning tea from her hands, he ate the meals she served, he gave her the requisite household expenses. He listened to her talking about wages for this year's harvest work, about the costs set by threshing mills, about home repairs, about their sons.

Everyday things. In the nights sometimes he reached for her bony back and after some brief, embarrassed scuffling, in moments of confessional tenderness, he stroked her oily hair and asked, was she contented, was she really contented? With his sons he was a father again. Not that the boys, in the age of savage tussling and tumbling, sought more than a moment's attention from him. It was enough for them that he tolerate their playfulness when they were around him. It was enough that he give them a smile. Giridhar's father was observant, though. His father wanted more from him: indications of control. And not receiving these, he seemed to doubt Giridhar. He sat on the wooden pallet in the front porch, and instead of reading the scriptures that lay open in front of him he looked at Giridhar through the thick glasses that magnified his eyes, and his scepticism.

Giridhar avoided his father when he could. And he could: if he moved and moved.

He left his house early each morning and went into the world, along the downhill path through the rice fields, to the bottom of the hill where the path forked either towards the Telecommunications Office or towards the People's Party office. This latter path he took without fail. At the end of this path, people were waiting for him. There were workers in the party office who turned to him as he approached, looked to him for direction, asked him questions, obeyed orders and did as he bid. He led and they followed. They confirmed him. They called him Giridhar-dai, Giridharji, Giridhar Sir. They reinforced his chairman's place. And if it was true that it was Nayan Raj's name and not his that had attracted all these workers, if it was true that their loyalties were to the cinema hero, even if it was true that the workers saw more to admire in the actor—it was nevertheless incontestable that it was Giridhar who knew, better than Nayan Raj, how to maximize the party's votes. On all matters pragmatic, the cinema hero turned to Giridhar. It was

Giridhar who planned the roadside rallies so that each one, gathering momentum, attracted larger and larger crowds. It was Giridhar who took Nayan Raj to the houses of important people, facilitating the only kind of talk that mattered in the end: person to person, face to face, with pledges made privately. It was he who briefed the cinema hero on the background of each person so that the actor could charm them. Giridhar's was the domain of the who and how and with what means, the results if so, the results if not, the what next and what after that. This was his home territory. His local knowledge counterbalanced Nayan Raj's grandiose talk. This man will be helpful to meet. This man might not back us, but if he doesn't oppose us it'll help. This man has been wanting to meet our candidate. This man says. This man claims. This man agrees. This man. This man.

Only a few men doubted him. Om. Om doubted him. This Giridhar could see from the allowances his friend made for him— allowances made out of pity. Allowances he thought Giridhar needed. Not that Om was ever unkind. Giridhar knew he must, one day, thank his friend. He must acknowledge how much he had benefited from Om's help in trying times. To placate Om, he must say how obliged he was.

But he couldn't do anything but flinch in Om's presence. The man had seen him—not just ill: what had happened? Drink had damaged his rationality. Yes. There had been a habit of drink, and now it was gone. This was a good way to explain it. But Om knew more. Om had seen him raving. If he talked to his friend, Om would ask probing questions which would take him back to the past. And the past was like a blot: to be discarded.

He moved away from it. He moved away from Om, from the party office, to Nayan Raj's house, to the roadside towns, to the houses of those who might vote for the party. Giridhar moved past doubting people and inhospitable spaces. He moved and moved.

And the world stood mercifully steady.

At night he lay on his bed looking with dumb gratitude at the brown water spots on the ceiling, which stayed just as they were.

27

It was to the schoolmaster's credit that Rishi had arrived at the right time to be of use to the party. It was to his own credit that he had made the right impression. His reticence in the midst of swelling, increasingly unwieldy crowds, his measured words and his qualifications impressed the senior party members. In their inexperience they took him for who he said he was, and began to rely on him. As the rallies progressed, Rishi was put in charge of a group of workers responsible for all publicity work: painting signs, sticking posters, pinning up party banners. 'The teacup,' Giridhar said whenever they met. 'The Congress tree and the UML sun, everyone recognizes. Now they must recognize our teacup symbol.' Giridhar was too busy to actually oversee Rishi's work. Nayan Raj rarely offered more than a few words meant to encourage him: 'I appreciate your efforts, Bhai. What would the party do without you?' Jimmawal-baaje had been struck ill, and had of late stopped coming to the party office. Chiranjibi Joshi rarely spoke, and Om Gurung was only at the office for part of the day.

The boys Rishi had been assigned to watch over included BB-Gun Thapa and his gang. Rishi had little respect for such boys of mindless flesh; he couldn't hide his dislike for BB-Gun. The disdain seemed mutual. BB-Gun never asked Rishi what to do. Each day he informed Rishi what his gang would do, and demanded the necessary materials—paints, brushes, posters and glue. Rishi handed him all that he asked for.

The rest of the boys formed a congenial group. Some were distant relatives of the party's senior members, others were family acquaintances, yet others were students at the nearby college campus—boys in the middle of their studies. They easily accepted Rishi's leadership, and they set off each morning carrying pails filled with paint.

The teacup in red enamel, the teacup in blue. DEMOCRATIC REFORM=TEACUP. VOTE FOR CHANGE, VOTE FOR TEACUP. Rishi supervised as the students painted the party's symbol and slogans on rocks and walls. 'Not there,' he said of a compound wall belonging to a masjid a short distance from the town. 'Not on religious buildings.' The boys accepted his logic. Rishi stopped at houses to ask permission from owners. 'A teacup with a saucer,' he said. 'In white on the side of your house. We'll take it off after the elections.'

Some said yes, some said no, most just shrugged.

Amid the trees, suns, ploughs and houses—symbols of the other parties—Rishi and his workers placed the teacup, writing the People's Party into the town's landscape. They slowly covered all of Khaireni Tar. The side of the government school where Rishi studied. The back of the Telecommunications Office. The watchmaker's canvas stall. Om Gurung's yellow house with stucco pineapples. Chiranjibi Joshi's wood mill. The woven bamboo walls of a landless settler's teashop: all covered with Rishi's signs of his loyalty to the schoolmaster.

Dust, debris, the smell of ripening rice fields, the teacup in a squalid highway town.

In all this time Rishi hadn't gone to meet the blind shopkeeper Shankar. He'd seen no need to; the schoolmaster's instructions sufficed for now. Prove yourself invaluable. Work your way into their trust. He was doing that, effortlessly. No one at the People's Party looked at him closely enough to see through his flimsy cover. There was no need to dodge anyone. Even if, by chance,

Rishi were to see the schoolmaster, if he were to meet the schoolmaster in a tucked-away alley, no one would notice.

With the Janamukti party's decision to run a candidate the election dynamics were set: Congress and UML would be in a close race against each other. This was Rishi's reckoning. The Janamukti party's ethnic rights platform would weaken all but the UML, for the UML candidate was a Magar man. The People's Party, with its base in traditionally Congress areas like Khaireni Tar, would weaken Congress. The more Nayan Raj's appeal grew in Congress areas the more the People's Party would help the UML win.

Rishi kept such calculations in sight as he lay, each night, in the dormitory room at the party office. The room now hosted shifts of out-of-town workers staying a night or two, sleeping doubled- and tripled-up on the rows of mattresses. Rishi kept a separate place by the corner. The party's driver was his one constant companion here, a heedless man whose sole pleasure lay in erasing the day's travails with whisky. He and Rishi exchanged no more than greetings. When Rishi entered the room at night he feigned exhaustion and lay in his bedding, turned towards the wall. He kept his radio on for the international news. Behind him workers talked and joked.

Rishi also preferred to stay alone in Binita's teashop, where he went for morning and evening meals, and for teatime snacks. Here, though, his group of painters often joined him, presuming friendliness. They talked about things that mattered very little: 'Should we try using red paint tomorrow?'

'What if someone paints over our signs?'

He answered as he had to, and heard from them about the latest speculations: 'You know, Rishi-dai, all of Khaireni Tar is leaning towards us already.'

Rishi-dai.

These same ties were created by the women of the teashop. 'Rishi-bhai needs more rice,' Pramila would say, adding to her stranger bhai's plate. Sani would ask, 'Shall I bring you more daal, Rishi-dai?' And he, in his avatar as a brother to her, would nod yes, he'd like more daal, Sani-bahini.

The widow Binita remained aloof, and Rishi liked her for it. Once, she asked Rishi if he wanted tea: that was their only exchange till now. She tended to keep away from the hullabaloo in her teashop. By now Rishi knew she wasn't as orthodox as she looked from her clothes and from the teashop's decor: a woman who had married across caste barriers. From certain angles she looked surprisingly young.

'Eh Sani, serve this bhai more rice,' Pramila would say. 'Have some more squashes, Rishi-bhai, they're fresh from our vegetable garden.'

'Where shall we paint tomorrow, Rishi-dai? Shall we paint in the southern end?'

Rishi-dai. Rishi bhai.

Even Giridhar addressed him as a brother. 'After the Khaireni Tar rally,' Giridhar said to him one night, 'we'll start our village tours, Bhai. We'll need two groups of painters then. One will go with our candidate. The Gaine singer, the girls—all of them will go with the candidate. Two weeks later I'll follow, forming booth committees. We'll need two groups of painters to go with both teams, do you think you can plan for that, Bhai?'

'I'll see to it, Giridhar-dai.'

'Good.' Giridhar spoke with more command these days. 'You come with my team, Bhai. When we go from village to village, you come in the team that goes with me.'

'I'll go with you, Giridhar-dai.'

Rishi-bhai. Giridhar-dai. Family ties of political expediency.

The hubbub at the party office grew steadily, and the rooms and hallways were now packed with restless, undirected hordes of young men all bursting with excess energy. Nayan Raj, Giridhar, Om and Chiranjibi tried to keep workers busy. But if there was any method to party work, Rishi couldn't make out what it was. What he could see was the swell of men hunting for better futures, trying to form useful bonds, or just whiling away time in dull or depressed lives that afforded little diversion.

Two days before the People's Party rally, BB-Gun Thapa picked a fight with a Congress boy. Rishi didn't see the fight take place. He was standing by the medical shop helping one of the workers paint a teacup when he heard the commotion. By the time he rounded the teashop and reached the flatlands, the fight had already broken up. BB-Gun was being fussed over by his gang members. The hooligan flexed casually, wiping sweat off his face. 'They were painting over our teacup,' he said to Rishi. 'They were erasing our teacup and replacing it with a tree.'

One of his gang members said, 'You showed them!'

BB-Gun laughed.

A short distance away Congress workers were stooped over a boy on the ground. If they retaliated things could get violent. 'Let's go,' Rishi said, pushing through the group. He was much smaller than BB-Gun's gang members, and he felt surprisingly anxious about his own safety. 'Let's forget about this, let's go.'

But BB-Gun wasn't willing to rush his moment of glory. He ignored Rishi and turned to glower at the Congress boys.

The Congress boys didn't take up the dare. They picked up the boy on the floor and led him away limping. He had blood on his temples.

'Let's go,' Rishi said.

BB-Gun said, 'Motherfucking corpses think they can challenge us.'

'Corpses saw their fathers' weddings.'

'Let's go,' Rishi repeated. 'Let's get back to the party office.'

To his relief everyone finally agreed.

When they reached the office BB-Gun began to brag about his victory as young party workers crowded around to listen. 'Now they know what happens when pups don't understand who's stronger.'

Rishi went up and reported what had happened to Om, who immediately set off to find the other senior members and to extend apologies to the Congress party.

After Om left the office, the atmosphere at the office became carnival-like. BB-Gun recounted, with greater and greater bravado, what had happened. 'And then I saw the terror in his eyes—like a calf seeing a tiger. He almost cried!'

'And he didn't hurt you?'

'What could the corpse do to me? This scratch—there's not even blood.'

Meat against meat.

Rishi went out and looked across the highway, at the UML office. Then, slowly, he walked across the highway and veered past the office, offering himself to the schoolmaster's sight, should he be looking for him. The building was still. The windows were dark. There was no sign of movement inside.

The next day he went to Shankar's grain store. The blind shopkeeper was sitting in one corner of the wood-panelled room, a small figure in the large interior. There was a group of women bargaining with him, and another man was waiting his turn. Rishi sat on a bench beside a few crates of local rice—mansuri, basmati, jarneli, pokhareli, dudhe. Sacks of corn, wheat, barley and millet lined the wall. The store smelled of chaff.

The women left in a group. The man behind them just wanted to buy a couple of candles. Shankar reached for shelves behind him, fetched the candles, and fingered the money to determine correct change. Then he turned, expectantly, towards Rishi.

'I want to talk to the schoolmaster,' Rishi said.

The man stayed still while he took in this new voice. He was an ancient, wizened man, and he sat in the posture of ascetics, with his spine perfectly straight. 'It's Rishi Parajuli,' he finally said. 'It's the comrade with sorrow in his voice.'

Rishi was startled by this statement. Was this how the schoolmaster had described him? He said, 'I want to meet the schoolmaster.'

Shankar smiled. 'Anything you need to tell him you say through me. So tell me. What have you done these past few weeks? Why didn't you come earlier?'

The blind man had a coy, ironic tone. Rishi said, 'Tell the schoolmaster that I'll be travelling with Giridhar Adhikari on his village-to-village tour. He'll be setting up booth committees then. I'll be able to report on them, and on the party's strategy at each voting booth.'

Shankar murmured, 'Yes, you are the comrade with sorrow in his voice.'

Rishi didn't like his theatricality.

Someone came into the shop then, a policeman who appeared to be in a hurry. 'Cigarettes, Shankar-dai. Cigarettes.'

Shankar reached for a packet of Khukuri cigarettes. 'Will you be needing a quarter-bottle of Everest whisky today, Sub-Inspector Sah'b?'

'Yes, why not? It'll come in handy. Here, take the money. I'm in a rush.'

Once the Sub-Inspector left, Shankar again turned to Rishi. 'In the meantime you've been painting signs? Yesterday you fought with the Congress party over signs?'

'That happened.'

'It happened. Why not fight with the UML workers?' The

blind man spoke now with distinct sarcasm. 'That'll prove your loyalty not just against Congress, but against UML too.'

'I didn't plan for it,' Rishi said. 'It was a personal fight between gangs. There was a rivalry—'

'It's always personal for the weak. For those lacking in ideology, it's personal.'

'In this case it was personal.'

For some reason Shankar cackled. Then he said, 'You'll come and paint a sign on my house tomorrow? A nice big teacup sign.'

Rishi decided he didn't like the man. 'I'd like to talk to the schoolmaster once.'

'You can't meet him.' Shankar kept grinning, as if at a private joke. 'I'm the one you report to now, I'm the one who'll tell you what to do. Come tomorrow, Comrade. Come and paint me a nice big teacup—in red! Prove your allegiance to me.'

Rishi stared at the man. Was he mocking Rishi's personal loyalty to the schoolmaster? The structure, not the person; systems, not individuals: the ethic of Rishi's schooldays.

'Talking to me is like talking to your schoolmaster,' the blind man said, becoming serious now. 'He and I are committed to the same cause; we're no different at all.'

Proletarians, workers and peasants, all.

'I'll come tomorrow,' Rishi said.

Outside the grain store, he caught a flash of silver and thought he heard someone moving, but when he turned no one was there.

28

By now the party office was constantly crowded with all kinds of workers, unruly boys many of them. They were creating too much mayhem. But given that he could spare only his afternoon hours, Om was helpless to bring the workers under control. That was Giridhar's job—but Giridhar neither listened to anything

Om said anymore, nor seemed to care about maintaining order
at the office. Not that Nayan Raj or the others seemed to mind.
Several roadside rallies had taken place by this time. In Tharpu,
the site of the next rally, Giridhar had decided to canvass the
town's leaders individually before the rally. They had given him
indication that—if approached with adequate ceremony, with
proper tact—they might be willing to stop backing the Congress
and start supporting the People's Party. The party might even
receive a block vote from the Congress belt in the north part of
the electorate. Giridhar and Nayan Raj began to spend all day
wooing this block vote, and in the evenings they came back to
Khaireni Tar exhausted, but still discussing what had happened
today, what might happen tomorrow.

Om limited himself to the small tasks that everyone else
seemed too busy to see to. He discovered, for one, that many of
the new workers weren't registered to vote. The deadline to register
was fast approaching. 'Collect the names of other unregistered
party workers,' Om instructed Juddha Ale. 'A week before the
deadline I'll take them to the district centre and get them registered.'

Sometimes it astounded him, the things that required his
attention. For instance, the party still had no posters or pamphlets.
So in his spare time he began to design a few posters, and to
scribble a line or two of text that would do nicely beneath
photographs of the candidate and the party's symbol. Sometimes
he got fanciful with the slogans: PARTY OF THE PEOPLE—PEOPLE'S
PARTY. PARTY FOR THE PEOPLE—PEOPLE'S PARTY. But the humblest
slogans seemed the best: DONATE YOUR VOTE TO THE PEOPLE'S
PARTY.

'See,' he showed the designs to his mita-son, whom he took,
every day, to the office. 'These will be printed as posters to be
put up throughout the electorate.'

Harsha Bahadur passively eyed whatever was put in front of
him. The boy didn't show any sign of interest, or even

comprehension. Poor sickly thing. Asha had suggested that it
might help the boy emerge from his dolor to accompany his mita-
father to the party office. 'The boy needs exposure,' she had said.
'Introduce him to other boys at the party office, teach him about
politics, give him small tasks that he can manage. I can't have
him at home always, moping like some abandoned woman.'

Harsha Bahadur followed Om about all afternoon, but all
he seemed capable of was answering questions with a nod or a
shake of the head. Mostly he seemed to want to sleep, which he
did till late every morning; and to eat, which he did in quantities
unlikely for a boy of his proportions.

He would recover slowly from his feeble state, Om figured.
A person couldn't function if he wasn't well in both body and
mind. Look at Giridhar. Now that he had regained his health,
Giridhar hardly ever met Om any more. The few times their
paths did meet, Giridhar was—preoccupied. He even seemed cross
with Om at times.

'I'm busy is all,' Giridhar said when Om mentioned, once,
that he looked tired. 'I've been in the field all day meeting people.
Isn't that a reason to look tired?'

'Ho of course, friend.'

Om wished Giridhar would stop acting so testy. Because at
the school there was trouble over the computers—he wanted to
share that with Giridhar. In fact he needed some sound advice.
The very day the new computers arrived from Kathmandu in a
rented minivan, one of them went out with a gassy pffft sound,
short-circuiting the school's electrical system. The technician who
had been hired to instal them immediately insisted that there
could be no refund. 'It's not our fault that your wiring is faulty,'
he had said before Om could even raise the issue with him. 'You'll
have to pay for repairs.'

'But we didn't even touch the machine,' Om had said
reasonably. 'You yourself plugged it in. You turned on the switch

which made smoke come out of the vents.'

The technician had the scrappiness of those who knew technical things that others couldn't even guess at. He said, 'You assured me that the electrical system could support it. Anyway'—he thrust the receipt at Om—'it says, above your signature, that you're responsible for all damages borne.'

'Yes, but.' Om stopped there. But what?

He was not only paying, now, for repairs, he was also spending extra for the technician to stay on in Khaireni Tar while the school's wiring got fixed. It turned out that the entire system had to be upgraded to accommodate computers. Om had to pay for electricians from Pokhara city. The escalating costs worried him.

But who was there to give him sound financial counsel? Not Asha: she'd just scold him for his poor business sense. Neither could Om turn to his other family or friends. He was alone with all his decisions, and they bore heavily on him.

Sometimes in a man's life, everywhere he turned he faced trouble.

One afternoon Jimmawal-baaje burst into the office room as Om sat with Harsha Bahadur, ruminating over these matters. The office was otherwise empty. Everyone had gone to attend a rally. 'Minding the office like a security guard?' Jimmawal-baaje asked. 'Very loyal of you, Om-bhai. But honestly, the sight prickles the eyes. A man of your stature—working as a security guard. It's not suitable.'

By now Om was used to the old man's ways. 'I'm an army man,' he said. 'I do as I'm commanded.'

Jimmawal-baaje sniffed. 'A British Gurkha security guard—the party is truly fortunate.'

Om shot him a hard glance. The old man had a bright flush to his face. The long saffron teeka on his forehead was askew, giving him a slightly daft expression. Om said, 'You're not looking well, Jimmawal-baaje. Trust the office to me. Go rest.'

'It's true, the stars are lined inauspiciously for me,' the old man said. 'I'm conducting prayers at the house, that's why I'm not at the rally...otherwise—. Our candidate's words...so inspiring.' He turned his gaze towards Harsha Bahadur, sitting beside Om. 'Eh boy. Sitting here idly instead of sticking up poster-pamphlets!'

Harsha Bahadur drooped in fright.

'He's not a party worker,' Om said. 'He's my son, my mita-son.'

'Mita-son?' Jimmawal-baaje frowned. He circled Harsha Bahadur, like a hawk circling prey. 'Your mita-son doesn't seem very able,' he said. 'He looks dull, his eyes lack brightness. Maybe he has worms in the belly? The boy lacks vigour.' He stopped and raised a finger. 'You know I've already talked to everyone about hiring my seventh son. He's high school passed...and smart, very smart. Everyone agrees—my son is all but hired.'

Om sighed. 'I've already told you, Jimmawal-baaje: why do we need a peon? There's no need at all. You go home and rest now. A man must mind his health.'

For a while, Jimmawal-baaje kept staring at Harsha Bahadur. Then, with the flightiness he was prone to, the old man wheeled around and started to crow about how useless their party workers were: 'Lord Krishna! I caught them sticking posters on rocks! The ones by the bar-peepal tree, they're torn already...but does anyone replace them? And is it really necessary to have ten of them in a row? The workers are squandering them—of course,' his tone became sly, 'certainly, you must be rationing them. Om-bhai, you must keep careful count of how many posters we have left. The workers, they'll want to squander...but you, our guide and guard—you must safeguard the party's properties.'

Om had no idea what posters Jimmawal-baaje was talking about, and he was getting annoyed at being called a guard.

'I'll do as you command,' he joked, but after Jimmawal-baaje left, his mood spoiled. Posters? Had the party made posters already?

Beside him his mita-son was staring into space. 'Eh boy.' Om jiggled Harsha Bahadur's knee. 'Are you all right, are you well?' Seeing his mita-son's panicked expression, he softened his tone. 'Buck up,' he gently exhorted the boy. 'You've left home in search of independence, you have to act smart now.' He placed the party ledger in front of the boy. 'Here: this is how you mark off each worker's attendance.'

Harsha Bahadur cowered at the sight of Om's thick black tick-marks.

Om offered him his pen. 'You do it. Go ahead, place a tick-mark beside this fellow's name. That's Juddha Ale, he's at the rally, we saw him this morning when he came in. Place a tick-mark after his name. That shows that he came to the office today.'

Harsha Bahadur held the pen in a stiff, illiterate grasp.

Poor boy. Om said, 'Ho yes, a smart young boy like you, you can take on the whole world if you try.'

For the rest of the afternoon Om felt upset. It occurred to him that he was doing the party's dullest, most uninteresting work. Nayan Raj, Giridhar and Chiranjibi Joshi—they worked hard, but they were always together, weren't they, enjoying each other's company. Om had to stay in the office while the rallies took place elsewhere. He was always left behind. He thought back to what Jimmawal-baaje had said. Had the party really made posters? How could he not have known?

When the workers began to return from the rally Om saw that indeed, they were carrying scrolled up posters. With Harsha

Bahadur close behind him he went to the hallway and found
Rishi Lamsal there. 'Was the rally a grand success?' he asked.
'Were the crowds large? Have we won the northern belt's block
vote?'

'It went well,' Rishi said.

'Excellent.' Om eyed the scroll in Rishi's hands. 'And our
Giridhar-dai—where is he?'

'At the teashop, with the others.'

'And this poster,' Om said. 'I don't believe there are any in
the office. Perhaps I might take this copy, Rishi-bhai?'

With Harsha Bahadur still following him he took the poster
back to the office room and spread it on a wall.

'Let's pin it up,' Om said. 'Son, let's decorate this room with
this poster of our candidate. You do it, in fact. Yes, go on, pin it
up.'

He watched in satisfaction as his mita-son stuck the poster
against the wall with swathes of Sellotape.

'Our candidate.' Om smiled. But looking at the portrait of
Nayan Raj in green, he was struck by how Chettri-Bahunish the
candidate looked. It wasn't a good picture; the lighting bleached
Nayan Raj's features and made him look very bony. The slogan
below wasn't inventive. Om read out loud: 'Vote for the teacup
party.'

He waited, then, for Giridhar, the candidate and others to
come to the party office. This they never did. Finally Om left the
office in charge of Rishi Lamsal, reached his mita-son home,
then headed to the widow Binita's teashop.

He found Giridhar, Nayan Raj and Chiranjibi huddled
together at a table, rapt in conversation. Om joined them, but
they barely noticed.

'And the thing you mentioned,' Giridhar was saying to Nayan
Raj. Chiranjibi added, 'Yes, yes,' and Giridhar continued, 'The
thing you mentioned, I'll see to it tomorrow. You're right about

that, you're right, we should be doing that.'

'It was your suggestion,' Nayan Raj said.

'The next time,' Chiranjibi said, 'we'll be perfectly set.'

Om listened patiently, trying to catch on. Finally he asked, 'So the rally today: it was a grand success?'

His question halted the flow of talk. Giridhar looked at him but didn't respond. Chiranjibi said nothing. It was Nayan Raj who answered, 'There was a lot of interest among people, we received a warm welcome.' He spoke politely, but his mind was clearly on other matters. With the patience of a teacher repeating something for a slow child he said, 'The local leaders haven't pledged us their support, but it looks like they will. We might get a block vote. It all depends.' Then he turned to the others. 'Let's go house to house in Khaireni Tar before doing our rally here, like you said.'

And the fast-flowing rapids of their conversation began swirling again.

'The group that met us afterwards, we should meet them again.'

'Yes, they're important, they hold a lot of votes, we must meet them again.'

Om tried to follow along, but as the conversation wore on, he got irritated. Why was he being left out of the talk? Why was Chiranjibi Joshi so much a part of the conversation—when he'd only just starting supporting the party? And why didn't Giridhar look at him at all? Didn't he think that Om would have something to contribute to the party's rallies? Jimmawal-baaje hadn't been wrong in calling him a security guard. That was how he was being treated.

When the conversation slowed Om turned to Giridhar. 'Is it the case that the party made posters?' His tone was sharp. 'But how is it that I, who stay at the office all day, didn't know about them? Why was I not informed? Isn't the matter part of my duty as office manager?'

Giridhar was turned away, as though Om's point was too trivial to even listen to. But Om wasn't, was he, being petty. Propelled by irritation, Om said, 'This shows a complete lack of coordination between us.'

Again it was Nayan Raj who replied. 'The posters came in yesterday night—I'd ordered them from Kathmandu. They're stored upstairs right now.' He spoke with all due apology, and Om immediately regretted his own shrillness. Nayan Raj said, 'You're right, we should have taken them to the office this morning and put them in your charge. It's important to have a system.'

But the assurance that these words brought was dispelled by the sight of Giridhar still turned away. Was it necessary for Giridhar to act so proud? 'And another matter,' Om said to his friend. 'I can't sit at the office all day minding the rooms like a security guard. To supervise is one thing, Giridhar-dai. But to sit all day when there's better work to do outside—. I haven't attended a single rally in all this time. We need to hire a party peon, I think.'

When Giridhar finally turned his way Om saw, to his amazement, that he was blushing. 'If you think we need a peon boy let's hire Jimmawal-baaje's son.'

'No, no.' This suggestion confused Om. 'That boy's too slippery, I don't think he'll serve us well. Let's hire someone else. One of our workers. Or—I know. My mita-son's father has disowned him. He's in great need of a job.'

'So hire him,' Giridhar said.

Was he dismissing the matter so lightly? 'Because I've got things happening at the school,' Om argued. 'I'm not free to sit idly, guarding the office. Not that I don't want to help the party. Especially with matters that require thought and planning. But I can't be asked to mind the office all day like a security guard. I am part of the party's inner core, am I not?'

For a long while no one spoke.

Finally Nayan Raj sat forward. 'You're right to identify our party's institutional weaknesses,' he said. 'Of course we don't want to spend more money than we need to. But a party peon we can certainly afford. Let's hire this boy you spoke about. Your mita-son.'

'That way I can help with the more important things,' Om said, feeling embarrassed. 'I can help you plan the rally, plan the village-to-village campaign.'

Nayan Raj said, 'I am counting on you to advise me about how to attract the Gurung-Magar vote.'

'I'll try my best,' Om said. Putting aside his ill feelings, he added, 'It won't be difficult with a candidate as illustrious as you.'

'The party needs the dedication of good men like you.'

'Men like us need the guidance of men like you.'

'Stay now—join us for the evening meal.'

But Om was embarrassed to have fought like a child in front of everyone. He stood. 'My old woman will be furious if I stay out, laughing and enjoying with friends.' Taking leave, he gave Giridhar a conciliatory pat on the back. He saw then that his friend's face had gone pale.

He was immediately struck by remorse. He had betrayed Giridhar by challenging him in public. This was a hard time for Giridhar. Shouldn't he be able to rely on Om's unwavering support?

'It's like we live in wartime,' Om said to Asha that night as the two of them nestled in bed. And he wasn't exaggerating. That was how he felt sometimes. 'All around us, people are being felled by circumstances which are completely unfair. Poverty, ill health, lack of basic amenities and services. A lack of opportunity.

Misfortune. But look at us—our prosperity, and more than that, our contentment. Sometimes I feel: do I deserve all this? Do I deserve this house, my family, do I deserve a wife like you? It's all random. It's all luck. So why hoard my fortunes? Why not help others survive their ill fate?'

'I never said we shouldn't help others,' Asha said.

'It's our moral duty to love others, see? Though sometimes it's hard to love. But the more you love, the more you can love. You know, love, I find that the heart expands to accommodate more and more love. The more you love, love, the more capacity you generate in your heart to extend more and more, more and more, more and more love.'

Asha sighed.

Om turned to her. 'Love?'

'Be quiet and go to sleep, love.'

29

On the day of the People's Party rally in Khaireni Tar, townspeople flocked to the ashen flatlands, eager to hear with their own ears the number one cinema hero making an appeal for their votes. The actor had made quite an impression in the rallies that took place in other highway towns. Word had spread of his humility, his charm, his skill at talking to ordinary people, and his vast knowledge about democracy. Could he be as impressive as everyone said? 'No, he's just acting like a perfect candidate, the way he played a perfect revolutionary in his movie,' some people said. 'I've heard he's not at all impressive in person.' Others disagreed: 'But he's much more than an actor, I've heard. He speaks very intelligently. They say he's read thousands of books.' 'I doubt it.' 'No, really.'

People turned out in droves to listen to Nayan Raj. Those

who were genuinely interested in him crowded up to the raised platform that had been erected near the church. Those who were more sceptical lingered back, as though they were just passing by. Congress and UML workers came just to see who else had come. The ashen plains filled with people, all turned to Nayan Raj.

Harsha Bahadur stood to one side of the crowd, dazzled by the glare of the sun, and jostling for footing as the hordes of townspeople pushed and shoved to get a better view of the podium on which stood the cinema hero—the candidate of the party which was also now the party of his employment. Harsha Bahadur had been confused by all the party's activities, but today the spectacle that presented itself before him was especially frightful. He stared in alarm at the men milling before him, men with hard faces, men jeering and leering and sneering, men smiling, men nodding, men clapping and men wearing scowls. He recoiled at the sight of a woman with blood-red lipstick who looked like she'd just eaten raw meat. Near by stood some boys his age who worked in the party, but whom he never knew how to talk to. He didn't like some of them. Why did they wear black shirt-pants—so inauspicious? Why those dark goggles that hid the eyes? The boy who beat up another boy the other day turned towards him and gave him a glassy, black-goggled stare. Harsha Bahadur shuddered at the sight of this man-sized fly.

The cinema hero was speaking, and his voice, amplified by electrical devices, bellowed through heaven and earth. What was he saying? And why were all these people pressing in to hear? Being, himself, the People's Party Peon, Harsha Bahadur felt he must understand what was being said. He tried to pay attention to the trumpeting words that were sometimes drowned in a terrible metallic scream: '*THE DEMOCRATIC REVELATION IS INCOMPLETE BECAUSE*

THE CURRENT SISTER DOESN'T SAVE AGAIN ELECTRIC PROD...THE PEOPLE'S
PARTY CAN DUCT A FAIR CHALK.'

But he couldn't follow the secret tongue of politics. He was
slow that way, he knew. His mita-father had been kind to have
him hired as a Party Peon, but he wasn't strictly qualified for the
job. It confused him, his work. What exactly was he supposed to
be doing with those books and ledgers? He mimicked his mita-
father's actions, but he didn't understand their meaning. And
now, listening to the cinema hero's blasting words, he couldn't
follow a thing:

'WINNER LOOSE IT. DOESN'T MATH SO LONG AS THE RESULTS TRULY,
BARELY REPENT THE PEOPLE...THE 1990 DEMOCRATIC MOVEMENT.'

A sweet breeze blew in from the northern hills, softening the
sun's glare. The long, wispy leaves of a willow tree stirred next
to Harsha Bahadur. The wind smelled of cut rice stalks. He turned
north and saw a ray of light catch a mote of dust swirling by
him, flickering, flickering. Sani. He hadn't felt her in the
atmosphere for four days now. It was Sani's pure essence. Where
was she?

Squeezing through the crowd he pursued the breeze, tasting
its bouquet of wildflowers in his mouth. The heat of the sun was
Sani's breath. The cool breeze was her freshness. He rambled
through the crowd, knocking against bodies soft and hard, and
though some people clucked in annoyance, he didn't stop till he
reached an opening where the motes of dust eddied in the light,
sparkling around him till he felt engulfed by Sani's grace.

'Leave all this and enter the kingdom of god,' a voice rasped
into his ear. A skinny man swooped on him, his face like a rusty
pan. 'Awaken, brother! Leave all this and join our church.'

The spit dried in Harsha Bahadur's throat. He shook off this
strange man's hands and backed into the crowd, only to bump
into a very fat woman. She turned to him with a glare, her hair
loose and her clothes filthy. 'Stop! Ho. You might open on a

joined by a turning,' she thundered.

A witch: he'd met a mad witch. Harsha Bahadur staggered in shock.

He looked about desperately for his mita-father, but there were so many people blocking his view. The loudspeaker kept blaring in his ears:

'THE SISTER NEEDS IMPROVEMENT SO THAT WE CAN ALL BOAT IN FREEDOM ACCORDION TO OUR OWN TREE WELLS.'

What secret tongue was this?

'BIG PARTIES THING IT'S THEIR HAIR TENSE TO RULE A BUS.'

What?

The words made him feel out of balance. Then he heard someone say, 'Brother,' and felt a strong arm wrap around him. He tottered into the embrace of his Maoist second cousin, who was saying in a faraway voice, 'Brother, are you feeling well?'

'Dai!' Harsha Bahadur clung to his cousin's heroic silhouette. 'I thought you went to live in a tunnel below the ground!' He reeled. 'Eh. I don't know where...My mita-father—I lost him. Where, where... This crowd!'

'Sit.' His cousin lowered him to the ground. 'You shouldn't be outside in this boiling sun. It's not like in the hills here, the town's air is thick. You shouldn't go out in the midday sun.'

Harsha Bahadur said, 'I usually...It's just today, the rally...I didn't understand, though—what was he saying? Dai, my stomach's aching!' And it was; his insides had suddenly hardened into stone. 'I'm sick, the Doctor Sah'b said I'm very, very sick!'

'Don't worry, I'm your brother and I love you.'

'I love you too, Dai.'

His second cousin patted him on the head, and spoke very warmly, 'Now I hear you've been hired as the People's Party Peon. Tell me, brother: what exactly do you do for that imperialist broker-capitalist parliamentary democracy-loving bourgeois reformist party?'

30

'Distinguished RPP members, respected elders, dear younger and older brothers, and dear younger and older sisters (shall I begin, then? Eh, all right. I'll start now. All right). Heartfelt namaste.

'In this our beautiful land, with sacred himals and fertile valleys, and with lovely rivers and thick-thick forests, and with peoples of four proverbial castes and thirty-six ethnic groups, but with unbreakable national unity nonetheless at the feet of the sacred himals, and joined under our King as a Hindu kingdom, furthermore having never succumbed to colonial powers due to our world-renowned Gorkhali bravery, and still fighting against outside forces, against which we Nepalis are always prepared to don khukuri knives, I stand before you as a mother-wife-sister-daughter of our motherland which has sacrificed her red blood and blue sweat for us, and remains united under our King as a Hindu kingdom, and which will never succumb to foreign influence, no matter how great the pressure exerted by our southern neighbour, and I ask you to vote for the RPP's useful election symbol, the plough. Long live our nation, our nation, our nation. Our monarchy is dear to us. We must never do anything to place the sovereignty of our soil in jeopardy. We are proud sons and daughters of Siddhartha Gautam Buddha and Mount Sagarmatha. Therefore I ask you, as a mother-wife-sister-daughter—we *really* must do something for the upliftment of women, though—who is willing to sacrifice all by joining politics for the sake of national unity.

'Vote for the plough!

'(Is that enough, can I go home now? My husband, children and in-laws will be waiting for their meal.)'

'Dear respected Janamukti party officials and members, brothers and sisters of all ethnic groups and all fellow countrymen:

'Namaste.

'Our country is home to over sixty caste and ethnic groups and seventy languages; and yet, a decade after democracy, only a few powerful castes rule, as they did in the former days. In every political party, in every organization, in every government office, in all sectors of society, Chettri-Bahun castes hold power while the ethnic Sherpa, Tamang, Magar, Gurung, Rai, Limbu people remain suppressed in the hills, and other ethnic groups remain oppressed in the southern tarai plains. Our ethnic cultures are looked down on, our languages are banned from offices, our numbers are under-represented in national census counts. With our constitution defining Nepal as a Hindu Kingdom, Buddhists and other religious minorities remain oppressed by the Hindu hegemony.

'But any time we address these issues, Chettri-Bahuns accuse us of trying to fragment the nation. They say that we want to go back to the age of twenty-four kingdoms, we want to foster ethnic strife. In fact we're only fighting for an end to discrimination against us—eh, and against the occupational caste dalit populations: great injustice they face. We have all lost our identities, in fact. How proud our peoples were before Chettri-Bahun caste domination. Originally we were egalitarian, peaceable folks. We had no hierarchies. There were no castes. Our women weren't oppressed by men. Really! Of course all this requires more research. Historians must verify. But basically, things were more ideal than now. We must restore our glorious past. But we mustn't go backwards. You know what I mean. Above all, we must assert our rights. Only when our people receive the respect they deserve will Nepal be truly democratic.

'Vote for the Janamukti house.'

fidget

31

Before an audience of relatives Kainlo-kaka's movements were choreographed to a show of fatherliness: he spoke fondly of Nayan Raj's parents, traced back their ancestry, boasted of bloodlines and declared everlasting loyalties. He took all the authority his position gave him. He took all the power his place as the head of the family allowed him. Binita stood in tense proximity to him, this man who had plotted—would still plot—to turn her into a wretch; this man who would readily punish her, if he got a chance, for her wilfulness. He would want her to move at his bidding. She clenched against him even as she followed form. She stiffened even as she let him reveal to her his duplicity. Without the least pause Kainlo-kaka would say in front of everyone, 'My sole concern is that our family stay together in this age of scattering—we mustn't erode our strong links to one another.'

It was as though he was oblivious to Binita—until the two of them found themselves alone in the private spaces that sometimes opened in crowds. Then he became skittish. He glanced at her, he glanced away. 'A man my age has to watch his blood sugar,' he snapped, refusing her tea. 'The saltiness of your snacks will make my pressure shoot up.' When he found no complaints to hide behind he adopted a sour silence. He looked at her, he looked away, he sat, he stood, he paced and he left.

Binita took strength from his unease. She could even, some days, laugh at him. By some mongrel luck she, a would-be whore, stood in society as the esteemed Binita-bhauju of his famous nephew; and Kainlo-kaka had to treat her civilly. 'Binita-bhauju,' Nayan Raj said each time he addressed her. 'Binita-bhauju,' other party members echoed his deference. Bhauju. Older sister-in-law. Wife of Nayan Raj's older brother. An older relation to all men, a woman to be respected. This link from husband to brother-in-law, from man to man, safeguarded her.

After the Khaireni Tar rally Kainlo-kaka came less frequently to the teashop. The initial thrill of his nephew's return had worn off. Also, it was time to help in the People's Party's campaign work, and suddenly there were home chores to do, there was business to attend to, there was harvesting to begin. 'Our field workers are clamouring for half the crops this year,' he groused. 'In this age of a hundred-and-one cheap liberation movements, if a man doesn't rein in his workers they'll claim his whole year's yield.'

Free of the bitterness and strain that came with Kainlo-kaka's frequent visits, Binita began to take an interest in the commotion in the teashop. Each morning party workers gathered to talk to Nayan Raj, filling each last bench and chatting endlessly about the party's prospects. Their voices hummed, buzzed, erupted in laughter and subsided into hushes. Binita, at the stove, caught snippets of their talk.

'And then one man said, all right, I'll vote for your teacup this time.'

'Will he bring his supporters too?'

'He commands a dozen villages.'

Binita had only to wait, and she heard everything.

'BB-Gun would have gotten kicked out at once if Giridhar hadn't personally vouched for him.'

And when the teashop emptied of workers, there was Pramila to fill the house with her vibrancy. 'Hare Shiva-Parvati, Radha-Krishna, Laksmi, Saraswati, Ganeshaya-namo,' she chanted theatrically as she began each day with a round of the poster deities. 'Protect us from Congress-Communists, bring us lots of money, give us good food and make us fat.' Pramila had much of the joker in her, hamming and jesting over the most trifling matters. The scarf on her head gave her an impish look, and her fariya was often askew, as though clothes were a bother to her. She had a blunt way that bordered, at times, on insolence. To BB-Gun she said, 'Your mother, she's dying with exhaustion trying to put food in front of you, while you walk about with rings in your ears.' Once, after Kainlo-kaka had spent a whole day loitering about the teashop, she said, 'Relatives grow like mushrooms at times of abundance.' The old man pretended he hadn't heard, so she addressed him directly. 'Isn't that right, Kaka? Relatives grow like mushrooms on a dung heap.'

Sometimes Pramila was too heedless in her speech; but her volubility let Binita take refuge in perfect decorum. While Pramila prodded Phool Devi—'Oho, rich lady, you honour us with the gift of your visit now, but will you give us your vote at election time?'—Binita would sit prim, keeping her own relationship to her neighbour polite. But Pramila's sharp tongue lashed at Binita too. 'How you plan to survive in this world being as shy as a new bride, I don't know,' she exclaimed. 'Those who speak can sell flour, but those who stay silent can't even sell rice. You have to tell people what you think. Otherwise this world will eat you raw.'

'The whole world's talking about women's development,' she cried once, for no apparent reason. 'Things aren't as they used to be—just listen to Radio Nepal.'

Another time she said to Binita, 'You teach me how to talk less, I'll teach you how to talk more. Both of us will be perfect then.'

Binita was glad to have her in the house. She didn't know much about Pramila—and any attempt to find out didn't yield much. Pramila was married, but never mentioned her husband beyond saying that he worked in India. She was old enough to have mothered several children, but she never spoke of any. She laughed that she'd been bored with an easy life, that was why she'd gone to work at Thakalni-aama's lodge. She evaded any more queries by joking.

It worked out that Binita took charge of cooking, while Pramila and Sani—who was now insisting that everyone call her by her real name, Madhu—served everyone and cleaned up after meals. Most days there were twenty, twenty-five workers present for each meal, and sometimes a relative or two. The teashop began to feel like a large, extended sitting room, and Binita found herself enjoying the cacophony of people's voices in conversation.

She began to notice each party member. With the exception of Jimmawal-baaje, whose failing health kept him away from party work, the senior party members came every day to the teashop. Giridhar Adhikari's moodiness intrigued Binita, and she liked Om Gurung's effusive ways. The contractor Chiranjibi Joshi had an unobtrusive way about him, and it was hard to believe he was so wealthy. The younger workers were interesting in their own ways, their faces turned towards the futures that the party might lead to. There were some female college students who came in now and then, and talked in charged, altruistic tones about equal rights. Binita liked these young women, unconfined by fear. She liked and envied them. The male workers formed their own cliques and circles. Juddha Ale sat with a group of men who were, like him, failed army recruits. The sign painters formed another group. BB-Gun Thapa sat off to a side with his rowdy gang, primping and preening. Binita kept Sani away from boys like them. There were other workers—college boys, a few stray older men—whom Binita knew by face, but not by name. The worker from Kathmandu, Rishi Lamsal, was aloof to the point of being conceited. He sat by himself whenever he could, as though determined to stay apart.

From her place behind the counter Binita also liked watching her brother-in-law. Her initial mistrust of him had passed. Nayan Raj-bhai was, overall, a pleasant man. He met every situation evenly: he promptly made all payments due to Binita, but he never acted as a customer or wavered in his courtesy as a younger brother-in-law. With Pramila he jested and kidded. With Sani he was encouraging, and with Tripti he was a playful uncle.

'Binita-bhauju,' he said, and his voice scratched exactly the way her husband's used to when he said: 'Binita.'

Once, Binita was serving the morning meal when Nayan-bhai said, 'I'm not sure my own Binita-bhauju will vote for us.' He spoke contritely, addressing the others at his table. 'With all the trouble we're giving her, she might vote for the opposition instead.'

Om was quick to follow the candidate's lead. 'It's true. Binita-bhauju might vote for Congress because they, at least, haven't given her any trouble.'

'That would be within her right,' Chiranjibi said. 'Congress, UML, RPP, Janamukti: she has the right to vote for whomever she wants.'

Then Om began to laugh, and her brother-in-law grinned.

Their bantering caught Binita off-guard: she blushed fiercely. She knew she should protest that of course she'd vote for her brother-in-law, but she felt too shy to.

She was rescued by a gruff comment from Giridhar: 'She'll vote for the teacup.'

She turned away, smiling at the good-natured laughter that followed her. Her abashment made the others laugh again. When she got back to the stove she too laughed at herself. And in her, that laughter turned into surges of pleasure as she did the rest of the day's work. Hours later she still felt the delight of that exchange. She heard again Om's mock seriousness, she saw her brother-in-law's grin. She let herself enjoy this delight among men—for slight though it was, it was rare.

She knew, though, that she mustn't show any of her enjoyment:

she'd learned this well in her wilderness years. And yet, surrounded all day by the party workers in the teashop, Binita dreamed all night of bodies in intimate enclosures and awoke, day by day, to longings that surprised her with their tenacity. She found, as the days passed, that her brother-in-law's voice in the morning could spark a memory of her husband's skin, and the feel of his lost touch could persist throughout the day as she went about the teashop. Later she would feel his hands stroke her at night. The sight of the party workers engaged in brassy exchanges could create in her a longing for laughter, for the abandon she'd felt as a young woman.

Binita had grown up in the district centre largely unsupervised, a single girl in a house full of brothers. She'd been told, too late, how she was supposed to act, what she was supposed to expect, what she was allowed to want. By then she was already ungovernable. She fought bitterly with her mother to attend college in Khaireni Tar, an hour's bus ride from home. And there she had reached for the world—. She strayed further and further from her parents' home till she arrived, one day, to stand centimetres away from her geography professor in the abandoned faculty room of the college campus. In that room the man who would be her husband had spoken in his scratchy voice, he had joked, he had flirted and had flattered her with his attention. He was a freethinking, unconventional man, unmarried well into his late thirties. Their attraction had taken him by surprise. Together they had conspired towards impermissible joys.

Joys which later trapped her—with his death—in a world more suffocating than the one she had fled.

Now suddenly this world was enlarging, thanks to her brother-in-law. In the teashop, these days, a few words exchanged with someone could plant in Binita a wish for communication. So many people—men. She had thought she'd feel nothing but fear amid them, but instead she found strange longings blooming insurgent within her.

Once, pleasure was married with risk, it came mingled with danger. It was she who had moved to her professor first. Then he leaned into her, his dark hands tracing the veins of her arms, the touch making them both reckless. An hour spent alone in a room resonant with the promise of pleasure. Binita was seventeen. The next evening she arrived, unbidden, at his home. She called him Sir when he opened her blouse. He laughed and said he was life's wayward student, not a teacher. He whispered a stream of words as he undressed her. He laid her on his bed and sat beside, looking at her.

'Sir.'

'Rajesh.'

'Rajesh.'

He addressed her familiarly as timi, and she returned that boldness. Timi. Rajesh. A fleeting rapture, here, evanescent, gone. There were surfaces on her body that still ached for his body against hers—for intelligent, spirited flesh to reach for her. There were places in her body wanting a flush of breath, wanting to be bewildered by a glut of sensation. Surrounded by men in the teashop she felt impossible urges come to the fore, and persist despite herself; persist. Outwardly she remained controlled. Inwardly she sometimes became giddy with a need for sharp, peopled pleasures entangled in chance and hazard, for pleasures half-light and half-dark. Voices chatting around her, the brush of an arm against her back, the feel of another person's hands through her hair. 'Binita-bhauju,' a man said, and she found herself distracted by the dip in his voice. 'Binita-bhauju,' another man said and she thought of him nearing her. A casual glance, a simple exchange, the most basic utterance that wafted from a table near by led to desires that came and passed, came and passed without ever manifesting themselves in her conduct.

'Binita-bhauju,' an unknown man said. His brows were

heavy and arched, his thin wet lips curved in the lines of a stone carving. 'Binita-bhauju.'

With perfect composure Binita replied, 'Yes, Bhai.' Bhai. Younger brother.

There were times when all the noise in the teashop disrupted Binita's own quietude; but she found means to avoid everybody then, to stay alone in the backyard plucking the last of the squashes and gourds, or tending to the buffaloes in the shed. Then she returned to the teashop, wanting to enjoy the exchanges there.

The voices of Pramila and Madhu formed a warm envelope around the stove area. Because of Pramila's presence in the house, Sani—Madhu—could continue her evening literacy classes uninterrupted. Most days she returned home full of gossip. 'The women of Dhorphirdi formed a mother's group and collected five thousand rupees! They sang and danced at every house, and built a temple with the money they raised. Sir said we should do the same thing here.'

'I'll be the first to dance.' Pramila twirled her hands. 'But who'd pay money to watch me?'

'There's a woman, Hom Kumari, who says she'll start a group.' Madhu laughed mockingly. 'Sir says if women don't organize, they won't be able to end patty-arcky. Nonsense he talks—and that Hom Kumari believes him. Tch!'

'How smartly this one talks,' Pramila exclaimed.

Missing her irony, Madhu beamed.

Tripti sat by at the counter, smiling at things she couldn't fully understand.

The voices of men buzzed from across the room.

'Really?'

'In my view, no.'

'But is the policy of giving land to the landless ultimately sustainable?'

A thin man with delicate features forming into adult definition. Another with rough gestures, fine talk. A man with a clean shirt and dusty shoes. A man glancing away from her. Binita noticed Rishi, the worker from Kathmandu. Given a choice of sitting alone he always did so, avoiding company. She was attracted by the intensity with which he stared down at his hands, as though studying his fate lines. His dry, papery skin spoke of neglect, but his clothes had an urban sophistication. Most days he took out a radio from his pocket and listened to the news. He looked sober and self-restrained.

Men. Was it safe to talk?

Binita went up to Rishi. His radio was tuned into some English station. Through the static and hiss she heard the words 'Nepal' and 'Kathmandu' spoken with a foriegn accent. When Rishi looked up Binita noticed that his eyes were of an unusual light colour. 'The food will be a little late tonight,' she said. It was harmless to talk about food.

It was never harmless to talk. There was a directness to Rishi's gaze which was moderated only by his serious expression. His eyes swept over the folds of her fariya, then shot to the posters on the wall, and back. He said, 'The rice Binitaji serves reminds me of home.'

'It's mansuri rice,' Binita said. 'I buy it from farmers on the northern hills. The soil there is richer; their rice is sweeter than ours.'

'Yes, it tastes like the rice from my home.'

Rishi was, in all likelihood, older than Binita, but his thinness made him seem younger. It felt all right to continue talking to him. Binita asked, 'Your home is close by?'

'It's close by.'

She thought to ask where; but he made an evasive, bridling movement, and a natural pause presented itself between them.

'The meal won't take much longer now,' she said, and she moved away.

When she got back to the counter she could still hear Rishi's radio—news of Kathmandu muffled by the voices of the men in her teashop.

That night, as she lay in bed with Tripti, Binita thought back to her husband. She'd broken with her family, and he'd thrown away his professional reputation for the thrill of his callused hands on her bare breasts, for whispered pleas in their breaths, for her thighs twined around his. She'd do anything to feel the pulsating river of veins on his arms now. His clean features. The way they were reflected in Nayan Raj-bhai's face. Nayan-bhai was sleeping upstairs right now. Binita saw her brother-in-law's jet-black hair and his affable smile as he talked to her. There was a sliding movement of his throat when he laughed, and she liked that. She remembered her lips on her husband's neck. But tonight her desire wasn't contained by memories of her husband. She saw Nayan Raj-bhai, his urban sheen. She saw the harsh cratered handsomeness of Giridhar's face and heard Om's dulcet voice. She saw Rishi's light eyes and dry, cracked lips. Men. She imagined the press of a warm chest against hers. Lips brushing her skin. Outwardly she lay still. She could allow herself the pleasure of a man only in her thoughts. Her phantom desires.

interval: i'm a person

32

'I wouldn't have gone to Nayan Raj's rally, but my relatives were going, and a whole group of friends was also going, and the flatlands are on my way home, and what harm would it do to give the man a listen? The crowd was thick, I was surprised. The microphone wasn't good but he sounded like a nice man, Nayan Raj—I don't know. He was handsome, modest, intellectual, all those things they say about him. He talked mostly about democracy—and once he got started on the subject... I didn't really listen carefully, but he sounded genuine. A cinema hero, though...How can we believe that he's not just acting? I was impressed with his style of speech: this much I'll say. Even amplified on the loudspeaker his words had a quietness to them. My son will talk like that one day when he gets a college degree—his words pronounced with such ponderousness you wouldn't know he was village-born. At the end of his speech, Nayan Raj thanked us for coming to listen to him. He was nice but a little too good to believe, maybe because he was so much taller than everyone else. His hair was extremely black. An actor. Vote for him? I don't know.'

'My son-in-law is a People's Party worker, and he said: Ba, come and meet Nayan Raj. So I went to his widowed sister-in-law's teashop one day. It turns out the house is just a mud structure—the cement part with the teashop was added later, it looks like. And I thought—why doesn't this hero make his sister-in-law a new house? And why should she have to serve tea to strange men to make a living? What, her brother-in-law doesn't have money? A number-one hit cinema hero has no money? My son-in-law says Nayan Raj will help him get a job after the elections. But this hero can't help his own people—so I don't think he'll find my son-in-law a job. Frankly, I should have never given away my daughter to that dung-brained gobar-giddhe turnip.'

'I met Nayan Raj once and didn't like him. He looked phony all the way through. It's silly to think that because he played a revolutionary in a hit cinema, he'll make a good leader. I mean, what does he know about governance? No, I won't vote for him. Anyway what do I care? I'm just visiting for a few days. I've lived in Kathmandu these past six years—I'm due to return tomorrow. And I won't come back to the district for something as pointless as elections.'

'I don't think it's fair to dismiss him because he's a cinema hero. Listen, I've watched every one of his cinemas, I went to his rally, I've met him several times now, and I can vouch for the fact that he's real. And I'm not an idiot; I'm an employee of His Majesty's Government, after all. Honestly, I find that there isn't much of a difference between the character Nayan Raj portrays in *Ma Manchhe Hun* and what he's like in real life. I'll tell you the story of the cinema and you judge for yourself:

'Nayan Raj plays the son of a poor farmer who lives next to the mansion of a powerful minister. At the beginning of the cinema we see the hero toiling in his fields. The minister's daughter is played by the heroine Kabita KC. Her father is very, very rich and has links in the underworld. Now Nayan Raj is a handsome youth who serves his aged parents well. He plays with neighbourhood children and attends fairs and gatherings. He's a popular lad. He's not a revolutionary at first. But then: trouble. One day the minister bulldozes Nayan Raj's fields in order to build a swimming pool—the minister's daughter likes to swim, I forgot to say. Right from the start we see her asking her father to build her a pool. Her father loves her very much and will do anything for her. Nayan Raj meets the minister and demands that his land be returned. He's treated very rudely by the minster's henchman, however, and isn't allowed to meet the minister. But while he's at the mansion, Nayan Raj sees Kabita KC and Kabita KC sees him, and they exchange tantalizing dialogues.

'After that Nayan Raj joins a group of democracy activists. His aged parents worry for his safety, but in a rousing speech he tells them that he *has* to fight for democracy. Now the cinema was made just after the 1990 movement, and everyone in the cinema hall clapped at Nayan Raj's speech. I clapped too. Meanwhile, Nayan Raj is beginning to see Kabita KC everywhere: on the streets, in the fields, in the jungles. Just before the interval, the two lovers meet in a flower garden and dance—but the minister, who's driving on his way to deforest some jungles, sees them.

'Interval. Now I saw the cinema in a shabby little town. It wasn't a nice cinema hall. The ventilation fan didn't work—and the roof was of tin, so it was sweltering. There was a mother with her baby son just behind me, and the baby must have dirtied his pants because something smelled awful. The mother was also irritating me. Throughout the first half she kept asking "Who's that? Who's that?" whenever anyone showed up on screen. If Nayan Raj changed his shirt from one scene to another she'd ask, "Now who's that?" So during the interval I turned to her and said—"Bahini, in a cinema hall you can't disturb others by asking who's that, who's that?" From her clothes and jewellery she looked like a village woman, and she went red in the face. Then I felt bad, so I asked, "Have you followed the story, Bahini?' She confessed that she hadn't understood a thing. So I told her, and the girl who was with her, what had happened. The woman said, "This hero, he's like Lord Krishna, he'll destroy those evil rakshasas, I know." If this election had happened then, she would have voted for the hero, I can tell you. "You have any questions in the second half, you ask me," I said. "La, I'll ask you," she said. Then her baby began to bawl, and she lifted her blouse and offered him a swollen dripping-wet nipple.

'Anyway, this is what happens in the second half of *Ma Manchhe Hun*: the minister decides that the only way to keep his daughter from cavorting with the son of a poor farmer is to marry her to his henchman, who kills people with a gold knife and has a thick, greasy moustache. The daughter says, no, never; but it's her father's will—. The date is set for a month later. Meanwhile the father finds out that Nayan Raj is agitating for democracy. With the help of his henchman he captures Nayan Raj and ruthlessly tortures him in his secret underground cellar. Nayan Raj suffers greatly but he never, never gives in. Even as he's being cut by the henchman's gold knife he turns to the minister and says—"I may die, but the fight for democracy will live on." The audience clapped again. "And what of your daughter?" Nayan Raj asks. "Her love will die with me too!" Then Nayan Raj gives the henchman a kick and grabs his gold knife. A fight ensues. It's Nayan Raj against ten, twelve muscular goons. He's surrounded! But he fights them all off with karate kicks, and in a dramatic scene he breaks through the window, shattering the glass, and escapes to freedom.

'The rest of the movie loses its flow. There are agitations, there are relay hunger strikes. Kabita KC also joins a protest—though her father has locked her in a room. Sometimes Nayan Raj and she are in the streets, sometimes she's pining alone in her room. It's a bit disjointed. Then the woman behind me started asking, "Who's that? Who's that?" and I had to keep explaining. But at the very end, when democracy is won, the movie becomes good again. That's when Nayan Raj and Kabita KC dance to that song—"*I'm a person, I'm a person. You're a person, you're a person. Let's share our personhood.*" Everyone clapped throughout that song.

'Thinking back to it now, it wasn't that good a movie. It's silly in places, I agree. But what do you expect: it was made in Kathmandu's Kollywood, and the plot was copied from a Bollywood movie that was itself a takeoff of a Hollywood film. But despite its flaws—as they danced the "*I'm a person*" number I saw a microphone protruding from the side—the cinema paid tribute to all those who fought to bring democracy to this land. Hundreds of selfless martyrs: they gave their lives for us. We owe them our freedom. We owe them our nation. We owe them our personhood. And even bad storylines can touch us, I find. All right, in real life Nayan Raj may not be a revolutionary. But when he speaks of saving democracy you remember his movie, and you remember what it took to win democracy, and you feel like protecting it now.'

'Forget America. Once actors start running for office in India, they'll run for office in our look-and-learn hinterlands too. Offer people an empty man who looks like a leader, who speaks like a leader, who acts like a leader, and they'll pour all their aspirations into him and give him their vote. In these days of satellite television power lies in images, they say. In my view Nayan Raj shouldn't win, but he will—if only because he looks like he will.'

the mystifying mathematics

33

The rice fields had ripened, the stalks were golden brown, and the sky a deep blue. Flocks of parakeets roved the skies. Poinsettia was in bloom. Sickles glinted in the hands of the youth and love songs rang in the air. The harvest had begun. In the fields surrounding Khaireni Tar, bands of girls and boys bent to work. Chaff flew through the air.

> *Me, I'm a boy from the flatlands,*
> *A boy from the flatlands...*

From amid a group of boys cropping a terrace, a most manly boy started this refrain. He was none other than the Rawal boy who'd come from India solely to find a wife. He lived up to his considerable reputation: his steely arms rippled and bulged as he sliced through rice stalks with his sickle. In one effortless move, he tossed the stalks onto a nearby heap and bent down to grab another handful.

> *Me, I'm a boy from the flatlands,*
> *A boy from the flatlands.*
> *Eh young girl, won't you run away with me?*
> *Let's ride off in a taxi-car.*

Harvest was a season of lenience, a time when social restraints got relaxed by the dizzying promise of storerooms packed full of grains. The girls on a nearby terrace ogled the Rawal boy. A man who worked in India! The bolder girls retorted:

> *You, you're a boy from the flatlands,*

A boy from the flatlands...

They were joined by other girls:

You can't earn enough for yourself, let alone for me.
I won't ride off with you in a taxi-car.

The Rawal boy stood, crossed his steely arms and smiled. 'Don't lie, eh girls. You'd be lucky to get good, strong men like us.'

'Heeh!' The girls cried cheekily. 'Twigs who'd topple if we blew phooo—bragging about being strong!'

There were cheers from the other boys, there was laughter from the girls, there was taunting and teasing and coquetry, there was an air of longing amid the half-coy, half-brazen voices in courtship.

But there was no Sani—no Madhu.

'You've *got* to come to the fields,' her friend Gaumati was exhorting her in a corner of the teashop. 'All the boys are complaining that the prettiest girls stay at home. They say, we'll finish our work and won't loiter a day more than we have to. You've *got* to come to the fields!'

Madhu didn't reply. She didn't want to go to the fields, she just didn't. How could she show her face to the world? She'd just found out that the corpse of a Khadka boy had blabbed her name in front of all his neighbours, all of Madhu's friends had been talking about the scandalous love tragedy. And everybody blamed her for encouraging him. She had enchanted the Khadka boy, her friends said. She was a most duplicitous girl. She met him along deserted paths, she talked to him in the fields, she made eyes with him at the water tap, she even let him come to her cousin sister's teashop when there was no one else there. She led him to believe she'd marry him, and then one day she told him, no, I won't marry you, and she broke his stupid heart.

That's what all the girls said.

'You've got to come to the fields,' Gaumati said.

'You think I don't know that?' Madhu snapped.

'Everyone's saying the Rawal boy wants to see you,' Gaumati said. 'A few days of modesty, all right: that shows you're not cheap. But if you never come to the fields, how will he ever choose you as his bride?'

Madhu bristled. 'What do I care about the Rawal boy?'

Gaumati took a frank, confiding tone. 'Nobody's told him about the Khadka boy, I swear. And besides.' She paused. 'Everyone knows it was one-sided love, nobody blames you for anything—though they always blame the girl in the end. You know it's not right.' She took Madhu's hand in girl-to-girl solidarity. 'Every time there's a love tragedy people always say it was the girl who encouraged the boy, that she acted as common as a cowherd girl. Not that—.' She turned bright red. When she spoke again her voice was unnaturally high. 'Not that anyone even *knows* about you and the Khadka boy. And even if they knew they wouldn't blame you. Who could believe you'd act so cheap?' She added, 'And if—by chance—they did blame you they wouldn't tell the Rawal boy. No one would ruin a match like that.' Here Gaumati sighed. When she spoke again she sounded forlorn. 'And if the Rawal boy finds out after marriage—well, that's the best you can hope for.'

This last statement was so demeaning, Madhu turned away in shock.

'A girl can't be weak-minded any more,' Gaumati cried. 'If the world accuses her wrongly, she has to say: I've done nothing wrong. How will we ever do women's development otherwise? You can't not come to the fields—you have to come!'

'I'll go, I'll go,' Madhu finally said, just to get Gaumati to stop nagging. 'But not today. Today I have—work to do at home.

So much work. I'll go to the fields tomorrow.'

The next day she said exactly the same thing.

Days passed.

Gaumati stopped visiting Madhu.

Madhu stopped doing anything.

A strange thing was happening.

She felt overcome by an intense malaise. She knew she should be doing things, but she didn't do them. Water, for instance, needed fetching. But she didn't go to the taps.

Must she go? Must she really go?

Pramila-didi went instead.

Firewood, too, needed gathering. The stock was running low. And then the buffaloes needed tending. There was grass to collect. And food to be cooked. One meal ended, another needed to be cooked. Tea, tea, tea. So much cooking. It was exhausting. If it weren't for Pramila-didi mealtimes would be delayed. And then clothes needed washing. The house needed sweeping. The vegetable patch in the backyard needed hoeing and planting and watering.

Must she really do all this?

It wasn't that she couldn't.

She didn't want to. She didn't see what good came of it. All her life she'd been meted hardship and punishment. All her life she'd been good. Her mother had died when she was just three. Madhu thought she remembered a time—though this might never have happened—when she queued up to meet her mother in a dark room. Of her father she had many memories. He loved her dearly till he died of encephalitis when she was seven. The uncle who took her in after that was a cold man, and his wife treated her like a servant. Madhu had taken it as a test of fate to serve her aunt and uncle; she had to prove her loyalty to her dead parents by meeting, with an even disposition, whatever hardship came her way. Even after her uncle and aunt sent her to her next closest relative, Binita-didi, Madhu had tried her best to be perfect. And had she ever failed in her duties to her cousin sister? Had she ever done anything wrong? To the contrary she'd put up with so much that she was too good for. Why was God punishing her now by snatching away her sole treasure of a good name?

When Binita-didi finally asked why she wasn't going to the fields, Madhu lied, 'My foot hurts so badly I can't work.' And it was true. The cut she'd got in the witch's land hadn't healed. The wound was infected now. There was a layer of skin on her right foot filled with a liquid of a brownish colour she'd seen nowhere else. Sometimes the liquid came out of the arch, sometimes from the side, and once from the space between two toes. Purple welters covered the arch and there was a tenderness to the heel. Each day after inspecting its latest abscess, Madhu wrapped the foot tightly in old, tattered rags.

Binita-didi made arrangements for others to cut the fields.

34

'Ours is a country of forty thousand villages,' Nayan Raj said to party workers after the rally in Khaireni Tar. 'We mustn't content ourselves wooing town votes. We must move into the hills, convince ordinary folks to support our cause. Let's walk from village to village.'

A sweet, baffled feeling arose in the heart whenever Chiranjibi Joshi heard Nayan Raj speak like this. So much had changed for him since Nayan Raj's arrival. He knew it looked odd, this decision to follow a man whom many mistrusted as an actor. Even to Chiranjibi Nayan Raj seemed unreal. He was like a gift, a boon, rather. He had stirred old, dormant passions in Chiranjibi. He had offered him hope. Or something grander. He didn't know. It was peculiar, the feelings he had these days. His faith in Nayan Raj—he couldn't really explain it to himself.

Nor could he justify it to his brother.

The day of the first village-to-village campaign, Chiranjibi sat at the teak desk in his wood mill, wondering how to tell his brother—his partner, his lifelong ally—that he was going to campaign for Nayan Raj in the hills, neglecting, even more than he had so far, his responsibilities towards their business. There were lucrative deals in the district centre—deals that Chiranjibi should be making. There were rounds to make in the private quarters of district officers; there was cheap or costly goodwill to generate. But Chiranjibi's heart was no longer in such work.

Couldn't a man take a rest from work? Couldn't a man just change? A father of six daughters he may be. A contractor. But wasn't he free to change? He was compelled by an uncanny sense that he'd stumbled onto something important just in time, if not too late. But it was impossible to speak like this to his brother, using inept and bungling words.

A short while later his brother entered the mill with a group of labourers. The labourers began to pull aside a pile of wood beams. Chiranjibi's brother stood by supervising. Chiranjibi watched uncertainly from his desk. It wouldn't do to leave Khaireni Tar without informing his brother. A month's absence would affect their profits next year.

Chiranjibi took off his glasses and checked the Sellotape holding them together. Then he said, 'This contracting work.'

'Construction begins in a week,' his brother replied.

What? Eh the school building. 'Eh,' Chiranjibi said.

From the odd timing of his reply, his brother sensed that there had been a miscommunication. 'The school for which we won the bid,' he said.

'The school.' Chiranjibi kept his glasses off. 'Yes.'

A silence settled between them. There was uneasiness in the silence, and stiffness, some questioning, a bit of accusation: some misgiving. His brother was disappointed with his negligence.

But there was more to life than the sum of simple math. Around him the smell of wet mango planks mingled with the crisp smell of pine. There were mysteries to act upon, visions to follow, Chiranjibi thought. There were things he needed to do.

For the first time that he could remember, he took advantage of their wordless way of communicating. 'I'll just be a while,' he said to his brother, and left the wood mill.

From there he slipped home, informed his surprised wife that he'd be gone for a month, threw a change of clothes into his eldest daughter's bunny-eared knapsack, and joined the People's Party team that was setting off on the village-to-village tour.

Chiranjibi had never ventured into the hills. He was of bazaar birth and bazaar breeding, and he'd never had to stray from the district's roadside areas. He had never wanted to. He wasn't really sure he could last a month without town amenities.

As the group left Khaireni Tar Nayan Raj walked ahead of everyone. Juddha Ale walked close behind him, as did the Gaine singer Thainlo Nepali and the party's small contingent of female workers. The female workers were only planning to go to the next village, and to return home before nightfall. Chiranjibi straggled at the back of the group, struck by the novelty of heading out of town on foot. The proportion of his body to the landscape seemed strange. His steps were too small. The land was too large. For some reason everything appeared stark. The flatlands looked particularly bleak today, the dusty surface cracking already, a month after the end of the rains.

The path led past the huts of the southern end of town, and through a dip towards the white, limestone-rich waters of the

Seti river. An ascetic lived in the caves by the river, Chiranjibi
had heard. He was once quite high in the Congress party's ranks,
but all he did now, people laughed, was to beg the gods'
forgiveness for his past corruption. Beyond the ascetic's cave a
few rotting planks were posted across the river. Chiranjibi had to
be helped across the waters, which were rushing madly below
the planks, ready to sweep away anyone who might slip.

Most of the electorate lay south of the river. The most remote
villages were three days' walk away; but the group would stop
at each village and take weeks wending their way through the
southern area.

Chiranjibi soon fell behind everyone, besieged by the
discomforts of walking under the scorching autumn sun. He was
sweating so profusely that his shirt was drenched. The bones in
his feet ground against his heels, and he wondered if his cuffed
leather shoes would last the trip. His daughter's knapsack
contained little, but it felt cumbersome on his shoulders. He tried
to walk briskly. He wanted to keep up with Nayan Raj, who,
with his long legs, was striding ahead with Juddha Ale.

Following a hero. Campaigning for democracy. Who could
have guessed that his life would be found in politics? Chiranjibi
had always sought it in the measurements and mathematics of
construction, in endless calculations. He had thought men moved
for money. But it seemed that there was another whole system
that he was only just beginning to discover. The mathematics of
zero zero zero sum no longer sufficed. No zero-sum mathematics.
Rather, one vote: there was a more mystifying mathematics, one
based on single individuals placing their one free vote. Was it
ludicrous to feel this way?

After hours of walking the team reached the village they
were to stay in tonight, a scattered settlement of forty or fifty
houses—all but a couple built with mud bricks, slate and straw—
perched precariously on a south-facing slope. There was a good

view of the himals from here. A local party worker had gathered a small band of supporters from his own family. 'I've arranged for our candidateji to give a speech,' he said, leading Nayan Raj through the village. 'Villagers are gathering just now.'

He took them to a clearing by a thin, blighted looking orange grove. Chiranjibi slowed when he saw the crowd. Only twenty people. They were slightly different from those who had come to the party's roadside rallies—more traditional in their clothes and jewellery. Some men stood to greet the cinema hero, but most of the crowd just looked on, tired from long hours in the harvest fields. It turned out that Nayan Raj had distant maternal relatives here; a few men shyly told him that they were blood relations.

The candidate at once launched a jovial exchange with them. 'You're my mother's aunt's own stepsons? Then I'm assured of votes here—with my own people here to support me.'

'You look just like your mother's aunt, Nayan Raj.'

'I'm your nephew. You call me Nayan Raj-bhadaa.'

'But everyone calls you Nayan Raj, the cinema hero.'

'But to you, I'm Nayan Raj-bhadaa.'

Juddha Ale took the rest of the workers to paint teacup symbols in the village. The female workers stayed on for the speech. Thainlo Nepali squatted to the side of the crowd and pulled a bow across his sarangi fiddle. Then he sang a song modelled after a love duet:

Eh love, I'll meet you
At the voting booth
The birds fly hu-ru-ru
Our hearts soar su-ru-ru
Eh love, the teacup
Is going to win this time
The birds fly hu-ru-ru
Our hearts soar su-ru-ru

The female workers clapped along to a steady beat. Attracted by the promise of merriment more villagers arrived at the orange grove. Soon, forty-five or fifty people had gathered. Most were men, but a few women also came and sat near the party's female workers. The son of the village leader also showed up, and the local party worker was quick to introduce him to Nayan Raj. The candidate, with his unerring sense of etiquette, invited him to sit next to him. The village leader's son settled down facing the crowd.

When Thainlo Nepali stopped singing, Nayan Raj began his address—by now a familiar, though still affirming one.

From the side Chiranjibi studied the crowd. The villagers looked small against the vista of hills and valleys and the distant himals. How lightly they lived on the land. Some of the women wore gold in their ears or nose. Others showed off their surplus income in layers of fat on the body. Most villagers were skinny, though. Their faces were leathery from exposure, and their arms and legs wiry from work. How hard they had to labour to live. Of course Chiranjibi had always known that farming was difficult: but walking through the hills today, he'd felt some of this hardship; his body had taken measure of it.

At the start the crowds watched Nayan Raj closely with narrowed eyes. When the candidate began to talk about democratic reform, they began to ease in their postures. Chiranjibi saw that though some of the villagers frowned through the candidate's loftier points, many nodded at his conclusion:

'We must make democracy ours. Some people say democracy hasn't benefited the poor, we should bring the king back to power. Others say we must have a Maoist republic. But neither of these alternatives lets people govern with liberty. And without liberty, what are we? Mere cattle spending our days serving a system we can't control. Democracy is the only way. But we must reform it, we must fight for both liberty and equality.'

'That's beautiful talk,' the village leader's son said. 'If any reform were possible—'

'But it *is* possible. It is in the hands of the voters to elect a party that will govern responsibly. It's in your hands to make politicians work for you.'

At this even the women nodded.

'Isn't it true, Sir,' one of them called out, 'that we should be able to vote for whoever works for us?'

Nayan Raj said, 'It's your right to vote freely, and your duty too.'

The village leader's son was more hardened. 'When they need our votes, all the parties say they'll work for us. But when they come to power they always let us down.'

Another man said, 'And it's the parties who do all the rigging on voting day. We care about democracy. But all we can do is sit and watch as party workers stuff our ballot boxes.'

There was a volley of questions after this:

'But which party ever says it'll rig votes? They just do it. Invariably, they do it.'

'Every party rigs elections.'

'What makes you any different?'

Nayan Raj responded forcefully. 'Many of our ills come from the influence of India's Bihar and Uttar Pradesh politics. In a big country there's less accountability. But we live in small villages here. We know each other, we rely on each other for our survival, we live by community rules. It's up to us—to you—to watch over each other and make sure that we don't infringe on your rights.'

As the meeting ended some of the elderly villagers in the group started talking about the candidate's family. One old woman with hair as white as the far-off himals came up close to feel his face: 'Jwalaraj's son, look how he's aged.'

An old man boasted, 'I was in his mother's wedding procession.'

Even those who'd never heard the cinema hero's name till today seemed won over by his ability to talk without the conceit of famous men. The village leader's son was also impressed by Nayan Raj. 'Stay at my house tonight,' he said. 'We've heard so much about you, Nayan Raj—I've seen your movies—my father's been hoping to get a chance to talk to you. Stay at our house.'

'Candidateji should stay in his house,' the local party member advised.

By the time they reached the village leader's house, Chiranjibi was exhausted. His muscles ached from the day's walk and his temples throbbed, auguring a headache. His neck was stiff from the weight of his daughter's knapsack, and most of all he was hungry. But no one else seemed tired. At the village leader's house a group of elderly men were waiting to talk to Nayan Raj. Introductions began. And before long Nayan Raj launched into a debate about human dignity.

Chiranjibi sat to the side again, trying not to let his haggardness show.

The party's female workers left when the sun reached the western hills. Having finished painting teacup symbols in the village, Juddha Ale and the other workers began to make arrangements for the night's food and lodging. It was fixed that Nayan Raj, Chiranjibi and Juddha would stay at the village leader's house. The other workers went to stay with other local party members.

As night fell the elderly men continued to discuss politics by the light of a kerosene lamp. Nayan Raj was getting into the intricacies of the party's platform. Juddha began speaking to one man in their common Magar tongue. It was shadowy in the house, and the drone of many disparate conversations lulled Chiranjibi. By eight he was nodding off. 'This is the first time I've ever walked in the hills,' he confessed when the village leader's son prodded him awake. 'My hair hurts from the heat of the sun.'

The man laughed. 'Well, what medicine could we offer?' He laughed again. 'Sit at ease, I'll get you a remedy which cures all ailments here.'

He fetched a jug of homebrewed rice beer.

'In these parts,' he said, 'this is what cures all ills.'

Chiranjibi tried to protest—but how could he refuse the man's hospitality? Besides, everyone else seemed happy to drink. The village leader's son served the elderly first, then Nayan Raj. Chiranjibi sipped cautiously at the milky liquid, finding it surprisingly fragrant, with none of the sour taste he associated with homebrew. He finished a glass, and found that the drink soothed his aching bones. When food was served later, he ate heartily.

Chiranjibi had never lain on the kind of straw mat that was set out for him on the hard mud floor that night. His bones jutted against the ground when he lay down. No posture was comfortable. He forced his eyes shut and tried to sleep; but he remained awake well past exhaustion point, becoming unpleasantly aware, as the homebrew wore off, that his muscles would be tender tomorrow. Juddha, near by, was snoring softly. Nayan Raj too was asleep. Late at night Chiranjibi's stomach began to cramp. His back was tight. His legs began to smart. It was hours before he slipped into a dazed, uneasy sleep.

Early the next morning Chiranjibi squatted precariously over a pit of swarming maggots which served as the village leader's latrine. He felt muddled from lack of sleep, and his stomach was upset from last night's meal. His every muscle throbbed. He felt shaky, and this worried him. There were gaping holes in the planks above the pit. He had to move with great precision.

He mustered the requisite strength. And he managed to conceal from everyone the fact that if no one were looking, he'd be hobbling. He was embarrassed to own up to his frailty. He felt absurdly out of place—a wealthy contractor playing at village politics. He didn't want to draw attention to the truth that he didn't belong here.

After receiving assurances of support from the leader's son, the group headed off to the next village. Nayan Raj and Juddha again led the way, speeding along the winding hill trail. Chiranjibi fell behind but found, as he walked, that his legs moved more ably than he'd expected. He didn't feel well, though. His stomach was still rumbling from last night's meal.

Walking past terraced fields, through patchy forest and up the rolling hills, it struck him again: the slow pace of human movement through the landscape. A step, a step, a step through a land crinkled into hills and valleys, into cliffs and plains and ravines and steep gorges. Horizon upon horizon revealed small, concealed settlements cut off from each other, by a days' walk sometimes. The group reached a ridge that offered a particularly good view of the himals. Chiranjibi had never been one for views, but he had to admire the crisp white edges of the distant snow peaks.

Every now and then they passed villagers harvesting their fields, and Nayan Raj stopped to talk to them. The workers handed out pamphlets to those who said they could read. To those who couldn't read they said, 'Ask your schoolmasters to read you what this says.' The tour had been planned so that the team spent the nights in villages that were strategically important. During the day they could only meet some key leaders in the villages—since most of the villagers would be working in the fields. It was after dark, often in the light of kerosene and petromax lamps, that speeches and debates extended well into the night.

The following days attained a good hard rhythm: early dawn skies, aching feet on uneven trails, fields stubbled with cut rice, bar-peepal trees to rest beneath, the riffs of the Gaine singer's fiddle, painted teacup symbols, crowds, words, exchanges, meals of the last of last year's rice, straw mats on hard mud floors. As the days progressed Chiranjibi's body learned to meet the rigours of the trail. His legs stopped hurting and his daughter's bunny-eared knapsack no longer strained his back. After a few initial bouts of diarrhoea his stomach started to accept whatever he ate, and he no longer got headaches in the sun. He even began to feel strong. Lying on the floor at night his body met the hard surface with a reciprocal hardness. On nights when there were no fleas or bedbugs in the bedding he slept soundly and awoke refreshed. By the end of the first week he was fit enough to keep up with Nayan Raj.

He still stayed in the background of village interactions, though. Deep inside he couldn't help feeling like he was masquerading as a political worker. What did he have to say to these villagers? He who'd made money off projects earmarked for the poor. At times he felt unforgivably dishonest, trotting about like a man of principles. Chiranjibi's cuffed leather shoes wore out one day, and he had to borrow a pair of Elephant Brand slippers from a local man. With a slap slap slap of his slippers he trailed the candidate, observing the spare economy which regulated people's lives and studying their attempts to live in dignity. They passed through Magar villages, through Chettri-Bahun settlements, through whole villages of occupational caste Sarkis, Damais, Kamis and Gaines, through Gurung settlements and through villages of mixed ethnicity.

Everything was instructive for Chiranjibi in this process, everything was significant. He found himself drawn by small details: the serious expressions on men's faces, the way they spat to the side before talking, the way the meekest ones waited to say what was on their minds, then did so with surprising poignancy. People spoke of hunger, they spoke of injustice, they spoke of the kind of changes they wanted to live to see. Their dreams weren't lavish. A bridge here would change their lives. A hundred-metres-long PVC pipe to bring drinking water to the village. A few benches for the school. A little more thought in the way they were treated by the district government. Who was talking of big sums? Small allocations sufficed. Perhaps the district centre could allot money for one medical camp a year?

An old woman in one village asked Chiranjibi, 'Son, when might we brighten our lives with electric lights?'

A teenage boy in another village said he wasn't studying. 'The high school is in a village two hours away. Who'll look after my family's fields if I spend all that time walking?'

Girls who should be in school were cutting the rice fields, singing in harmony.

In one village a woman had just died birthing a breached baby.

In a village of Kami blacksmiths everyone was harvesting the land of their high-caste landlords, and they had no time to talk of politics. A man there said, resentfully, 'The same people who tell us there's democracy still say—you're polluted, don't touch us, don't come into our houses, don't use our water taps, don't defile our temples, you're low of birth. The law may say we're equal, but we still live like slaves. That's the kind of democracy we have.'

Chiranjibi felt unable to respond to such bluntness. He felt personally accused.

In one village the monsoon rains had transformed a small gully into a raw, open cleft capable of taking the whole village down with it in a landslide. 'We need a supporting wall,' said the village leader. 'I'll vote for any party that helps us build a gabion-wired supporting wall here.'

In another village a man with cataracted eyes asked if it was true that an operation could fix his eyes.

As days passed, as they walked deeper and deeper into the

electorate, the rest of the world became remote. How far Khaireni Tar seemed from these villages. The district centre seemed centuries away. Chiranjibi thought of all the men in those shabby government offices exchanging favours with each other, making deals, reaching agreements, siphoning off percentage cuts for whichever project brought them the most benefit. They too felt deprived, he knew. They complained of low wages and spoke of a day when they might build a house in Kathmandu, when their children might go abroad, when they might live at ease with servants to look after them. They looked at those richer than they, and dreamed bright dreams. No one looked at the poor. No one looked at Kami villages, generations-old sharecroppers who were entangled in debt, their self-esteem trampled on by centuries of bigotry. No one looked at the villages of women waiting for their men to return from abroad. No one looked at the school-aged girls fetching water from streams an hour's walk away. No one looked at the elderly being carried in baskets to health posts miles away. No one looked at the disadvantaged, at the burdened, at those whose desires were thwarted at birth. No one looked at the meek. Chiranjibi himself, in his years near power, hadn't.

Nayan Raj, though—unlike him, Nayan Raj turned to the poor. As the tour progressed the Nayan Raj of Khaireni Tar—slightly dreamlike, a little too polished—gave way to a more unaffected man who spoke in the language of villagers about economic democracy and social justice, who rallied against a politics of money-grubbing and power-hoarding. 'Poverty is anti-democratic,' Nayan Raj argued. Chiranjibi walked behind his candidate, his heart aflame. Yes, of course Nayan Raj was just a man—a former actor—not a visionary, not a miracle worker, not a saint. Many people probably thought he wasn't for real; he spoke well, he was a pleasing sight, they said, and that was his job, wasn't it, the reason he had been given the ticket. This election, they said, it was a novelty for him, or perhaps he was only extending his years of stardom. A cinema star, a politician, where was the difference? 'At best,' a government official had told Chiranjibi over an exchange of money, 'he is a naive, deluded man. He's trapped in his role in *Ma Maanchhe Hun*. He mouths that old script he learnt by heart, Chiranjibi. He understands none of those fine-fine ideas.' But Chiranjibi trusted Nayan Raj. And more than that, he realized, what he felt for his candidate was in fact a kind of devotion.

Because the mystifying feelings that Nayan Raj evoked were so tender in him, people's cynicism struck Chiranjibi hard.

Two weeks into the tour one village leader talked acerbically about the way elections were conducted in his village. 'Votes are bought here, cinema heroji,' he said in the bullying tone of a man with the advantage in a bargain. He was angling, perhaps, for a sum of money. 'A few nights before voting, the selling and buying begins. Your talk is appealing,' the man smirked, 'but it's of no use. The villagers will vote for whichever party pays them the most.'

Nayan Raj replied: 'Our party won't participate in such activities.' The village leader had a large following, and could bring the party many votes. But Nayan Raj didn't pander to him. 'Those who sell their votes have no right to complain, later on, that their government isn't working for them. They've sold their citizenship.'

'But people are poor,' the leader retorted, becoming self-righteous. 'You can't blame them if they want to convert their votes into cash.'

'We're all to blame for making a mockery of democracy. Those who buy votes, those who sell votes, and those who broker that exchange.'

It filled Chiranjibi with a childish glee to witness such integrity. Overcome by conviction he too stepped forward and added, 'The teacup party will do nothing to harm the cause of democracy.'

And then he retreated in embarrassment.

Later he spoke at another village: 'We stand for the cause of true democracy.' He noticed that he sounded exactly like Nayan Raj. He felt self-conscious about this; his admiration for the candidate showed so openly. His attempt to partake in politics was inept. He was just a fraud. He was vulnerable to criticism. He was standing up to be ridiculed. And yet—.

The uneven surfaces of the trails, the hot harvest sun, the scent of the harvest fields, the hard floors to sleep on, the under- or overcooked rice, the meagre vegetables, the water that tasted of earth, the words that people uttered—all these became part of his apprenticeship to Nayan Raj. People, the old and young, women and men, those harvesting golden rice crops, those who were sick, those who were singing, those fetching water, those resting in the shade became his teachers.

But as the tour progressed Chiranjibi began to see that it was complicated, this matter of democratic reform. At the village level, party politics became mired in histories of personal loyalties, generations-long debts, family patronage, and ethnic and caste rivalries. One night, while resting after a particularly taxing walk, Chiranjibi heard about the violence that marred the last elections. 'Each party got its workers drunk and told them to do as they pleased to scare away voters so that they could stuff the ballot boxes,' a local worker said. 'There's an old rivalry here between Gurung-Magar and Newar boys. They've joined different parties. That day they hacked each other with khukuris in the name of politics.'

Stories like this started to crop up as the group headed from village to village. Tales of captured booths, stuffed ballots and burned ballot boxes began to emerge from the simplest exchanges. Each voting booth had a distinct way of rigging elections. Proxy voting was the simplest and most rampant form of rigging. 'Even *I* voted thrice last time,' a local party worker admitted with a grin. 'Once in my name, once in the name of an uncle away on work and—tch!—once in a dead man's name! Even my twelve-year-old son voted. And I told my wife, go, go, vote again, but my woman, she was too scared.' He caught Nayan Raj's expression and grew sober. 'Of course now that I'm a member of the teacup party, I won't do things like that.'

In some cases the villagers themselves participated in the rigging. This often happened when a whole village—or a majority of its population—supported one party. They allowed party workers to take over the booths and stuff ballot boxes. Voter turnout was thus recorded at ninety per cent in some booths. Or, in the last days before the vote, the village would pass an ordinance on whom to vote for; on voting day party workers made everyone comply by examining their ballot slips as proof. In one of the villages where the group stayed at overnight, two men had been knifed for defying such an ordinance. 'How can you talk of free choice,' these men cried, 'when party workers force us at knifepoint to show whom we voted for? Could you guarantee our safety if we voted for you? Are you strong enough to protect us afterwards?'

In other places the parties rigged elections against the wishes of the majority. When a party knew that it wouldn't garner many votes at a booth, its workers created a scare to discourage voter turnout. Or they destroyed the ballot box as it was transported on the long walk to the district centre where votes were counted. It was also common for party workers to threaten voters of rival parties. 'If we vote for you, and if the other parties find out, will you guard us afterwards?' the people of such villages asked Nayan Raj. 'Will you stay with us always, and make sure that the others don't retaliate?'

It was safety people sought when deciding which party to vote for: protection from the local power brokers of rival parties. In one village three families voted against the leader's party, and they were banned from using the only water tap in the village for five years. 'We'd like to vote freely,' one member of these families said to Chiranjibi, mistaking him for the candidate. 'But our women can't spend another five years going all the way to the river for a bucket of drinking water. Next time we'll vote for the village leader's party. So don't waste your time talking to us. Go to our leader.'

These stories disturbed Chiranjibi. From far away each village looked like a peaceable idyll; and yet the people conducted themselves rowdily come election time. In these tucked-away villages the parties became marauding armies. Territories were carved out, protected, defended and ruled over. For what? All the development contracts awarded by the party in government? Chiranjibi wondered: so this is all it takes to rob people of all their humanity?

The most powerless were most easily controlled. 'No question of free choice here,' one man from a settlement of Damai tailors said with a smile. 'We'll vote as our landlord tells us to.' A village of Sarki cobblers didn't even meet with party members. Juddha Ale picked up a rumour that they'd been threatened with violence if they met Nayan Raj.

In the face of all this Nayan Raj only became more ardent in his call for reform. It touched Chiranjibi to see this. Nayan Raj said, 'It's this very abuse of power that our party is seeking to end.' He spoke with increasing ardour. 'What is needed are citizens' groups who refuse to let the parties act like the middlemen of democracy, taking steep percentage cuts in return for the favour of letting you vote for them. We live in small villages, where accountability is easy to ensure. Democracy will empower us only if the parties are held accountable. Everyone must fight to be free.'

In most villages Nayan Raj managed to convince people as to his sincerity. Invariably a few men stepped forward and volunteered to help the party supervise the booths on election day. 'Our chairman Giridhar Adhikari will come in some weeks' time,' Nayan Raj said to these new recruits. 'He'll meet with you and form the booth committee. You must help him in whatever way you can.'

With a slap slap slap of his slippers Chiranjibi followed Nayan Raj, and as the days passed, he felt like he'd reached the edge of another world. He felt moved to ardour at the thought of a single free vote. How lucky he'd been to find Nayan Raj. An actor: an unlikely agent of democracy. And Chiranjibi, a contractor, was his unlikely supporter. Yes, there were questions about his business ethics in the past. He had profiteered. The cynical could laugh. But a sweet, baffled feeling arose in him when he thought of people entering voting booths with a real choice at hand.

The tour wended its way through remote villages that got increasingly impoverished: tumbledown clay huts with leaky thatch roofs, and vegetable patches with one or two squash vines, and straw mats ridden with lice. Unwashed children with skinny limbs and swollen stomachs stared as the group walked past. Women with night blindness groped about after dark. These were the people, Chiranjibi thought, whom he'd cheated for years, whom he'd siphoned money from, whom he'd used as a means to his own enrichment. Mercy was what Nayan Raj was offering him: a chance at redemption.

35

In Khaireni Tar Madhu continued to malinger in her household chores. So many things needed doing. But every day there were more and more things that she didn't do—and all these undone things heaped on top of each other till they became a himal of her failures. Sullenly she watched Pramila-didi fetching water. She watched her sweeping the house and courtyard. She watched her washing the dishes. She watched Binita-didi prepare the meals and serve everyone. Binita-didi milked the buffaloes every morning now. She had hired help to harvest the fields, and paid Pramila-didi to fetch grass and firewood. The two of them were now doing all the work Madhu used to.

Sometimes Madhu did one or another chore, if she felt like it. Sometimes she swept the house and backyard. Sometimes she made tea for customers. But she hated having to lift a finger. More than once she burned the milk. More than once she broke china cups. Binita-didi wasn't strict; she never admonished her. All she did was watch Madhu. Pramila-didi, too, watched her from the corner of her eyes. Neither of them said anything to her. Why didn't they say anything? Why not just admit they'd heard about her love tragedy? Why not just laugh at her for having been brought down to their level?

She was being punished for nothing she'd ever done.

Madhu countered her cousin's watchfulness with a show of studiousness. When Binita-didi was around, she pored over her literacy textbook, frowning earnestly at all the words and sentences. When Binita-didi approached her, she frowned more mightily. When Binita-didi turned this way, she turned the other way. When Binita-didi faced her directly, she looked down. And once, just as Binita-didi opened her mouth, Madhu shrieked,

'Hah!' and ran to chase off some birds from the vegetable patch. Whatever it was that Binita-didi intended to say, she wanted not to hear it.

But how long could she silence Binita-didi? One day her cousin spoke. Binita-didi, Pramila-didi, Tripti and she were in the teashop, waiting for the pressure cooker to cool. The evening meal was later than usual tonight. Outside, the night was dark. The light from the naked bulb sharpened Binita-didi's features as she said, 'Madhu.'

Madhu scowled.

'Madhu,' Binita-didi said again. 'Something's happened maybe. You've changed.'

Madhu reeled at the accusation.

'You're getting quiet, you look unhappy.'

'You're upset that I didn't work in your fields,' Madhu said. 'I'll go tomorrow, don't hire anyone to crop the fields, Binita-didi—I didn't even know the harvest had begun, I've been so busy learning letters. But now that I've remembered my duties I'll definitely go. From tomorrow I'll go.'

Binita-didi looked at her queerly.

Could she tell she was lying? Madhu reached for the pressure cooker. Excitably she said, 'But first—we're all hungry—let's eat.'

When she opened the pressure cooker's lid there was a sludgy mass of overcooked rice paste inside.

She should have put in less water.

'It's all stuck together,' she said.

Then, oddly, she chortled.

Black and gold. Heat and cold wracked her.

When she opened her eyes, her cousin's face hovered over her. The face of a hussy.

That face said things she didn't want to hear. 'Madhu,' it said. 'Madhu.'

The face said, 'After your parents passed away you had to grow up fast. With only your uncle and aunt to guide you. Now you're here. I haven't known how to steer you well.'

The face said, 'At a certain age needs arise in a person. I heard about the Khadka boy. I don't know what happened, but if you want to tell me, you can.'

The face said, 'You don't have to hide anything from me.'

The face said, 'I'll try my best to guide you, if you only stop hiding things from me.'

Hiding things? Who was this whore and what was she saying? How did she know what had gone wrong?

The woman kept saying things. Again and again. Again and again. Till Madhu could bear it no longer.

'I just want to study,' she said one day. Her voice was wild. She could see his thin, pinched face. He was an ugly boy. She rummaged about for something to say. 'I want to be educated,' she said. 'I don't like the girls of this town. They're so dull, so uneducated. I'm sick of them.' The truth was that her body burned sometimes, and she shivered violently. Her mouth was parched and there was a strange buzz in her head. She was being punished—' for what?

Madhu laughed unpleasantly. 'I just want to be educated and learned and knowledgeable like you. I just want to be left alone to learn letters.'

'You can do that, you can study,' the woman said slowly, looking at at her strangely. 'I want you to study, I want you to learn all you can. I'll teach you more than your textbook contains. You can study as much as you want.'

Madhu smiled as though appeased. 'That's all that's wrong.'

'Are you sure, Madhu? Is that all you want?'

'I just want to study,' Madhu groaned.

the laughter of women

36

When food entered the body—good, healthy food—it melted into thousands of particles like tiny gobs of healthfulness which caressed each solid bone and tissue, each lean muscle and slippery organ. The waters of the body accumulated, and their moisture prevented wildfires. The spirit radiated a steady warmth, sustained by the breeze of the breath. Spaces for love came into existence, and the soul resided there.

This was what Harsha Bahadur felt as he feasted, day by day, on meals prepared by his mita-mother, meals which made his skin smooth and his hair lustrous, which made him walk upright and talk in less squeaky tones, and which made his body suited to holding love. Fish heads simmering in gravy, watercress with burned fenugreek, plump cauliflower slathered with spices, daal scented with jimbu herbs, buttery beans, potato-and-sesame pickles, fluffy rice grains. Meal by meal his mita-mother offered him affection. Meal by meal he suckled at her love, and he grew strong.

All the while his mita-father taught him how to conduct himself in the town. Harsha Bahadur's duties were slowly becoming clear to him. As the People's Party Peon he had to do such things as registering workers' attendance and stocking the party's posters, pamphlets and banners. Only the worker Rishi Lamsal should have unlimited access to these materials, his mita-father had said. Harsha Bahadur dutifully recorded the number of posters and pamphlets Rishi Lamsal took, and told everyone else, 'I have to ask my mita-father. My mita-father said I should say I have to ask him.' The only person Harsha Bahadur couldn't say no to was BB-Gun Thapa, who easily muscled his way past him. But despite this failure his mita-father praised him. 'If I'd been like you when I was a lad,' he said, 'I'd be much better off now. I'd know how to make the school yield a profit.'

Was he really a boy of great skill, a boy of great worth? Harsha Bahadur doubted this. Yet everyone praised him . . . When he went home after work his mita-mother and many mita-relatives fussed over him no end. 'We must fatten the boy.' They smoothed his hair when it spiked up, fixed his collar and patted him on the back.

Home to party office. Party office to home. He hardly strayed from this path. He really didn't have to. In his mita-father's sitting room was a shelf filled with splendid objects from all over the world that held his attention. There were pale fan-shaped objects with irregular ridges. Sea animals lived in them, his mita-father explained. Then there was a glassy ball with ribbons trapped inside which, catching the light, refracted rainbow glitters. Next to it was a lamp that his mita-mother once turned on for him. It radiated dully and a gob of ink at the bottom rose and fell on its own. There was a doll with blue eyes and several other curiosities: beaded cloths and painted boxes, curved glass vases and dishes woven of bamboo. All these things were from Hong Kong, his mita-mother had told him. This was the island where his mita-father had served in the foggy white British Gurkha forces.

In his mita-parents' house there was also a television set covered with a pretty scarf. It stood in a corner of the sitting room, and was always on, showing images of exotic overseas lives that astonished Harsha Bahadur. He didn't understand much of what flickered and flashed on the screen, but he watched reverently, gleaning valuable information about the world from these undreamed of apparitions.

The town seemed a kind place now. These days he rarely thought of Sani. Harsha Bahadur felt blessed at last, and thought— well, no—but yes—maybe he was fated for a little bit of happiness.

37

Even after Nayan Raj left for the hills, the structures of social esteem he had created for Binita held remarkably well. When she went to the bazaar townspeople turned to her, smiled, inquired after her and murmured bland, appreciative words about her brother-in-law. The vendors at the bar-peepal tree loaded her with free cheeseballs, peanuts and bananas. The shopkeepers of the bazaar discounted their wares for her, and blind Shankar gave her a free fistful of rice for every kilo she bought. One day Tripti asked why her friends at school were being so nice to her.

Pramila explained, 'You've got a cinema hero uncle and now you're famous too. It's only till the end of elections.'

'Unless the teacup party wins,' Binita laughed. 'Then people will have to be nice to us always.'

To her it seemed unlikely that her brother-in-law's party might upset the bigger parties. Her newfound respectability would vanish the day elections ended. Veneers collapsed fast in this town. She mustn't get used to all the strangers who came to her teashop and treated her with such respect. She mustn't be seduced by their politness. She liked it, though, that men called her Binita-bhauju and were courteous to her. This was the strange gift her brother-in-law had given her: he had brought society back into her life, but also shielded her from its baser aspects. He had given her people, and also protection from them.

But Madhu's sudden turns in mood worried Binita. Whatever had happened between her and the Khadka boy, Madhu had reacted badly to it. The girl bridled when Binita tried to talk to her and pretended that nothing was wrong. For a few days she looked feverish, but once her fever passed, she sat alone in the backyard leafing through her literacy textbook. Some days she came into the teashop and desultorily performed a few chores. She never spoke much to Binita. Pramila did her best to cheer her, and sometimes Madhu responded with a tight smile.

Binita spent more time in the teashop. From the party workers who remained in Khaireni Tar, she heard of Nayan Raj-bhai's impact in the southern hills. Sometimes Om Gurung came—'The tea here is so special I couldn't resist dropping by'—and he chatted, in his ebullient way, of the victory that seemed imminent. 'The northern areas were already abuzz with Nayan Rajji's name,' he said. 'And now we're penetrating the southern areas. Binita-bhauju, people all over the district—all over the nation—are disillusioned with the big parties. They're crying for an honest alternative.' Binita liked his easy smile, his easier optimism. 'All we need now are strong booth committees at each voting booth. And these our Giridhar-dai will set up when he begins his own village tour. I tell you, Binita-bhauju, our victory is all but assured.'

The rest of the workers were also touched by a similar optimism. When the younger workers came to the teashop they huddled in groups, gossiping. Binita could overhear them from the stove. Once, a boy said, 'An uncle of mine came from Kihun yesterday and said the whole village is ready to give us its votes.'

The workers laughed. 'The other parties thought they owned the southern belt, well, now here's a challenge to them.'

Rishi didn't take part in such exchanges. He waited for his meals in silence, he ate in silence, and afterwards he stayed on in silence, listening to his handheld radio. Binita could tell by now that he wasn't being arrogant; he was just too pensive to enjoy such bluster. His aloofness seemed sane. She sympathized with it.

'They say Nayan Raj-bhai is doing well,' she offered one day as she gathered his empty plate.

Rishi said, 'Elections are unpredictable.' His light eyes

skimmed her face.

'True.' She lingered on to see if he'd say any more.

'The southernmost regions are controlled by UML.' He spoke as though Binita would know the electorate's voting pattern. 'They know how many votes they can rely on, they know how many Congress votes they need to cancel, how many extra votes they need to steal.' He looked her in the eye, with a boldness checked by his politeness. 'A lot depends upon the booth committees that Giridharji establishes. Your brother-in-law is a charismatic man, Binitaji, but he can't win without strong committees at every booth.'

Binitaji: a formal but not unpleasant term which refused family ties. Binita too addressed him formally: 'Rishiji will go to the hills with Giridhar Adhikari?'

'In a week or ten days.'

'Won't it be hard for a city dweller to walk the steep hills?' she asked.

Rishi smiled for the first time that Binita could remember. He said, 'I grew up in these steep hills.'

She too smiled and moved away, still smiling. Later she found herself going back to that conversation: a brief back-and-forth exchange, but enjoyable.

Binita didn't enjoy every interaction that came her way, though. Nowadays her neighbour Phool Devi came by with increasing frequency, sometimes carrying fresh green beans or tomatoes, and always launching on the hectic nattering that wearied Binita. 'Yesterday my relatives were saying, that poor widow, how does she feed all those party workers every day? I told them, you think that poor widow doesn't know how to run a kitchen? She's not a village lass, she's intermediate passed. She looks like a helpless girl but she can do anything, just anything.'

Binita always tried to send her neighbour away as briskly as possible. Pramila too tolerated little from Phool Devi. 'Eh rich lady,' she said one day, 'the poor widow will do very well with a larger supply of vegetables next time.'

Phool Devi never knew how to react to Pramila's barbs. 'We close friends help as we can,' she said, arching her brow. 'That's how it is, isn't it? You help me, I help you. Neighbours help each other in times of need.'

Pramila opened her mouth to say something, but Binita cut her off. 'That's how it is,' she said.

Afterwards Pramila strutted about, impersonating Phool Devi. 'Fresh from my garden.' She picked at her fariya with mock daintiness and stuck her nose in the air. 'I'll bring you some more tomorrow. And after the cinema hero wins the elections, I'll come to collect the interest. Isn't that how it is with neighbours? *That's* how it is.'

A few days later two women came to the teashop to visit Binita. This was new, Binita thought, showing them to the back porch where they could sit at ease, away from the party workers. She spread a straw mat for them. One of the women was Hom Kumari, the wife of the Sub-Inspector, who was in Madhu's literacy class. Hom Kumari was in her forties, with square features and the plump build of one who could afford servants. The other woman was the wife of the ascetic who lived by the Seti river. She was a bony, wizened old woman decked in a bright red fariya.

'Madhu's resting,' Binita said to dispel the initial awkwardness between them.

Hom Kumari blushed for no reason. 'We're in the same class,' she said.

'I know, she said you pressed the Sir into starting the class. She's getting to learn letters because of you.'

Hom Kumari smiled shyly. 'A girl her age picks up everything so fast. If a mother of four can learn letters, why can't she? You studied till college, didn't you?'

'I did my intermediates.' Binita gestured in the direction of the college campus, but didn't say more. The other women surely knew that she'd met her husband there.

The ascetic's wife sat forward. 'That's why we want you. We need lettered women like you in our mother's group.' She crossed her legs, smacked her lips and continued, 'The group is still very new, the two of us are heading it. But we don't have anyone who's educated, who can write letters—what if we need to write or read documents? A group of blind, deaf, dumb women—what can we do? Educated mothers like you must join.'

Hom Kumari said, 'We're asking all the mothers of the bazaar to come. All our members are going house to house. We wanted to talk to you ourselves, to make sure you'd say yes.'

'Young mothers like you must join the group,' the ascetic's wife said. Then she said something which sounded quite false to Binita: 'A widow like you—you need other women to guide you through your dark times. A widow's life is pitiless, we know. You need friends. You must join our mother's group.'

Binita tried not to bristle. Where were these kind, solicitous women even a few months ago, when she was alone? Where were they before that, in her most difficult years? Where were they before Nayan Raj-bhai returned to Khaireni Tar to loan her some respectability?

'I'll bring you tea,' she said, leaving them on the porch. By the time she returned, Pramila had joined them, and was teasing Hom Kumari about becoming a lettered woman. Binita served everyone tea and went back inside to prepare the evening meal. She was able to avoid the whole issue of the mother's group.

That night, after coaxing Madhu off to her literacy class, Pramila settled at the stove and told Binita about Hom Kumari. 'Ten years she's married to the Sub-Inspector, and her husband suddenly brings home a Magar girl of eighteen, says this is my younger wife.' It was hard for Pramila to keep her voice low, and her face strained with the effort. 'He says, it's not that I don't love you, it's just that I've ruined this girl, and her family says I have to marry her. So what does Hom Kumari do? She starts a court case to get the second marriage annulled. Because by law the older wife can annul her husband's second marriage if she finds out in thirty days. And Hom Kumari's brothers are educated, see, and they help start the case at the district court. But the girl—the second wife—holds on to Hom Kumari's feet and begs her not to annul the marriage. Where will I go, she cries, who'll take me now that I've been used by one man? Everyone knows your husband's made a wife out of me . . . All this in front of the district court—people have gathered, everyone's shouting, the police are trying to separate the two wives. An uproar! The second wife bawling at Hom Kumari's feet, pleading for mercy.'

'And did Hom Kumari annul the marriage?'

'Could she throw out a ruined girl?' Pramila shook her head. 'No, she ended the case. But she made her husband transfer his land to her name—to protect her children's inheritance. Just in time. The younger wife was already carrying a son.'

For some reason this story lessened Binita's mistrust of Hom Kumari and the ascetic's wife. But she still didn't want to join their group. The group didn't want her—they wanted Nayan Raj's sister-in-law. Had the group formed a few months ago no one would have bothered to invite her. She was quite sure of this.

The next day another woman paid Binita a visit. Binita was brewing tea at the stove, and at first she didn't think she knew the woman. Then she recognized Laksmi, Giridhar Adhikari's wife, a timid, insecure woman who confined herself to her house in the northern hills. Binita figured Laksmi was looking for her husband. 'He hasn't come here for days, he must be in the party office,' she said.

Laksmi shook her head. 'I came to talk to you.'

Binita gestured for her to take a seat. Laksmi shied away from everyone and chose a corner table. Binita took her a fresh cup of tea.

Laksmi sat hunched over at the table with a harassed air about her. Her oily hair was slicked into a bun, and her arms were clasped tightly against her thin chest. With a pointed chin, drawn eyes and overly sharp nose, her face was quite plain. She had a tense way of watching people, as though scared of them. She spoke in a soft chiming voice: 'There's a mother's group—'

'Headed by Hom Kumari and the ascetic's wife,' Binita interrupted. She instinctively disliked Laksmi, and her tone was short. 'I know about it.'

Laksmi said, 'They're meeting tomorrow in the flatlands. Maybe you and I could go.'

Binita looked away to avoid saying no.

Laksmi kept studying Binita's face as though needing to meet her eyes. 'I won't go if I can't find a friend,' she said, and her begging tone put Binita off. 'I thought you could be my friend and we could go.'

Laksmi wasn't the kind of friend Binita sought. 'I've got too much work,' she lied.

The woman hung her head like a rebuked child. This irritated Binita. Everything about Laksmi elicited pity. Well, perhaps there were reasons to pity her—but Binita didn't want to know them. Her own reserves of happiness were so scant, she didn't want to deplete them by befriending a woman like this.

Laksmi said, 'And how could I go without a friend?'

She sounded so sad. 'It's just that I have work,' Binita said more gently. 'I'd like to go, but can't.'

Laksmi left quickly soon after that, without touching her tea.

Binita remained at the table, brooding. Why should she join the mother's group? Women didn't, on the sole basis of being women, form trustful unions, she thought. They often acted as the loyal agents of punishing men. Hadn't Binita suffered her mother, who would much rather follow tradition than take her own daughter back? Hadn't she suffered Kainlo-kaka's wife? And what of the townswomen who had rigorously ostracized her until her brother-in-law came back? She had no need to subject herself to their false camaraderie now.

She suddenly felt movement at her table. Rishi had sat down across from her. He was fiddling with his radio. From this proximity Binita could see just how dry his lips were. He twisted the dials as the radio cracked and popped.

Binita liked talking to him. 'Rishiji is always listening to the radio,' she said.

He glanced up. 'You don't like to?'

'There's always some woman crying.'

Rishi laughed long at that, transformed, for a moment, in his whole bearing. 'I only listen to the news,' he said, still smiling. For a while he twisted the dials, but there was no reception. Then he switched off the radio and asked, 'Are you going to join the mother's group?'

He must have overheard her talking with Laksmi. Binita shook her head.

'They're a good thing, mother's groups.' He took in a sharp breath and made as if to say something, then stopped. For a while he looked down at his hands. Then he took in another sharp breath. 'They help women who've been mistreated find each others' support.'

It was a strange, melancholy statement, and it made Binita recoil. A mistreated woman: was that how he saw her?

'You should join the group,' he said.

'And you would know what I should do?'

Binita abruptly left the table. Pramila was at the counter chopping onions, so Binita went to the stove, where she'd set aside the rice for the evening meal. Turning her back to the room— to Rishi—she began to sort through the grains.

Women who've been mistreated: that was how she looked— like Laksmi? Briskly, she picked out stones and stray husks from the rice. She couldn't help feeling upset. This was what people thought when they saw her—that she was a mistreated woman? Did she bear evidence of Kainlo-kaka's invasion, did she look like she'd been used by him? She glanced at Rishi. He was listening to his radio now, absorbed by the news of the world. He couldn't guess at what she'd been through. Nobody could. She was unsociable, yes. She feared men. She had retreated from their world. But she wasn't defeated, like Laksmi appeared to be. She did not look mistreated.

The next day Thakalni-aama came to the teashop, and Binita knew at once that she'd come to fetch her for the mother's group meeting. 'Let's go,' the old grandmother said, entering the teashop. It was rare for her to leave the Himal Lodge Restaurant Bar anymore, and Binita rushed about clearing a table for her. But Thakalni-aama was more interested in inspecting the teashop. 'You've done well with this room. Nice benches. Strong wood. The posters—I should get some for my hotel.' Catching sight of Tripti she exclaimed, 'Eh, the baby's grown up so fast.' She clucked to see Madhu on the back porch. 'I didn't recognize the orphan girl, she's a woman now.' Then the old woman turned to the party's driver, who was sipping tea at a nearby table. 'Eh boy, are you a party member? Mind the teashop while we're gone.'

The driver gaped in surprise. 'I've got to drive workers to Mouriya.'

From the next table Rishi said, 'I'll mind the shop.'

'There.' Thakalni-aama turned back to the back porch. 'You—orphan girl—stay and look after the daughter. Binita, Pramila, let's go. The meeting's already begun.'

There was no way for Binita to refuse. She followed Thakalni-aama out the front door. Laksmi was waiting outside, and she smiled anxiously at Binita. She was dressed in a bright yellow fariya which did nothing to ease her fretting look. Binita noticed that she was terribly small: a woman the size of a girl.

'Mothers forming groups all over the country. Why shouldn't *we*?' Thakalni-aama led them past the highway, towards the bar-peepal tree. The old grandmother was dressed festively in a pink fariya and polka dotted Chinese shoes. 'Old mothers like me and young mothers like you getting together and creating a ruckus—I tell you there's no big objective. Even after you've lost all your teeth it's important to have fun. You'll find out when you reach my age.'

At the bar-peepal tree she called out to those on the path: 'We're off to the mother's group meeting. Ho, it's being held today, in the flatlands. Thirty, forty of us getting together and creating a ruckus. Come and see.' She admonished some women passing by with basketsful of dung. 'Are you so busy you can't come with us? Have you no time for fun? What, you're carrying the weight of the whole world on your backs?'

Binita fell behind as they neared the flatlands. A group of women had formed a rough circle in the barren plains, sitting on the bare ground. They were all bazaar women, women she recognized by face but didn't know. A few Newar women were clustered at one side, across from some Gurung and Magar women. The rest were Chettris and Bahuns. No one from the town's well-to-do families was present. Phool Devi wasn't there. Neither was Om Gurung's wife, nor the wives of Jimmawal-baaje or Chiranjibi Joshi. The poor and the lower castes from the nearby Gaine settlement weren't here either. It was a middling group.

Hom Kumari stood up when she saw them. 'Thakalni-aama's come.'

'Mothers, I've come.' Thakalni-aama walked into the space that opened as women made way for her. Pramila followed her to the centre of the group, and Laksmi also chose a spot near her. Binita remained at the edge, taking a seat beside a woman who looked, from her jewellery, to be Magar.

The ascetic's wife had been telling a story when they arrived. She resumed it now. 'Thakalni-aama, I was talking about Akala-mai.' She was decked in an orange fariya which made her look devout. 'Akala-mai wasn't happy with the town for many years,' she said in the confiding tone of a gossip. 'She wreaked droughts in the land and made people starve. She was extracting revenge for the neglect people had shown her. She made every one of the townspeople suffer. She made men, women and children cry.'

It was a story Binita had heard before: only after the townspeople repaired her shrine did Akala-mai relieve their suffering. Everyone in the group had probably heard the story before, but they listened attentively, enjoying the way the ascetic's wife spun a tale. 'And so one day Akala-mai appeared in a dream...'

Binita examined the group. She didn't know many of the women. Women never came to her teashop the way men did, and Binita took little initiative herself to meet them. Besides, every woman here was from another part of the country: a daughter-in-law who had come, only by marriage, to call Khaireni Tar home. They didn't have lifelong links here, the way the town's men did.

The ascetic's wife ended her story with a declaration: 'The first thing the mothers' group must do is repair Akala-mai's shrine. The shrine's got cracks in the side and the roof leaks. It won't last another monsoon.'

'Let's repair it and make our mother happy,' Thakalni-aama agreed.

There was a murmur of assent in the group.

The woman next to Binita called out, 'Why should we build temples?' There was a marigold in her hair which set off her round, attractive face. She said, 'Let's repair our water taps, let's make a water tank, let's do something useful with the money we raise.'

Pramila cried, 'Hah, then all the men will see we're developing the nation and clap!'

The women broke into laughter.

'Let's just repair Akala-mai's shrine,' Hom Kumari said. 'It won't cost much; we can do it fast. Then we'll think about what to do next.'

The ascetic's wife raised her hands in supplication. 'Eh Akala-mai, your daughters are ready to serve you!'

With this the crowd broke into chatter.

'That way we'll have a place of our own to meet.'

'But how will we raise the money?' a woman called out.

The ascetic's wife laughed. 'By dancing, like all the other mothers' groups.'

'But what will people think?'

'Who cares what they think?'

'Dancing in public like whores, they'll say.'

'Dancing for Akala-mai's pleasure, we'll say.'

A woman near by shouted, 'My old man won't let me.'

'How can he stop your devotion to Akala-mai?'

'Think of our fathers-in-law!'

Binita liked hearing women talking with so much jest. It felt mirthful, it felt light, it felt like it was taking place outside of her life.

The woman with the marigold in her hair turned and smiled.

Then she reached for Binita and began to undo her hair. Binita turned to make it easier. The other woman's fingers combed through her locks, then rolled her hair back up, pinning it expertly into a bun. Then the woman sat back, resting her hand on Binita's lap.

Somewhere, a woman in the group began to hum. Binita saw Laksmi looking around anxiously, as though to assess what was about to happen. Next to Laksmi, Thakalni-aama stood up. 'Let's dance for Akala-mai. Let's create a ruckus for our mother.' And, despite her age, she went up on her toes and began to step in rhythm, swaying with surprising agility.

The other women began to clap, laughing. Hums spread from breath to breath, and gave way to song:

By the far-off river let's sit and talk.
The sun over the hills, let's you and I walk.

Suddenly some women were up and dancing. Hom Kumari protested as Thakalni-aama coaxed her up. A Gurung woman joined the dancing, then another woman also got up. Soon, seven or eight women were dancing in the arid flatlands, kicking up dust with their shuffling, thumping feet. Passers-by stopped to stare, grinning openly at the revelry.

Instead of enjoying the dance Binita found herself stiffening. She was supposed to be having fun, she knew. But it seemed to her that women who could do little to improve their circumstances were settling, now, for the suppleness of chapped feet, the sway of bony hips, the swaying of arms wiry from overwork. It irritated her. Laughter pealed through the clapping. 'There, there!' Women twirled with an abandon they couldn't have in the rest of their lives. It all felt false. Hom Kumari started spinning nimbly, and the ascetic's wife swayed her hips in a way that would have been unseemly in a younger woman. Across the crowd Laksmi was

smiling widely, like a child. Her yellow fariya end had fallen off
her shoulder. Something like disdain flashed through Binita.

But then Pramila got up, and for a moment Binita was taken
by the sight of her transformed. Pramila's dancing betrayed none
of her everyday cloddishness. The reds and purples of her fariya
swirled elegantly. Around her, women's bodies were revealed in
the lift of a blouse; their modesty was tossed aside in a fanciful
whirl of the hands. For a moment Binita surrendered to the laughter
of women.

The Magar woman next to her kept making lurching
movements with her legs, as though wanting to get up and join
in the dancing. Her hand was still on Binita's lap, and she seemed
to want her company. This unnerved Binita. A widow dancing
for the whole town to see: it would look grotesque.

She slid away from the woman, and hoping that no one would
notice, hurried back home.

Rishi was still minding the teashop when she returned, and though
Binita knew she should say something to thank him, she felt loath
to explain why she'd left the meeting. Neither did she want to
hear from him how she—as a mistreated woman—should seek
solidarity with other women. She went past the teashop without
a word. Madhu and Tripti were in the back porch, hunched over
a copy book. Binita wanted to be alone. She went to the alcove
they all shared now, with its rows of beds. She was overcome by
a sudden, urgent need to cry.

Rajesh. Timi: you. When they married, she had made him
her world. He had satiated her with his talk and filled her with
his touch. She had let him. That had been a mistake. When he
went, there remained nothing concrete in her life, only gaps, and
shadows.

There would be no one in her life who'd seduce her with his

words and let her seduce him with hers. No one who'd allow her to discard her caution and bare those desires which set her alight.

After a while Tripti came in and began to talk about her day at school. Pramila returned from the flatlands an hour later, sweaty and flushed—hollering, 'You should have seen the ascetic's wife dance afterwards!' Binita murmured something about a bad headache. She didn't want Pramila's effervescence, she did not think she could deal with it today.

That night Binita excused herself from work. She spent the evening alone, cleaning her brother-in-law's room upstairs. There was a pair of pants and a shirt hung on a chair. On the table lay an open notebook with some lists and scribbles. The air had gotten stale in the room. Binita opened the window. She straightened the bed covers and tucked in the sheets, then stood awhile looking at the room—no longer hers—where, years ago, she'd lain with her husband night to night. A familiar scent, from her past, emanated from her brother-in-law's belongings in the room.

Her thoughts strayed to men, to one man. To Rishi.

Not that she'd—. She couldn't.

She thought back to the mother's group meeting. There was laughter in the group. There were intermediate pleasures amid women—.

A bitterness arose in her. Intermediate pleasure was all she could have any more.

38

The day Harsha Bahadur received his first month's salary, he stared at it in disbelief. 'Keep it safe in your pocket,' his mita-father said, and for one incredulous moment he thought he was being told to hide it because his mita-father had stolen it. But no:

his mita-father then wrote the sum of five hundred in an accounts ledger, and asked him to sign it. This Harsha Bahadur did, feeling amazed. He was an earning man.

After work he went straight home and laid the bill on the kitchen table.

His mita-mother was chatting at the dining table with some distant aunts. They all looked at the five-hundred-rupee bill as though they'd never seen so much money.

'What's this?' his mita-mother asked.

Harsha Bahadur said shyly, 'For you, my earnings.'

His mita-mother picked up the bill, folded it in half, then placed it in his shirt pocket. 'You silly boy,' she chided him. She wasn't, of course, angry. Her voice was kind. 'Go spend it on something nice. That's what boys your age do. With no family to feed you're free to spend that money as you like.'

'Go buy booze like a real man,' one aunt said.

The other aunt laughed. 'Eh these Chettri-Bahuns don't drink— and if they start, they never stop. The boy will be stumbling all over town, throwing away his caste.'

'In this age which Chettri-Bahun doesn't drink?'

'Ho, you're right, they've all thrown away their caste.'

The two aunts started to howl in laughter.

'Tch.' His mita-mother hushed them. Then she took Harsha Bahadur by the hand and led him out of the kitchen. 'Go to the bazaar,' she said. 'And don't come back without spending some money.'

Harsha Bahadur had never wandered the bazaar by himself. He walked a few paces from the house, shying away from the shopkeepers who were looking at him as though challenging him to buy their wares. He avoided the aggressive vendors beneath the bar-peepal tree, and kept away from Congress party workers. He was just about to head into an alley when he saw a ruffian there, so he veered away. Suddenly he found himself at a crockery store filled with UML workers, glaring at him as though he were personally responsible for all the world's wrongs. Quickly he headed back to the bar-peepal tree, where he took shelter next to a peaceable looking woman bangle seller.

Much to his delight his Maoist second cousin appeared, then, from behind the bar-peepal tree. Dressed in old army fatigues he cut a heroic figure. 'Come, brother!' He placed an arm around Harsha Bahadur and led him to a narrow side alley. There he stopped awhile. 'Look at you,' his cousin said. 'You work a month for a reformist bourgeois party, you already look like a reformist bourgeois boy—but I'm your brother and I forgive you.'

Then he led Harsha Bahadur through the alley past a plain as dry as dung, and onto the southern end of town. They ducked into a seamy, slapped-together teashop. His cousin sat him on a bench. 'So you're not missing home?' he asked. 'I thought for sure you'd have quit working by the time of the harvest, but look: the fields are cut, yet you're still here.'

Mention of the harvest immediately reminded Harsha Bahadur of Sani. How strange that he hadn't thought of her for weeks. A pang of love shot through him. Ssss! 'Has she—has she married the Rawal boy?'

'Your Sani?' scoffed his cousin. 'She's so precious she didn't even work in the harvest fields.'

'She didn't cut the fields at all?'

'Now that she's learned a few letters, she thinks she's above manual labour.'

'Perhaps she is,' Harsha Bahadur said.

His cousin suddenly exploded in Maoist rage. 'Bourgeois girls see themselves as commodities of exchange,' he cried, his eyes turning red. 'Your Sani is happy to be exchanged like a cow between father and husband. Where is her will to fight? Where is the rebellion, where is her revolutionary fervour? With women like cows how will we ever wage guerrilla war?'

It hurt Harsha Bahadur to hear Sani being called a cow. His cousin probably thought of him as a cow, too. This made him feel sad. It was all related to the doctrine of Maoism, he knew. He stayed silent, not wanting to provoke any more of his cousin's Maoism.

The teashop owner brought them tea.

After a while his cousin gruffly conceded, 'Of course I may be wrong about her.'

Harsha Bahadur smiled, happy to reconcile. 'It could be that I don't know how the world works.'

For a while they both stayed silent, sipping their tea. Then his cousin started to ask about his work.

Harsha Bahadur talked happily about the workers, the posters, the party's future plans, and the way his mita-father guided him in his work. He also talked about his mita-mother, he talked of the unidentifiable foreign objects on his ritual parents' shelves, and he talked of television. It was nice to be listened to. His cousin paid great attention to everything he said, and gave him excellent advice:

'Take your work seriously, brother. Be diligent, make people happy, make them trust you. The men you've come into contact with—big men like Nayan Raj—they're important. They can give you a job just like this'—he snapped his fingers—'if they want.'

'I don't really deserve the post of Party Peon,' Harsha Bahadur admitted.

'You do,' his cousin said gently. He looked again at Harsha Bahadur's clean, pressed shirt and trousers. He said, 'And even though you're working for the reformist forces of the multinational imperialist broker-capitalist system of multi-party democracy, I personally support you, brother. To tell you the truth, my comrades would criticize me if they saw me now, talking to you. You must hate your class enemy, they say. You must wage war on them. You must work tirelessly for a wholesale landslide gale-storm kind of cultural revolution.' He leaned over and took Harsha Bahadur's hands. 'It's true, you're lacking in consciousness. But you and me, we're brothers, and we must stick together. I'll always look out for you.'

'And I'll look out for you,' Harsha Bahadur said, touched by his cousin's warm love.

When it came time to pay Harsha Bahadur pulled out his five-hundred-rupee bill.

'So much money.' His cousin peered at it suspiciously. 'Where did you get that much money?'

'It's my first month's salary,' Harsha Bahadur said proudly, handing the money to the teashop owner. He got back a fistful of change.

Afterwards they walked through a few back alleys, his cousin taking an older brother's advising tone as he explained, at random, the town's novelties. 'These are cheeseballs,' he said, pointing at the tin foil packets on sale in a wayside shop. 'There's nothing in them but air, just like parliamentary democracy.' At another shop he said, 'Those are rubber dolls that bourgeois girls play with to learn how to become submissive objects.' They reached the watchmaker's canvas stall. His cousin said, 'Those are digital watches from abroad that break in a month so that you have to buy another one, draining money from the country.' At the bar-peepal tree he said, 'Here, let's buy a packet of chips.'

Harsha Bahadur handed some bills to the cheeseballs-and-chips vendor.

His cousin opened the bag. 'These are made of Nepali potatoes, Nepali oil and Nepali salt. No multinational capitalist exploitation is perpetuated by eating them.'

Harsha Bahadur liked walking about like this, buying things.

It made him feel older somehow. Passing by the lane to the medical shop he asked exuberantly, 'If one were to eat all the medicines in the Doctor Sah'b's shop, would one be cured of every ill? If one were to take all the blue pills, white pills, red pills and yellow pills, would one become extremely strong?'

His cousin stopped and turned his face skyward, striking a heroic pose. 'That would only enrich imperialist multinational broker-capitalist pharmaceuticals,' he bellowed. 'What our people need is food, plenty of food. They need land to farm on, seeds to sow, irrigation canals, fertilizers. They need equality, justice, liberation! Our skilful guerrilla warfare has liberated four-five districts already! We'll liberate the rest of the country with our workers-and-peasants violent armed people's revolution!'

'Eh,' Harsha Bahadur said.

'Our government is an agent to multinational broker-capitalist imperial forces that exploit the poor! We're all being sold to corporations which pay the highest percentage cut! We're being treated as chattel!'

'Eh,' said Harsha Bahadur.

'Guerrilla warfare is the way of the future!'

'Eh.'

Then, as they reached the edge of the bazaar his cousin said, 'Don't tell anyone you saw me, brother'—and abruptly disappeared into a mulberry bush.

That must be where he lived in his tunnel below the ground.

Harsha Bahadur looked around in befuddlement, wondering what to do next. Despite his cousin's Maoist opposition he still liked the idea of buying medicine. Because, having thought of Sani after a long time, it struck him that maybe she rejected him because he was so sickly. For being sickly, while understandable for those born into misfortune, failed to attract love. Why wouldn't a girl as splendid as she prefer a strong, healthful and—ssss—

steely-armed boy like the Rawal fellow?

He patted the money in his pocket. Then he walked back towards the medical shop. Blue, white, yellow and red pills. He was going to buy health-giving pills.

inebriation

39

In the haze of anger befogging her days and nights, Madhu felt an intolerable bitterness, a kind of blind envy towards Binita-didi. She could hardly bear to be near her. She could hardly bear to do anything. She had tired of all her friends. Tripti was a bore. And Pramila-didi was just an uncouth woman.

And getting to the literacy class was such a chore. She would have stopped going, if she hadn't lied about wanting to be educated. So she sat every evening on a straw mat in the school room, listening to Sir. Sometimes he spoke in ways that seemed right to her—his tone, more than his words—though she still didn't care much for what he said.

Sir was a frail young man with an expression of great panic on his face. He spoke rapidly, rushing to spew out all that was in him. 'Gha,' he said one day. 'What words begin with gha?' His eyes flashed about the room. 'Gha. Some words that begin with gha.'

Madhu always sat at the back of the class, and she shrank to avoid Sir's eyes.

Sir's eyes landed on the woman sitting next to her. 'Gha. You live in a—.'

The woman said, 'Ghar?'

'Yes. Good. And what's that on Madhu's foot? A—.'

Madhu tucked her foot beneath her.

'Ghau.'

'Yes. Ghar, ghau.' Sir turned to the blackboard and wrote out both words. He circled the first and turned to the class. 'Ghar. A man without a house isn't a man, and a woman without a baby isn't a woman. Is that expression right?'

The students were always shy to launch into discussion. A

few women giggled. For a long time no one spoke. Then Hom Kumari raised the end of her fariya to cover her mouth, and ventured, 'That's what the old people say, Sir. A man isn't a man till he settles his own house.'

'Every man has to make a house,' said another woman.

The wife of the ascetic disagreed. 'But my son's father gave up the one house he had. He said, you come too, let's live in a cave and give up this corrupting world. Me, I said, you give me your house, if you don't need it. You write your house in my name.'

'So your husband's a man, though he doesn't have a house,' someone laughed.

'He's not a man, he's a jogi.'

Sir said, 'And is a woman without a baby a woman?'

The ascetic's wife said, 'No, women are born to be mothers.'

'It's true,' Hom Kumari said. 'God sent us to this world to birth children. A woman without a baby isn't a woman.'

'In this time of overpopulation?' Sir said. 'In this time of birth control? A woman isn't a woman without a baby?'

'No.' Hom Kumari was adamant. 'She's not a woman in the true sense.'

'Wrong,' Sir said. 'Just because this is an old saying doesn't mean it's true. So many men in the cities live in apartments. They can't afford a house. But aren't they men? So many women can't have babies. Yet don't they live full lives? Getting educated doesn't just mean learning letters. It means you have to think!'

Madhu found most things that Sir said quite silly, but there was something in his tone, a vexation, an impatience, that she liked. She was tempted to emulate it.

Sir turned back to the woman beside Madhu. 'The next word. Ghau. That wound on Madhu's foot. What makes it fester?'

'She's probably been mounted by a spirit,' the woman declared. 'The only way to cure her is to have a jhankri perform prayers, ritual blowings and blood sacrifices to drive off the spirit.'

A chill swept through Madhu.

'Wrong.' Sir glowered at everyone. 'There are minuscule beings causing the infection, called bacteria. If you don't kill these bacteria in a timely fashion, they'll make the wound fester. We must be scientific. The age of believing in spirits has passed.'

Hom Kumari said, 'But Sir, there are ghouls who plot deep into the night about how to harm others, there are witches who suck their husband's blood till they die, who wreak havoc on other women by mounting them and torturing them. My own sister's youngest daughter-in-law was mounted by a witch.'

'All blind belief!' Sir snapped. 'Only modern medicines can drive out whatever has taken possession of Madhu's foot.'

Through all this Madhu stayed absolutely still. It made perfect sense now. She had been mounted by a witch. Why else would she be feeling so ill-tempered, so rebellious all the time? Here she was. She looked normal. But deep inside she was being steered by an evil woman keen on seeing her suffer. Because she'd been so perfect, she'd attracted the witch's envy. She was being punished because she'd been so good. And because all women were made to suffer, in this land cursed by women.

40

The morning that Rishi was to head to the hills with Giridhar, he spent hours at the teashop waiting for a chance to talk to Binita. A fatuous sense that she liked him had taken hold of him. Not that he imagined her liking to be more than simple human companionship; but two people meeting, individual to individual, was a surprising enough event at this time, in this place in his life. Just to talk. Across the crusted buffers of society the two of them had talked, now and then—and in that talking they had communicated something more elemental than the words they traded. From Binita's first tentative words to her bristling reticence after he told her to join the mother's group, he had noticed how she hid and revealed herself, how she reached out and withdrew, how she protected and risked herself cautiously. Nights in the dormitory room with the radio on, he thought of her ways of guarding herself. With boys like BB-Gun she never talked. With other party members she adopted the role of Nayan Raj's Binita-bhauju. With Nayan Raj's relatives she took the stance of a daughter-in-law. To Madhu she was a sister, and to Tripti a mother. To the larger town she showed the face of a reclusive widow. But to him she seemed to come less restrained; she came as herself. Binitaji, he'd called her. Rishiji, she'd returned. Rishiji. In some small way—but in a way that surely meant something—she strayed from social confines when she talked to him.

But since they had spoken about the mother's group Binita had avoided him. Rishi recognized this as chastisement for having pressed her to join the mothers' group; but he thought she might soften to say something—even small—to acknowledge that he would be gone, now, for several weeks. But the morning he was to leave Binita remained resolved to ignore him. Her back was turned as she worked at the stove. Her face was also turned away; he would be at the edge of her peripheral view. Rishi waited after his meal. He thought that if she gave him an indication he would go up to her and take leave. But after she stopped cooking Binita still moved from chore to chore turned—purposefully?—away from him.

That too was a message: I have thought of you and want to keep you away.

Out to his banishment he went, then.

Outside, the sun was dazzling. Rishi headed to Shankar's grain store. The town looked bedraggled. Sun, trees, ploughs, houses and teacups marked every free wall. Torn posters fluttered from tree trunks. The banners strung on branches and electric poles were faded by the sun.

There was a crowd of villagers at the grain store, bargaining to sell the grains they had just harvested. 'Look, Shankarji,' one of the villagers was saying, 'we can't sell at the price you ask. No matter how many fertilizers we use our harvest keeps thining each year. If we don't get a fair price we'll starve before winter's end.'

'Without any profit how can I survive?' Shankar said. 'I'm not the government which can live on foreign aid.'

Then a rustling voice said from inside the shop, 'Surely our Shankarji will make concessions for my own people.'

Rishi recognized the voice at once. He circled over to the side door. And there he was, the schoolmaster, turned away from him on a bench. A moment of uncertainty passed through Rishi. The schoolmaster's silver hair was covered by a crumpled black cap. He sat stooped, as though he were too tall for the room. He was acting as the intermediary between the farmers and Shankar: 'Surely our Shankarji will reconsider—such sweet, fragrant mansuri rice.'

Rishi realized, then, that the farmers were from the northern hills—men he had called uncle as a child. A village neighbour was standing next to him. The neighbour glanced at him, but turned away without recognizing him. Rishi felt strangely hurt. He surely resembled his mother—. The other farmers didn't take any note of him either as they negotiated, in the leisurely and longwinded way of villagers, for the price they sought.

When Shankar finally agreed to pay two rupees extra per kilo the farmers disbanded, satisfied. The schoolmaster stood to leave. Rishi, a few feet away, thought that once the farmers left they might exchange a word—the schoolmaster, Shankar and he.

'Shankar-dai,' he called out.

The blind man turned.

'It's me, Rishi Parajuli.'

The schoolmaster walked out the door.

Shankar broke into smile. 'The comrade with sorrow in his voice.' He seemed to sense, and to enjoy, Rishi's dismay. He cackled unpleasantly. 'Come! Sit. Tell me what you're planning to do for me in the hills.'

Outside, the schoolmaster veered towards the UML office.

Rishi took the schoolmaster's bench. The structure, not the person. Systems, not individuals.

Rishi handed Shankar a sheet of paper on which he'd written the itinerary for Giridhar's tour.

'For your schoolmaster's eyes only,' Shankar laughed, flapping the sheet. 'Only for your schoolmaster's eyes.'

Rishi shrugged off the man's sarcasm. He looked outside. The schoolmaster was already at the crockery shop, joining a group of UML workers. The workers were young: students, like he'd been, of the schoolmaster. Their bodies formed a tight enclosure. For a moment Rishi thought of sauntering over to force the schoolmaster to pay attention to him, his recruit and comrade.

'You can meet him during the festivals,' Shankar said, as though he'd seen where Rishi was looking. 'During the festivals he'll come to meet you at home.'

'I never said I would go home.'

'It's too risky to meet in town. You go home. Your schoolmaster will come there.'

Rishi felt sickened by these words. 'No, I want to meet him here.'

'Your schoolmaster said you must go home.'

And what the schoolmaster said Rishi must do. He took in the hard feel of being used. Then, without another word to Shankar, he headed out to his drunken master Giridhar.

Not having touched a drop for months, Giridhar knew he was prepared now for the test. The true test was here. His body felt in balance at last, and he was able to focus on whatever required his attention. After Nayan Raj left for the southern hills Giridhar had even planned, village to village, whom he'd meet on his own village tour—what he'd say, how he'd ensure votes for the teacup party. The test of his chairmanship was here. With his own tears and sweat, with his own blood and flesh, with only the effort of his bones and the fortune lines scarred on the palms of his hands he would make the party. This was his ambition. Tracing Nayan Raj's tour through the southern hills he would form committees wherever he could summon local support. Ideally he'd form thirty-three committees, one for each voting booth. The task would require all his acumen. While he met with village leaders and rounded up the right kind of men—strong party soldiers—the workers would add to the posters, banners, slogans and symbols that the earlier team had painted. Rishi would supervise these boys. This trip—test—would last a month. And at the end of that time Giridhar would have made a future for himself.

He was entering the hills. Given his deteriorated physical state it was hard, though, to walk the narrow dirt trails in the dazzling post-harvest sun. The terraced fields were covered with the unsightly stubble of cut rice stalks. The sunlight hurt Giridhar's eyes, and he had to blink constantly to ward off the glare. His bones felt slothful and his body felt like just so much heaped-up flesh. His breath was loud, his face felt hot, and he wanted very badly to rest.

Rishi, who stayed a few paces behind him, seemed to be having an easier time: slim young men like him would. BB-Gun's gang was scattered along the way, some boys charging ahead to the next village, others lagging behind sticking posters along the trail. Giridhar paused now and then, overcome by lethargy. But he didn't let himself rest. Walking would get easier as the days wore on, he knew. His body must keep up with his mind, which spun from village to village, person to person, thought to thought, over possibilities.

The thoughts that came to him were sometimes idiosyncratic. Like: there was time enough for everything. There was time enough to lock himself in his room, and time enough to learn again how to go back to the world. There was time to talk and plan and execute according to design. Ages passed—time was always ticking—but not so fast that there weren't interstices for muddling.

Another thought: there was no such thing as a mocking god. In his youth Giridhar had been an atheist. Later he'd become agnostic. But lately he'd begun to act as though the gods were everywhere—and were laughing at him. Unreasonably, he attributed hostile intentions to inanimate objects, he sought assurance in signs and omens, he scraped before the gods of vengeance and fear. There was no reason to behave like this. He was a modern man. He mustn't think in absurd terms.

And: whatever became of the Elephant Brand slippers he'd bought from the cobbler? Had he taken them home or left them at the party office? Had he lost them? Forty rupees gone just like that.

They were not very useful, these thoughts.

Rishi, behind him, stayed silent. He seemed disposed to be that way. This suited Giridhar, who needed the time along the trails to think. There were strategies to be made in every booth, there were tactical battle-plans to prepare. Voting wasn't about talking sweetly, the way his dashing cinema hero candidate thought. Elections were about doing whatever it took to place votes in the ballot box.

When they reached the first village, Giridhar heard from local party members that the candidate had made a good impression here. The village leader's son came to meet Giridhar, and insisted that he stay in his father's house tonight. This would prove very useful, Giridhar thought.

At the leader's house a few elders were waiting for him, asking about Nayan Raj, about the party's history, about their vision of democratic reform. Exhausted by the day's walk Giridhar replied to their queries as best he could. 'Our candidate doesn't mean drastic change,' he said when the leader's son asked him what exactly the candidate had meant by reform. 'We all need to improve. The parties, party workers, each one of us, ourselves: we need to reform, that is what our candidate says.'

'The reform that he's calling for,' said the village leader's son, 'it must come from the parties and not from any change to the structure, right? He's not opposing parliamentary democracy, is he?'

'Eh we're not Maoists opposing the whole system,' Giridhar snapped. 'You think, if we were Maoists, we'd come and ask for your vote?'

At this point Rishi stepped forward to explain. The boy—man—seemed quite intelligent. 'Our party is determined not to let democracy succumb to anti-democratic forces,' he said. 'Those on the far left and far right say that democracy isn't serving the poor. Others who are committed to democracy still ask if the parliamentary system works for a country like ours. There is demand for a federal structure. These, too, are valid questions. But our party believes that the failure of Nepal's democracy is the fault of the parties. That's what Nayan Rajji means. The success of the 1990 movement was only the beginning of the democratic revolution. We have to follow through by bringing better parties into power.'

'That's what we were wondering,' the village leader's son said, apparently relieved. 'That's what we wanted to know.'

'That's what Nayan Rajji means,' Rishi said.

This Rishi Lamsal, it seemed he'd learned the party's message by heart. An MA-passed boy from Kathmandu: he was useful to have. Giridhar was glad for the chance to sit back as people asked questions and Rishi answered, praising the cinema hero in words that Giridhar knew he himself couldn't say.

The next morning Giridhar felt fresh. The village leader's son was willing to help form a committee for the local booth. When the two of them were alone, Giridhar asked him, 'You foresee any irregularities here?'

'About three thousand votes fall in our booth,' the other man said. 'If we have a strong team we can make sure the booth isn't captured, as usual, by UML workers.'

Giridhar had always known that people were like deep, dark wells. Their secret motivations had to be fished out from the murky depths of their hearts. He cast a net: 'The important thing is to conduct a fair election. So tell me, what can we do to help you ensure that the elections will be free and fair?'

The village leader's son looked at him, and their eyes locked, and it was clear that he'd understood Giridhar. He looked down, and after a while said, 'To win, the party must spend a little here.'

And he named his price.

Giridhar listened intently, calculating the costs. Several thousand rupees to hire enough men to fight off UML workers; a few thousand more to buy key votes. 'The whole settlement farms my father's lands, they'll vote for you if he tells them to. I can personally guarantee at least five hundred votes for the teacup.' After a brief pause, the man said, 'Myself, I don't want anything. But my father, he's getting old. Last month there was a hospital bill totalling thousands. How can we afford it?'

'Our party will amply reward its supporters,' Giridhar said. 'You must come to Khaireni Tar just before the elections so that we can talk about this in depth.'

It was decided that they would finalize their transactions then.

By the time they left Rishi and the others had covered the whole village with a fresh batch of teacup symbols and party posters.

And again the long, hard walk.

Again odd thoughts came to Giridhar on the trail. Like: if indifference was the matter from which all of creation arose—and really, wasn't the world basically an indifferent place—why did he care so much about himself?

And: being overweight was like carrying death in the body. A morbid thought; he tried to put it aside. Yet that was what it felt like to carry so much inactive flesh as he laboured up steep, sun-soaked hills to the next village and the next.

Always it surprised him, the swell of people who met him in each village. So many villagers were willing to help the teacup party, based on just one speech by Nayan Raj. Giridhar supposed it was good. This public support would build the platform from which he would stand for elections himself next time. But it also annoyed him to see people go agog for the cinema hero. He was forced to parrot Nayan Raj's lines about democratic reform. He was forced to listen to Rishi lecture, again and again, on the People's Party's vision. How could Giridhar not despise Nayan Raj? At each village people kept talking about how full of integrity he was. 'That's what an MP should be like,' elderly men crooned. 'Incorruptible.' Younger men stopped him along the trail to say, 'Eh your candidate talks big. Does he act accordingly?' And before Giridhar could bring himself to say something true and cynical, they answered their own question: 'Seems he will, though. A number one hit cinema hero—he doesn't even brag about himself.'

Even women praised him: 'He helped us carry water from the taps. And he made his workers do the same.'

'That's what all men should be like.'

'Ho yes,' Giridhar said with ironic exaggeration. 'That's what I myself aim to be like.'

From village to village it remained constant, this ludicrous enthusiasm over Nayan Raj. People were basically stupid, Giridhar thought. The literacy rates in these areas were low. There were no televisions, there was no cinema. Folks were easily manipulated by a man who could act.

His own work was strictly pragmatic. Village to village Giridhar cut deals. After a mandatory talk about how illustrious his candidate was, he turned all his attention to gathering real supporters. He sought out past acquaintances who owed him, people who needed connections to a larger world, friends, distant relatives and villagers who'd taken loans from him at the bank. He met them alone, he met them in groups, he assured them about the help they'd receive after the elections, and he convinced them to serve in the People's Party booth committees.

Thanks to Nayan Raj's popularity his work proved easier than expected. Some people wanted jobs in return for their help, others were content with money, and the foolish just wanted to earn prestige by aligning themselves with a cinema hero. In every village there were leaders and power brokers who could guarantee so many votes in return for favours, so many votes in return for cash. This many votes they could command. This many votes they could steal. This many votes they could stuff. These were the rules of war. Giridhar executed his battle plans more smoothly than he'd thought possible. It wasn't difficult to convince seven, eight men to volunteer as committee members for each booth.

With these men he conducted secret meetings. He asked about past elections in these parts, he asked about the hold of the other parties: did they tend to capture booths here, did they intimidate voters, did they resort to violence? What was the best strategy for the teacup party? He sat long hours with the booth committee members, working out the best tactics for their particular booth. An ease came into his body. He knew what he was doing. He listened carefully to what everyone said. And what they said was this: 'All the other parties will be rigging votes.'

After some hesitation they invariably admitted, ' So should we. We'll never win otherwise.' Eventually they said, 'Why should we sit around and watch the other parties loot us of our votes? At the very least we need strong boys to make sure the booth isn't captured.'

Strong boys. Giridhar understood such words. His years at the bank had taught him how to nod at just the right time, showing that he agreed without actually having to say so. He nodded just so when people said, 'We need boys who can help us stand our ground.'

Or, 'A battalion of workers.'

And, 'That settlement, their loyalties have to be bought.'

At the end of these drawn-out meetings Giridhar leaned forward and said in confidential tones: 'I'm going to count on you to see to these important tasks.'

And the men of the booth committees replied, 'We'll count on you to remember us afterwards.'

And it all came back to Giridhar: the lowering of the head, the raising of a brow, the pursing of his lips which indicated that he had made a pact. There was a way of taking in a breath and blinking the eyes that signalled concurrence. There was a movement of the torso that signalled trust. There were ways for him to move. There was a glass of homebrew offered late at night that expressed camaraderie. How could he not drink it? He drank. And he said, casually, 'Let's celebrate our understanding,' which left open the question of what the understanding was. These understandings could grow and grow in people's minds. These were the ways, Giridhar knew, that a chairman made a platform for himself.

He was good. He knew he was good. As he formed one booth committee after another he came alive with gestures. He shrugged, he sighed, he emanated significance with the slightest movements. With a prolonged stare he reminded people of past favours he'd done them. He patted a relative on the back, letting cordiality unloosen formal blood ties. He let his knee rub against the knee of another man. He looked at men directly, or he turned away. Some perfect moments he became all nuance.

Along the trail his disjointed thoughts diminished. Why think of things that weren't useful? Why think of uncertainties, frailness, fear or failure? With growing aplomb he went along with everyone's elevated talk about Nayan Raj. 'Our candidate isn't just an actor, he's a grand philosopher,' he said to villagers. 'He really means what he says.' For the truth was, Nayan Raj was a fake and a fool, and people would see this soon enough. The overly-philosophical timbre of Nayan Raj's voice, the overweening expression on his face when he spoke: how could they take it for real? The man even dyed his hair.

And in the end, what did it matter what people thought about Nayan Raj? The decisive factor was Giridhar's work. What mattered were strategies whispered late at night in smoky kerosene lamp-lit rooms. Rishi was with him, BB-Gun and his gang members were with him. Villagers respected him and saw that he had power to wield. All was in place.

Then two weeks into the tour, as Giridhar made his way out of a village, the blue sky warped.

Rishi, walking a few paces behind, caught Giridhar as he buckled, but the man's weight threw him off. They both landed hard on the ground.

A local party member rushed to their aid. 'It's the heat,' he said, pulling up Giridhar. Giridhar was limp and couldn't walk by himself. As BB-Gun and his gang crowded around to gape, Rishi and the party member supported him back to the party member's house. They laid him on the front porch. The party member said, 'The sun these days is harsh, it drains the body.'

Rishi agreed, 'All this walking has been strenuous.'

'He must drink water.' The party member called a daughter standing by. 'Go fetch a glass of water. Bring a mat, bring a pillow. Your uncle's fallen ill.'

Giridhar's eyes were darting about to assess where he was. The party member kept asking questions: 'Feeling better? Need some more time? The midday sun has too much fire, the body quickly gets parched.' Giridhar didn't reply.

Rishi sat off to the side. He had scraped an arm in the fall, and blood was trickling from a gash at his elbow. He could feel a soft pulse at the cut. Disgust arose in him—not at the blood, but in bleeding for Giridhar—for this.

He'd been sickened by his own work since he'd left Khaireni Tar and entered the villages. Amid the masses, amid those for whom he'd become a communist as a boy, amid the absolute poor he led this counterfiet life... *Will it come*, he'd asked the schoolmaster in his student days: will the revolution come? And the schoolmaster had replied in the voice of the poets: *It'll come spreading brilliance like the morning sun . . .*

A mockery.

Lying to those who'd once inspired him to revolutionary fervour, he now followed a drunken master whose goal was to rig elections in his own favour. He was abetting an unscrupulous man who played his power over the poor. When Giridhar whispered into the night with members of the booth committees he sounded exactly as the schoolmaster had, years ago. The same low tones of secrecy, the same muffled accord, the same hums of evasion: like something Rishi had lived through in a previous life. He hated where he was and wanted to extinguish his being here. But he was a good comrade. He had watched Giridhar meeting people, coaxing, wheedling, negotiating, cutting deals. He'd kept notes of all he'd overheard, he'd jotted down the names of booth committee members, he'd written down strategies and diagrammed plots. Giridhar, oblivious to all but his own ambitions, hadn't even noticed when Rishi began sitting in on booth committee meetings. He hadn't noticed when Rishi started to take notes in a copy book. Rishi's presence hadn't registered at all with him.

Giridhar fell asleep on the porch as the party member fussed and clucked. BB-Gun and his gang watched on, entertained, it seemed, by the spectacle. The afternoon deepened, and the sun reached the western hills.

From the courtyard of the party member's house the himals were visible. Rishi sat and watched the mountains at sundown: a senseless abundance of rock and snow for those who dreamed of arable land. There were blue hills between here and there, and settlements scattered over the distance. As the himals took on the last deep oranges of the setting sun, village windows in the distance lit up with dim kerosene lamps. Deceptively pastoral villages at a time of the globe: this was a land of peasants dreaming of foreign goods, foreign enlistment, foreign currency—and slouching towards citizenship. Who was bothered with the poor inhabiting the world's peripheries? Not the parties who'd brought democracy: their futures were mangled by the past. Not any lofty international. And not independent leftists like him. Rishi, a good comrade, brooded: after communism, anarchy.

The next morning Rishi watched over Giridhar, who lay rigidly on the straw mat with his eyes closed and his forehead knitted. Sometimes Giridhar fluttered open his eyes, and at other times he drew his lips into a grimace. He seemed to have bloated. There was a blue-grey pallor to his skin. He lay stiffly, as though at attention.

'I've seen it before,' said the local party member, dabbing

Giridhar's face with a moist rag. 'Bazaar men underestimate the sun—they've never felt its fire. A day's rest and he'll be all right.'

Rishi nodded as though in sympathy, but everything about Giridhar repulsed him.

He left the porch and went to the party member's front courtyard. BB-Gun and his gang were lolling there, admiring the view of the himals. Rishi avoided their closed-off circle. They'd herded together throughout the trip, and this suited Rishi. He was supposed to supervise them, but they ignored him and he ignored them, and this was fine.

He gathered some posters and picked up a container of gelled rice. Choosing a boulder on the side of the party member's house, he pasted a poster there, with a photograph of Nayan Raj in blue. VOTE FOR THE TEACUP. He pasted another poster on a nearby wall, then another one on the back of a house. VOTE FOR THE TEACUP. The day was hot, with a scorching sun welded into the deep blue sky. A stultifying lowland wind shifted indolently. The village's clay huts wavered in mirages. As he put up posters Rishi was strangely aware that he was in BB-Gun's field of vision; there was a theatricality to his actions. He felt like a bad actor on a poorly set stage—all performance and no conviction. His steps were light as he walked, and it occurred to him that he was free to walk away, right now, and leave behind all this subterfuge. Choices. In two days he could be back by the highway. He could avoid Khaireni Tar and catch a bus to Kathmandu and put all this behind him.

At the foot of a small hill he was drawn by a distant sight: at the top of the hill a boy was painting over one of the teacup symbols that he had painted yesterday. The boy had wiped out the cup and was turning its rim into a spoke-edged UML sun. Little wastage of paint: his design was good. Rishi climbed midway up the hill, watching the boy.

The UML worker finished painting one sun, then began

erasing another teacup. The cup disappeared and the rim began to turn into a sun. The boy must be following the itinerary Rishi had given Shankar in Khaireni Tar. Giridhar's illness had thrown everything off schedule. Ideally Rishi wouldn't be here, now, to witness this erasure.

A few spiky rays on the edges produced another UML sun. A quick emotion flashed through Rishi: envy. The boy was working openly for his party. While here he was, an impostor.

Overcome by disgust he tossed the remaining posters of Nayan Raj into a nearby ditch. The UML worker was now erasing a third teacup. Rishi wanted to go up to him, take the brush from his hand and complete his task himself. Choices. He headed up the cobbled path.

Then he heard a cry. Both he and the UML worker turned. BB-Gun and his gang members were standing at the bottom of the hill, shouting.

Rishi didn't even have to think about what he had to do. He strode to the UML worker, taking him by surprise. He was just a boy. Rishi reached for his shirt and pushed him against the red sun he'd just painted. 'You're ruining our sign.'

The boy picked himself up, and took a few steps back. BB-Gun and his gang remained at the bottom of the hill, watching. The UML boy studied Rishi's face, looking uncertain about what to do. Rishi too faltered. He hated what was happening.

Awkwardly the boy stooped for his can of paint, but then he suddenly lunged forward and pushed Rishi, sending him reeling by a tree stump. A can toppled over and red paint splattered over Rishi's shoes. The boy began to pull away, but now Rishi reached for him.

The boy lashed back with every intention to harm. He struck Rishi against the cheek, then wrestled him to the ground, his legs a squish of flesh, but surprisingly forceful. Rishi tried to push him away, but the boy's elbows jammed his ribs. He felt a pummeling at the sides. By the time he thought to grab the boy's hands the boy was being pulled away by BB-Gun. 'Let him go, let go, we'll have a go now.'

Outnumbered the UML worker recoiled as BB-Gun hulked over him. 'Eh corpse,' BB-Gun said in a casual drawl. 'You want to see your father's wedding?'

Rishi crawled away to the sound of dull thuds.

When Giridhar came to attention later that day, all the workers were buzzing with excitement. Apparently there had been a fight and Rishi had beaten a UML boy and the whole village had been in an uproar. A meeting had taken place, and the village elders had denounced both the UML and the People's Party. Eh. This was serious. But Giridhar was thinking that if he could get a few swigs of homebrew he'd feel much more fit and sound. Because after his vision of warping sky it wasn't clear if he could go on. The floor of the party member's house undulated when he moved. The wood beams in the ceiling wavered, and the heavy air resisted him. He had a persistent pain on the right side of his belly. There were difficulties that he needed to allay. Around him people were saying things that he should pay attention to—the UML wasn't playing fair, they shouldn't touch other parties' signs and posters, they went seeking trouble—but all Giridhar really wanted was a sip of strong homebrew.

How many days had passed? It was after nightfall now, and they'd moved into the main room of the house, where the party member had set up a few makeshift beds. BB-Gun and his gang remained on the porch. Rishi had a cut to his face from the fight, and he moved slowly. He said little about the fight.

'We must give our two invalids a night of peace,' the party member said.

A few other local party supporters had come to visit. They

agreed, 'Our chairmanji will be walking tomorrow. We must give him a night of peace.'

With all the will he could muster, Giridhar sat up and attempted an offhand kind of buoyancy. 'Are we so sick that we need to sit around like corpses?' Inside he felt gutted. He said, 'We'll get worse if we're treated like corpses waiting to be burned by the riverside.'

One of the members of the booth committee said, 'That's true, the sick need to laugh, they heal faster that way. The more you mope the worse you get.'

Why was it that when he wanted alcohol it took so much effort to talk as though he didn't need a drink? Giridhar nudged his host. 'Look, get us a glass each of homebrew and let's celebrate our victories ahead. Otherwise we're already mourning defeat.'

The party member guffawed. 'My wife brewed a batch yesterday.'

Giridhar smiled briefly. Rishi was sitting near by. The boy was always so inward, so serious. He always seemed lost in thought. But now Rishi turned, and for a while he held Giridhar's gaze. Something—not accusation, but something similar—got communicated. Giridhar looked away guiltily. Everyone knew he was a drunk.

But when the homebrew came Rishi came to sit beside Giridhar and poured himself the fullest glass. Giridhar tried to focus on the party member's explanation about why the party needn't worry about a small squabble with the UML. 'The members of our booth committee are a-hundred-and-one per cent solid. We'll do what it takes to make us win.' That was all very well, but Giridhar was distracted by the fact that Rishi, beside him, was drinking so fast. Each time Giridhar looked in his direction the boy—man, what, he must be thirty, thirty-five?—seemed to be pouring himself a refill and topping off Giridhar's glass as well.

How astonishing that Giridhar had never identified this thirst in the boy before. Of course. His quietness: the boy's withdrawn manners came from a secret need for drink.

As the evening wore on the men began to lose their focus and to slur their thoughts. Propped up by alcohol Giridhar stopped doubting himself. He felt stable enough to sit forward in his bedding, the pain in his belly overcome by a tingling in his blood, a loosening of joints. He enjoyed the bravado of the party members' gay words: 'If they try to steal our votes, ke, we'll pull out our khukuris!'

'They won't even dare when they see how popular we are!'

'They'll see that we're serious and they won't dare!'

Two rounds, three, four rounds inspired increasingly voluble speculations of victory. 'We can get all the votes if we hire the right boys!'

'Just a dozen.'

'Not even.'

Words without weight which flew skyward, boosting the mind. Giridhar felt confidence surge through him, a confidence made more urgent by the threat of ill fortune lurking. It was vital to squeeze solace out of life.

Rishi poured himself another drink and filled Giridhar's empty glass.

Eh, Giridhar thought. This boy was useful to have.

After that day Rishi slipped into an intimacy with Giridhar that was entirely of his own manipulation. The next day, despite everyone's doubts, Giridhar declared that he was ready to continue the tour. They set off in the morning to avoid the midday heat. From what Rishi could see, Giridhar still wasn't sure on his feet. Rishi too felt a tenderness in his ribs. Giridhar seemed to need reassurance, and as they walked he kept turning back to keep an eye on him. A few times he even spoke to Rishi, offering the kinds of words he must have thought Rishi wanted to hear: 'The UML boys might seek retaliation. You'll be safer if you remain by me, Bhai.' They held no mass meetings in the afternoon. When they settled into a party member's house at night Giridhar suggested that Rishi and he sleep in the same room. Feebly he joked, 'We two invalids must stay together.' Later, in his meeting with volunteers for the local booth committee, Giridhar made space for Rishi by his side.

Rishi knew it was alcohol Giridhar wanted. Each night he obediently poured alcohol, first into his own glass and then casually into Giridhar's. Barley beer, rice alcohol, thick brews of fermented grains: he poured and poured, serving his drunken master. 'Mero bhai,' Giridhar started to call him affectionately. My younger brother. 'Mero bhai, come and sit beside me.'

And in the forgiving clarity that intoxication brought, Rishi thought: Giridhar's need for him was genuine. An absurdly incompetent man, Giridhar was unable to contain his wants, and grasped desperately for a salve. Some nights when Rishi had made no move to procure him a drink Giridhar sat looking at him with an expression of confusion, as though he didn't know what to do to appease the gods of drink. Rishi was less disgusted by him than he had been. The man was pitiable.

And he?

He'd been brought down to the brutal world of flesh attacking flesh.

As the tour progressed in a haze of inebriation the nightly booth committee meetings reduced to a hush of voices in Rishi's mind. He tried to follow discussions, but felt lazy. He hardly took notes any more. Sitting beside Giridhar he thought coldly that it was dangerous, the feeling of being let in. It was so transfixing that it obscured the question: being let into what? His dislike of Giridhar had lessened only because the man made room for him. He even, sometimes, worried for Giridhar. The man still wasn't at ease. No matter how confidently he talked—and there were times, during late-night meetings, when he sounded impressively clear—he remained abnormally withdrawn. He always walked alone, and rarely uttered more than a word to anyone other than Rishi. Sometimes he even seemed mad. Once, when the trail was blocked by stacks of harvested rice, Giridhar paced skittishly, muttering, 'It's a small thing, it's a small thing,' as though any small problem might avalanche into disaster.

Rishi helped the man through such times. Then at night, if he was sober enough, he would betray the same man, jotting down notes on his work. Did it matter what he did any more? If he didn't betray Giridhar he'd betray the schoolmaster. If he didn't betray the schoolmaster he'd betray Giridhar. Either way he was betraying himself, erasing himself with either choice.

His handheld radio ran out of batteries eventually. No new ones could be bought in these parts. With no news of the rest of the world to give him a larger perspective, Rishi went from village to village in a state of inebriation, helping prepare to rig elections—and serving, in this way, the cause of revolution. How? With an elliptical, self-serving logic. It had become counterfeit, his communism.

A long and very indistinct age after leaving Khaireni Tar, Giridhar returned to his home town in triumph. There were some aspects of the campaign that were out of control, he knew. Rishi's fight with the UML worker: not good. And the budget to pay off the booth committee members, the local headmen, and hooligans: he had yet to calculate the costs. Ho, there were uncertainties. Tremors sometimes shot through him. The threat of the ground suddenly opening beneath him was real. But in the end—when it mattered the most—he would prevail. He was no less capable than that cinema hero. He had proved it with thirty-three booth committees and all the strategies worked out.

As he walked into Khaireni Tar the dusty town looked quietly welcoming. The town would give him his due. 'You go ahead, inform the candidate we've arrived.' With a wave he sent BB-Gun's gang ahead—these mindless bazaar boys bursting with tales of their village exploits. Rishi, Giridhar kept by him. Rishi he wanted with him, still. Rishi had helped him through hard times, and for this the boy deserved a few pegs' reward.

By the time they reached the southern end the sun was down and the crickets were beginning to chirp; soon they would screech like irate wives. But this evening was meant for celebration.

'Come.' Giridhar lead Rishi into a derelict lodge next to the ashen flatlands. Rishi-bhai's presence made it easier to enter the lodge. People wouldn't assume he'd come to drink.

Inside, he greeted the lodge owner, a young woman with long, elegant bones. 'Bahini, a glass of your best for my Rishi-bhai and me.'

The woman smiled coyly. 'It's been months, Dai. We thought you'd become a big man now and forgotten all your friends.'

Giridhar said, 'I've had too much to do.'

The woman nodded towards the inner room. 'Some of your own people are inside.'

Giridhar headed to the inner room and saw, past the door, the Agriculture Officer. A gathering of friends. He was cheered to see the Sub-Inspector too, and forgot at once about Rishi. 'Eh turnip, ullu ko pattha,' he said, sliding into the terms of their long and feral friendship, 'you going to keep the juice all to yourself?'

Rishi sat at the table and waited to be introduced by his Giridhar-dai to the Sub-Inspector and Agriculture Officer, but Giridhar was busy protesting his undying loyalty to his friends—'I've had hardly a drop all these months, it's enough to drive a man mad.'

Drinks came—no orders for cheap homebrew when there could be Everest Whisky or Khukuri Rum drunk neat. The men started on topics that excluded Rishi—each speaking of his woes, caring little whether the others were listening. Tales of long hours, arduous work, demanding wives and ungrateful children. Tales of their sacrifices, talk of their fortunes, small brags and claims.

Rishi sat amid these companion strangers, not touching his drink. He no longer wanted oblivion. He wanted the schoolmaster now. The Dashain and Tihar festivals were coming up: the schoolmaster would come to meet him at his home.

Home was a difficult place, though, a stubborn anachronism. For Rishi, now, all places were hard to be in. Khaireni Tar—the dormitory room, the teashop. His pathetic happiness at being noticed by a woman he hardly knew. Perhaps he could return to Kathmandu. Choices. If he could be anyone he wanted . . . It was no use thinking. He didn't know anymore.

He felt in his shirt for the copy book in which he'd taken notes on Giridhar's deeds: the document of his excellent work for the masses. He wished he could just disappear. For him who loathed himself all places were hard to be in.

41

Madhu returned to her tasks one by one. She began to fetch water again, to sweep Binita-didi's house and teashop, to collect grass for the buffaloes, and even to accompany the other girls to the hills north of town in order to cut firewood. With increasing regularity she helped serve party workers their meals. She wasn't the same girl she used to be, though. She felt moody much of the time, and she often had ungracious thoughts. She heard once, in

the teashop, that thanks to his mita-father Om Gurung, the Khadka
boy had found employment in Nayan Raj-kaka's party: and she
sneered at the thought. A party peon! The lunatic boy wasn't fit
to be a doorkeeper! He'd never have gotten a job if he hadn't
used his mita-father's connections.

Then, another day, Madhu heard from some girls that
Gaumati was fixed to marry the steely-armed Rawal boy; and
she raged against her old friend as a traitor, a schemer and a
cheat. How could Gaumati have gotten the Rawal boy—when
she wasn't half as beautiful as Madhu, and nowhere as flawless
in character? Gaumati was obviously a whore: she had ensnared
a choice boy using the most vulgar wiles!

While she herself languished.

A wild urge sometimes took hold of Madhu, a longing which
had no particular aim, an inquietude so strong she felt she couldn't
get through the day without screaming at someone, shaking
something. She wanted to go away somewhere, do something—
she didn't quite know what. She was falling behind.

And so one day she slipped away and stole across the highway
towards the bazaar. She felt compelled to wander. A bus had
pulled into the bus stop at the bar-peepal tree, and vendors were
swarming to the windows. Beyond, groups of boys stared
impassively out of party offices. Men and women were scuttling
by. People were tending to their inscrutable, unknowable lives.
What did they do, all these people?

She turned into an alley and found herself in front of a medical
shop. Without any forethought she stepped inside.

An old man was moping in a corner.

She said, 'I want to get better. I'm sick.'

The man looked pained. 'Don't take precautions in time,
illnesses ripen,' he droned. 'You have to come to town you have
to buy medicine and spend money but what's the use if you don't
take precautions.' He frowned deeply. 'Sit.'

Her heart pounding, Madhu chose a shady corner bench beside a shelf crammed with dust-covered bottles. At the prodding of the old man, she stuck out her tongue.

The man peered into her mouth. 'Gastroenteritis indigestion acidity and ulcers, you neglect your health you'll need operations. Tapeworms ringworms hookworms and stomach bugs. Fevers shock shivering shaking quaking hallucinating. Can't prevent you have to treat. Antacids deworming pills vitamins minerals nutritional supplements. A girl who's anaemic. Iron tablets. Costly? Let an illness ripen its treatment gets expensive such are the basic principles of primary health.'

So many illnesses breeding inside her! Madhu's heart was set racing.

The man got up and shuffled to a shelf, and took out a glittering array of medical objects: a bottle of pig-pink lotion and another dark syrup, several sheaves of pills and a plastic bottle. He placed the whole display on the countertop. 'This one thrice a day at six-hour intervals this one four times a day at three-hour intervals this one twice a day only after food this one two spoons once a day this one one spoon a day and the rest once a day. Never on an empty stomach. Never take less than prescribed. Dizziness may result. You forget a dose you'll have to repeat the whole treatment again and if this doesn't work there's no choice but to operate.' He sighed. 'The cost is two fifty.'

'Two fifty!'

The man shrugged. 'Two forty, then. Special discount for you.'

Madhu had no money. Perhaps she'd finagle some medicine for free? She wrung her hands in a show of despair. 'Poor folks like us, how can we dole out money for so much medicine? Are they even needed? Who knows? We live in darkness. We have no choice but to believe what we're told.' She was fascinated by her own words. Where had she learned to talk like this?

Unmoved, the old man droned, 'You don't take the medicine we'll have to operate for that you'll have to go to a hospital. Hospital bills transportation medical fees and extra charges. You want to heal, do as I say.' He thrust out a hand, looking morose. 'Final price two thirty.'

Madhu stared at the thrust-out hand. There was no use wasting her efforts on a man as stubborn as this. She said, 'And if I don't have any money right now? Can I come back with the payment?'

'You can come back.'

'I'll come back, then.'

Madhu left the shop feeling strangely elated. She would ask Binita-didi for some money and come back for the medicine. She should roam the bazaar more often. Yes, she should roam the bazaar.

trajectories

42

By the time of the Dashain and Tihar festivals Khaireni Tar resembled a tatty old notebook used by a schoolchild for handwriting exercises. There were posters and flyers stuck on every free wall, their edges fluttering in the wind. Torn banners hung from the trees and dangled from light poles, blocking out the sky. Crudely painted slogans were visible everywhere, the same messages repeated over and over: Vote for the tree! Vote for the sun! Vote for the plough! Vote for the house! Vote for the teacup!

The air, though, was crisp, and smelled of freshly threshed grains. There were the echoing tuk-tuk sounds of diesel-fuelled threshing mills in the distance. The terraced fields surrounding the town had all been harvested. It was autumn. In the front yards of the bazaar's houses bright marigolds were in bloom: and from this alone it felt like the festivals had arrived.

Beneath the bar-peepal tree the banana vendor was finishing his stock of local bananas and beginning to hawk Indian fruits: 'Bananas so large they make a whole meal!' The peanut vendor and the cheeseballs-and-chips vendor continued to push their all-season wares. Business was slowing, though. The party workers who had poured into Khaireni Tar in the past few months were leaving, one by one, to celebrate the festivals with their families in the hills. The party offices were all but closed, the schools and government offices had shut, and only a few men loitered any more in the bazaar. Instead, the townsmen were busy seeking out distant relatives and long-lost acquaintances and catching up on gossip—who married whom this year, who gave birth to a son or daughter, who went abroad, who came back, who earned, who lost, who passed away. They reviewed their harvest yields, they reminisced about shared yesterdays, they renewed allegiances and spoke sentimentally about all that was good and gone all that was bad about these fast-changing times. And they indulged in the favourite pastime of the season ...they gambled with cowry shells, they rolled dice for games of pasa, they moved pieces for the board game bagh-chal, and they shuffled one after another card game, making increasingly reckless bids.

With the men cleared from the bazaar the Musalmaan bangle seller finally started doing brisk business. For while the town's men gambled, the women combed the bazaar's shops for new clothes for their families. What Chinese rayons had come to the market this year, what Indian cottons, what imported gabardines and wools? With their purchases tucked under their arms the women fingered all the other tempting items on sale—shoes and belts, lipsticks and nailpolish—'But who would wear *blue* polish?'—and they haggled over the price of handkerchiefs and hair oils and scents. On their way back home they invariably stopped by the bangle seller's stall.

'These look like they'll break the first time I wear them.'

'Have I ever sold shoddy wares, baba?'

The bazaar was also taken over by out-of-school children running ragged, chewing sticks of sugarcane. Bands of boys and girls wove in and out of alleys inventing fierce new games. 'First one to that tree gets to hit everyone!' Some of the older boys had put together a roti-ping ferris wheel in the flatlands, and long queues formed as children waited their turn. Those who ran out of patience pieced together crude kites from polythene bags and spent their days trying to make them catch the wind.

This year there was some confusion in the Gurung and Magar families of the town about whether or not to celebrate Dashain and Tihar. In his rousing speeches the candidate of the ethnic rights Janamukti party had stirred much sentiment against Hindu subjugation of minority religions. Many Gurung and Magar families felt it was time to return to their roots. 'We're Buddhist in origin,' said some, citing as proof the way they turned to Buddhist lamas for death rites. 'That's what historians say nowadays, we were originally from Tibet, and Buddhist in faith.'

'No, we're animists,' said others. 'Our people are indigenous to this land, we were Bon-po long before we became Buddhist. We worshipped nature. We prayed to trees, rivers and rocks.'

'It isn't a question of what we are but a matter of what we aren't,' said those who felt it more urgent to oppose the Hindu hegemony than to bicker about hoary origins. 'It's clear that we weren't originally Hindu, so we must boycott Dashain-Tihar.'

Then there were others, like Om. Om believed that there were surely powers greater than he, but he wasn't chained to any particular religion. Believing the country's diversity to be its most wonderful asset, he supported the resurgence of pride in ethnic identity, but he wondered, nevertheless, if it wasn't a bit, well, unhappy to stop celebrating the festivals that his family had observed for generations. 'Why rebel now against hundreds-of-years-old oppressions?' he mumbled good-naturedly, neither able to dismiss the call of the Janamukti candidate nor willing to accept it. This year Asha's whole family was boycotting the festivals. Om said, 'The festivals aren't about religion, they're about getting together and enjoying the company of one's near and dear.'

But Asha felt it was important to prove allegiance to one's own people. 'Ethnic minorities must stop stooping before Chettri-Bahuns,' she declared with a firmness Om knew he could never match. 'All the bazaar's Gurung families are saying let's be proud of who we are, let's not celebrate Dashain-Tihar. All over the country not just Gurungs—but Sherpas, Tamangs, Magars, Rais, Limbus—are asserting their identities. But you, love, want to pretend you're a Chettri-Bahun.'

'Tch, love, don't call me Chettri-Bahun.'

'You've agreed then?'

Om wasn't yet willing to concede. 'So we'll sit gloomily as the rest of the country celebrates?' The thought of the festivals vanishing from his life was strange. 'While all the people around us enjoy the company of their loved ones and bless each other, while everyone feasts on wonderful meals—we'll just sit and look at each other? The children . . .' He gestured towards the sitting room. His sons and daughter, on leave from school, were watching television with their mita-brother Harsha Bahadur. 'And our mita-son is Chettri-Bahun. How can we deny him his Dashain-Tihar?'

But Asha remained firm. 'We mustn't tolerate our continued oppression by the Hindu majority,' she said, echoing the Janamukti candidate's words exactly. 'How proud our peoples were before Chettri-Bahun domination. We must honour our glorious pasts. All over the world minority populations are asserting their rights. But we here in Nepal remain happy to be discriminated against.'

Then she stopped and glanced towards the hallway. 'It's true that the children will want to eat well at festival time,' she conceded. 'We could cut a goat. There's no harm in that. And I was planning to buy the children new clothes.' She smiled. 'We could still invite our relatives, couldn't we? We could do everything but actually celebrate the festivals, love.'

'Yes, let's do something celebratory, love.'

'La, all right, that much we can do.'

Elsewhere, the Hindu households of the town were bustling with activity. At Jimmawal-baaje's house, a family of Damai caste tailors was busy sewing clothes for the old man, his wives and their considerable progeny. Push-pedal sewing machines whirred in a frenzy of stitching. Meanwhile Jimmawal-baaje sat on a straw mat in his front porch listening to the pleas of all the impoverished wretches who'd borrowed money from him and wanted their interests pardoned. The old man's frail health forced him to keep lying down, though. He was experiencing an imbalance of the digestive fires; how he'd suffered these past few months. It had all begun with a simple upset stomach. Then his mouth had become ulcerated, his skin had developed rashes, and soon he couldn't take a morsel of food without having to run to the outhouse. He'd dutifully ingested the bitter herbs and metal ashes prepared by a trusted ayurbeda baidhya, but his stars were badly lined. The illness had proved intractable. By now the spleen was aflame, and the excess wind in his system was causing his attention to fly and his hands to shake. It seemed that all the bitter herbs in the world and all the metal ashes couldn't douse the anger in his blood.

Still, it was important to do one's duty without attachment to the results. Niskama kama. The town's cobbler was one of many who had taken loans from Jimmawal-baaje. Despite the innocent expression on the cobbler's rusty face he was sly, Jimmawal-baaje knew: it was said that he'd taken money from cow-eating Christian missionaries to hail their foggy white god. 'Eh generous merchant,' the cobbler pleaded in front of Jimmawal-baaje, 'the mealy bugs ate half my landlord's harvest this year; my share won't feed my family for three months. I try to make a living mending shoes but no one repairs shoes any more, they just go to the stores and buy new ones. My pockets are empty, hajoor. I beg you, cancel my interest this year.'

'Cancel your interest I can't.' Jimmawal-baaje dismissed his plea with a wave of the hand. 'But it's true that it's festival time and I'm a religion-minded man, so I'll let you pay this month's interest at the beginning of next month. Go now, can't you see that I'm seriously, seriously ill? It aggravates the spleen to hear your miserable moans and complaints.'

The cobbler bowed deeply in mock gratitude. And Jimmawal-baaje, pleased with his own benevolence, sat back and pontificated to his seventh son: 'At this time of Dashain, when Mother Kali defeated the demon Mahisasur, good must triumph over evil.'

'Good will triumph,' said his son.

Not far away, in his house attached to his sprawling wood mill, Chiranjibi spent Dashain time wondering how to reach an understanding with his brother, who was by now displaying unmistakable frustration at his neglect of family business. Of course his brother had been too deferential to actually voice any resentment. But ever since Chiranjibi had returned from the village-to-village campaign he had noticed a tightness in his brother's expression, and he'd realized that he must now account for his newfound—love?—no, commitment to Nayan Raj.

But how to explain the way he'd been suffused with the light of a pure ideal?

The only way was to speak. Speak to his brother?

He must speak.

For a few days Chiranjibi followed his brother around the house, waiting for the right opportunity. His brother seemed to sense that he was trying to communicate. He slowed to let Chiranjibi remain in his company. He lingered to allow him to speak. He waited, he dallied, he paused. Still Chiranjibi didn't know how to begin. Just blurt and babble like an idiot? How could he?

Just speak.

'It looks like I'll have to give up my share of profits from this year's work,' he finally said one evening, as his brother tallied the profits of the completed school building. They were at the teak desk in the woodmill, surrounded by a batch of freshly cut redwood planks. Chiranjibi's brother was turned away from him, which made it easier to talk. Chiranjibi said, 'I haven't done enough work to justify taking profits this year.'

His brother maintained a steady, consenting silence. To hide his discomfort, perhaps, he continued to add up figures. Looking at him, Chiranjibi felt sorry for him. A man passing his life counting figures. Was this what his brother wanted? Did days of calculation suffice? Chiranjibi said, 'It might be best if we make public that we're no longer partners. That way my politics won't interfere with your livelihood.'

His brother looked up from his papers, flashed Chiranjibi an agreeing look, then turned back to his accounts. But how unfortunate a figure his brother cut, counting and counting. How devoid of joy was his life, how—impoverished.

'Come my age,' Chiranjibi added, 'a man wants to start doing things that fulfil the soul.'

His brother shot him a quizzical look. But Chiranjibi couldn't restrain himself. He said, 'All these years you and I grew up in the bazaar, in privilege. You should have seen the villages we went to.' He took off his glasses and put them on the black surface of the teak desk. This made it easier to talk. 'One person after another, one person after another, all participating freely in an act of government. One, one, one, one person. Each with separate dreams and desires.' He fumbled for a pack of Yaks and pulled out one stick. But he forgot to light it. 'Look,' he said to the blurred and out-of-focus figure of his brother. 'I've made enough to eat well, live in comfort, educate my daughters. At a certain point in a man's life he wants to stop thinking about worldly matters, he wants to do what's finally right. You know,' he pointed at him with the cigarette, 'you should think about it too. This life,' he gestured vaguely, 'all these unfinished wood planks, they get turned into things like this desk, so polished, so fine. In the same way democracy is crafted out of unfinished people. All those unfinished people—there's a gleaming vision they'll become part of.'

For a long while the blurred figure of his brother said nothing. Then he reached for Chiranjibi's glasses. 'The watchmaker must have fine screws,' he said, examining the Sellotape. It seemed to Chiranjibi that he was trying, awkwardly, to respond as best he knew how. 'I can take these to him and have them repaired.'

'That would be helpful,' Chiranjibi said. 'There are times when it becomes a bother.'

To his surprise his brother didn't end the conversation there. 'I'll take it to the watchmaker tomorrow.'

'I've been meaning to fix it for years.'

'One fine screw is all it'll take.'

'You think the watchmaker can do it?'

'I think so. Just one fine screw. I'll take it to him.'

'That would be extremely helpful.'

'It's no trouble at all.'

In his house on the hills north of town, Giridhar was spending festival time reacquainting himself with long lost drinking pals. The Sub-Inspector and a few other government employees came to his house every day to play gin rummy and flash and marriage, and to gossip about the People's Party. 'Surprising how big an impact your candidate's made. Everyone's charmed,' they said, throwing back stiff pegs of whisky and rum.

'The Congress, UML will be amazed at the numbers of votes they'll lose.'

'Thought they'd inherited the country, they did. They'll see!'

To Giridhar, surrounded by old pals, it felt like a long time of exertion since the announcement of elections. He felt taken back to his years of unemployment—which had afforded their own kind of crashing, careening fun, hadn't they? Now he sat in tight circles of nudging, cajoling, bantering, smoking, guffawing, knee-slapping men, some intense in their pursuit of card-game victory, others more interested in lively, garrulous talk—'Have you noticed that all the Hindi movie heroines wear hot pants beneath their mini-skirts?'

His wife Laksmi applied herself to serving fresh rice flour

sel-roti and frittered bara. Giridhar's sons sat beside their father, placing fifty-paise bets on his cards. The Sub-Inspector entertained everyone with vociferous complaints about his younger wife, whom he was already tiring of. 'She's so spoilt she acts like a queen.'

At this someone said, 'The only way to solve that is to act like a king.'

The Sub-Inspector let out a long, indecent chuckle.

Giridhar radiated a drunken smile.

But it wasn't all easy for Giridhar, no. Since his return from the hills he was sometimes numbed by a malaise which eventually distilled into dread. One day he stayed in his room all day, focusing on the minutiae outside the window: a patch of rogue thistles, the fluttering of a dragonfly's wings, a millipede slinking on the window pane. He drank all morning to ward off apprehension. But even as his arms and legs tingled with rum-sodden strength, he could see that no matter how confident he acted in public he was faking it. That whole day his blood flowed sluggishly in his veins. He heard his wife calling. She knew he was hollow. She said don't drink. Her words were euphemisms.

Underneath everything there was a bloodier pustule of sense: bile and sloughed-off skin. Giridhar's body felt rotten. He stayed in his room for days, alone. When he slept his mind was free. Awake, he trained narrowly on the present. This cotton rug here, weighing on his chest. Those water stains on the ceiling. That light bulb blackened with dust. Steady.

For Binita festivals were always a mean time of exclusion. Even the regular customers abandoned the teashop and in the empty hours she was forced to confront her isolation. A woman without a family. This was the price she had paid for love. This year, though, people still swarmed to the house so long as her brother-in-law remained in town. Local townsmen posted all over the country had returned home for the festivals, and they dropped by to meet the cinema hero who was wooing their votes. Far-off relatives too came to talk to their clan's most famous son.

Binita had come to like Nayan Raj-bhai. To her his sensitivity didn't seem put on. By now Nayan Raj-bhai had picked up on subtle family dynamics, and he found ways to keep Kainlo-kaka from the teashop. When Kainlo-kaka did come, with his army of relatives, Nayan Raj-bhai treated Binita with special courtesy, signalling to them his respect for her.

Binita liked having Nayan Raj-bhai in the house. But then, a few days before Dashain, he left to spend festival time with his wife and children in Kathmandu. Pramila left soon after that to be with her family. The house and teashop suddenly emptied of people, and Binita listened in shock to the padding of individual footsteps as she made her way around. She heard the silence surrounding each utterance by herself, by Madhu, by Tripti. A sober gathering of mother and child and orphaned cousin: this was what the festivals meant for her.

She reacted badly to this silence, several times losing her temper for no reason at all. She couldn't bear the quietness this year. For her there were no families to visit at festival time. For her there were no visitors. This was the hushed ostracism awaiting her if her brother-in-law were to lose the elections and leave Khaireni Tar.

She decided to force this Dashain to be different. Surely this wasn't impossible? On the day of Dashain teeka she put on the silk fariya her brother-in-law had brought when he first came. She saw in a hand mirror that it suited her. By some lights it took on the liquid shades of deep water or the fur of wet moss. She liked the way it looked on her.

Even Madhu seemed pleased to dress well for the festival. She and Tripti wore identical rayon kurtha-sural sets stitched by a local tailor. Madhu also put on the red sweater that Nayan

Raj-bhai had brought for her, and she spent a long time examining herself in the hand mirror.

Once they were all dressed Binita laid out tender green wheat sprouts and vermilion, and a container of yellow teeka for herself. At the time deemed auspicious for blessings she offered teeka to a picture of the goddess Durga, then put teeka on herself and the girls.

After their meal they headed to Kainlo-kaka's house across the Seti river. The three of them walking to meet relatives presented a warm picture. The day was bright, the breeze cool. The flatlands were cracked dry, and though the expanse was uncultivated, it smelled of hay. Binita let herself enjoy the feel of Dashain, she pretended that she was walking towards an extended family which welcomed her. Tripti ran ahead, eager to reach the river. Madhu charged after the girl, and Binita was glad to see the girls laughing. But as they crossed the Seti's waters, Binita began to get nervous. She braced for a visit which she knew would be unpleasant. For Madhu and Tripti's sake, she forced herself to believe that questions of belonging were answered yes. For the meanwhile, yes.

It took over an hour to get to Kainlo-kaka's house, far beyond the river. The settlement around it was sparser than she remembered, and several houses looked abandoned. Kainlo-kaka's house stood out in the cluster, washed with fresh red clay for the festivals. There were relatives swarming about, and Binita bowed before each one. No one hid their surprise at seeing her: 'You came this year? Finally you remembered us?'

As everyone looked on, she, in her green silk fariya, bent to receive Kainlo-kaka's teeka. Her whole body went rigid to feel his fingers on her forehead. She balked at his mumbled blessings: 'May you fulfil your dharma. Keep the gods in your heart. Find solace in piety.' Binita tried to stay defiant, inside, as she stooped at his feet.

It was only after she stood up again that she was overcome

by disgust. Was it worth enduring this humiliation for the appearance of fitting in?

As Kainlo-kaka went on to bless Madhu and Tripti, Binita stood aside watchfully, trying not to let her fears overtake her. But it was difficult to stay calm in this fortress of family power. A lone woman had no protection here. This was the place where she had been violated and shown absolute contempt. This was the place from where she'd retreated, looking for safety. She was still looking for safety. Safety, always.

May you fulfil your dharma.

This wasn't the place for her.

43

A room in an empty office building; rows of mattresses, each one smelling of use: Rishi's place. A cold blue light filtered in from the window. It could be any day, anyplace, anytime. But it was Khaireni Tar, it was the day of Dashain teeka. The party's driver, who had been Rishi's one constant companion in the dormitory, had gone home to Kathmandu. No one else had stayed on. Till a few days before Dashain the peon Harsha Bahadur came every morning, and after sitting quietly all day in the upstairs office room he left at four. Sometimes Om Gurung would come to supervise him. Now no one came at all.

Rishi had his radio for company, but it had become painful to listen to headlines about Dashain. 'Families all over the nation are gathering for the festivals': the blare of the norm drowning out his difference. For some days now Rishi had stopped going to Binita's teashop. He wanted to, but he felt embarrassed to be the only party member there. He'd chosen instead to eat in restaurants in the southern end. On the day of Dashain, though, even these restaurants would be closed. He had nowhere to go.

At midday he looked out from the office door as families—whole, extended—made their way in tight-knit groups from relative to relative. Their choking closeness repulsed Rishi. With vermilion-and-rice blessings on sun-wrinkled foreheads and wheat sprouts tucked behind the ears, people who belonged, belonged thickly today, celebrating their clannishness with red fariyas, new trousers, readymade shirts and flashy gold. The security of groups, of hoards, of clans. There was no place for the individual at festival time.

Without any particular forethought Rishi had bought biscuits the day before. He ate them in the afternoon—Glucose, Thin Arrowroot—surrounded by mercifully unseeing walls. Despite his godlessness he felt ashamed to be alone at festival time, eating stale biscuits instead of a traditional feast. This was for him: additives, colour, preservatives instead of milky rice grains. The thin taste of crumbs in the place of spiced daal fried in ghiu. No pinch of salt estimated to taste by his mother's hand. The dry biscuits stuck to his throat, but he forced himself to keep swallowing the insipid taste of himself here, now, eating biscuits at a time of family feasts.

Buses were operating; he might still escape to Kathmandu's anonymity.

But the schoolmaster wanted him to go home.

He didn't want to.

He spent the day feeling out his isolation, daring his loneliness within bare walls. How much barrenness could he subject himself to? Spending Dashain teeka without human company: a way of enduring culture.

But he could bear it no more, and early on the second day of Dashain he left for the northern hills.

Yet his mind tore away from home. As he walked he kept turning on his radio, wanting a diversion. Then he kept turning it off at any mention of the nation's festivities. It felt false to return. He couldn't go back to being a son. He mustn't want to. He was going back only to give the schoolmaster the information on the booth committees. All for the masses. He was a good comrade: no more than that. But if he could be anyone he wanted, who would he be?

The day had a leisurely feel. Rishi slowed as he neared the settlement that was built along the northern hills. He passed a few huts, cut across a gully and headed to a low-lying hillock. He had dressed for his return in a white shirt and navy blue corduroys and a matching blue cardigan tied around his neck. His eyes, lit up by the morning sun, scanned the surroundings. The path home was lined with bottlebrush trees. To his right was the old water tap. He could almost taste the gritty water of his childhood. Further along, the lemon tree that he used to steal from as a boy was smaller than he remembered. The path, winding along a brook, also seemed narrow. He felt big here, his adult proportions jarring with boyhood memories. He felt remorse at the wrongness of his body here. What stubborn nostalgias drew him to this place and convinced him that these brooms and ryegrasses smelled of his belonging?

Rishi stopped by the swish and purl of the brook. The schoolmaster's house was on the other side, nestled in a ravine. Not far from it was Rishi's father's house. The day's bright sunlight illuminated the small structure, but the porch remained in shadow. A dark figure moved there. Was it? His mother. She bent over, then stood, carrying something. She walked to one side of the porch, then turned and walked to the other side. Then she bent again, attending to some chore. Tucking blankets.

If he could be anyone he wanted, he would be her son.

Rishi was almost upon his mother before she looked up. Her square face was hardened by the sun, and startlingly aged. She was thinner than he remembered, with bones protruding at the elbows, and blue veins on her forehead. Her sunken eyes were milky with cataracts. Her forehead was criss-crossed by frown lines. She studied him impassively, then called out to Rishi's father, 'Our eldest son has come.' She spoke as though making an everyday observation.

Rishi bowed to her. She blessed him without touching him.

His father rushed out of the house, armed, as always, with words, declarations, opinions. 'Finally he's returned.' Rishi bowed to receive his blessings. 'At last our son has remembered us.' Rishi's father too had become elderly: his skin had taken on a watery, deathlike translucence. 'Why didn't you tell us you were coming? Why didn't you come in time for teeka yesterday? Where were you all this time? Why didn't you at least write?'

His mother remained outside and continued what she had been doing: tucking blankets.

Inside the house there was and there wasn't change. Some things had altered—there was a bed in the front room, a wood veneer table, metal bars on the windows, and posters of Hindi cinema stars taped on the walls. Had the room always been painted in this cream coloured wash? It seemed bright. But it had the same small proportions, the same sooty smell. Rishi stopped himself from making comparisons with the past. The house had changed. It didn't matter.

Rishi's father kept talking, beginning, in his roundabout way, to make a few tentative claims on him. 'Your brother said he saw you in Khaireni Tar. He said he saw you there working for a party—the cinema hero's teacup party. Is that true, Son? Did you leave the communists? Your brother, you know, joined

Congress. Always doing the right opposite of you. You must talk to him, advise him, show him the right path. He's at that age, ready to spoil. You must guide him. Take him to the city. Get him a job.'

Suddenly, there it was: family. Suddenly he was locked into it again.

His father studied Rishi cautiously, then forged ahead with talk about filial duties. He spoke anxiously, as though trying to convince himself. He said, 'Even in this age when it's hard to get government service, many work abroad, they do business, they invest, they send their profits home. Even in this dark age it's possible to look after one's parents.' Did he think his son looked receptive? He went on, 'Old age is like this, it's a time of wanting assurance, wanting ease. In our time we thought—do your duty, get rewarded. This era isn't like that, I know that too. But we served our elders, we brought up our children, we looked at every side of things. We had our own difficulties, we faced hardships— but we bore them all with honour. Now tell me, Son, how long will you stay?'

His mother came in just then, carrying a tray of teeka and wheat sprouts.

'We must bless our son.' His father shot up to duty. 'This way is east. Here, face that way. Let's bless you, after all these years.'

He led Rishi by the arm and made him stand to one side of the table. Rishi could see his mouth moving, heaping his blessings on him. His mother followed her husband without uttering a word.

It had been a mistake to return. That day and the following days, Rishi tried to keep free from his family. He kept listening to the radio, fixing on whatever news he could find. Unseasonal floods, mudslides, earthquakes measuring seven on the Richter scale: a catalogue of disasters. He waited for the schoolmaster to come.

In the beginning his father persisted in asking questions and offering opinions. He kept questioning Rishi about what he'd done all these years, how much he'd earned, what conditions he lived in in Kathmandu, what his future plans were, didn't he want to get married? What businesses could he do, what prospects did he have?

Rishi lied in response. He was a teacher at an English-medium boarding school, he said. He earned six thousand a month, enough to live on, but not to send home. He lived with friends in an apartment house. The party he now worked for was powerful; it would help him get a new job with a greater salary. There was a girl he liked, Radhika. They would get married once he found a better job.

His father received each utterance carefully, with his eyes narrowed. Did he actually believe him? When neighbours and relatives came by, he slipped into role, declaring, 'Our son's come back to look after us.' The myth of honoured fatherhood. When they were alone he was more tentative. He said, as though in rebuke, 'It's important to look after one's parents.' His eyes fluttered away from his son, turned to the ground. He said, 'The old man's son the next house over, he never came back but sends his family money every now and then. They say he's in Korea. And the jhankri, both his sons joined the Indian Gurkhas. The other day I heard there were openings in the government, you have to take a test and they'll employ you.'

As though he might still harangue his son into serving him.

From the day of Rishi's arrival his brother, seventeen now, stood at a distance staring mulishly at him, making no effort to talk. He had grown to be swarthy, and Rishi saw he had BB-Gun Thapa's veneration of flesh. His brother didn't try to hide his resentfulness. The burden of family happiness had fallen on him.

It was he who had given up his studies to look after the family. It was he whose hands and feet were black from working in the fields. He was still trapped in all that Rishi had escaped. He held a fixed, begrudging look in his eyes. Rishi knew he should talk to his brother, try to share his responsibilities; but he found he wasn't capable of extending himself. The boy had joined the Congress party just to spite him. Rishi found it impossible not to share his brother's hatred of him.

All the while Rishi's mother attended to chores that had occupied the whole of her life. Rishi could hear her wake up at dawn, and he followed her movements through the day as she prayed at the family shrine, fetched water, swept the floors, cooked, washed dishes, ground flour out of corn and sat on the porch mending torn clothes. She stayed unresponsive when Rishi approached. Even when he stood next to her she acted as though she were alone. He kept looking at her protruding bones. She had shrunk in old age, and looked slighter than she used to. He couldn't tell what went on inside her. She had receded into permanent solitude. Or perhaps she was reproving him by ignoring him so studiously. Did she wish that he hadn't come back? Or did she know, already, that he hadn't come back for her? Rishi watched her spread red peppers out to dry in the sun, he watched her grind fresh lentils, he watched her pick stones from the rice. When he was young he'd seen her bony back turned to his father. Now it was turned to him.

Had his father beaten the defiance out of her? His father—Rishi began to loathe again with a young boy's hatred. His father had founded his social respectability on the pain of his family. As a younger woman Rishi's mother had come to Rishi at night, bruised and scraped by her husband, her hair dishevelled, her clothes in disarray, her face bathed in sweat and dirt and snot. In the dark she had cried. She had clung to Rishi and muttered desperate pleas and supplications into his ears. He'd felt her convulsions, and he'd felt her bones pressing into him. He was her boy, she'd whispered. He was her king, her god. When he finished studying he would get a job in the city; he would become a big man. Her legs had clamped around him. He would come back and rescue her.

He had said: I'll take you away from all this.

And now—. Now Rishi spent his nights trying not to listen for evidence of his mother's suffering. At the heart of the good comrade, a paltry personal failure. *For the weak it's personal.* As a boy he'd asked: Is the revolution coming, Mother? And the poets had replied for his mother:

> *Yes my dear it'll come.*
> *It'll come spreading brilliance like the morning sun.*
> *You'll see a weapon shimmering*
> *Like mist at its waist.*
> *With this it will fight impiety . . .*

He had failed as an avenging son.

The radio saved him from wanting to try and rescue anyone anymore. There was no sound as important to him as the BBC world service: news of plane crashes, news of natural disasters, news of rescue and relief missions. A new government elected. A popular revolt. Shootings and organized crime. The radio's noise distracted him from impossible longings. To bring happiness into his life, or his mother's. To bring back love. To bring back a foetus aborted years ago.

He waited for the schoolmaster to seek him out, thinking: surely there were trajectories that could rescue him from his past.

Trajectories:

He was flinty and hard-eyed. He believed in the goodness of nothing. There was a birthmark the size of a coin on his breast. Sometimes he closed his eyes. Once a man had asked, 'What do

you know?' and Rishi had replied, 'Everything you know is a
falsehood.' He took uneven steps. His socks were ribbed and his
shirt polka-dotted. He bleated in laughter.

Trajectories:

His manifesto was dedicated not to Marx or Lenin but to
Bakunin. 'But anarcho-syndicalism,' he would say to a confidante,
'doesn't actually solve a thing.' Circulation was his fond pastime.
Circulation fascinated him. He marked each rupee note that
passed his hands. He borrowed his friends' clothes and loaned
his own. When people served him a plate of rice he passed it on.

Trajectories:

Once he counted all the people he had ever known. But he
forgot many—for instance, the boy who sat behind him in class
ten. If one was the sum of all the interactions one had ever had,
he had unaccounted for debits. Did it matter?

Did anything matter?

Trajectories: He must put an end to family.

A week past Dashain the schoolmaster still hadn't sought him
out. By now Rishi was desperate to leave. His father had started
to go back to his daily card games. His brother went to the fields
to till the ground for the next planting. Rishi stayed at home,
watching his mother turned away from him. He had left her to
her fate. She now left him to his.

Another day passed, and another, without the schoolmaster.

What desiccation had he been living with, so that he could
tolerate even this?

The next morning he took a trail through a nearby banana
grove, and skipped over the gully which opened onto the
schoolmaster's properties. A narrow path led through the yard.
Rishi remembered being small in this yard. He walked cautiously
now, feeling out of place. The house was still. Why, at festival

time, would the house be still? He entered the front porch. The
door was closed. He pushed it open and peered in. The darkness
inside had no movement at all. There was no one in the
schoolmaster's home.

All for the masses.

By the time he scrambled across the ravine, he was ready to
leave.

He went back to the kitchen for his last meal. His mother
was at the wood stove. She was blowing into the fire, her face
puckered in effort. The embers cast an orange sheen on her cheeks
and sparkled in beads of sweat.

His father was sitting near by, waiting for his meal. Slowly,
over the past few days, his father had fallen silent, countering
Rishi's reticence with his own. He could tell, perhaps, that his
admonitions were glancing off his son without effect. He was
bracing, Rishi thought, for offence.

His brother hadn't come back from the fields. He wouldn't.
This Rishi recognized: a brother seeking to avoid him. Rishi took
a seat beside his father. His own slim bones came from this man.
The two of them waited as Rishi's mother ladled food onto two
stainless steel plates.

And this too was familiar: accepting a plate of food doled
out by an indifferent hand.

Rishi said, 'I want to sell my share of the family lands.'

His father turned to him.

'You can buy it from me,' Rishi said. 'Twenty-five thousand.'
He looked at his mother, who was looking at the floor, listlessly.
Didn't anything faze her? He said, 'If you want the land I'll go to
the district centre, prepare the deed and come back for the
payment. The price is more than fair.'

His father frowned. The price was less than half what it
should be. His father would buy the land, Rishi knew. But first
he had to follow form. He said, 'But why?' He spoke without

conviction, not wanting his son to change his mind. Rishi hated him. 'Why sell the land?' his father repeated. 'A man needs a small plot. A place where he can return. The place of his ancestors.'

'You want the land?'

'Why do you speak so curtly to your own father?'

'If you want the land I'll prepare the deed.'

Rishi's father sighed. He spoke like a man sacrificing his happiness for the sake of his son: 'Do as you want. Cut yourself from the land. But your arrogance, boy—'

'I'll come back with the deed.'

Rishi ate quickly, hardly tasting the food that wasn't meant for him anyway. By the end of the meal his brother hadn't come back from the fields, and he was grateful for this. When his father finally left for his card games, Rishi took out of his pocket his life's savings of six thousand rupees. His mother was still at the stove, keeping the food warm for her younger son. She sucked in her breath when Rishi reached for her. Ashamed of the inconsequence of his action, he placed the money in her hand and closed her fist around it. Six thousand rupees. It compensated for nothing. 'I'm leaving,' he said.

She shot him a terrorized look. Then, without a word, she rose and put the money in a tin can on a nearby shelf. Would she keep it for herself? Would she give it to her husband afterwards?

Rishi left without asking for, or receiving her blessings.

As he walked down to Khaireni Tar he kept a hand on the copy book in which he'd taken notes on Giridhar. He felt suddenly unburdened. He conjured up in his mind the trajectory of a new Rishi Parajuli, at the far edges of this society, a man released from the despotism of the past. A man completely unshackled, living in a future freed of meaning.

He could be no one he recognized.

44

At Binita's teashop Pamila had returned from the Dashain festival visibly upset, and after a few days of tending stoically to housework she sat on the back porch one afternoon, and started to cry. When Binita asked, she told her, between sobs, what had happened. She had hoped to hear from her husband in India, she explained. He'd sent no word for the last four years, and now no one knew where he was any more. 'Has he fallen ill, is he in need, is he in trouble, has he died?' Her forehead knitted in distress. 'Has he found another wife and started a new family? How could he forget us like this?'

Madhu listened on, riveted by the older woman's story. Then she surprised everyone by launching into a tirade against Pramila's husband. 'He's probably loitering uselessly in that foreign country,' she said. 'That's what men are like, they're all useless. It's a curse placed on women that we should need them at all.'

Tripti tried more gently to assure Pramila. 'We'll ask Nayan Raj-kaka to make the police look for him.'

'Ho, the police will bring him back.' Pramila smiled through her tears.

'Just leave him. You leave him,' Madhu said, her eyes flashing.

'I'll leave him,' Pramila agreed.

When she was alone with Binita, though, her grief returned. Binita asked about her family, and this time, unable to joke and laugh it off, she told her. She had two married daughters and two unmarried sons in their twenties. Her husband's family was kind to her, but poor. After her husband went to work as a Bahadur servant in Delhi, he sent part of his earnings every few months. Eventually he was hired by a restaurant. But his communications became infrequent as time went on, and one day he stopped sending money. That was when Pramila started working for Thakalni-aama.

'If I only knew that he was all right,' she groaned. 'The last we heard of him he left Delhi saying he was coming home. But it's been four years now. Has he fallen into bad company, has something happened to him, is he even alive any more?' Then her voice took on harder tones. 'If that corpse has taken another wife, I swear by Kali-mai I'll find him and cut him to pieces.' She cried a while, then stayed silent for a long time. Finally she sighed. 'I don't know whether to grieve for him or to be angry at him.'

On Binita's advice Pramila left, a few days later, to meet her brothers. They had offered to help trace her husband, using some contacts of their own. She would return after the Tihar festival, she said.

And the house and teashop returned to silence. Pramila's grief had affected Binita, adding to her own sadness. The whole town appeared full of damaged lives. What could these ashen flatlands offer Tripti? She deserved more than Binita could provide. And Madhu? In the empty teashop Binita brooded over the curtailed lives ahead of them all.

Then, to her surprise, Rishi showed up at the teashop one day, in time for the evening meal. He must be the only worker staying in the party office, she realized. Why wasn't he at home? Rishi didn't explain anything, and hardly even greeted her. He sat by himself paging through a tattered copy book. His skin seemed drier than ever, and his curly hair was untidy. His clothes still bore some urban refinement. He remained superior in his aloneness, even defiant. There was, about him, the look of someone devoid of worry.

There were no other customers in the teashop. Madhu and Tripti were at a table writing passages from their textbooks, distracted by their task. Rishi's heedless air intrigued Binita. 'You came back early?' she asked as she served him his meal.

Rishi rested his light eyes on hers. 'I broke with my family,' he said. He looked about the empty room, as though acknowledging how out of place he was. Then he asked, 'You have brothers coming for Tihar? I'll be intruding if I come here to eat.'

Binita shook her head.

'And your brother-in-law,' he asked, 'he'll spend Tihar in Kathmandu?'

He was exposing her loneliness to forestall her from exposing his.

'Me, Madhu and my daughter are alone,' Binita said offering him the honesty he sought. 'Everything is as it was before.'

Rishi shook his head. 'But everything's changed. You're relying on your brother-in-law to support you. You've withdrawn into family, and you're not independent any more.'

Binita was startled by this statement. She shrugged, uncertain about what to say, and when Rishi made as if to say something more, she asked, 'Is the food all right?'

Rishi smiled, accepting her evasion. 'The mansuri rice of the northern hills is always excellent.'

She left him alone after that, but she thought back, later, to what Rishi had said: You're not independent anymore. He had observed the changes in her life over these past few months. She felt flattered by his attentiveness, and unnerved by the intimacy it implied. Yet, when Rishi came to eat the next morning, she found herself wanting to continue their conversation. 'For a man it's easy to be independent,' she said as she gathered his plates.

He understood at once what she was referring to. 'For a man it's easier to break from family,' he agreed. 'But for a woman it's more important. For our women.'

That was all they said to each other that day, but lying between her cousin and daughter that night, Binita gave in to improbable fancies. Rishi had turned to her twice or thrice through the day, with a neutral, but lingering look. His forthrightness was disarming. When he spoke so frankly, was he flirting with her? Was she reciprocating by talking to him? In her thoughts she might wonder about his light eyes and thick eyelashes. She might think of brushing her hand against his skin and putting a finger to his dry lips. But in her behaviour she mustn't be foolish enough to breach the distance between them.

How surprising to be cut free. Rishi felt a peculiar strength amassing inside him. He felt capable of moving in any direction and doing anything. He felt light. Things that hurt him earlier now slid past him with hardly any impact: the musty air of the dormitory room, his place amid sweat-stained sheets, his waiting, his purposeless waiting, his aimless wandering. And there were options he saw. He could give Shankar his notes on the booth committees and leave, just like that. He could stay on and try to meet the schoolmaster. He could reveal the schoolmaster's plans to Nayan Raj and help the People's Party in earnest. He even thought, sometimes, of asking Om Gurung for a teaching job at the Pure Hearts Boarding School. He could be anyone. An underground worker, an unemployed tutor. Rishi-bhai, Rishi-dai. Nothing mattered but the desultory rambles of a life without weight.

Binita, though, had begun to pull him with a seductive gravity. Now that she was alone—though never far from her cousin and daughter—she spoke to him, allowed him to speak more openly, without fear of her retreating. She would say something, then equivocate and pull away. It occurred to him that she was, in some controlled way, dallying with him. 'Rishiji,' she called him. Not Rishi-dai, not Rishi-bhai. A man to her woman? He couldn't tell.

The first day of Tihar was kaag puja, the day of the crows. When Rishi reached the teashop Binita and the two girls were in the back porch, scattering grains of cooked rice over the backyard. He went to stand by the door to the porch, watching them quietly.

'Look, Aama, there's a crow, there's another crow,' Tripti cried, tossing rice towards the ravens perched on the banana plants. 'Here, kaag, this is for you. Eat some rice.'

'Those are kauwa,' Rishi said, noting how Binita turned to him, startled by his voice, with a direct, searching look.

Rishi bent down to Tripti's level. 'Look, that's a dhobini bird,' he said, pointing at a bird picking at the offerings. 'There's a fiste, and there's a chaanchar.'

Tripti was in a boisterous mood. 'We just saw a flock of parrots! They flew that way. Maybe they'll fly back.'

The four of them remained on the porch feeding birds, almost as though they were a family. And in a moment of abandon, Rishi thought he could sink into this place and rest, he could remain in Khaireni Tar for this.

When Binita went in to see to the meal, he followed her, leaving Madhu and Tripti in the porch. Instead of waiting as usual at a table, he sat at the counter and watched her move, in her precise way, from counter to stove, towards him and away from him. She didn't seem to mind his proximity. She even slowed, he thought, to extend it.

She served him his meal at the counter, and then sat on the other side, watching him. A woman to his man?

'At this time when there isn't party work,' Binita said as he ate, 'perhaps you could supervise my cousin and daughter as they write letters.'

'Be their tutor?' Rishi laughed sardonically.

Binita gave him a surprised look. But she didn't back off, as she might have. 'It would be helpful to them, I thought. Only during the festivals, if there's no party work.'

She was offering a place for him in her life. Rishi accepted the offer. 'I used to work in Kathmandu as a private tutor,' he said. 'I taught boys in ninth, tenth class, boys doing their intermediates. Most of them I taught history.' He looked over at Madhu and Tripti, still on the porch. The four of them would spend more time together if he tutored the girls. It would be a means to sidestep prohibitions. He said, 'Of course I'll supervise their writing.'

'They'd benefit from that,' Binita said. She smiled by way of thanks, and then pulled away again, in her usual rhythm of coming and going.

Later, as Rishi looked over the girls' notebooks to assess what he might teach them, he kept noticing Binita's movements as she moved in and out of the teashop.

Binita, Madhu, Tripti and he—sitting together at ease.

It was Binita's back that he thought of at night, alone in the dormitory room. The bone at the back of her neck, the curve of her shoulders, the sinews along the part of her spine that showed above her blouse. There was personality in her back, and expression. He could read her mood from its ripples, its movements from taut to slack. It was her back that he thought of touching when they were alone. He would move upon her, gently, his lips on the back of her neck, persuading her with his caresses out of her exile.

On kukur puja, the second day of Tihar, Binita wore the green fariya that she'd worn on Dashain. In the morning Madhu and Tripti tossed food scraps to stray dogs, and Binita watched on, noting how she waited for Rishi to appear and join them. He must be at the party office right now. Yesterday he'd come to the teashop by this time. She felt jittery. Then she checked herself. She was indulging in an unreasonable whim. What she wanted—

what she thought she wanted—was ridiculous.

She left Madhu and Tripti, and went to clean the alcove.

'Alone again?' Phool Devi dropped by as Binita began to straighten the beds. She stared frankly at Binita's green fariya, and pursed her shiny, lipsticked lips. 'Your brother-in-law, what, he's not here for Tihar and you're all alone, just like before?'

'He'll be back as soon as the festival ends.'

Phool Devi sat on Binita's bed and watched her finish tucking in the sheets on Madhu's bed. 'Silk,' she said, reaching over to rub Binita's fariya. She sat back again. 'You could start wearing more colours. No vulgar reds or pinks—but blues and greens, you could wear.' She brushed off her own vermilion-flecked fariya. 'Widows from the ethnic groups, of course, have fewer restrictions. And in the cities they wear anything. But I think it looks cheap, you know, when a widow wears bright colours—like she's advertising herself, showing men she's free.'

Binita tried assiduously to ignore her.

'So, the other day,' Phool Devi said in a high, knowing tone, 'all these women danced in front of half the town. To raise money for a temple, can you believe?' She emitted a short laugh. 'They jiggled and shook while half the town watched, and then they went about asking for money!'

Binita turned to her in dismay. 'Was it the mothers' group?'

Phool Devi made a face. 'The older and younger wives of the Sub-Inspector, moving together like dancing girls, you should have seen his face! There were others—I can't even recognize all the town's new brides. Jiggling and shaking as though anyone wants to look at them casting away their decency. So unsightly it was. More shameful for those watching than for those doing it!'

'It was the mother's group?'

'A group of fools. Asking for money like whores in the name of women's development.'

Binita wished, just then, that she could say something rude

to jettison Phool Devi out of her life forever. Something crass, something true. But her habit of restraint was strong. 'Do you want tea?' she asked with a bluntness that she hoped would end the visit.

Phool Devi blinked several times, deciding whether to take Binita's tone as an affront. 'Eh no, I can't linger,' she finally said. She took another long look at Binita's fariya, then picked herself off the bed.

For civility's sake Binita followed her out.

'I just, you know, wanted to see that you weren't too lonely,' Phool Devi said on the back porch. She couldn't seem to resist peeking into the teashop as she passed the door. 'No one there,' she announced to herself. Finally she turned back to Binita with a sugary smile. 'La ta, I'll be going.'

For a long time after her neighbour left, Binita sat in rigid silence.

Then she left the house in Madhu's charge and headed to Thakalni-aama's.

She felt upset and agitated. Why hadn't she been invited to the mother's group meeting? Why hadn't anyone told her?

Emptied of Congress workers, the Himal Lodge Restaurant Bar was quiet. Thakalni-aama was sitting cross-legged on a bench in the courtyard, talking to someone—as she approached, Binita saw it was Laksmi.

'Eh, Binita,' Thakalni-aama said, squinting in the sun. 'Come. Take this cushion. Sit.'

Laksmi turned and scrutinized Binita, as though trying to read something in her face. Then she turned back to Thakalni-aama. 'If we go ward to ward that will be better,' she said in her low, lisping voice. 'Otherwise we'll miss some houses and repeat others.'

Thakalni-aama nodded. 'People will criticize us.'

'So far nobody's opposed us, really.'

'We give them a chance, they'll laugh at us. We mustn't give them a chance.'

They were speaking only to each other, and Binita felt a chill of exclusion. When there was a pause in their conversation, she said, 'I would have come. If I'd known about the meeting I would have come.'

Laksmi shot her a strange look. She said, 'You left early last time. We weren't sure you wanted to join.'

Binita didn't like feeling rebuked. She said, 'I want to join.'

'Young mothers like you—you must join,' Thakalni-aama said. 'What, you think this group is for those nearing death, like myself?' She repositioned herself on the bench to offer her back to the sunlight. 'The next meeting is after Tihar. We'll start with dancing in the first ward, raising money house to house.'

Laksmi was still looking accusingly at Binita. 'You left early, so we thought . . .' Then she suddenly brightened. 'Will you really join the group, then? If you come to the meetings, you can be a friend to me, and I'll be a friend to you.'

Her needy, pleading tone put Binita off. But she thought of all the other women in the group. Their laughter...She wanted to be among women. She said, 'I'll come.'

With her eyes still fixed keenly on Binita, Laksmi then started talking about the last meeting. Only a few women had danced, she said. They'd raised a few hundred. From next time on, they must raise at least five hundred per meet. Binita listened on, and wondered even as she did: was this really the kind of company she wanted? Was this her place? Among unsure and insecure women, among women defeated, crushed and bound, among women easily ridiculed for their clumsy attempts at freedom: was that where she belonged?

After debating his course all morning Rishi headed, that afternoon, across the highway and towards Shankar's grain store. He would send a message to the schoolmaster. The bazaar was silent today, and the UML office seemed closed. Was the schoolmaster in the northern hills, then? The crockery store was open, but there was no one there. The Congress party office, beyond the fruit stall, was closed. Rishi found Shankar's grain store shuttered, but he saw the blind man sitting by the side of the shop sunning himself on a straw mat.

'I recognize your treading walk,' Shankar said as Rishi approached. He turned his face towards him, squinting past him. 'Comrade. You've met your schoolmaster, then? You've reaffirmed your loyalty to him? You're no longer sorrowful?'

'I had to leave,' Rishi said curtly. 'I'll have to meet him here, now.'

The blind man laughed. 'But you were to meet him there.' Then he grew serious. 'You, Comrade, you must do as you're told. I'm not your schoolmaster, I don't have his charisma, I don't have his flair. But I have his authority, I am his voice. You must go back and wait for him at home.'

'I can't.'

'Then give me the notes.' Shankar raised his hands like a beggar asking for alms. 'You said you'd taken notes. I'll give them to your schoolmaster.'

Rishi shot back, 'My notes are for the schoolmaster's eyes only.'

For a moment the blind man looked lost. Then he laughed in his cackling way, not upset, it seemed. 'You're rebelling? You'll only give us the notes if you can meet your schoolmaster? You're bargaining on the sale of your notes?'

'I don't want to work for the party any more.'

'But you'll give us the notes?' Shankar smiled. 'For the price of a meeting you'll give your schoolmaster the notes?'

'Tell him I need to talk to him,' Rishi said. Then, not wanting to subject himself to any more of Shankar's heckling, he left.

There was a sweetness to not knowing where things led from here. He reached the bar-peepal tree and sat on its stepped platform. There were no vendors here today. The town was still busy celebrating the festivals. Rishi leaned against the twined-together tree trunks and stared down at the lines on his palms.

He hesitated to go to Binita's. He'd awoken, this morning, to the sense that it wasn't impossible to make a place for himself in her life. Love. He felt reckless and rash. All morning, in the quietness of the dormitory room, he had entertained dreams that defied reality, fantasies of undressing Binita. Not impossible to set up a life with her in the anonymous spaces of Kathmandu. He, Binita, Madhu and Tripti becoming a family. Not impossible in today's Nepal.

But neither was it likely.

He wanted this impulse to pass before he went to the teashop today.

But as he sat at the platform he saw Binita coming out of the Himal Lodge Restaurant Bar. She was wearing a muted green fariya. She walked with her face turned down, inward in her bearing, intentionally ignoring those who might be looking at her. When she neared the bar-peepal tree, Rishi stepped down from the platform and joined her.

They'd developed an agreeable way around each other, and his presence, when she noticed it, didn't startle her. They reached the bougainvillea tree. There Binita stopped in the shade. She was turned slightly away, and Rishi couldn't read her expression, but he sensed an emotional tumult. For a while, neither of them spoke, then suddenly Rishi said, 'Binitaji must tell me if I've made a mistake.' The intimate timbre of his voice surprised him. He saw Binita had stiffened. Feeling a need for restraint, he folded his arms. 'I broke with my family,' he said more evenly. 'Throughout my childhood my father mistreated my mother—he beat her, he threw her out of the house.' He paused. 'I promised to come back for her, but once I left, I never returned. Till this Dashain. Years too late.'

They were standing in plain view of the bazaar, sharing a startling privacy. Binita hadn't turned to face him, but she hadn't walked away either, and Rishi was grateful for this.

He said, 'Do you need to correct your original failure? Must you return to your early mistakes to make up? Or can you correct wrongs elsewhere—to make up?'

Finally Binita turned her face to him. A look of confusion passed briefly through her eyes. Rishi could see her deciding to accommodate his confidence.

She said, 'One day you might go back and help her. What seems impossible now might suddenly become possible. Paths open where it seems there are only walls.'

It was electrifying to have Binita talk so directly, in her soft clear tone.

Rishi said, 'Do you remember I told you to join the mother's group? I was thinking of my mother, hoping that she might have found some strength from other women.'

'Everyone has to find their own means.'

Rishi stepped closer to her. 'But do you wait for those means to arrive, or do you go looking for them?'

Binita gave him a long, questioning look.

He said, 'A kind of person is struggling for birth in this land. A free person.'

She nodded uncertainly. 'It's difficult to know how to be free.'

'Do you wait for situations to free you, though,' Rishi said, 'or do you force your own freedom?'

At these words Binita looked away, and Rishi couldn't tell what she was thinking. Then she turned to him with a smile. 'Perhaps it's a mystery,' she said lightly. 'You spoke of birth.

Who gets conceived, who survives, who dies—these things can be up to chance.'

She was evading him.

She made as if to leave, and Rishi reached for her.

When his hand brushed her arm she shot him a hard look.

He stepped back.

Without any indication of how she felt, Binita abruptly said, 'Come, you must be hungry, Rishi-bhai,' and stepped past him towards the house.

Rishi felt the warm air set swirling after her movement. She'd called him a younger brother. Bhai: with one swift word she wanted to curb any risk from him. So deftly, like fingers pinching a flame; it didn't hurt.

He would not be a brother to her.

He followed her home.

All the next day Binita tried out having Rishi in her life. Rishiji. Rishi-bhai. Or just Rishi: an improbable fancy.

When he came in to eat, when he tutored Madhu and Tripti, and when he stayed on, listening to the radio, Binita examined the feel of having him near by. His interest in her was unmistakable. He still refused family titles and called her Binitaji. In no other way did he force his intention on her. Instead, he acted like someone who had made an offer, for her to accept or reject. Was he for real?

Binita thought: she had lived many years now in hiding. She had mourned long over the brutality of her world. To protect herself, she had knowingly stunted her own life, deprived herself of pleasure. She remembered Thakalni-aama's advice to her months ago: use the hero's return to your advantage. Sooner or later she must break out of her stupor, she must move, of her own volition, towards happiness.

But was the love of one man something to risk reaching for? About this she remained uncertain. Rishi—*a free person struggling for birth*: did that make him someone who could love a widow? A free person: a man who wouldn't shrink from the difficulty of love—in this land of unreliable men?

It was the third day of Tihar, goru puja, the day of worshipping bulls. The day after tomorrow was bhai teeka, the day when women made offerings to their brothers. Binita's brothers had long stopped coming to receive her blessings. Rishi showed no signs of going to visit his own sister. Binita might place teeka on him, making a ceremonial brother of him. Rishi bhai.

But imprudent longings made her prefer Rishiji. She liked the way he taught Madhu and Tripti. He was grave, but kind with them. Rishiji.

Or just Rishi: in less flawed circumstances, in less perilous times.

On gai puja, the fourth day of Tihar, Rishi was leaving the People's Party office when someone brushed up from behind and asked, in a rustling voice, if he had a light. He turned in shock to see his schoolmaster standing next to him, holding an unlit cigarette. The schoolmaster's face, burned by the sun, glowed beneath his flash of silver hair. He appeared taller, and more rangy than in Kathmandu. Without a hint of familiarity he repeated his question, 'Do you have matches, Comrade?'

Rishi shook his head, too taken aback to speak.

'I need the notes you took.'

On instinct Rishi felt in his shirt, where he was carrying the copy book. He said, 'I need to meet you.'

'Leave the notes with Shankar.'

'I need to talk to you.'

'Then come to the Moonlight Hotel in the southern end.'

With this the schoolmaster left. Their exchange was as brief as a casual chat between strangers. It left Rishi stunned.

When he reached Binita's teashop, Madhu and Tripti were finishing the assignments he'd given them yesterday. Binita was at the stove, her back to him. She did not turn around. She had drawn into herself since their talk beside the bougainvillea plant. Rishi studied her, but he couldn't interpret her mood. When she brought him lunch, she wouldn't meet his eyes. She served him, he noticed, on the same cheap plastic plates that she reserved for family. Was this an allowance?

'You must be hungry, Rishiji.'

Rishiji. One day away from the festival of brothers and sisters, she was releasing him from family ties. A woman and a man. She was feeling out their restrained courtship to see how it suited her. He would wait.

Rishi thought of the schoolmaster. At the Moonlight Hotel was his past. On this side was Binita He spent the rest of the day at the teashop supervising Madhu's lettering and the math sums he had assigned Tripti. He didn't listen to the radio today; he wanted to look for signs of Binita's consent. He felt a long forgotten thrill when she finally looked at him briefly, before averting her gaze. He wanted to talk with the same openness as before. He wanted to touch her, to feel her and make her feel out his life. He waited.

But all he received was her evasiveness.

Madhu and Tripti were lighting candles at the windows when he left without eating. It was gai puja, the eve of the new moon. Not wanting to go straight to the dormitory, Rishi sat by the edge of the Telecommunications Office, crouched against the wall. An autumnal mist was falling over the town. He pulled his cardigan to him. He could hear the radios playing in the bazaar houses. Around him everything was in shadow. Straight ahead, beyond the black shadows of the bar-peepal tree, was the UML party office with its windows lit. He saw figures flitting in the yellow rectangle of the front door, but he couldn't make out anyone in the dim illumination.

He stayed a long time, feeling the coldness of the night set into his bones.

She must step out of this cramped life and find her footing in another. It was bhai teeka; Binita would not put the teeka on Rishi. She would not make a brother of him. With much deliberation she had examined all possibilities before her, and yet . . . There was no way for her and Rishi to be together than to elope to Kathmandu, taking Tripti and Madhu along. Even if this were possible—if she gave up her present security and placed herself in Rishi's custody—how reliable would he prove? He felt trustworthy to her. But if, one day, he vanished like her husband had, became a spectre—what then?

And things had improved in the past months. Nayan Raj-bhai's arrival had opened doors: people did not shun her anymore, her business had grown, and within her husband's family, too, her position had improved. There was the mothers' group, which promised a life less solitary. She might find a place for herself amid women. Manageable risks, manageable pleasures. Wasn't that enough of a change in her life?

But the brush of Rishi's hand on her arm—she remembered that. So much desire had come alive at that glancing touch.

No amount of reflection could help her decide.

When night fell, Madhu and Tripti lit a row of candles by the back porch, then moved to the front of the house to light up the front porch. By the time Rishi arrived for his meal the house was lit up like a temple.

Binita was sitting in the back porch. Rishi joined her there, sitting so close that she was just inches from him. She caught the new-wool smell of his cardigan. They were shaded by the darkness of the new moon night. He was looking at her. This close, she saw the light, golden colour of his eyes, the sweep of his thick eyelashes. She could hear his even breath. But he did nothing—he just sat beside her, looking at her. He would wait for her.

Was his personal integrity safeguard enough?

She wondered how his dry lips might taste.

'It's easier for a man to be free,' she said.

And he seemed to understand her dilemma: 'It's more important for our women.'

Then—because it was the only thing that felt judicious to do—Binita got up and walked away.

Rishi turned down to study his palms.

Tomorrow Nayan Raj would return. Other party workers would return, and party work would begin again. Only a few weeks remained till election day. Party members would pour into Binita's teashop and eliminate their privacy. The time for their courtship was over.

love, soil and pathway

45

Pramila-didi's misfortune had reinforced Madhu's new conviction that truly, there was no justice in this world. Pramila-didi should forget about her husband. She should forge ahead alone. Or even elope with another man! Why not? What was gained from following a straight line? Even Binita-didi—what had she gained by being so faithful to the memory of her dead husband? Had she won the love of friends and relatives? Madhu herself had been so good—and look what people said about her now. Madhu began to look coldly at her own idiocy. She began to look outside with an unforgiving eye. And what she saw surprised her.

The bazaar she saw from home each night, glimmering like a sky of stars. She had never much admired that view. But the town had power, Madhu noticed. Its winding pathways led to all four corners of the world. Its shops displayed foreign items which cast spells, making people pay money for them. Strangers met, here, at crossroads, carrying places inside them—places they were from, places they'd been to, places they'd go one day.

For hours every day she wandered the bazaar like a girl of low birth. She couldn't help it. There was so much to see. Like the watchmaker at his canvas stall, bent over a plate full of tiny metal parts. He was always tinkering with metal bits. To Madhu the whole town seemed like this man—capable of understanding things she couldn't even form questions about. She'd lived, all her life, by a traditional ethic, and she had been left out of all this. She felt tricked and cheated. It bothered her.

A basic sense of unfairness raged in her. She had been left behind by the world. Look at Gaumati, married now to the Rawal boy. Look at the Khadka boy, office-employed. Things were awry. Her anger was bolstered by the things Sir said at each night's literacy class. 'Cheli,' Sir said when reviewing words that began with the letter cha. 'Are girl students better or worse than boy students? Are girls more intelligent or boys?'

'Girls are more emotional,' one of the older women replied. 'Girls aren't as intelligent as boys, but they understand people better.'

'No, I'm more intelligent than my husband,' quipped one woman. 'But he got to study, he's employed by the government, whereas to me, till this class, black letters were as good as buffaloes. But I'm more intelligent, I say so honestly.'

It made Madhu think: was she intelligent? She'd never assessed herself on such merits. It had been more important to be simple, agreeable, and virtuous. To be intelligent one had to be cunning. One had to be sly, canny, shrewd. One had to be suspicious of everything and to think the most unpleasant thoughts. One had to argue, bicker, and quarrel. One basically had to be bad.

Not that being bad was so hard now that she'd been mounted by the spirit of an evil woman. By now there was no doubt that the witch had cursed Madhu for trespassing on her land. Otherwise why would she keep having the most unrefined thoughts?

She made her way through the bazaar each day, and felt rancour at the sight of all the boys dressed smartly in trousers and collared shirts, wearing leather shoes on their feet. Why did they get to strut about so uselessly? What made her fated not to strut? What made it possible for these uncouth boys to judge her and mock her? She hated each one of these boys. They were stupid and base, but they could strut because they had power and privileges that she did not. And she wanted their—their freeness. The freeness of the bazaar was something she must have.

And walking through the bazaar one day, seething with resentment, it occurred to her, quite out of the blue, that the Khadka boy could give her his freeness. Yes. Maybe. He was an earning man. He was an ugly boy. But he had a freeness that she very much wanted. Of course he was a skinny corpse. And of course she did not love him. Love was a despotic thing, she knew. She wouldn't be indentured by it.

Pramila-didi and Binita-didi had both been chained and ruined by love. Love was best fled.

46

After the festivals party workers flooded back into Khaireni Tar and began to stumble, as though in a daze, back to conducting their parties' campaigns. There wasn't much longer till voting day. Every day was critical now. But the festivals had diverted everyone's attention. There was a sluggishness to the pace of campaigning. All the parties did the obvious: slapped on fresh posters to cover old, faded ones, walked through town screeching slogans over a loudspeaker, repainted old party symbols with fresh paint.

The days were sparkling clear, the air crisp with the winter sun. Flocks of cranes flew south amid a riot of inelegant squawks. Those with choice irrigated fields began to hoe their fields for a round of winter maize or wheat. But there was time yet for planting. In the town people were neither busy nor altogether free: though there was work to do, there was also time enough to sit back and enjoy the theatre play of politics.

When Nayan Raj returned from Kathmandu, the People's Party office filled again with workers. Juddha and the other failed army recruits set about replacing old posters. Rishi's group of students took charge of repainting faded teacup symbols all over town. The female workers went from house to house talking to women about voting for the teacup party. BB-Gun and his gang took to the town with hand-held microphones: 'Vote for the teacup!

Vote for the teacup! Vote for the teacup!'

But the elections now had an unmistakable air of being part of the season's merrymaking. The most gruelling aspects of the campaigns were over. Each party had canvassed the electorate, made public speeches, and formed booth committees for voting day. What remained was the subtler work: to court local leaders and come to private understandings with them, making promises in return for their support, arranging for them to buy and sell votes, seeing to ballot rigging and booth capturing. The campaign work that remained was very important; but it was invisible to the eye.

And so the senior members of each party huddled in their offices making plans, strategizing, considering options and revising plans. Could this village be bought, could it be intimidated? Could the government's election authorities be persuaded to overlook stuffing at this booth? How many registered voters in this village were absent—could proxy votes fall in their names? Which ballot boxes should be destroyed if voting didn't go as desired? And how likely was it that international election observers might visit this booth?

Every now and then party workers could be seen scurrying across the highway to place urgent STD trunk-calls. The small interior of the Telecommunications Office was crammed with men assiduously listening in on each other. The operator briskly put through their calls. But everyone knew that her supervisor, lolling in his stained, soft bed, was listening in on their talk from his room above the office. When it came time to step up to the receiver, people spoke cautiously:

'We've run out of *it*, Comrade, we need more of *it*.'

'*That it* or the *other it*?'

'Ho, you're right, I mean the *other it*, not *that it*. We need two lakhs more, urgently.'

'No need to specify amounts, Comrade.'

'Did you hear? We need two lakh rupees more.'

All the men in the office room shuffled about, pretending not to have heard a thing.

No such messenger came scurrying from the People's Party office to place STD trunk-calls. In fact there was no plotting to be seen at the party's office. Nayan Raj had come back rested from the festivals, already with the glow of victory on his face. Unlike the other parties' candidates he neither huddled in the office, nor did he rush about meeting people to cut last-minute deals. Such was his confidence. Instead he spent his days meeting ordinary townspeople, going from house to house accompanied by Chiranjibi, and sometimes by Om.

His confidence aroused the town's curiosity. Was the cinema hero being overconfident? Or did he have reason to be so assured? His poise made the other parties look frantic—almost desperate, as though they were sure to lose. 'They say Nayan Raj made a real impact in the southern hills,' people said, chatting beneath the eaves and awnings of the bazaar's shops. 'They say in all the villages, even in the towns, people are talking only of Nayan Raj.'

'The big parties, they're running here, there, everywhere, shaking in fear.'

'They'll be trounced by the teacup, ha ha.'

Giridhar could almost hear everyone talking about the teacup party, and asking: where is the teacup's chairman, what is he doing at home, why is he so incompetent? He knew he had things to do. But he'd tried, after Dashain-Tihar, to stop drinking—and found that he couldn't. Or he could—but at the cost of his sanity. For when the juice was thin in his blood, there was no solace for him. Violent derangements scared him back to the bottle. Giridhar knew these last weeks of the campaign were decisive. All over

the electorate, booth committees awaited his command. Village
leaders needed persuading. Votes needed buying. Boys needed to
be prepared. It was now or never, make or break, do or die time.
The true test was here.

But the only thing he was capable of was procuring bottles,
hiding them in the corners of his room, and when he needed,
lifting them to his lips. Sometimes his wife tried to hide his bottles,
or to throw them away. Desperately he explained to her that
alcohol wasn't the cause of his sickness, but a salve for greater
madnesses. 'Don't tell anyone—I've gone crazy,' he confessed.
'Don't tell my father. Don't tell my sons that their father is going
mad.'

Then, overcome by Laksmi's tormented look, he wept till
she brought him a quarter bottle of rum. And another quarter
bottle. And a half-bottle. Laksmi's thin face diminished with the
treachery he begged of her. Still she cooperated. Without a word
she brought him the bottles he asked for, and handed them to
him with her small bony hands. She kept her eyes turned down
throughout the act. Was she trying to kill him with drink? Wildly,
Giridhar threw away a bottle one day, smashing it against the
wall. When Laksmi came in, wide-eyed, he lunged at her and
shook her till she moaned. 'You want to kill me, whore? You
want to poison me with drink?'

The next day he had to beg her to bring him another bottle.

Without a word she complied.

With rum, Giridhar pulled out of his bed, careened out of his
room and walked towards the world. The teacup party. An
election. But he was degenerating into mindless blood, bile, skin
and bones. He paced the length of the front porch and finally sat
on the wooden pallet. Why was it so hard to think clearly? Beyond
was a view of the town. Elections: strategy. Strategy. Strategy.

Om arrived one day, obviously to snoop on him, 'Oho,
friend,' he sang with unnecessary cheeriness. He was sporting

the colour of his school's uniform: white shirt, grey pants and a maroon cardigan. There must have been some event at his school. For a while he puffed from the strain of the uphill walk. 'It gets harder each time,' he said. He wiped his forehead with a polka-dotted handkerchief. 'Remember when we were boys, we scrambled along the slopes picking berries? How nimbly we ran! But look at us now.'

Om's copious cheer depressed Giridhar.

Om took a seat beside him on the pallet. 'My old woman was saying, our Giridhar-dai must be preparing his fields for the winter crops. Otherwise why wouldn't he come to the party office? I told her, you think our Giridhar-dai has time for the fields? Workers, field hands, labourers: our Laksmi-bhauju manages all that. No, our Giridhar-dai is planning our election strategy. He's drawing the plans that will lead us to victory.'

Giridhar pulled into himself.

'Eh friend.' Om placed a hand on his back. 'You've done a wonderful job. Everyone's saying that. A few months after Nayan Raj decides to run, we've got workers, booth committees, supporters everywhere. Our candidate—a fine man. But could he have set up thirty-three booth committees? It's a matter of separate skills. He talks, you act. Everyone's saying that.'

So much pressure. It was wearying. 'Tell them,' Giridhar said. Tell them what? 'There'll be a meeting tomorrow at twelve noon sharp.'

Om nodded.

'Go tell them now.' Giridhar wanted to be left alone. 'Now is the time. Go.'

Om stopped smiling.

What, he wanted to sit and chat? Tch. Why, always? Why so much friendliness? 'Go,' Giridhar growled.

'All right, friend,' Om said curtly, obviously hurt, but just as obviously trying not to show it. Of course. 'I'll set a meeting at

the office tomorrow at twelve noon sharp. Don't you worry,' he
added, softening. 'I'll inform everyone.' As a gesture of farewell,
he reached for Giridhar's hand.

Giridhar drew away. He was done. He stumbled back into
his room and took a swig at a bottle of XXX Khukuri Rum.

In town, some people were indeed beginning to wonder about
Giridhar's absence. Chiranjibi was wondering. It was irresponsible
for Giridhar to stay at home now. Nayan Raj spent all his days
meeting people, urging them to use their votes to make their
government work for them. His words were always incisive, his
demeanour charming. But Chiranjibi worried. Fine speeches alone
wouldn't ensure the party's victory. People made their choices
based on complicated community, caste and clan loyalties; they
would want to be assured of their safety if they were to vote for
the People's Party. The ideals that Nayan Raj spoke of were
important—they were true. But soon booth committee members
from all over the electorate would come to Khaireni Tar, asking
for final instructions. Only Giridhar knew who they were. Only
Giridhar knew how they might translate people's admiration for
Nayan Raj into votes. In this final hour Giridhar should be taking
charge.

Chiranjibi himself was of little help to the party, but his
dedication was unquestionable. Today, three of his brother's
labourers were carrying his teak desk out of the fragrant mill
and to the People's Party office. Chiranjibi had decided to donate
it to the party. The labourers were straining, now, with the effort
of keeping the desk off the ground as they made their way through
the bazaar lanes. Chiranjibi led the way.

At the party office a swarm of party workers and some idle
townspeople gathered around as the labourers struggled to fit the
desk through the front hallway. The hallway proved too narrow.

'We'll have to pull it up the front, then manoeuvre it in through the top window,' Juddha said. BB-Gun and his gang stepped forward. 'Let's pull it up the front of the building on ropes.'

It took an hour to have the desk hoisted by ropes and pulleys through the meeting room's window, and when the workers placed it squarely in the centre, the desk looked measured for the room. For a while, all the workers came in to look at it, and to admire it.

'Real teak, it must have cost a fortune, Chiranjibi-dai.'

'So dark, so rich in hue.'

Chiranjibi remained in the meeting room after everyone had left. All over the walls were scraps of paper that Giridhar had taped: lists of the electorate's VDCs, scraggly maps, notes made in his uncontrolled and scrawling script. The paint on the walls had flaked off in a powdery mist, exposing the cement below. There was dirt on the overhead bulb, dust on the window sills and finger marks along the walls. The desk stood apart from its surroundings, a liquid field of black, like a gleaming vision.

47

At twelve noon the next day Om skipped the school's lunch hour and headed to the party office for the meeting that Giridhar had called. He was feeling unhappy. He hadn't liked the brusqueness Giridhar had shown him yesterday—practically ordering him to leave and do his bidding. Not that a little effrontery would harm their friendship, of course. Om's love for his friend was a thorn tree; it clung to inhospitable terrain and survived by growing thick, tenacious roots. But friendship was a delicate thing. Too much inconsideration could atrophy love's roots, it could cause the entire plant to wither and waste away. This was what made Om feel bad.

'And it's hard, love . . . but we mustn't give up,' he had confided to Asha last night. 'For people like us, a life without love is as barren as the surface of the moon. A desert one can dig a well in; but you tell me—who wants to live on the moon?'

'You speak as though serving Giridhar-dai is your whole karma,' Asha had said. 'There are others who would benefit more from that same love. Look at our mita-son. He's another boy now.'

'Someone suffering in front of me, someone placing himself in danger. In a battlefield, in combat—would you abandon a friend?'

'What combat are you talking about? What war is going on?'

'Tch, love. All the harshness that fells innocent people . . . There's an undeclared war being waged, in our country, against the unfortunate.'

Asha had sighed. 'You mustn't think in such big-big terms. You and I, we're small people. We can only do small things.'

Now Om entered the party office, and pushed his way through the crowd of workers in the narrow hallway. 'Namaste, namaste,' he greeted Juddha and the party's female workers.

He found Harsha Bahadur in the upstairs office room, guarding the remaining stock of posters. The boy was dressed smartly in a sweater that was only slightly big for him, and neatly pressed black trousers. Asha was right: he was transformed now. Harsha Bahadur was at that age when boys finally gain looks; his features were filling out.

'Come, we mustn't be late,' Om said. His mita-son would take minutes at the meeting, he had decided. Doing such things would boost his confidence.

'Come, Son.' Om went next door to the meeting room, and when he opened the door, he was surprised to see a teak desk so large it left hardly any space at the sides.

And what was this: Giridhar was sitting in a corner, slouched forward on the desk.

'Oho friend,' Om squeezed his way to the chair next to his friend. He patted the desk. 'Quality furniture to suit our stature, finally. And why not? Everyone's saying what a fine job you've done. Everyone's saying the teacup party will win. I'm eager to learn about our final strategy.'

Giridhar sat up and looked blankly at him.

Om smiled widely to show that he held no grudges from yesterday.

Giridhar turned to Harsha Bahadur, who was still standing at the door. 'What do you want, boy?' he said.

Om explained, 'He'll take minutes, see?'

'No.' Giridhar shook his head. 'The boy takes no minutes, you do.'

This sort of behaviour was entirely inappropriate. 'No,' Om said firmly. 'Harsha Bahadur is our peon, and he'll take the minutes for us.'

'Then what's the purpose of you managing office work?'

From Giridhar's garbled speech it was obvious that he was drunk. 'It's not my job to take minutes,' Om said. His voice wavered, for he wasn't used to disagreements. For all his army training, he had never mastered the art of striking, even in defence. He felt, even now, that he was being too quarrelsome. 'Harsha Bahadur is a capable young man,' he explained apologetically. Then without giving Giridhar a chance to say no, he turned to his mita-son, who was staring at the two of them like a startled goat. 'Take a seat, Son. Here, sit here beside me, and if you have any questions you can just ask your mita-father.'

Timidly, Harsha Bahadur perched by Om.

Giridhar slouched forward again and lay his head on the desk.

Tch, Om thought. It would be a disgrace to let him start the meeting drunk. 'I was thinking,' he said, 'I'd really like some tea.' In the interest of convincing Giridhar he made a show of looking at his watch. 'And it seems there's plenty of time till the meeting starts. What do you say, Giridhar-dai? Let's go and surprise my old woman by demanding a cup of tea.'

Giridhar scowled.

'She'll be thrilled,' Om said. 'I'll tell her: make us a cup of tea, quick.'

He stood up to get his friend to do the same, but Giridhar didn't budge. Awkwardly, Om remained squeezed between the desk and the wall.

When Giridhar finally spoke, his words had a snarling tone. 'You want me to be late for the meeting that I myself called?' He shook his fist, holding up his watch. 'It's past twelve and nobody's come. Don't they think what I say is important?' He narrowed his eyes in a way that made him look very unattractive. 'I know what you think, you think—what does he know, he's a useless lout out of work for years, he got fired, don't you know?' He suddenly roared, 'A drunk! You think Giridhar Adhikari's a drunk! You think, what does he know about running a campaign, we'll win without him based just on our candidate's acting skills. Hah! You think people will vote for a man just because he can act? You think he can win without me?'

'Ssss.' To Om's great dismay Giridhar was looking quite savage. Om sat down, protesting, 'Nobody thinks like that.'

'That's what you think!' Giridhar was still shouting, and Om feared that the workers downstairs would hear him. 'That's what everyone thinks—the cinema hero will win based on his fine talk alone! But only I know'—he waved at the scraps of paper that he'd posted, irregularly, over these months on the wall—'only I know what it really takes to lead us to victory!'

'Exactly,' Om said, feeling desperately unhappy. 'Your expertise is without a doubt most critical to our party. Only you know all the villages, Giridhar-dai. You belong to this soil. Only you know all the strategies we need to prepare for every voting booth.' Then, because there was no choice but to speak the difficult truth, he gingerly added, 'Perhaps, though, you might want to rest awhile before the meeting. You've been working hard, Giridhar-dai, a cup of tea might erase whatever—ha ha— whatever merriment you enjoyed over the festivals.'

'Don't call me a drunk!'

'I'm not calling you a drunk, I—'

'You always underestimate me, you condescend to me, you talk to me like a child!'

'Eh no, I—'

'Always meddling, meddling, meddling, you! Asking this, asking that, offering all kinds of advice as though I couldn't function without you!'

A pool of injury collected inside Om. 'Tch, let's not fight,' he said. 'Let's just—not fight, Giridhar-dai.'

Giridhar pointed at him with a thick forefinger. 'Never talk to me like an idiot!'

'I—'

'Never!'

Om was so hurt by these unkind words his eyes watered suddenly, and he had to turn away.

Eh, the intensity with which the impermanence in the body piqued one's lust for life! The revenue collector of yore Jimmawal-baaje was recovering from his protracted illness—Lord Krishna protected the religious-minded from harm. No longer laid flat by a raging imbalance of the digestive fires, he had begun to strut about his properties as part of his daily constitutional, treading nimbly through his front courtyard to the nine-stalled cow shed, and back. He wasn't as fit as he used to be, true. There were rashes on his skin, he sometimes trembled violently, and he still frequented the outhouse more than seven, eight times a day. But the bitter herbs and metal ashes he'd faithfully ingested these past months had brought back some of his old vigour. How short was the span of man's life in this earthly realm, he thought as he prepared for the party meeting today. How pressing the need to make each year, month, day, every moment yield, like a lemon, all its abundant but hidden juices.

'You're the only one who causes me some worry,' he said to his seventh son, who was helping him get dressed for the meeting. 'Yama Raj's chariot will come for me one day,' he said, slipping his legs into the white pajamas. 'There's no escaping the Lord of Death. Me, I've led a devout life, I'm prepared to take that final ride...I'll leave all my family behind and cross over to the next realms.' He grew sad just thinking of that inevitable passage. 'Eh it will be hard,' he said as he let his son tie his drawstring. 'There'll be ice and fire to endure, there'll be physical and mental torture to bear, there'll be ghouls and demons to flee, there'll be a river of pus to row across.' He pointed at his house, and at his nine-stalled cow shed. 'Will I be able to take all of this with me? Will I be able to enjoy it up there? Have I put together all this for my own satisfaction? It's for *you* that I've worked so hard.'

'Your kindness is immeasurable, Father.'

'The times, they are degraded.' Jimmawal-baaje sighed. 'Don't worry, Son. Lord Krishna will see to it that I don't die...till I see you gainfully employed.'

When the boy finished dressing him, Jimmawal-baaje put on his Chinese shoes and picked up his umbrella. He was leaving his home for the first time in months. He hurried towards the party office looking preoccupied. In these changing times, this kaliyuga, caste and position were not an adequate defence against the corrupt world of men. Money, that was what mattered in this dark age. Lord Krishna, he thought, how might he serve his family by amassing just a wee bit of wealth?

He received his answer the moment he saw the party office.

Lord Krishna, the building was ragged already! He approached it aghast. He poked at the flaking doorframe with the butt of his umbrella. A few months and there was filth all over. You'd think the house belonged to heathens!

Alarmed, he rushed into the downstairs corridor. There he stopped in shock. Who were all these people? Why were they loitering thus? 'Out, out,' he shooed away a few college boys. Beyond was a gang of hooligans…what kinds of godless ruffians had the party enlisted? To his horror one of them spat against the wall just as he passed. Direct provocation! Jimmawal-baaje slunk by as though he hadn't seen this. His condition was frail…he must avoid agitation. But he must be compensated for all damages borne!

He burst into the meeting room in a high state of agitation.

There, he once again stopped in shock. A very pricey desk stood before him, occupying the whole room. Pure teak: thousands and thousands it must have cost!

The drunkard Giridhar was sitting at the desk, next to rich, moneyed Om. To Jimmawal-baaje's irritation Om's idiot mita-son was also in the room. How lethargic the group of them were! How listlessly they sat in the room!

Jimmawal-baaje spun onto a chair by the door. 'Who would call this a new house!' he spluttered. His heart beat erratically. 'How will I fetch a fair price from the next tenant! A man came yesterday, wanted to know—would I rent him the house after the elections? I'm willing to pay a generous rent, he said. Me, I said: my loyalties to my party are firm, don't tempt me with offers of double rent, no matter how much you pay me, I couldn't tell the party to move!' As he spoke, Jimmawal-baaje lost his breath. 'The man,' he panted, 'he said—Baaje, your house is so good I'll pay *thrice* what the party's paying!'

Strictly speaking, none of this was true. But there was no

reason why such a conversation might not have taken place. The house was—it used to be—worth much more than the party paid in rent.

But neither Giridhar nor Om seemed to be listening.

'*Thrice* the rent,' Jimmawal-baaje squawked. The rashes on his face began to itch. 'Now my loyalties to the party are firm; I'll let you keep renting the house. But it's not fair for a poor Bahun like me to be made to suffer such a loss!'

'When have you ever incurred a loss?' This Om muttered under his breath. Nevertheless, because it was so unlike him to speak angrily, it was stunning. Om said, 'For a religious man you think too much about money, Baaje.'

'Who wouldn't!' Jimmawal-baaje thumped the new desk. 'A party which can afford such fine-fine tables!' He swept his eyes over Om's imported-wool sweater. Even the peon boy was dressed in newfangled foreign cloths. He said, 'I'm not like you, Om-bhai. I'm a poor Bahun with two wives, seven sons and twenty-two grandchildren to feed. You with your foreign-earned affluence, you think everyone's well-to-do?'

Om snapped, 'We should have rented a cheaper house in the first place. Then we could have hired more staff so I needn't have wasted my time in the office.'

'It's not as though you *have* spent much time here,' Jimmawal-baaje shot back, all righteous anger now. 'Our Om-bhai looks like a straight and simple Gurung, but he's as crafty as any Bahun, it seems. Crafty enough to hire his own mita-son to do all the party work.' He turned to glower at the boy. 'Everyone's taken advantage of the party, everyone's profiteered but me!'

At this the Gurung man did something truly frightening. He stood up—the whole bulk of him heaving—and slapped his hands so hard on the desk that its wood vibrated with thunder. 'Will your greed show no bounds!' he bellowed. 'Will you never stop thinking of your own selfish profits, your own selfish needs?' He leaned forward, and it looked like he might actually lunge for Jimmawal-baaje. He cried, 'To accuse a man like me of having taken advantage of the party—there must be limits, Jimmawal-baaje, to your mindless utterances. I will not tolerate this!'

Jimmawal-baaje steadied himself on his chair. 'Lord Krishna.' He realized he was shaking. His intestines growled. Eh gods! The winds of agitation had stoked his digestive fires. His system was in danger of igniting. Such brutes there were in this world full of defilement. And he, in his fragile health! Not wanting to provoke any more of the Gurung man's rage, he remained quiet at the desk.

But what a desk. Ten, twelve thousand it must have cost—twelve, fourteen, maybe more. He must raise the rent somehow.

Couldn't everyone just quieten down? When it came time to prove his worth, there was no one to support him. Giridhar stood alone. Still, he would show everyone that he was capable. He felt in his pant pocket for the sheet on which he'd scribbled the strategy for each booth committee. He felt the sleek curve of a ballpoint pen, a crumpled velvety rupee note, coins, a months-old cigarette stub, wood splinters, dust and lint. No strategy chit. How could there be no strategy chit? In his other pocket was a quarter bottle of Khukuri Rum. But no chit. Tch. A failure. No, it didn't matter. He knew by heart what he'd written on that chit. The only thing was, he needed to remember something . . . The memory would return as he talked, maybe.

For a long time they waited—Giridhar, Om, Jimmawal-baaje and the peon boy—for the cinema hero to make an appearance. At long last there was a scraping at the door, and the candidate walked in alongside Chiranjibi. The two of them were smiling in unison, and Giridhar was immediately struck by their camaraderie. Both men were dressed in identical homespun shirts.

Chiranjibi sat right next to the candidate. Giridhar thought: why stick to the man when the whole rest of the bench was free?

Nayan Raj said, 'People are full of questions these last days. Who will win, they ask. Whom should we vote for? We'll vote for whoever's going to win, they say. They fear they'll be punished later if they vote against the winning party.'

The contractor said, 'People look to political parties for patronage, for protection. This notion of freedom—of free choice—it hasn't found the right conditions to proliferate in yet.'

Giridhar thought: So? Didn't everyone know that? What was so profound about that?

Everyone turned to Giridhar. He saw that Om was staring at him, and thought maybe he should say something amusing to start off, the way Om always did. 'They're right,' Giridhar said, but his throat dried. He coughed, then continued, 'Those who come to power always punish those who didn't vote for them.'

'There's been much misuse of power,' Nayan Raj agreed.

'Which is why—' Giridhar couldn't go on. Not with this fake sitting before him, talking as if he was still a hero in some stupid cinema. And then Giridhar remembered that he needed to talk about each booth committee. He felt about his pockets. No strategy chit. Abruptly he said, 'Anyway, it's the booth strategy that counts in the end, not these big-big ideas. Let's turn to practical matters.' He meant to sound authoritative. Everyone was staring at him expectantly. A dull yellow flame flickered in the periphery of his vision. He feared, for a moment, his body's betrayals. 'In my village-to-village tour,' he began, 'I found that people responded well to our candidateji's personality, his message. They truly believe he'll—'

Affably, Nayan Raj cut in, 'We'll.'

'*We'll* offer them an alternative to the big parties. This means—'

Jimmawal-baaje chimed, 'Everyone's mesmerized by our

candidateji!'

Giridhar faltered. These interruptions seemed a questioning of his authority. Once again he felt in his pockets for the list of booth committees. He would have looked more impressive if he'd brought the chit. He felt the cool edges of the Khukuri Rum bottle. 'For each booth, I established a committee.' Then, without warning, the room suddenly tottered, and it was apparent that he was going to slide. He held on to the side of the desk. 'Our boys—'

'Men and women,' Chiranjibi said.

'—in each committee will protect our votes, now this isn't easy.' Giridhar closed his eyes and saw villages obscured by darkness. Words filled his mouth, making it hard to talk. Thickly he said, 'In Phirdi there's a Congress majority, the boys there get rough, they're going to try to capture the booth for sure. We've gathered a battalion to counter them, and they'll need to be paid for their efforts. In Puttar we're strong, we've got boys lined up and ready to capture the booth by noon. We can make eighty per cent of the votes fall in our name.'

'You—'

'And.' Giridhar forced himself to stay where he was, to keep talking as though chasms weren't yawning beneath him. 'In Chhang we must create a disturbance at the booth to keep voters away. That'll be best for us since we're not expecting votes there. Give our boys some drinks, set them loose, that's all it takes. There's a local boxing champion who's agreed to help.'

'You—'

'Now Mijethum is still puzzling me. Workers there say we should rely just on proxy voting, but I feel,' Giridhar opened his eyes, and the walls swayed, and he felt like he was falling. 'I feel that a little cleverness may be needed here. Now the nearby villages have waited for months for a bridge, and will vote for anyone who gives that to them. I propose—'

'Giridharji.'

'—we drop a few planks off a few days before elections, saying we've brought in a project to build them a bridge and here's proof of that. A few thousand rupees worth of planks will buy us thousands of votes.'

'Giridharji.'

The hardness of the candidate's tone this time halted him.

Everyone was staring at him.

What? Wildly, Giridhar looked at Om, who was looking away. His face was red.

'What?'

The candidate looked disgusted. 'You're not planning to steal votes?'

'Steal?'

From beside the candidate Chiranjibi remarked coldly, 'Our strategy, as you know, must simply be to protect votes already coming to us, not to steal votes that should go to other parties.'

This truly irked Giridhar: a contractor lecturing him on ethics. He snapped, 'This isn't the time for lessons on democracy.' He shook his head to clear his blurring vision. 'I'm not talking about the importance of free choice, or liberty and equality. I'm not using fancy words to talk about fine-fine ideas. No. I'm talking about how elections get run by everyone else, how we have to run them ourselves.'

Nayan Raj said firmly, 'But our principles have always been clear.'

'Principles.' Giridhar sneered. 'Our candidateji talks as though we live in a cinema.' In his pocket he gripped the bottle of rum. 'Every party has beliefs. The Congress says socialism but means free market. The UML says communism but means socialism. What does it mean? In the end they'll win only by rigging votes. Why shouldn't we?'

'Because our party stands for free choice.' This nonsense came not from Nayan Raj, but from Chiranjibi. They were the cinema hero's utterances, though.

'Now I have—had—a sheet,' Giridhar shouted at the contractor. 'I had it with me till this morning, I'll find it after the meeting. It has the strategy of every booth committee laid out, and if we don't follow these, we'll lose.'

'We may lose anyway.' This the contractor said sternly. 'Our objective, as Nayan Rajji has said many times, is not necessarily to win. Our objective is to impress people with our fairness. Our goal is to reform the whole system, Giridharji. We'll win next time, if not now.'

This last bit confused Giridhar. 'We'll win next time?'

'Because Nayan Rajji isn't here just to gather votes,' Chiranjibi lectured on, and suddenly Giridhar looked at Om— still turned away—and understood that the world was squeezing thin at this final hour, forcing him out, just as he always suspected it would. His hands started to shake. Chiranjibi continued to speak, but Giridhar saw fire at the edge of his vision. The desk in the room pushed against him, making it hard to breathe. The walls took on yellow and brown hues. The ceiling was buckling. He needed a drink.

His body slackened. Everything seemed far away. Somewhere, someone said, 'Now let's find out who's in our thirty-three booth committees and decide how they might protect our voters.'

'Yes let's begin.'

'Giridharji?'

'Giridharji?'

'Friend?'

Giridhar sat limply, allowing the desk to push against him. Madness. He needed a drink.

Never one to miss the opportunities created by shifting power balances, Jimmawal-baaje realized that he'd gravely erred, all these months, in pursuing the drunkard Giridhar—when it was Chiranjibi who was ascendant in the party. How unfortunate that he had failed to see this earlier! How fortunate that he saw it now! Ho: one look at the contractor, and one could see that he was a man of quiet capability. He looked so ordinary—a man who'd made millions off district-level bids without ever giving the impression that he was rich. Chiranjibi knew how to earn discreetly, save discreetly and spend discreetly. One had to admire such discretion. With his money he'd bought his way into Nayan Raj's confidence, and now spoke of high ideals—*this* was what a man must be like!

As soon as the meeting ended, Jimmawal-baaje edged up to the contractor. Giridhar was sitting within earshot, so Jimmawal-baaje couldn't say anything *too* obvious to express his respect for the man. He just indicated his support for Chiranjibi with an avid nod.

But Chiranjibi turned away.

The man demanded grovelling—naturally. Such were the rules of power; the meek must abide by them. And Lord Krishna, why not abide? Niskama kama, Jimmawal-baaje thought as he followed Chiranjibi, who was following Nayan Raj, out of the room.

Alone in the meeting room with Giridhar and his mita-son, Om dithered over what he should do. He watched his friend slouched in his seat, and he braced himself against his own impulse to comfort him. Why help such an unscrupulous man? Giridhar had betrayed all the party's ideals . . . he had planned to inflict harm on voters. Om thought: a boy skipped school to steal oranges from his neighbour's backyard . . . but that was long ago. Now he was heedless about people's feelings. He was arrogant, and he refused help. He poisoned all that was good in him with drink. And he hastened his own demise. He looked . . . unwell. Wasted. And before he knew what he was doing, Om had shifted over to Giridhar. He put his arm around his shoulder.

'Friend?'

Giridhar shrugged his hand off.

Om felt a broad, unfocussed pain in his chest.

Giridhar: his old, old friend. Abandon him to his barbarous battlefield. Leave now, Om told himself. Leave Giridhar.

'Come, Son.' He rose from the bench and led Harsha Bahadur to the door. From there he gave Giridhar one last look. His friend was glaring hard at the table, as he'd done throughout the meeting. The top of a bottle was visible from his coat pocket.

Tch. Om said, 'Friend . . .'

Giridhar snapped to life. 'Don't think I don't know what you people think of me!'

You people—this was who he was to Giridhar?

The bottle, a sparkle of gold and white, shattered against the wall.

And Om walked out the door, severing his oldest link of love.

48

Jimmawal-baaje died the next day. He was at the party office pestering Chiranjibi to raise the rent when he collapsed and lost consciousness. Party workers rushed to call the Doctor Sah'b, but not even the Doctor Sah'b's father could have jogged the revenue collector back to life. He stopped breathing long before his seventh son flagged down a taxi-car to transport him to the hospital at the district centre.

'The old baaje passed away with the name of Lord Krishna on his lips,' said the townspeople, generous and reverent in the face of death. 'May his soul find liberation from the cycle of rebirth, may he find a place in the upper realms.'

The following day the candidate and all the party members attended his cremation by the shores of the Seti river. Rishi followed the funeral procession through the southern end. Before reaching the river, though, he veered towards the shacks of landless settlers. He wanted to find the Moonlight Hotel to meet the schoolmaster. He would explain his lapses and terminate their collaboration. He would end his spell underground.

He found the Moonlight Hotel without much difficulty, in a quiet alley wedged behind the Agriculture Office. It was one of the larger lodges of the southern end, with two separate rooms for dining and lodging. The woman who ran the hotel said that the schoolmaster hadn't come today. 'He'll come tomorrow,' she said, surveying Rishi brassily. There was an infant in her arms. Her breasts were scantily covered by a too-tight blouse, and she exuded the careless sexuality of a breastfeeding mother. 'One o'clock most days the schoolmaster comes here.'

From there Rishi took a bus to the district centre to arrange for the transfer of his land into his father's name. The deed could take months to transfer if he didn't allot all the necessary cuts, so he did. He spent a few hours by the river near the district centre, sitting on an embankment of sand and schist. By the time he returned to Khaireni Tar that afternoon, the party workers had returned from Jimmawal-baaje's cremation.

That night in the teashop the party workers kept talking about the cremation. Jimmawal-baaje's death had animated everyone; though no one seemed upset by the loss. 'Just yesterday he came to the office, threatening to raise the rent,' Juddha said. 'He didn't look well, but I never thought—.'

Another worker said, 'At the pyre, his seventh son looked

just like him. For a moment I thought it was him.'

'All his older sons also looked the same.'

'Their white clothes.'

'Why did Jimmawal-baaje always wear white?'

The inconsequential chatter that followed a man's death: a man's fleeting afterlife. Rishi was turned, subtly, towards Binita. When her brother-in-law returned from Kathmandu, Binita had slipped into the guarded role of the town's Binita-bhauju. Rishi and she had reverted to greater distance, as though agreeing tacitly that their intimacy must stay suspended for now. Rishi continued to tutor Madhu and Tripti, and felt quite sure that he was still included in Binita's thoughts. He was willing to wait for an opening when they could talk.

Tonight, for a short while before the meal, he looked over the assignments he had given the girls. Madhu, under his supervision, was becoming interested in studying, though she was an excitable girl, and easily distracted. Tripti's greatest weakness was math. She didn't understand the simplest divisions, and though she could copy the fractions in her textbook she couldn't figure out what they meant. Rishi was patient with her. 'Pay attention, now,' he said. 'Two more fractions and you're done.' From time to time Binita glanced their way as they sat—tutor and students—bent over their notebooks. Rishi felt that through the din of the teashop, she was listening to them. 'Two more fractions,' he said to Tripti. 'Listen to me. You can do it.'

The next morning he returned to the district centre to follow up on the land deeds. He had thought he might return to the Moonlight Hotel that afternoon, but when he returned to Khaireni Tar he found a commotion taking place outside the People's Party office. Giridhar had been dismissed, that morning, as the party's chairman. Om had been asked to replace him, but he had declined. For lack of a better alternative, then, Chiranjibi had reluctantly accepted the post.

In a disorderly scene that extended all the way to the highway, Giridhar was now taunting Chiranjibi about his inexperience. It was obvious, from Giridhar's dishevelment, that he was drunk. Chiranjibi stood in a crowd of workers trying to reason with him; but Giridhar entertained no reasoning. 'You do whatever you want, let's see how many votes you bring,' he yelled at Chiranjibi as the whole bazaar watched, with craned necks, from the bar-peepal tree. His words were grotesquely slurred, and he cut a ridiculous figure. He was obviously beyond caring. He gestured obscenely at Chiranjibi. 'Eeeh, pubic hair. Eeeh! Run your elections like the cinema hero wants, and let's see you win, motherfucking corpse!'

Juddha Ale was trying to restrain him. 'Leave it be, Giridhar-dai, leave it be.'

'Eeeh!'

Rishi watched the spectacle from a distance. The day passed in uproar as Giridhar returned again and again, in greater states of inebriation, to curse and swear at the injustice done to him. Every time he returned to the party office, he was prevented by workers from getting into the building. 'Let me in you motherfuckers, I built this party with my own blood and sweat. The teacup is mine, you can't kick me away like a stray dog now!' For a long while he raged. Then, maniacally, he started to sing the song featured in *Ma Manchhe Hun*. '*I'm a person, I'm a person,*' he sang off-tune, swaying his hips obscenely in burlesque mimicry of the revolutionary that Nayan Raj had played. '*You're a person, you're a person.*' He skipped towards an imaginary heroine beneath a flower tree. '*Let's share our personhood.* Eeeh!'

The townspeople laughed openly at the fracas, and their audience inspired Giridhar to greater outlandishness. 'Can a cinema hero do politics?' he shouted across the highway, demanding their witness. 'A Kathmandu intellectual! Pretending to love villagers! He thinks no one's going to see that he's just acting the role? The teacup party, hah! I'll piss in the teacup, I'll break it to bits! I dare the cinema hero to win! The man dyes his hair black! But he can't fool me! Eeeh!'

It was only towards evening time that the Sub-Inspector of Police finally lured him away with a promise of drink.

In the party office, the party workers were scandalized. The things Giridhar had said—the ravings of a drunk—had nonetheless set off disquiet and doubt. An impulse to cynicism, reined in till now, was suddenly unleashed. Workers sniggered, recalling Giridhar's imitation of Nayan Raj's dancing. Did Nayan Raj really dye his hair black? Was he just acting like a politician, as Giridhar said? The candidate was, after all, an outsider to the district. And a cinema hero. He seemed sincere. But didn't he seem, well, *too* sincere? Wasn't he too perfect to be real?

By the time of the evening meal the workers had grown solemn. It was too late for them *not* to back Nayan Raj now— they might as well follow through with their commitments, and collect due compensation after the elections. Besides, even if Nayan Raj was a fake, he wasn't a bad man. He was nice to everyone. There was nothing to dislike about him. He refused to condemn Giridhar for his antics, and seemed more—well, unreal for it. Still, the man couldn't be entirely fake. He probably didn't dye his hair. And what he said about democratic reform—it was glib, but true.

But there was a more serious problem facing the party. Giridhar hadn't told anyone his plans for the booth committees; and no one else knew what these were. As he tutored Madhu and Tripti that afternoon Rishi heard other workers worry, without saying so directly, about Chiranjibi's inexperience. 'We don't even know who's in our booth committees,' Juddha said at a nearby table. 'How can we instruct them what to do?'

To Rishi this seemed to afford an opportunity—to put all the falsehood behind him. He thought all night about what to do: how to act in freedom. And the next morning he handed Nayan Raj the copy book from his village-to-village tour. 'These are some notes I took,' he said, ending his collaboration with the schoolmaster. 'I was with Giridharji in the villages. I know what he planned for the booths.'

Rishi spent the day with Nayan Raj and Chiranjibi, poring over the lists of names. 'Ram Bahadur Ale, Harka Prasad Pun, Devi Nath Parajuli, Karna Dhoj Malla,' he read out from his copy book. 'They wanted to hire ten boys at that booth. At the next booth there was Lal Bahadur Thapa, Romani Regmi, Hit Man Gurung. They were going to buy a hundred-odd votes.'

'And in the Rayapur booth,' Chiranjibi asked, 'who are the members of the Rayapur booth?'

Rishi read from the copy book. 'Bhim Nidhi Shrestha, Harihar Rawal, Jetha Thapa Magar and Kirtiman Gurung. That area has a majority of UML voters. The Congress was planning to create a scare to keep them away.'

'Dhor? What about Dhor?'

'Laxman Mahat, Chudamani Aryal, Keshab Pun and Shyam Prasad Adhikari. That's a Congress stronghold. We can expect a lot of violence if Congress doesn't look set to win.'

All of Rishi's excellent work for the masses. He felt like he was releasing himself as he read aloud his notes. He was gaining the gratitude of Nayan Raj, he knew: a favour in stock. But it wasn't for Nayan Raj that he was making this choice. It wasn't even to manoeuvre closer to Binita, not really. He was doing this to unfetter himself.

He tried to get away the next day to meet the schoolmaster, to let him know that he had betrayed him—but Nayan Raj and Chiranjibi detained him with questions on his notes. The two of them formed a thick bond now, whispering over sheets of paper.

Om sometimes joined in their discussions, but the other younger members were never asked to participate. Rishi preferred not to be consulted anyway. In a few days his land deeds would be transferred, and he would get the money due him from his father. There would be nothing tying him back any more. The only thing he wanted of politics, now, was to meet the schoolmaster once, to explain. Why? To receive his sympathy? Impossible. The older man would never condone his anarchy.

By the time he managed to slip away from the office that day, it was already four.

'He waited for you yesterday, he waited for you today,' said the woman who ran the Moonlight Hotel. 'I told him maybe you'd come at one, and he waited for you.' She pointed to a bed next to the kitchen stove. Her baby was sleeping there, bundled in a flannel sheet. 'Sit, Bhai. I'll make you tea.'

'I can't.'

The woman came up to him. 'There's what—a copy book you have?' She flashed him a dimpled smile. 'The schoolmaster said you could leave it with me. But first I'll make you hot tea.' She took his arm and nudged him towards the bed. 'I've called the schoolmaster my dai for years now. You can trust me. There's no need to feel uneasy with me.'

Rishi saw that her too-tight blouse—the same one she'd worn before—wasn't a licence of motherhood; it was an offering. She wanted to effect an exchange, turning him, and herself, into ornaments in the schoolmaster's design. The top hook of her blouse was unfastened.

Rishi shook free. 'I haven't brought the copy book,' he said.

'Bring it tomorrow, then.'

Leaving the hotel, he thought: Binita. At that proximity, with such permission, he would have unfastened her blouse.

49

When Rishi entered her teashop, Binita tried not to look at him. She tried not to look at him when he left. Sometimes he would look at her, and she had to turn away. She feared that their affinity would show. When Madhu and Tripti took lessons with him, she looked at the girls, not at him. But she saw Rishi. She saw the way he taught her cousin and daughter, and she took note of the attentiveness he showed them. Madhu, Tripti, Rishi. They looked unusual together. But not wrong. They looked interesting. Rishi looked interesting. She heard his measured words through the more unruly sounds of the teashop, and she felt, somehow, that he was addressing them to her.

She made an effort to busy herself in her work. Pramila had delayed her return, and there was much to do. From the time Binita awoke till the time she went to sleep at night, she moved from one practiced chore to another. She overheard the workers in the teashop talking of the goings-on in the party. But she didn't pay attention. She was focused on her own questions.

A life of desires held in check.

Binita's workload eased when Pramila returned from her family and resumed her work at the teashop. 'You go and rest,' Pramila said to her, tying a scarf around her hair. 'I'm back now, you can sit with your arms folded like a princess.'

Pramila was happier than she'd been at Dashain time. Her brothers had asked around about her husband, she said. They found someone who'd seen him in a hotel in Lucknow city two years ago. Now they were trying to trace him, relying on men who worked as private guards there. 'The lout probably spends all his earnings on booze and whores,' Pramila grumbled. 'Doesn't he know I'm working day and night to support his family—his father, his mother? Doesn't he care?' She joined her palms and raised her arms theatrically towards the posters on the wall facing her. 'Eh Radha-Krishna, Shiva-Parvati, give him the brains to think of his family too, and not just of himself, his booze and his whores.'

Madhu and Tripti were delighted to have her back. 'There's no justice in this world, Pramila-didi,' Madhu said. The girl had grown less stuck-up of late. She said, 'You're better off without your husband. You're better off being free.' Binita was glad to see the girl changing. She had never known how to penetrate Madhu's mind. Pramila seemed more skilful at befriending her.

With Pramila back, Binita could take things easy. But she felt too restless to stop working. She busied herself in the teashop, waiting for Rishi to come. And when he arrived, she found herself glancing at him again and again. She was being careless, she knew. She tried, sometimes, to stay away from the teashop. All one day she carried buckets of water from the tap to irrigate the backyard for the winter vegetables. She shored up the beds and cleared them of weeds. She mixed dung into the soil. But when she rested, at the end of the day, she found herself thinking of Rishi's light eyes, his quiet words. She went back into the teashop to see if he had come.

A mother's group meeting was scheduled for a few days later. Binita found that she waited for that too.

On the day of the mother's group meeting, Binita went to Thakalni-aama's Himal Lodge Restaurant Bar and found Laksmi waiting for her there. 'She's already gone,' Laksmi said, pointing towards the kitchen. 'I waited so that you and I could go together.'

They headed together into town. Binita noticed that Laksmi hadn't changed in her conduct towards her, despite the altercation between Giridhar and Nayan Raj-bhai. She had washed her hair today, and had combed it back neatly. But her eyes were lined

with shadows. Her husband was clearly straining her. The two
of them walked in what seemed a mutually desired silence towards
the town's first ward, which sprawled past the ashen flatlands.
Binita rarely ventured to the southern end. The mothers' group
had begun raising funds there, and would move on to the second
ward after a few weeks. It would take maybe three months to
raise money in all the town's wards.

The women had gathered in front of a house that belonged
to an old Indian Gurkha lieutenant. Hom Kumari and the ascetic's
wife were standing in front, with Thakalni-aama. Other women
shuffled about shyly. Binita saw the Magar woman whom she'd
sat next to at the first meeting. She went to her, Laksmi following
behind.

The other woman recognized Binita: 'You didn't come to the
last meeting.' She was wearing a marigold in her hair, as she
had before. 'I looked for you, but you didn't come.'

The lieutenant was sitting, with folded arms, on his front
porch. The men of the house were squatting near by, while the
family's women lingered at the front door, covering their smiles
with the ends of their fariyas. The lieutenant joked, 'I'd heard the
mothers were going from house to house, and was wondering
when they'd come to us.'

The ascetic's wife raised her hands. 'The mothers have come,
Laf'tan Sah'b! The mothers have come to your house.' She turned
to the women, then broke into song:

> *How beautiful she is, our Mother.*
> *How bright and full of force.*

It was a prayer to the goddess Durga that many were familiar
with. A few women picked up:

> *With the lion at her feet.*

Others began to clap.

With her spear poised to fight the evils of the world.

The group hedged forward uncertainly. Binita lingered behind, next to the woman with the marigold in her hair. The woman was singing along. Laksmi was clapping. Binita also clapped. No one was dancing yet, and everyone was glancing at each other for cues on how to begin. There was a stiffness in their smiles; the audience of men was intimidating them. Laksmi kept turning to look at Binita, as though she wanted to see if Binita was enjoying herself, and if she was expected to be enjoying herself too. A few women giggled like schoolgirls.

Thakalni-aama and the ascetic's wife suddenly swept up to the men of the lieutenant's family. 'The mothers are dancing,' cried Thakalni-aama. 'See how our old bones dance!'

The other women began to sing louder:

How beautiful she is, our Mother.
How bright and full of force.

Their clapping grew louder, but they still hesitated to join the older women. Binita thought of what Phool Devi had said— women jiggling and shaking as though anyone would want to see that. The women of the mother's group were afraid of eliciting such judgment: it was awkward for them to dance. Binita herself would never dance in public before the whole town.

Thakalni-aama and the ascetic's wife swayed for a while to the religious song. Then someone interrupted with another song, which was more appealing: a soulful lament on lost love. Drawn out by the wavering calls of an abandoned lover, Hom Kumari and a few other women joined in the dance.

By then Pramila had arrived at the meeting. When the song

of lament ended, Pramila stepped forward. 'I have a song.' She
placed her hands on her hips. 'Eh,' she began. Then she launched
on the number one hit song on the radios:

Me, I'm a boy from the flatlands.
A boy from the flatlands.

The other women started to laugh.
'You're not a boy,' cried the woman next to Binita.
Pramila stroked a make-believe moustache. 'Ho yes, I am.'
She winked bawdily at the woman:

Me, I'm a boy from the flatlands.
A boy from the flatlands.
Eh young girl, won't you run away with me?
Let's ride off in a taxi-car.

'Ho what a handsome man!' The woman stepped forward.
Without a trace of abashment, she retorted:

You, you're a boy from the flatlands.
A boy from the flatlands.
You can't earn enough for yourself, let alone for me.
I won't ride off with you in a taxi-car.'

A group of women began to rally behind Pramila, singing
along with her:

Me, I'm from a bazaar town,
But you're from the hills.
Eh young girl, how pretty you are!
Let's ride off in a taxi-car.

Another group of women rallied back:

You, you're a boy from a bazaar,
A boy from a bazaar.
How can a hill girl trust a boy like you?
I won't ride off with you in a taxi-car.

The lieutenant gave them two hundred rupees at the end of this duet.

Laughing at their crazy success, the women headed to the house next door. Here, Pramila and some other women danced to a song about an unripe jackfruit. The household head stood at formal attention as he watched the women dance. 'You must continue to organize,' he said as he handed Hom Kumari his family's contribution. 'You must do what you can to develop women.'

The women moved from house to house, singing, clapping, dancing, entreating each family for help with Akala-mai's shrine, and counting gleefully as people made donations. Eventually they lost their inhibitions. The younger and old women began to dance together; religious songs gave way to love songs and duets. At one house Hom Kumari and the woman with the marigold in her hair started to dance together. Binita saw Laksmi laughing at the sight.

Binita asked her who the woman was. 'I've talked to her but don't know who she is.'

Laksmi met Binita's eyes. 'That's Lalita, the Sub-Inspector's younger wife. Hom Kumari and Lalita: the man's two wives, dancing together.'

Binita turned back to watch them, remembering that Hom Kumari had tried to get the second marriage annulled. *Who'll take me now that I've been used by one man? Everyone knows your husband's made a wife out of me.* That mustn't have been many years ago. Now here they were, the two wives, dancing together. Hom Kumari perspired with the effort of keeping her plump body in motion. Lalita was less supple, but more abandoned in her movements. Binita saw a long yellow mark—an old bruise—at the back of Lalita's blouse as she lifted her hands.

'How these old bones can move,' the ascetic's wife cried, joining the younger women. 'How they can sway in service to Akala-mai.'

Lalita laughed, 'What devotees we are.' She had an irreverence that Binita liked. 'Sacrificing our time, energy and good names for Akala-mai.'

'It's all for Akala-mai,' the ascetic's wife said, missing the irony.

When Lalita stopped dancing, she came back beside Binita. She couldn't be over twenty-five or twenty-six, Binita figured. Her face was flushed and she looked striking with the marigold in her hair.

'We are devout, aren't we?' Binita said to her.

'Devout as priests who perform rituals for pay,' Lalita said. They laughed together.

'What?' Laksmi turned eagerly to them. 'What?'

'Women are devout,' Lalita said.

Laksmi smiled uncertainly, eyeing the two of them.

Then Lalita called out to the group: 'Let's count our money, let's see how much we've earned.' She left Binita's side, and Laksmi followed her.

Binita took this chance to leave. It was past ten, and she needed to get back to the teashop to help Madhu with the morning meal. Pramila was enjoying herself, and Binita didn't disturb her. Nor did she take leave of anyone. The group would meet every week. She would come to its meetings. She was glad she had joined in now. She liked Lalita. Perhaps they would become friends. She remembered the yellowing bruise beneath her blouse. The hard-won laughter of women: wasn't this change enough in her life?

She felt buoyed making her way back through the southern part of town. Though she hadn't danced, she felt she'd done something sassy, even impudent. She could hear the cries of the mothers even as she made her way past the bamboo-and-thatch huts of landless settlers. In a short while she passed a line of brewhouses. This was a part of town Binita never came to, a settlement of migrants from other districts who probably didn't know her, whom she didn't know. From a thatched teashop came the sound of a woman laughing frankly. A man was saying something. A few teenage boys loitered on the path, as though waiting for their lives to begin.

Binita followed the path into the heart of the neighbourhood. Beyond was a fork in the road: she could either head towards the highway or take the path past the Agriculture Office. She was about to turn onto the path when she caught sight of Rishi.

He was in the front room of a hotel with his back turned to her, sitting next to a tall man with an upright posture and bristly silver hair. Binita recognized the man at once: the old schoolmaster of Khaireni Tar, renowned for his lifelong dedication as a communist. He was the secretary of the UML's district committee.

She stopped to take in the sight. Was she mistaken? No. Rishi and the schoolmaster were sitting so close that their sides touched. Binita couldn't see their faces, she couldn't see whether they were talking or not. Rishi was looking down at his hands listening to the other man speak. He often sat like that in her teashop, listening to the radio. Binita stood a long while watching the two men side by side. Their affinity was unmistakeable. Then she turned past the Agriculture Office.

It didn't surprise her, deception.

All the unreliable men: spectres changing form. Rishi had
been spying on her brother-in-law's party. *A kind of person is
struggling for birth. A free person . . .* Had he been deceiving her
too? What of the way he turned to her; what of the way he waited
for her to turn to him? The way he lingered, giving her all the
leverage. Hadn't he been true with her? Rishi's papery skin, the
delicacy of his bones. His loneliness bordering on arrogance.
His dry lips. She was sure she knew him.

When she reached the far end of the Agriculture Office, she
turned back to take another look. Rishi had stood up and was
turned this way. He was too far away for Binita to make out
whether he'd seen her, but there was a sudden alertness in his
posture. She paused, feeling an uncomfortable thrill at being
included in his conspiracy.

What was she to do about what she'd seen? She turned back
and left the path of the Agriculture Office. At the edge of the
bazaar, she looked about at the society which rationed her meagre
pleasures. A few men were gathered around the watchmaker's
stall, looking at him as he worked. Others were gathered in the
doorways of shops, gossiping. Beyond, the bus stop was teeming.
The whole bazaar seemed taken over by men.

Binita then saw her brother-in-law coming out of the People's
Party office across the highway. There was a crowd in front of
the office building, but Nayan Raj-bhai stood out because of his
height. He was heading to her teashop for his morning meal.

A free person. Binita headed home to take up the guise of
Nayan Raj's Binita-bhauju.

50

It was time and he needed to know. He needed to know: where
was he going? Rishi rushed into Binita's teashop, thinking it was
time. A roomful of watchful men. At the stove, Binita's back was

turned to the room. She had communicated something to him when he saw her from the Moonlight Hotel: I have recognized you. He had taken leave of the schoolmaster and followed her, but too late. She must have just arrived.

Rishi took a seat at a nearby table occupied by Om, who was talking to men at the next table. When Rishi sat, Om turned to him and began to talk in his longwinded, loquacious way. 'Oho Rishi-bhai. Come, sit. You look hungry. Things have been so hectic. All of us are so busy we forget to eat. All of us, working as one, we belong to one family—and I don't mean just the party members. We, all of us—the town. We belong to the vast and interlinked family of humankind, isn't that so?'

Rishi could hardly bother to listen. He swept his gaze across the room. The fariya she wore today had black and white triangle shapes.

'It's our duty to extend love to each other,' Om said, for some reason. 'Of course this is difficult. Love isn't easy, love takes work.'

What was Binita thinking, turned away like this? Would she tell her brother-in-law? Had she already told him? Or would she protect his secret? And would they meet, in secret?

'Do you think I'm being unreasonable, Rishi-bhai?' Om asked. He waited for an answer, so Rishi shrugged. There was a resoluteness to Binita's stance. Om said, 'Sometimes, I wonder if it's me. But doesn't man's very morality stem from his capacity to love? We live in such a hard land. Our soil—we must nourish it. We must love the poor, the hapless. We must love friends in need. But—.'

Impatient with such effusive sentimentality, Rishi glanced back at Binita. A sign: Binita was just standing at the stove; she wasn't preparing his meal. Was she stalling?

Meanwhile, Om continued, 'But what Giridhar-dai did to the party Tch. How could he? Where's the heart? If a man can only take love, but can't give any back—what good? Really, I feel sorry for him.'

Binita was stalling for time.

Om finally seemed to notice that Rishi wasn't listening. He followed Rishi's gaze towards Binita. 'The rice may have run out,' he suggested tactfully. 'I'm sure our Binita-bhauju will prepare more for you.'

Rishi flushed at having been caught in his desire.

Om seemed oblivious to his embarrassment. Genially, he said, 'She's been a blessing for the party, Binita-bhauju. Her excellent food makes us all feel at home. Feeding hundreds of workers over these months: the party owes much to her.'

Rishi saw that Om had finished eating and was waiting for the right time to go and wash his hands. At another table Nayan Raj and Chiranjibi had also finished eating, and were beginning to stand. Binita turned at the sound of benches scraping. Her first glance was towards Rishi. Her eyes were still. She was waiting to talk to him.

Rishi said, 'Do wash your hands, Om-dai. You needn't wait for me.'

Om glanced from Rishi to Binita, to Rishi again, then looked away discreetly. 'Are you sure, Bhai? If you don't mind, then, I'll go wash my hands.'

'Yes of course.'

Left alone at the table, Rishi fidgeted. The room suddenly felt cold. Winter proper was setting into the town, and the long dry season had begun. The cold was something Rishi wanted to feel right now. He took off his blue cardigan and laid it on the bench. This time of year it was frigid in Kathmandu. He thought back to the last room he'd occupied there. The bed, the table, the dank cement floor, narrow hallways in and out. Places where he didn't matter. Now his shoulders hunched in cold. Around him people were taking turns leaving after having finished their meals.

Rishi could hear some leftover gossip about Giridhar. He didn't bother to follow. Binita was still at the stove. Rishi tried to harden himself against a shudder of cold bones.

And then, as the room buzzed with conversation, as the rest of the workers talked among themselves, Binita came. Without looking at him, without uttering a word, she set down the rice, daal, vegetables and pickles. She was a hand's reach away. She had waited for him. That too was an intimacy. The black and white triangles on her fariya were still. At the cusp of losing her trust, Rishi knew he could not make a new life for himself without her.

'It'll be best if you leave.' Her each soft word fell into place.

Rishi said, 'Yes.' In a flash he understood. She had protected him. She wouldn't tell anyone. She wouldn't betray him; but neither would she betray her brother-in-law. Rishi's leaving would be justice enough. She had thought it through. She had opened his door out. She stood, black and white triangles, a hand's reach away.

There were others around them, but no one was paying them any attention. In the small private space that opened in the midst of this crowd, Rishi said, 'And if I come back after the elections and prove I've committed no deception?'

Binita looked hard at him.

'Will you trust me then?' Rishi asked. 'Will you come to Kathmandu with me? You, me, Tripti—Madhu. Will you marry me, will you give me your life?'

Binita stayed absolutely still, looking at him.

'Or will you keep playing Binita-bhauju to the world?'

Binita glanced towards the kitchen counter, at Madhu. Tripti was at school right now. Impossible to read Binita's thoughts. Then she looked back at him, calmly meeting his gaze. She said, 'Have you been true to yourself?'

'I've been true to you.'

'You'll show yourself honestly?'

'I'll show myself to you.'

Then Binita glanced, again, towards Madhu.

Rishi said, 'I'll come in a month.'

'Two months.' Binita had thought it through. She looked back at Rishi, intent and grave as they conspired, in the middle of the teashop, towards their happiness.

Rishi agreed, 'I'll come in two months.'

Binita looked down, and then the black and white triangles on her fariya shifted as she stepped away.

Rishi bowed his head and started to eat his last meal of mansuri rice from the northern hills. He was ready to put behind him his childhood of shielding his mother, his school days of desiccation, his romantic youth in the communist party, his young blundering love, his spiteful adulthood, his homesickness for the schoolmaster. He would finish all the paperwork at the district centre, then go home and collect the twenty-five thousand his father owed him. And then—.

There would only be the ever-shifting present. There would be no more nostalgia.

51

An idea had fixed in Madhu's mind of late: she must find the Khadka boy and tell him she'd marry him. Ho. So all right, all men were useless and he was an ugly boy. But his prospects were good. And his freeness—she must have it. A husband—every girl eventually ensnared one. In this day and age, what was the headache? She must find a husband too, and build a free life upon him.

The pills she'd bought from the Doctor Sah'b had fixed her foot, and made her feel strong; it took her no time to run across the highway and into town. In the past months Madhu's face had lost some of its full-moon lustre, but she was still far from plain. Rose shades still blushed her body—and wasn't there a mole on her chin? She'd begun to wear her best kurtha-sural and her hair was combed with a left part, which suited her best. She had realized that a girl needed looks to get a boy.

Almost every day she skirted the town's front alleys, heading towards Om Gurung's yellow house with stucco pineapples. She had to find that boy. There were countless pathways he must take to work; she checked them all in the hope of meeting him. And as she wandered about, she saw things that gripped her with a queer mix of wonder and bitterness.

Look: a group of girls walked by singing a song that sounded like a love duet, but was actually asking for votes:

Earthquakes, famines, landslides, floods.
Vote for the sun, we'll end this sweat and blood.

One of the girls had short-cropped hair and was wearing pants like a boy.

Madhu got agitated.

She had to find that ugly boy.

'Where is Harsha Bahadur Khadka, son of Krishna Bahadur Khadka?' This she asked with great bravery of the blind shopkeeper Shankar. Shankar turned and his gaze settled on a spot behind Madhu. She repeated, 'Harsha Bahadur Khadka, son of Krishna Bahadur Khadka.'

The shopkeeper kept staring past her. 'What is it for?'

'I had something to talk to him about.'

'About?'

Madhu blushed fiercely. 'Just something.'

'And you would be?'

Suddenly she panicked that perhaps he wasn't blind after

all. Perhaps he could see her!

'And you would be?' he repeated.

'Nobody.' A girl looking for a boy—. 'Never mind,' Madhu said, and fled back home.

But she returned every day, and began to sit in a sheltered niche by the watchmaker's canvas stall, looking out for the ugly boy. Each time she came to the bazaar, she grew more and more resentful. She'd been cheated from so much. The more modern women in particular angered her. They marched about the roads, not at all bothered about how strange they looked or what people might say. Madhu kept staring at them. There was a woman at a cheap tea stall serving men with a smile. Another woman sat on a front porch with a baby strapped to her back, reading a magazine. One woman was manning a shop all by herself. Her customer—herself an unmarried girl—was talking without the least modesty to a boy in line with her. No one seemed to find such behaviour irregular. The atmosphere of the bazaar was so free.

After spending hours in the bazaar, she asked the watchmaker, 'What time is it, Dai?' and regardless of his response, she knew that it was time to leave all this, for today.

one one one one vote

one one one one volt

52

On the afternoon before voting day, as Harsha Bahadur walked
home from a day of work, his Maoist second cousin stepped out
of a mulberry bush and took him to a side alley. There he delivered
stunning news of an utterly un-Maoist variety: Sani was walking
through town looking for him.

All at once the breath rushed out of Harsha Bahadur's body.
He stammered, 'Sa-Sa-Sa-Sani?'

'She calls herself Madhu these days.'

Sani. Her face as radiant as the moon on a summer's night.
The well-placed mole on her chin. Her modesty, her grace, her
perfection. His love. Sani, looking for him. Stunned, he asked,
'Did you talk to her?'

'Talk to her?' his cousin scoffed. Each time Harsha Bahadur
saw him, his cousin looked more and more heroic. Today again
he was dressed in army fatigues, and his wispy beard was neat
and combed. He said, 'A girl whose only aim is to be exchanged
like a cow? No, I didn't talk to her.' For a while he turned his
face skyward, and Harsha Bahadur braced for him to rail in
Maoism. Instead his cousin turned to him with a flash in his
eyes. 'I needn't have told you, you know.'

Harsha Bahadur bowed his head. 'I know you never liked
her, Dai.'

His cousin's beard waggled as he said, 'It's all because I
love you, stupid bourgeois boy.'

'I know you love me, Dai.'

'Love.' His cousin sneered. 'An imperialist broker-capitalist
reformist bourgeois waste of a human being's life, love. You
have to engage in guerrilla warfare.' Again he turned to the sky.
'The revolution needs warriors, not lovers. The revolution needs

thinkers, not feelers. How will the workers and peasants ever be liberated if their warriors are busy loving?' Then he sighed and turned back to Harsha Bahadur, his face soft like a disappointed child's. 'But it's too late, brother: I love you and find that I'm willing to do anything for you.'

Harsha Bahadur was touched. It was true that his cousin loved him. Taking time away from his work beneath the ground, his cousin had shown up when he needed company, and had boosted his morale, talking to him, encouraging him, listening to his tales, advising him and inducting him into the town's ways. Truly he was more than a second cousin—he was a friend. Harsha Bahadur said, 'I love you too, Dai.'

His cousin grunted. 'I'll take you to meet her tomorrow,' he said. 'Come here in the morning, I'll take you to her.'

The whole world slanted and whirled around Harsha Bahadur. 'Take me to her?' he squeaked.

'I'll take you to her.'

No, he mustn't dream to want Sani any more. 'But the office,' Harsha Bahadur protested. 'It's my duty to mind the office when everyone is at the voting booth.'

His cousin smiled for the first time that Harsha Bahadur ever remembered. He looked very nice when he smiled. He said, 'At shops, in houses, she's been asking: where is Harsha Bahadur Khadka? In my opinion, brother, your bourgeois fantasy of being a happy husband, father and grandfather is on the verge of coming true. Now I can't deny you your happiness, counter-revolutionary and reformist as it may be. You are a lumpen mass; you severely lack consciousness and you can't be righted without an armed struggle. So.' He placed an arm around Harsha Bahadur. 'I'll mind the office for you. That's how soft I've become in the heart for you. Now go. Come here tomorrow morning, I'll take you to her.'

Then, suddenly, he disappeared into a mulberry bush.

Harsha Bahadur stood by the bush, shaking and quaking, cradling his head in his hands. How? The distant star of his dark life with a mole on her chin who was flawless and whom he loved but who he thought didn't love him was now asking for him by name so that she could choose him in a free and fair manner as all choices must be made if they were to be called truly democratic according to the cinema hero Nayan Raj whose teacup party he worked for as the People's Party Peon. Sani choosing him? Without his even campaigning? How?

True love. He shivered. Harsha Bahadur thought of his mother, whose love made her give up her life birthing him. He thought of his father, who might not even be his father, whose love was as miserly as water emerging from a stone. His mita-father and mita-mother had offered him a love as nourishing as milk for a starving child. Their affection had strengthened him—but was he ready to hold love in the liquid emissions deep within him, was he ready for true love to ventilate his soul? His heart beat erratically. But the heat of his body was constant, and the solid spaces within him were maybe capable of love now. After all these months of feeding on the love of his mita-parents, maybe there was a place in his body steady enough to receive Sani.

He shook violently. He must be strong. He knew what he must do.

He crossed the bar-peepal tree and headed straight for the medical shop, where he'd been before many a time.

There he looked the dour Doctor Sah'b square in the eye. 'Give me medicine,' he said. 'I have to do something for which I need capsules and capsules of strength.'

The Doctor Sah'b made his usual unhappy face. 'A lifetime of hunger malnutrition and disease,' he said. 'And you want an overnight cure. You want strength.' He looked disparagingly over Harsha Bahadur's lean frame. 'You have to eat. Meat vegetables rice milk. This I've told you many a time it's prevention not cure

what's the use I've made too much money off of you I can't do it
anymore a man like me has scruples too. No I won't sell you any
more medicine.'

'What?' Harsha Bahadur blinked in alarm.

Even the Doctor Sah'b looked surprised by what he'd said.
He stared back with a baffled expression.

But Harsha Bahadur was determined to get what he needed.
He took out all his money and slapped it on the counter. 'I'll pay
you all this,' he said.

The Doctor Sah'b raised his eyebrows. But he shook his head.
'Come every two weeks asking for medicines vitamins
supplements you'll turn into a pauper in all my years working in
the field of public health I've never seen a boy spend so much on
medicine what's the use what's the use it's preventive care you
need a man like me has scruples too I won't give you a single
capsule tonight.'

'What?'

Harsha Bahadur waved in panic towards the dusty shelves
crammed with bottles, pills, bandages and potions—all beyond
his reach. 'But I can pay, I can pay all you want!'

The Doctor Sah'b eyed Harsha Bahadur's money. Then he
said, 'What's the use what's the use what's the use.' And, much
to Harsha Bahadur's relief, he got up and went to fetch a pale
green box.

'Glucose powder,' the Doctor Sah'b said, placing the box on
the counter. 'For free. Take as many spoons as you want mixed
with water you'll have all the energy you need. Now a man like
me has scruples too I won't give you a single capsule but glucose
you can have for free.'

Harsha Bahadur grabbed the pale green box. He was going
to tell the Doctor Sah'b how kind he was, but the old man made
a sour face and waved him away. 'It's no use it's no use go
away.'

Glucose water: Harsha Bahadur knew it would be of use.

Early the next morning, on voting day, after downing four glasses of glucose water Harsha Bahadur headed to the first mulberry bush he could find. 'Dai,' he called out. 'Are you there? I've come like you said. Are you there?'

And his cousin stepped out of the bush.

Without a word he led Harsha Bahadur through tucked-away trails that led, eventually, across the highway. He was wearing the same army fatigues as yesterday, but he seemed like a different man. He said nothing at all to Harsha Bahadur, and he clutched a string bag, as though he was afraid of losing it. His beard was unruly today. He gestured when they reached the party office. 'Open it, moola,' he hissed. He kept his face turned to the walls.

'There's no one here,' Harsha Bahadur said, trying to reassure him. 'The door wouldn't be locked if the party driver was still inside. One of the workers, Rishi Lamsal, used to stay here at night, but he left a few days ago. The other workers all stay at their own homes. There's no one here, Dai,' he said.

'Open the door, moola. We've got to move fast, don't you see?'

The glucose had made Harsha Bahadur jittery. His hands shook, and he couldn't seem to place the key in the lock.

'Quick, quick,' his cousin said.

'I'm trying, Dai.'

After a long time of fumbling he finally opened the door.

Once they entered the narrow hallway his cousin relaxed. 'I'll wait here,' he said. For some reason he was whispering. 'You go wait at the watchmaker's stall. That's where your bourgeois girl will come. Wait as long as you need to, don't worry about leaving me here. I love you, brother, and I'll wait as long as it takes for you to meet your girl.'

'We don't need to whisper, Dai.'

But his cousin preferred to keep whispering. 'You can go now, brother.' He looked up and down the hallway. 'Go to the watchmaker's stall. Go wait for her.' Then he turned to Harsha Bahadur and embraced him. 'And think of me every now and then, and remember that I've loved you in my own way. I've taken very little advantage of you; I've spared you from real harm. But now my path leads me elsewhere.' He sounded profound, like a poet. 'We've liberated four-five districts already, and we won't stop till we liberate the whole country in a wholesale landslide gale-storm kind of cultural revolution! The future lies in guerilla warfare, brother. Yes it's dangerous. But don't worry for me. Don't cry for me if you hear I'm in jail, or I've been captured by the police, or I've given my life for the revolutionary people's war.' His cousin then adopted a revolutionary posture with one fist raised. 'Now go.'

His cousin's tone had brought tears to Harsha Bahadur's eyes. His hands were trembling and he felt panicky. 'Go to the watchmaker's stall?'

'That's where your girl will come. What time I'm not sure. But I tell you she'll come.'

'I love you, Dai.'

'I love you too, moola. Now go.'

And Harsha Bahadur went.

53

Chiranjibi woke up loath to face voting day. He'd felt averse to facing the elections ever since things began to go out of control. He hadn't wanted to be put in the place of Giridhar. He didn't want to hold a responsible post. Party chairman for the district—what was his qualification? He'd stayed up nights agonizing. He preferred to follow than to lead. He had preferred to stay in the background all his life. Now he was standing at the centre, and everyone could see him and say—what does he know? He felt idiotic. What, in fact, did he know? With Rishi's sudden, unexplained departure there had been no one he could turn to for advice. Alone with Om and Nayan Raj—who like him knew almost nothing about the villages—Chiranjibi had guessed at strategies each booth committee should adopt. Protect the votes: this was the message they'd sent out to all thirty-three booth committees. And when members of these committees came into town asking hard questions—'Our voters are asking, will you at least hire enough boys to protect us from the other parties on voting day?'—Chiranjibi wished he could hide behind another, more experienced chairman. He didn't know what to say.

From early morning on voting day, the sun shone brilliantly, as though this was a day like any other. But there was an eerie stillness over the town. Vehicles had been banned on the highway to prevent the trucking of proxy voters from other districts. The bus stop was empty, and there were no vendors on the stepped platform beneath the bar-peepal tree. Across the highway the Telecommunications Office was closed. Rumour had it that the Congress candidate had leaned on the head of the Telecommunications Office, and he—obliged to obey the party which had given him his job—had told everyone else that the lines were down.

Chiranjibi reached Binita's teashop early. Nayan Raj was already waiting for him, and after a glass of tea they headed to the Khaireni Tar booth. The candidate was silent today, but calm: he hardly seemed to care whether he won or lost. Surely he was just acting collected? Chiranjibi himself felt nervy. He fumbled for Yak cigarettes; he kept taking off his glasses and examining the frame. He felt as though a knot had formed in his guts. He wished he weren't responsible for anything that would happen today. He wished, in truth, that he didn't have to go through the day. He shouldn't have followed this ridiculous calling. Politics. What foolish impulse had moved him to want to play politics?

Om was already at the government high school which was to serve as the booth for the town. Juddha, BB-Gun and the party's other workers had also gathered there. 'Well, friends, we've done our best, and there's no doubt that the people will repay our efforts,' Om said brightly; but his cheer seemed forced to Chiranjibi. Chiranjibi gave everyone a quick glance, then—doing what a chairman was supposed to—he went to meet the government officers who had come to supervise the Khaireni Tar booth.

'Are you from the People's Party?'

Chiranjibi produced the necessary documents. 'We're the booth committee.'

'Stand by.' The election officers turned to watch the Sub-Inspector set the booth's security arrangements in place. Six skinny policemen armed with rust-coloured guns were posted around the school building where voting would take place. The premises had been roped off, and two ballot boxes had been placed in front of the schoolrooms, in plain view of everyone. Members of the other parties' booth committees were also present, standing in watchful groups.

Once all the policemen were in place, the election officers turned to them. 'Two people from the booth committees sit at the booth.'

Juddha and another worker stayed on as planned. Chiranjibi went to stand a short distance from the booth. He wasn't sure that he was doing everything he should be. He watched intently as the government officers checked the ballot boxes, then took a seat at the entrance to the roped-off area, where voters would have to identify themselves. It would fall on Juddha to ensure that there was no proxy voting. Juddha would do a good job,

Chiranjibi assured himself. He had proved serious and hardworking throughout—even though it wasn't certain that the party could get him into the army. This no longer seemed Juddha's prime motivation, though. Somewhere along the process of campaigning Juddha had just begun to feel a part of the party; he'd begun to support Nayan Raj out of habit, out of association. Was that why people spent six months of their lives in this way? Not for principle—but from chance associations? Chiranjibi smoked several Yaks in a row. Some kind of personal drive compelled people. It was luring, politics. It promised company, and it promised drama in dull times. It gave a man a chance to define himself. Politics entangled people. It had entangled Chiranjibi. Seduced by its shining ideologies, he'd gotten mired in its sludgy net.

No, he mustn't lose faith. The party needed him. Nayan Raj needed him. That was why he'd accepted the chairman's post. A hollow sensation of being without a body came upon Chiranjibi. He'd had too little sleep these past few weeks. His eyes were red, and his thoughts were unfocused. Battling his reluctance he watched as the first voters began to gather at the booth, anticipating—what? In the past weeks whole villages had been bought, bribed, tricked, intimidated, coerced by all the parties. Promises of money, of jobs, of futures had been distributed like so many cheap pamphlets. Armies had been prepared and arsenals stocked. No expense had been spared: such was the profane mathematics of buying and selling liberty.

Voting was due to begin at eight. By seven-thirty workers from each party had gathered at the booth, and they banded together in separate groups, eyeing each other. The candidates for the other parties were in their home booths elsewhere. Despite all the turmoil of the past weeks Nayan Raj was expected to do well in Khaireni Tar. He had the strength of his whole extended family behind him; and the townspeople were taken with his celebrity. At the booth he commanded everyone's attention. His smallest movement was scrutinized by rival party workers, and his every exchange was listened in on. When he walked one way, the eyes of rival party workers followed him, and when he walked back they followed him back. Nayan Raj no longer exuded the fresh, glossy air with which he'd arrived in Khaireni Tar. Yet he was calm, much calmer than Chiranjibi. Did he really not care if he lost? And then, absurdly, Chiranjibi thought: perhaps Nayan Raj wasn't of this world at all; the toiling, compromising, uncertain and awkward world of imperfect people like himself, like Giridhar, this whole town—perhaps Nayan Raj was above it.

Slowly, the small crowds of voters began to trickle into the booth. There were two roped-off lines leading to the school building: one for men and another for women. One by one people lined up in them, smiling self-consciously at first, and then becoming comfortable enough to squat on the ground, waiting their turn.

Ordinary voters. Their normalcy cheered Chiranjibi. The women, in particular, gave him faith. They were dressed for the occasion, wearing their festival best: bright reds with gold filling, polka dotted blues, pink flowers on green cotton. There were shawls on their heads to shade them from the sun, and threads in their hair, flowers behind their ears, black gaajal in their eyes, bangles on their wrists, beads on their necks, and flashes of gold on their ears and noses. Some held hands, some leaned against each other and some started off on long tales, as though they weren't here to vote but to chat with friends. Some of the women were more impatient and they called out to the Sub-Inspector:

'Police-dai, we've got so much to do at home! Quick, just let us vote and we'll be off.'

From the men's line someone retorted, 'What about us? There'll be two women going in for every man, it'll take us twice as long to vote.'

The women cried, 'But you have all the time. You don't have children at home waiting for their meal. You don't have work to do.'

'Enough, enough: we've seen the work our womenfolk do, always working, working with their mouths.'

'You think your wives would be able to feed you if they played cards and drank booze like you men?'

The men turned away laughing.

It soothed Chiranjibi to see people behaving so normally. Everyone seemed ready to enjoy themselves. The booth had taken on the atmosphere of a village fair. The sun had brightened. The day was fine.

The mood of the crowd stayed jovial even as the lines lengthened. A few younger men started pressing against some older men, trying to get ahead of them. The older men shoved them back. 'Eh, wait your turn.' Many people had brought along umbrellas to shade themselves during their long wait.

There was a sudden commotion just as the polls opened. 'Make way, make way,' a man cried, pushing through the lines. He was stooped over, carrying an old woman in a basket. 'Make way, let us through.' The woman in the basket—his grandmother probably—sat looking resigned to her debility.

'An old grandmother coming to vote,' someone remarked. 'She's the mother of the UML candidate.'

The watchmaker, who was standing in the middle of the line, said, 'No, of the Congress candidate.'

'She must be allowed to vote first,' people said. 'It will be auspicious if we begin with a grandmother of her age.'

The crowd murmured in consent as the man carried the elderly woman to the head of the line. The Sub-Inspector removed the cordon and let them through, and everyone watched as the man identified his grandmother. The members of each party's booth committee checked her identity, and then the government officers inked her thumb and gave her a ballot. Unsteady under the weight of his grandmother, the man carried her towards one of the classrooms where she could vote.

But someone cried out from the men's line: 'How can two people go into the booth at once? Isn't the vote meant to be confidential? Won't the grandson be violating the grandmother's right?'

'Ho yes,' cried the watchmaker from the line. 'The radio says this is a violation of human rights.'

The man carrying his grandmother stopped and turned. The Sub-Inspector and the members of the booth committee looked around in a quandary. 'It's true,' one of the election officers said. 'This goes against regulations.'

The crowd looked from officer to Sub-Inspector to the grandson and grandmother, assessing the situation. The old woman, sitting limply in the basket, obviously couldn't walk into the booth by herself. Staggering under her weight her grandson shouted, 'An hour I've carried her on my shoulders, how long should I stand about? I'm her own grandson, let me through!'

And so the election officers looked away, the Sub-Inspector looked away, Juddha and the other parties' booth committees looked away, and the crowd turned back chattering as the man carried his aged grandmother into the voting booth.

The reasonable consensus of folk justice. Wouldn't this same kind of reason govern as people voted, Chiranjibi thought. Human beings were essentially fair-minded; people were basically just. Or would clan, caste, ethnic loyalties prevail now? Would a narrow self-interest rule? Would fear reign supreme today? Would people vote as though making offerings to appease the wrathful gods of power?

Om and Nayan Raj went to join in the men's line, but Chiranjibi remained where he was, anxious to watch over everything.

'Eh Police-dai, let us through,' a group of young, colourfully dressed women called flirtatiously from the women's line. 'We have work to do at home.'

The Sub-Inspector struck a gallant pose. 'If you had work to do at home,' he said, 'why would you dress like you're headed to a fair?'

The young women giggled.

Chiranjibi took heart.

The man carrying his grandmother came out of the booth, stooped to let her cast her ballot into the box, then carried her outside the roped-off area. He finally set down the basket on a patch of dry grass. The old grandmother stepped out and sat like an obedient pet, squatting on the ground. The grandson wiped his brow. 'All the way from the northern hills we came,' he recounted to the people in the lines. 'I asked, Bajai-aama, do you want to vote? And she nodded yes, so what could I do? A grandson's got to do as a grandmother bids.'

The banana vendor had set up shop near by. 'Bananas so yellow they dazzle the eye,' he called out, waving a bunch in the air.

'How much for that bunch?' asked the son.

'Ten rupees, just for you.'

The women in line heard this, and cried out, 'Ten rupees for a handful of Indian fruits!'

The vendor shouted back, 'They're brought all the way from the southern plains—what can I do?'

The women laughed. 'Tasteless Indian bananas, who'll spend money on them?'

Again Chiranjibi felt comforted. As long as there were women at the voting booth, everything would be fine.

As the morning matured, most of the townspeople showed up to vote. Thakalni-aama arrived with a large group of women, including the Sub-Inspector's two wives and other women from the mothers' group. Binita and Pramila came together with a crowd of Nayan Raj's relatives. Om's wife came with her family and friends. Chiranjibi's brother came with his wife and sister-in-law. Some voters stayed only long enough to cast their votes; others lingered at the booth afterwards, analyzing the turnout and speculating on results. Chiranjibi stood apart from everyone, not wanting to be distracted now. He noticed that Giridhar hadn't come to vote. Giridhar's aged father came, though, and he spoke with Chiranjibi. 'My son isn't well,' he said with a sorry tone. 'He wouldn't have behaved the way he did if it hadn't been for his—his sickness.'

'Giridharji is a capable man,' Chiranjibi said, not wanting to burden the father with his opinion of his son.

'It's just that he's sick,' Giridhar's father said, his large eyes blinking. 'He'll get better if he receives the help of friends like you.'

Chiranjibi felt guilty to hear this. 'Yes Ba.' He'd never thought himself Giridhar's friend. But he said, 'After the elections I—we—we'll come and talk to him.' He added, 'I never wanted this post, Ba. It would have been much better for Giridharji to stay. If—' he faltered. He realized he was lying. But Giridhar's father seemed comforted by his words. Chiranjibi said, 'If there hadn't been that slight misunderstanding at the end.'

Nayan Raj and Om left soon afterwards to spend the day at the teashop. The rest of the party's workers stayed on with Chiranjibi, forming a tight group like the ones formed by the Congress and UML workers. The atmosphere at the booth remained genial, though. Chiranjibi himself slipped into line. In the women's line across him he saw the RPP lady candidate, hiding behind female relatives.

The candidate for the Janamukti party, who was standing a few paces ahead of Chiranjibi, called out to her. 'I'll vote for you if you vote for me,' he said pleasantly.

The crowd around them laughed.

The lady candidate blushed, as though embarrassed to be caught voting for herself. 'How can I trust a politician's word?' she said. 'All they do is lie to the people, our politicians.'

'But candidateji,' the Janamukti candidate said, 'you yourself are a politician.'

The crowd guffawed as the lady candidate protested: 'The party had to fill the five per cent women's quota so they told me to fight so I fought, but I'm not a politician; don't call me that.'

And Chiranjibi thought: as long as there are women in line everything will be all right.

It took more than an hour for him to reach the head of the line. There he identified himself, had his thumb inked, received a ballot and walked into the dark schoolroom. His eyes adjusted slowly to the darkness, till he made out a table in front of him. There was an inkpad and a rubber stamp on the table. On the ballot he saw all the parties' symbols: the sun, the tree, the plough, the house and the teacup. The teacup looked shrunken in this small format. Perhaps he'd gotten used to seeing it splashed on the town's walls. He inked the rubber stamp and placed his vote on the teacup. His one free vote was gone.

He emerged from the booth, blinded by the sun. He finally caught sight of the way out of the roped-off area, and began to head out, ballot still in hand.

A hand tapped his shoulder. 'The ballot box is over there,' said the Sub-Inspector.

'Eh ho.' What kind of party chairman was he? 'That's what

I was looking for,' Chiranjibi lied.

In the afternoon the women's line shortened and the men's line grew longer. People from further away began to arrive at the booth. Groups of voters arrived from the northern hills. Voters came from the nearby Gaine settlement. The bangle seller came with a group of Musalmaan women. The number of party workers milling around the area also increased as the day wore on. This worried Chiranjibi. Thankfully, there was a lassitude among the party workers, who seemed content, right now, just to find a shaded patch to sit in. Though the mornings and evenings were cold these days, the afternoon sun was still warm.

Chiranjibi stayed tense, watching over everything. Was he doing everything he was supposed to? By now Juddha had been replaced at the booth with another party worker. Juddha too sat near by, speaking in low tones with the party's female workers. BB-Gun and his gang stood at a distance from them, flexing and flaunting their muscles. They were dressed more fashionably than usual, in jeans that were torn and patched together outlandishly, and T-shirts that bore designer logos. Looking about with a theatrical nonchalance, they eyed each other, they eyed the booth, they eyed a group of Congress party boys.

Chiranjibi noticed that they hadn't voted. He didn't like the menacing picture they presented: they made the People's Party look like a gathering of thugs. He suggested to Juddha to find a way to remove them from the booth. 'Tell them to man the party office,' he said. 'There's no one at the office today except our peon boy.'

But BB-Gun bridled at the suggestion that they leave. Juddha returned to Chiranjibi, shrugging. 'They said they're waiting to vote. They won't let us stop them from voting; they say it's their right to vote.'

BB-Gun was staring hard at them. Chiranjibi took in the boy's challenging expression, and he felt oddly disembodied, as he had this morning. Here it was, his failure as a leader. He would have to accept it. He wished he weren't here. He much preferred to be with Nayan Raj at the teashop. What kind of chairman was he? But then, what kind of chairman had Giridhar been? How sloppily Giridhar had put together a party, relying on boys like BB-Gun. Now here he was, at the centre where everyone could see him, having to right the other man's wrongs.

The Congress party boys were mirroring BB-Gun's overly virile stance. The rivalry between the two gangs was evident. If there would be any violence at this booth it would start with these boys, Chiranjibi realized. It was the Congress's legacy to resort to booth violence here. At this moment, though, BB-Gun looked equally capable of starting trouble. A People's Party worker starting a fight...under his chairmanship.

Chiranjibi tried to combat his dread by thinking back to the village-to-village tour, when he had been so moved by the need for people to be free. All these people waiting in line, he thought: all the wriggling, writhing aspirations wanting expression. A water tap, a bridge, a polyethylene pipe, a blackboard and a few benches in the local school. Medical camps. A gabion-wired wall to stay a landslide. This was all people expected from their government: and still it couldn't be done without having rival armies battle for power over development contracts. He must not lose his belief. But no sweet wonder washed over him now. Nayan Raj's vision was right, but naïve. Chiranjibi was trapped in a position he didn't want to occupy. He would be much more effective in the background. In the background was where he belonged.

Voting was still proceeding normally in the late afternoon, when two Land Rovers pulled into the narrow lanes leading to the school, kicking up a cloud of dust. International observers. Chiranjibi went through several Yaks, watching them. Three foreigners got out of the vehicles, accompanied by Nepali officials from a human rights organization. While the officials went to talk to the election officers, the foreigners stared uncertainly around them. There was an Indian woman, a British man and an American woman. The American woman produced a camera from her handbag and took pictures of children who had gathered to stare at them.

The Indian women scoffed. 'These children, they're not here just to look, they're here to vote.'

'They're obviously underage,' the other woman protested. 'How could they get into the booths?'

'You have no idea, the kind of rigging, violence and fraud that takes place in our parts.'

The American put away her camera, eyeing the children suspiciously.

The Indian woman continued, 'What good is it anyway, us coming and looking at lines like this?' She pointed at Chiranjibi. 'These people, they've voted twice, thrice already. It's all the same in India-Nepal and the whole subcontinent. Proxy voting, rampant election fraud.' She made a knowing face. 'We come like this to observe—but what do we see? Not a thing. What's happening remains invisible to us.'

The man, meanwhile, had wandered to the women's line, and was grinning at some women wearing stick-on teekas shaped like tiny trees. 'Rook, rook,' he said clownishly, mispronouncing the word for tree.

The women in line, ardent Congress supporters, cried back in Nepali, 'Place your vote on the tree!'

The Indian woman turned on him. 'But why is our British MP friend campaigning for the Congress party? This violates observation rules.'

The man rolled his eyes, and the American woman turned away as though she hadn't seen anything.

But the Indian woman grew indignant. 'All the western world trembles at the thought that leftism is alive in our parts! If they only knew how deeply people resent their colonial attitudes! Their divide-and-rule legacies, the strife they've sown all over the region! India-Nepal, all of South Asia. All our troubles began thanks to you!'

The Nepali officials returned from talking with election officials. 'Everything here is proceeding smoothly,' one of them said.

The Indian woman was determined to make her point, though. 'But didn't we all see our British MP friend violating our own rules? What kind of typical behaviour! I want to report it at once!'

'Madam,' the Nepali official replied, 'let us go now, otherwise it will get dark and there will be violence.'

At this all the international observers banded back into their Land Rovers.

Everyone at the booth watched them leave in a cloud of dust.

'They'll be having dinner in their five-star hotels when all the trouble begins,' a man remarked loudly, and the men in line snickered.

Just as the sun dipped behind the western hills, a group of People's Party workers came running to fetch Chiranjibi. 'The office,' they said, panting out of breath. 'It's been wrecked, come and see.'

A sick feeling washed through Chiranjibi. Was he supposed to know what to do? He followed the party workers into town, wishing Giridhar were still the chairman.

When he reached the party office he saw a crowd around the building. Someone was murmuring about Maoists. Chiranjibi slowed. Inside the building workers were thronging the front hall, reading signs that had been scrawled in black paint on the walls: WE DON'T WANT REFORMIST DEMOCRACY. DEATH TO THE BOURGEOIS PARLIAMENT. LONG LIVE THE REVOLUTIONARY PEOPLE'S WAR.

Nayan Raj and Om were also in the hall reading slogans.

'We heard an explosion,' Om said. 'The windows upstairs, they're cracked.'

The three of them looked at each other, and Chiranjibi knew it was his time to lead. He headed up the stairs with Nayan Raj and Om behind him. He tried to walk confidently. But he felt afloat in the currents of a river that he was helpless to control. Slogans had also been scrawled in the upstairs hall: DEATH TO THE AGENTS OF IMPERIALISM. DEATH TO THE MURDEROUS PARLIAMENT. LONG LIVE THE REVOLUTION. There was a mangled look to the door of the meeting room. One of its hinges was undone. 'Careful,' Nayan Raj warned from behind as Chiranjibi pushed the door open.

There was black smoke on the walls, and shards of metal strewn on the floor. His teak desk, with one leg blasted off, lay askew against a wall.

'A pressure-cooker bomb,' Om said, pointing at a makeshift stove. 'Someone lit it and left.'

Someone outside in the hallway said, 'A downstairs window was open, they must have come in from there.'

'Why wasn't anyone guarding the office?' someone else said. 'Where's the peon boy? Did everyone have to go to the booth?'

'Someone should have stayed here for security.'

Chiranjibi kept staring at his desk.

Om nudged him. 'Let's not stay, there might be other bombs in the building.'

Chiranjibi nodded. The watery surface of the desk had been scratched ferociously: DEATH TO THE REFORMISTS.

This was the kind of politics he wanted to do?

A sense of violation moved through Chiranjibi—and he suddenly felt completely immaterial. Hatred had been aimed his way. This hatred swept through him, but didn't hurt him because—because he wasn't of the solid world, was he? People weren't all meat and blood. At the core everyone was a spirit, untouched by gross violations.

He shut the door behind him and motioned for the workers in the hallway to clear the building. 'Let's go back to the voting booth,' he said. He had decided: he would resign from his chairman post as soon as the elections were over. This was not his place. To Nayan Raj he said, 'Nayan Rajji should go home. The booth will close in two hours' time. Omji and I and our workers will accompany the ballot boxes to the district centre for vote counting.'

'I'll tell the driver to get the van,' Om agreed.

Downstairs, Jimmawal-baaje's seventh son had arrived at the office building. Dressed in spotless white mourning clothes, he looked exactly like his father. 'My father's house!' he lamented, approaching Chiranjibi. 'Blackened and burned...even as he passes into the heavenly realms!' He flitted in horror through the length of the downstairs corridor. Then with his father's same self-serving indignation he cried, 'How will we poor sons of pure Bahuns recoup the cost of such damage?'

'The party will compensate your losses,' Chiranjibi said.

The boy's eyes widened. 'It must! I've got two widowed mothers, six brothers and and twenty-two nephews to support! You must raise the rent at once, Chairmanji.'

Chiranjibi brushed the boy aside and headed back to the booth.

As twilight set in all the women cleared away from the voting booth. The men's line also emptied, and the aura of a village fair passed. A hush fell over the surroundings. All around the school building bands of rival party workers stood in the shadows. The sky above began to show the first stars. Crickets began to chirp from the darkness, and men's voices murmured in the settling air.

At the head of the line the Sub-Inspector had become grave. The police were badly outnumbered by the bands of party workers surrounding the school; if trouble were to begin, they would be helpless to prevent it. BB-Gun and his gang were strutting like cocks to one side. The Congress party boys were strutting across from them. A little further away stood the UML workers, gathered around their leader, the old schoolmaster of Khaireni Tar. No one was doing anything untoward. But people were glancing at each other warily, ready to react to the slightest commotion.

Juddha had been moving back and forth between the booth and the town, finding out what had happened at other booths. He was the first to bring reports of rigging throughout the electorate: 'A fight's broken out in Mijethum. Congress workers captured the booth.'

'Someone's been knifed,' another worker reported. 'Someone who voted for us. Om-dai is arranging for him to be taken to the district hospital.'

'Eh,' Chiranjibi said. What was a chairman supposed to do now? Giridhar would have known.

Chiranjibi just remained where he was, watching darkness fall over the booth.

After some time another worker came running from town. 'A ballot box was burned in Bhimad—they think it was the UML.'

'In Chhang, the Congress made all the voters show whom they were voting for—and beat those who didn't vote for them.'

'Eh.'

As the darkness deepened the workers around Chiranjibi started spreading speculations and rumours. 'The Congress candidate sold his land to fund his campaign.'

'The communists threw around lakhs and lakhs.'

'The Congress gave sheets of tin to Baari village last night. And five bags of cement.'

'The UML promised a bridge over the Seti river.'

'If we'd given Baari five thousand, they would have voted for us.'

Chiranjibi kept his eyes trained on the booth, in shadows. It was getting cold, and he pulled on a sweater, but he still felt cold.

Across from him the other parties' workers were also discussing events in other booths. Juddha Ale continued to move between the booth and town, coming back each time with news from other polling stations. 'Both booths in Dhorphirdi have been captured by Congress party supporters,' he reported, 'and one booth in Manapang. Congress boys surrounded the booth, beat up the police and stuffed the ballot box. The village leader ordered them to.'

'We were expecting trouble in Manapang,' Chiranjibi said. Suddenly he felt defiant. How bad could things get? He wanted to see. 'We were expecting trouble in Manapang, that doesn't surprise me. That area is controlled by Congress hooligans.'

The night turned black. A grey mist fell over the booth. The only light that fell on the area came from a few bare bulbs on the outer wall of the school building. Men, shuffling in shadows, surrounded the booth. But all the parties had equal numbers of workers present. That would prevent trouble.

Another worker came running. Another booth had been captured, this time in Dulegauda. 'Someone's been injured badly there, he was running to town to report the burning of a ballot box and they split his skull with a brick.'

manjushree thapa

'A gang of Congress supporters there are saying they want to stone you and Nayan Rajji.'

Was that all? Chiranjibi felt oddly unafraid. Mere violations of the flesh. He said, 'Tell our workers to watch out for their safety. But tell them not to retaliate, not to strike back at all. We must stay true to our beliefs.'

He turned towards another worker, coming with more news. What was the worst that could happen? The electorate was turning into a war zone. What freedom could there be? He wanted to know.

At six the Sub-Inspector cordoned off the booth and summoned all the parties' representatives to oversee the sealing of ballot boxes. The schoolmaster of Khaireni Tar, a Congress worker, the Janamukti candidate, an RPP worker and Chiranjibi took turns stamping their party's seals. Then everyone followed the police as they carried the boxes out of the booth. Around them the dark figures of men took on menacing silhouettes. Everyone watched the ballot boxes pass, as though this were a solemn ritual. It occurred to Chiranjibi that each of these men were capable of wreaking harm on each other. Each was expressing, in his stance, a potential for violence.

And violence there was; as they left the booth BB-Gun and his gang began to slap and shove the Congress boys. Cries rang out; Chiranjibi heard a groan, a stream of abuse, a bottle smashing, and the sound of bodies falling hard on the ground.

'Gang rivalries,' the Sub-Inspector said, prodding along the skinny policemen. 'Keep the boxes safe, boys. We don't have enough manpower to bother with gang rivalries right now.'

The ballot boxes were swiftly whisked away to the highway and placed securely in the back of a government truck. They would have to remain there for a few hours yet. Ballot boxes from several other booths in the hills would arrive here throughout the night. Then they would all be driven to the district centre to be counted over the course of the next few days.

Chiranjibi met Om at the People's Party van parked near by. The old schoolmaster of Khaireni Tar and the representatives from the other parties formed separate groups. Thankfully the fighting that had broken out at the booth didn't extend till here. The ballot boxes from Khaireni Tar were safe. But the other ballot boxes that were being carried, sometimes for hours, through dark hill trails—Chiranjibi had no doubt that many of those boxes would be destroyed, replaced.

Votes won, votes lost, votes bought and coerced and stolen. One one one one vote. All looted. Such were the rules of power, Chiranjibi thought. Such were the profane mathematics of zero-sum politics. He was going to resign tomorrow, and follow instead of lead. Working quietly from behind; that was his way. He sat in the front seat of the party van, and started to do calculations, working out his estimates for the People's Party votes in the various booths, from the Majhkot VDC Building booth to the Barahi Primary School booth; the Rajpur Middle School booth to the Ratna Jyoti High School booth. Thirty-three booths in all. He counted and calculated on his fingers.

The sound of distant yelling and shouting floated in through the night air.

The party would have had twelve thousand people behind them if all conditions had been fair. That was Chiranjibi's estimate. But conditions hadn't been fair. Only the crudest calculations could take place now. The price of people, the price of their votes. The monetary cost of coming to power: it would be recouped by the winning party, later—by a government working on contract.

But there were, still, mysteries to serve. There were ideals to follow. Small and gleaming visions which survived brutal attacks.

Chiranjibi smoked a Yak. If Nayan Raj kept leading him, he would follow his vision of true democracy: one free person, and another one, and another. For if the world was corrupt, it was also, finally—it had to be—at its core, noble.

54

When Madhu returned home that the evening, her conversation with Harsha Bahadur was still ringing in her ears.

He had said the most ridiculous things. 'Sani, I don't want to bother or pester or harass you,' he'd blurted out as soon as they met. 'First and foremost I want to say that what I did was very, very wrong. I stained your good name and for that I can never forgive myself. It is understandable that you hate my air. Plus, it turned out I was being undemocratic in not giving you any choice but to love me. It's all my fault, I now know. I wanted love but didn't care if you wanted to give it. But a girl needs a choice. A girl needs freedom, a girl needs to make up her own mind. It turns out that that's what democracy means.'

Madhu had thought that the stupid boy was just nervous. She had forced herself to smile, and to say nice things to him. She had even told him he looked nice. He did look nice. He looked taller than before. His hair was combed and his face had filled out. His complexion was polished. He was almost handsome now—though it could just be the clothes he'd worn: a collared shirt, clean, pleated trousers and shiny leather shoes.

But the friendlier she had become the stranger the boy had acted. For what seemed like hours he stammered on and on about the importance of free votes. Madhu had listened very patiently. But finally she'd fluttered her eyes at him to show him her true intention. And he'd stepped back from her. Odd. Was he being shy, she'd wondered. She told him that she'd been thinking about him, that she'd been wondering if he had been thinking about her. She needed his freeness. She had moved close to him.

But the boy kept saying a lot of disjointed things; he had stammered on and on about democracy. 'It is no longer my intention to force you to love me, my only goal is to accept that you don't. Just because I stained your good name doesn't mean you have to love me. You hate my air, I accept. I thereby let you know that, and wish you to make your own free choice from hereon about what it is you want to do with your life. All I want now is to say I was wrong for my earlier undemocratic behaviour. I do not want to force you to marry me any more.'

Madhu had said, 'But you can marry me.'

And the boy had said, 'But do you—do you love me?'

Love? He wanted her to marry him—and to love him, too?

'There must be love,' he had said.

What?

Madhu had told him the truth.

She had told him she hated him.

It wasn't his fault, she had said calmly. She just hated him, she was like that, that was her, hating him for possessing a freeness she didn't have. 'But you can marry me,' she had said. 'I forgive you for vengefully babbling my name in front of the whole town, and now agree to marry you.'

'That would be undemocratic,' the stupid boy had warbled. For a moment he looked just as he had back when he was chasing after her. He was an ugly boy. His face contorted with the effort of speaking. 'This thing called democracy,' he had said, 'it gives us choices, see. There are so many choices in the world for us to make, maybe it would be wrong to make this one choice if there isn't true love.'

Love? Madhu had chortled sarcastically. Love?

They had parted, then. After that she had waited for hours by the side of the highway, thinking stormily that maybe she could just go somewhere, escape forever, just ride off in a taxi-car. But the highway was still; there were no taxi-cars today. Not a bus, not a minibus came by. The night sky finally obscured the point at which the highway met the horizon.

And so here she was now, back in front of Binita-didi's house. The teashop was packed with party workers. Its windows were lit. Binita-didi was inside, leading her life of ostracism. Perhaps she was content with her widowed life. But Madhu—she was aching for freeness. She didn't love the Khadka boy. Why need she? She had been mounted by great, restless passions, not by love.

In his room in his mita-parents' house, Harsha Bahadur trembled at his narrow escape from what could have been a serious lifetime mistake of staggering consequences. How diminished Sani looked now that he'd spent time away from her. How vulgar, how crass was her behaviour—so unlike the way he'd seen her before. Where was that lunar radiance he'd been in love with? Where was her grace, her perfection? She'd once seemed endowed with the thirty-two qualities of unblemished womanhood. But today she'd smiled shamelessly baring all her teeth, she had squirmed and twitched, she had spoken in high-pitched tones like an improper girl, and she had fluttered her eyes at him. Where was the—the romance that he had seen so many times on television? Where was the love, Harsha Bahadur thought. And besides, it was—well, a little unthinkable, wasn't it, for a smart boy like him to marry a girl like her who hadn't even studied till class five? What could he have been thinking earlier? How wrong he had been! With his kindly mita-parents and his paying office job, he had far better options available to him. Harsha Bahadur trembled at his narrow escape. Fortunately he was still free. He was hale, he was hearty.

His mita-parents loved him, they would lead him into the wide
world. He must not look back at all, he must only look forward
and take every chance to improve his station in life.

desiccation

55

'Election report was released today at Election Commission, and international election observers reported at press release that barring "only a few incidents of irregularities", the elections were conducted in a free and fair manner. Leading intellectuals have supported this finding despite claims from losing candidates to have suffered election fraud. Several cases are pending in court. Anyway, mood is not positive in government. With hung parliament there is very pessimistic prospect of coalition round-robin governments, with each party staying in power for short periods before breaking up again in a snap election. "Stability" is of grave concern, declared the leader of the Congress party, who is speculated to become the next Prime Minister if he is supported by the former Congress Prime Minister, his brother-in-law. Currently all parties are conducting secret negotiations to see who will form coalition government. Leading intellectuals opine that an unstable government will lead to frightening bilateral and multilateral donor agencies and discouraging multinational corporate business partnerships in the private sector. Informally there is lots of bribing and MP-buying going on, with rampant power-mongering. Bids to buy each MP's loyalty are said to be ranging to lakhs of rupees, houses and properties, foreign travel and international hard currency cash.'

56

A month after the Congress candidate had been declared victorious in Tanahun three, Nayan Raj went back to Kathmandu with plans to return soon. Strangely, the cinema hero had lost badly, garnering no more than three thousand votes, the bulk of them from Khaireni Tar. But he remained determined to dedicate his life to grassroots politics. Or so he said. He was, after all, an actor, the townspeople now said. He had said the teacup party wouldn't rig elections—but come voting day he'd set BB-Gun Thapa loose on the Congress boys. Could anyone really trust the words of a Kathmandu intellectual? Could anyone really believe a cinema hero? His own party's former chairman Giridhar said he dyed his hair black. And indeed Nayan Raj's hair was extraordinarily black. His personality was too pleasing. He was too humble, too affable, too intelligent. He spoke too eloquently. Wasn't he just mouthing fine, scripted lines? He had fooled them all.

The People's Party office had been closed after the elections, and it stood vacant now, with no tenants willing to take rooms in a building bombed by Maoists. No one had been arrested yet in connection with the bombing. For a while the Sub-Inspector questioned Om Gurung's mita-son, but only because the boy kept babbling about a Maoist who lived in a mulberry bush. The boy could never substantiate his claims, though. The bombing investigation remained ongoing, but the Sub-Inspector had stopped working on it. Who really wanted to catch a Maoist, after all? The only way to end the Maoist people's war was for the government to actually function; and working for the welfare of Nepali citizens was something no politician seemed willing to do. So why should the Sub-Inspector hurt his head over capturing armed guerillas? Hopefully, the Maoists would move on to another, poorer district that was easier to take over—and then the Sub-Inspector could go back to living in peace.

Giridhar rarely came into town any more. There were rumours that he was drinking hard. Om busied himself further improving his private school, first buying a large tract of land, then hiring a bulldozer to convert it into a football field. News had spread through town of the computers at his school. Six gleaming Korean computers in Khaireni Tar! People lauded him for bringing them into the twenty-first century.

As soon as the elections ended Chiranjibi had resigned as the chairman of the People's Party. He still remained strangely committed to the party, though, and he could be seen making his way through the bazaar to the houses of teacup party well-wishers. He made an odd sight: a millionaire who wanted nothing more than to follow the leadership of a cinema hero. The townspeople looked at him and thought—a man with six daughters and no heirs, giving up all his contracting work to run after a party that has come to nothing. They felt sorry for him.

At the stepped platform beneath the twined-together bar-peepal tree talk still veered, now and then, to the night of the elections. 'Those hooligans knifing each other,' the banana vendor said, clucking in disapproval. 'I saw them with my own eyes! I thought they'd killed themselves that night, I thought they'd met their deaths. After all that talk of reform, it was the teacup's hooligans who started the fight.'

'That's what all parties are like,' the peanut vendor said. 'Their leaders may say they're honest, but you can't trust a word they say.' He spat emphatically. 'And to think I wasted my vote on the teacup. With the Congress candidate being the nephew of the Prime Minister—of course he'd win! What was I thinking?' He turned to a passerby. 'Peanuts?'

The watchmaker was taking a break at the platform. 'I knew that Nayan Raj was just acting all along,' he said. The man who had stopped to buy peanuts was closely associated with the new Congress MP, he knew. It was important to show allegiance to the party in power. The watchmaker said, 'We're different, Nayan Raj kept saying. We won't deprive you of your free choice. But our new Congress MP—born to a most illustrious dynasty of democrats—now *he's* the one who'll bring us any reform we need.'

The Musalmaan bangle seller, near by, ignored all this useless chatter. Now that the small-town hubbub of elections had subsided, the bazaar had emptied of all the useless men, men, men. She sat back at her stall, displaying a hundred glass bangles of the latest designs which would attract lady customers around her. All around her, the other vendors called out:

'Peanuts? Peanuts? Peanuts?'

'Bananas so ripe they taste like sugar!'

'Cheeseballs-chips-a-locket!'

'Peanuts?'

There were of course others who had remained indifferent through the entire season of elections: the town's cobbler, for instance. He had proselytized passionately these last few years, and had finally saved some lost souls: his own wayward teenage sons had accepted the word of Christ. 'A god in whose eyes we're all equal is the only god who merits the faith of our Sarki caste.' The cobbler had returned straying flock to their father's kingdom—what did he care about the miserable groups in the kingdom of Nepal?

The ascetic in his cave by the Seti river also remained unmoved by the buzz about elections. Nor was he bothered that his former party, Congress, had enjoyed victory at the polls. Like the cobbler, he was on a higher mission, a mission which he got closer to achieving every day. Had even one of Nepal's politicians learned to control his appetite? Was any Congress party member truly free of greed? May every man learn to control his stomach, the ascetic thought. Om.

Another person who cared nothing about the teacup party or any other party was the madwoman of Khaireni Tar. As always, she spent her days making senseless but earnest pronouncements: 'Upon the unnatural holler down an inspection for the general left so we darkly go in the profession above of house,' she said to anyone who came near her. 'Break only the argument in some power of darkly dislike.'

She wasn't in the least concerned about who had won in the elections and who had lost.

Across the highway, Binita's teashop had slowly returned to normal. When Nayan Raj went to Kathmandu, party workers dropped away, one by one. Some returned to their own lives. Others headed to Kathmandu to make good on the party's promises of jobs, recommendations and connections. For a few weeks after voting day Om came to Binita's teashop, as though this were still the centre of party activity. Then he got too busy expanding his school. Chiranjibi stopped by once or twice to meet with party workers. Then the teashop emptied of all party members, and Binita opened it again to regular customers.

At first only a few townspeople came to buy tea. In the beginning they asked after Nayan Raj and sat politely, as though they were invited guests rather than paying customers. But as time passed the town seemed to take back the teashop. More and more townspeople crossed the highway for a glass of Binita's fragrant milk tea, and eventually bus passengers also found their way back. The teashop stayed open through the day and closed promptly at evening time, as it used to.

Binita had made arrangements to move the teashop, though. Her brother-in-law wanted to erect a more modern house in his ancestral properties, and he had made a fair offer for Binita's half: 'I won't let your business be hurt by my politics, Binita-bhauju. You move your shop closer to the bazaar.' Family: some give, some take. Binita had accepted his payment and had arranged to buy a small plot of her neighbour Phool Devi's land. She hadn't yet bought the new plot, though. She wouldn't; not till she knew what her future might be.

After the elections Pramila returned to working at Thakalni-aama's Himal Lodge Restaurant Bar. She still visited Binita frequently, filling the teashop with her cheer. 'That husband of mine, the day he comes back I'll kill him myself,' she swore, staving off with her laughter the fear that he might never be found. 'It's better for him if he doesn't come back—the day he comes here, he'll be killed by his wife.'

Madhu still acted a bit erratic sometimes. She could be moody, defiant, or occassionally cross with Binita. She was clearly at an age of upheavals. She visited Pramila often at the Himal Lodge Restaurant Bar and seemed to enjoy the older woman's company. Pramila was equally fond of the girl and treated her warmly, as a younger sister. Binita liked their closeness. She encouraged it, thinking, with the pragmatism that had taken hold of her these days, that if Madhu didn't want to go with her and Rishi to Kathmandu—if Binita were to elope with him—the girl might turn to Pramila.

Binita hadn't told anyone she wanted to leave. She couldn't; there was too much risk involved. Concealing her intentions she encouraged Madhu to enrol in a more advanced literacy class. She let Tripti continue, unburdened, with her life of school and family. In secret, though, Binita plotted. In secret she prepared. She kept the money Nayan Raj-bhai had paid for her land at home. She also withdrew money from her bank account. She was readying to leave. Tripti would pose her no problem. Madhu, though—Madhu was unpredictable. Would she go to the city as the cousin of a remarried widow? Would she want to give up her place in this town to follow Binita into an outcast life?

If Rishi were to prove himself to be true.

The day he left Khaireni Tar Rishi had left behind a cardigan, deep blue in colour. Binita wore it often on these cold winter days. She was wearing it as she made her way, today, to the Akala-mai shrine for a mothers' group meeting. The shrine lay a short way beyond the flatlands. Binita walked there alone. Thakalni-aama wasn't coming today, and Laksmi had stopped coming to the meetings weeks ago. Binita had been relieved, in truth, to be freed of Laksmi's strained and insecure friendship. She much preferred to befriend women who had some nerve, some resolve.

The brown, uncultivable flatlands were cracked and charred by the midwinter sun. The long dry season would extend for a few months yet. Binita liked this desiccation; she preferred it to the deceptive lushness of monsoon. There was no illusion of ease in this aridity, just the harsh, honest truth.

Past the church there was a cleft in the flatlands which led to a grassy slope. A few members of the mothers' group were already at the shrine. Binita saw that the Sub-Inspector's younger wife Lalita hadn't come yet. Without much effort, she and Lalita had become good friends, and they usually sat together at the mothers' group meetings.

By now the mothers' group had raised close to eight thousand rupees. In a few weeks they would finish raising money in every ward. An overseer was expected today, and he would work out an estimate for the cost of repairs to Akala-mai's shrine. The shrine was almost entirely broken down on one side, where a young banyan tree had pushed out its walls. The roof had caved in and needed repair. Hom Kumari was sitting to one side of the shrine with the ascetic's wife. A few women were clearing weeds from the surroundings.

Then Binita saw Laksmi, picking weeds at the front of the shrine. Hunched over, she looked smaller than she actually was. There was a nervous expression on her face, a dry look in her eyes. Her oily hair looked untidy, as though she hadn't combed it for days. She was obviously worn down by her husband's drinking.

Out of pity, Binita joined Laksmi, uprooting a small patch of dandelions by her feet.

Laksmi looked up. 'For Akala-mai,' she said in a subdued chime. She reached for a patch of thistles growing on the shrine's cracked wall.

Binita said, 'For Akala-mai.'

Laksmi kept at her work without talking. Binita never knew what to say to her. They both continued picking wildflowers off the shrine's back wall. After a while Laksmi turned to the idol of Akala-mai in the arced opening at the front. The deity was a concave stone smeared with vermilion and rice and smothered with marigolds. With the sharp edge of a stone Laksmi scraped moss off the ridges of the idol.

Binita stopped and watched the small, bony woman moving up and down at her task. She could smell the mustard oil in her uncombed hair. An odour of unwashed clothes came off her fariya. She wasn't wearing much else in this cold.

Fighting off her aversion to the woman Binita sat down next to her. 'Your husband,' she said. 'He's still ill?'

Laksmi stopped scraping the moss. She was squatting, and she dropped down onto her haunches. She turned to fix her eyes on Binita, searching for something in her uncertain way.

Binita tried not to be put off by this. She said, 'With an old father-in-law, and two sons to take care of, and no help—. It must be difficult for you.'

For a moment Laksmi kept looking at Binita, as though she didn't trust her to really care. Hard not to accept her judgement. Binita looked away. A more generous woman would console Laksmi. A more giving friend would guide her, day to day, through her hardship. Binita hoarded her own happiness, afraid that the other woman might deplete her scarce reserves. She acted tightfisted with Laksmi, she knew.

'It's been years my husband's been sick,' Laksmi finally said. 'But now he's dying. And I'm helping him die.' Her voice lowered. 'I used to think he'd stop, you know. He's been drinking since I came here as a bride. Now he asks for more and more, and'— she thrust out her hands in a gesture of offering—'I give him death.'

Binita looked at her hands: bones and purple skin.

'I'm turning myself into a widow,' Laksmi said.

Then she turned away, staring past the slope of the ashen flatlands.

A cold breeze began to stir. Goosebumps arose on Laksmi's arms. Binita reached for her hand.

Laksmi turned and looked at her with her dry eyes. Binita again looked away. She couldn't—she wasn't willing to—offer Laksmi any true companionship. All she could offer the other woman was to sit together awhile, holding hands as though they were friends.

And this too was a way to live in this town. Women migrating here by marriage could forge a life amid strangers—and, if they were lucky, find themselves embraced, eventually, by one or two like-minded friends. Binita could stay with Laksmi till the woman found better friends, perhaps. This wasn't much; but it was all she could think of.

From somewhere far away she heard a tinkling of temple bells. She settled more easily against the shrine. Soon all the women of the mothers' group would gather around in a group. Soon the Sub-Inspector's younger wife, Lalita, would come to offer Binita her friendship. Laskmi might be able to lose herself amid them.

This was the women's society that she had only just discovered. She had only just found women; and she would give them up for Rishi. For the pleasure of one man.

And if he were to fail her?

She had some money; she'd use her wits.

Beyond that there were no safety measures.

57

The apartment that Rishi now rented was at the top of an old brick building, and it had north-facing windows that looked onto a modern housing complex. Concrete and glass reflections outside. Inside, a bed, a shirt hung on the door, a neat stack of clothes on the floor. A tube light on the ceiling, its wires bald and black. There was a bathroom down the hall where water had to be carried. The kitchen had running water in the rainy season. Rishi had also rented an additional room. He had told the landlords—a farming Newar family—that his family would come from the village.

It was an apartment of conventional aspirations—husband, wife and children living together. A place where more aberrant forms of happiness might be disguised. Two months, Binita had said. She needed time to prepare. Two months had passed. He, too, had prepared. Upon returning to the city he had found work at one of the many substandard private schools that had cropped up in the past decade: the Hardvard International Boarding School. Answering Rishi's phone call the principal had asked, 'Who are your references?' Rishi had said he tutored the actor Nayan Raj's niece. 'Let's meet,' the principal had replied. 'We need teachers. You said you had a Master's degree?'

To his students—lower-middle-class girls and boys—Rishi taught how to live off the discarded scraps and fragments of world history. 'Where is America, Sir?' they asked him before and after class time. 'Sir, where is Japan? How do they make televisions? What is a computer, Sir?' Outside, the machinations of power ground on. The parties still wrangled savagely for power. The far right was calling for a return to absolute monarchy, the Maoists were continuing their guerrilla war, and the markets were continuing to birth hordes of ill-informed customers. To his students Rishi offered his only remaining conviction: in a life lived thoughtfully, they might yet retain their dignity.

It was a conviction that proposed no larger solutions. For Rishi there was no more revolution—just the permanent unrest of those who moved unseen through the land. Where once he had dreamed of collective liberation, he now contented himself with the private dignity of individuals. Himself. His students. People who passed through his life:

Binita.

The school where he taught was opening a centre for pre-nursery-age children. There was profit in daycare, the principal speculated. 'My wife is looking for work,' Rishi had said. And the principal, a casually conscienceless man, had replied, 'We'll hire anyone who'll work for our wages.'

On a foggy winter morning exactly on the day that Binita had set, Rishi left his apartment to return to Khaireni Tar.

The morning was frigid. When he left the old brick house the city appeared like a chimera, cloaked in mist. He entered its formlessness. Buildings emerged from the fog as he walked, darkness and light glistened by. Around him he heard the shuffle of steps, vendors standing in the fog hawking yesterday's vegetables. On the streets dogs curled into sleep. Rishi smelled vapours of tea, dust, piss. He could hear footsteps behind him, footsteps in front: leather shoes clacking against asphalt. A man pushed against him, rushing for a taxi. Children ran helter-skelter on the way to school. He walked past a diner and caught a whiff of its oily cooking smells.

At the bus park Rishi bought a ticket for the next bus: a half-an-hour from now. On the sidewalk was an old woman selling freshly brewed tea. He went to sit on a low wall near her, and the woman turned with a smile. 'You want a cup of tea, son?'

Her fond tone startled Rishi. He said, 'I don't have any money, mother.'

She turned away, no longer bothered with him.

A hard confirmation spread along Rishi's skin, like a shiver. He sat, turned away from the old woman, and thought of Binita.

Her slim back, rippling from taut to slack. It was her back that he would move upon gently. The bone at the back of her neck. He would trace her collarbone and turn her towards him till her eyes finally steadied on his. Binita's desire. His love. Their happiness, forcibly wrenched from society. When the two of them were alone at last, with her consent he would move in, in love, to kiss her.